GETTING TO KNOW YOU . . .

Colonel Slayer let go another mecha-to-mecha missile across the bright green landscape as the radar locked onto a blurred target. The sensors would lock on briefly and then would lose track for a microsecond. That microsecond was enough advantage to the Chiata ground trooper that it morphed its body away from the missile. The missile passed through the alien blur like it wasn't even there, and then a tentacle jutted out from the creature, wrapping itself around the missile. The alien then spun the missile about like an Olympic hammer thrower, letting it go at just the right moment, sending it back at Max. Maximilian fired the thrusters on the tank's feet and leaped upward into a forward roll, all the while firing his guns.

Max's bot-mode tank pounded through the giant fir trees at a pace of nearly one hundred kilometers per hour. His first and foremost target was the mecha-to-mecha missile he'd fired only seconds before. His guns struck home on the tip of the warhead, setting it off and blasting him backwards just as the Chiata ground trooper closed in on him, stretching out amorphous tentacles. In a red-and-green oscillating blur it spun about him as if trying to put him in a straitjacket.

"Not this fucking time!" he said as he shoved the barrel of his giant cannon into the thing's front orifice and fired several rounds. The close proximity to the alien's shield armor was enough advantage to the guns that after several rounds the barriers failed. Amor-piercing rounds tore through the back of the creature, scattering its internal bits across the battlescape with a splash of green glowing goop. Colonel Slayer thought for a brief second that he was getting better at killing these alien bastards, and then as his targeting locator pinged wildly, he thought again that he was going to have to get a *hell* of a lot better.

KILL BEFORE DYING

TAU CETI AGENDA SERIES

✦ ✦ ✦

TRAVIS S. TAYLOR

Copyright © 2017 by Travis S. Taylor

A Baen Books Original

Baen Publishing Enterprises
P.O. Box 1403
Riverdale, NY 10471
www.baen.com

ISBN: 978-1-4814-8310-0

Cover art by Kurt Miller

First Baen paperback printing, January 2018

Distributed by Simon & Schuster
1230 Avenue of the Americas
New York, NY 10020

Printed in the United States of America

10 9 8 7 6 5 4 3 2 1

I've dedicated each of the books in this series thus far to heroes of various sorts. At least they were heroes as far as I was concerned. This book is no different in that regard. I'd like to dedicate this one to all of the fallen heroes that CrossFit Workouts of the Day have been named for such as Murph, Badger, Blake, Dragon, Erin, Gallant, and the list goes on and on. Just Google the "hero WODs" and you'll see. Next Veterans Day or Independence Day, go do one of them in their honor.

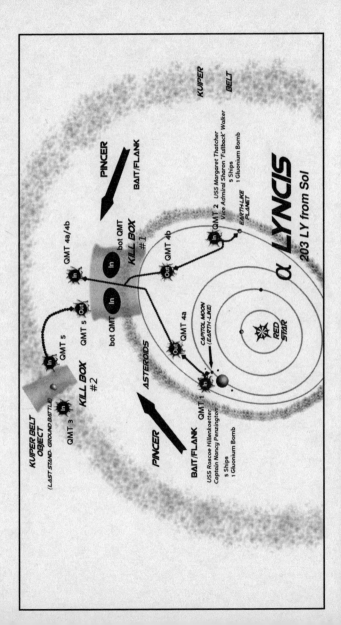

PINCER

BAIT/FLANK

QMT 4a/4b

bot QMT

KILL BOX #1

In

In

bot QMT

KILL BOX #2

Out

QMT 5

QMT 5

In

In

QMT 3

KUPER BELT OBJECT
(LAST STAND GROUND BATTLE)

Out

QMT 4b

In QMT 2 *USS Margaret Thatcher*
Vice Admiral Sharon "Fullback" Walker
5 Ships
1 Gluonium Bomb

KUPER

BELT

EARTH-LIKE
PLANET

Out

QMT 4a

CAPITOL MOON
(EARTH-LIKE)

In

ASTEROIDS

PINCER

BAIT/FLANK

QMT 1 *USS Roscoe Hillenkoetter*
Captain Nancy Penzington
5 Ships
1 Gluonium Bomb

α LYNCIS

203 LY from Sol

RED
STAR

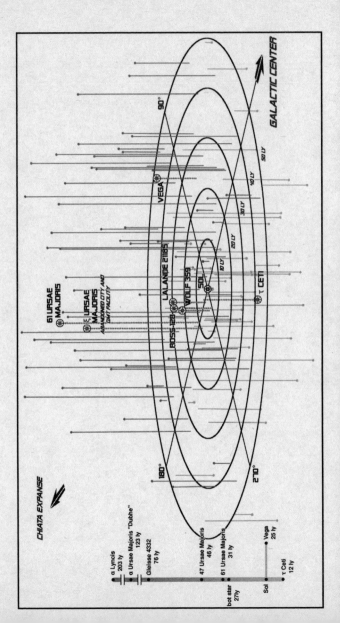

KILL BEFORE DYING

TAU CETI AGENDA SERIES

Prologue

November 13, 2407 AD
61 Ursae Majoris Oort Cloud
31 Light-years from the Sol System
Tuesday, 11:30 A.M. 61 Ursae Majoris C Capitol
  Standard Time

"It will only be a moment now." The strange expressions on the alien-controlled clone body always unnerved Alexander Moore, and he was pretty certain he'd never get used to it. "I am receiving a QM ping from our guests."

"I hope they have some insight or magic weapons they might let us borrow," Alexander said smugly as he looked out the clear panel at the large QMT transmission system's exterior. The facility was the size of a Kuiper Belt object and was artificial. That fact alone had always amazed and startled Alexander. The alien had somehow managed to send bots to this system centuries, if not millennia, before and had them build the mammoth device. The wall around Copernicus continued to ripple but it didn't cloud Moore's view of 61 UM. It was very small at the Oort Cloud distance where they were. It was almost a light year away but it was still the brightest star in the sky.

"Don't count on it, son," Sienna Madira grunted pessimistically as she adjusted the long, white-streaked lock of her otherwise jet-black hair that curled down her forehead and left cheek. "One thing I've learned over the years is that you can always count on people not to really help when they offer to. Especially if it means they have to put their own necks onto the chopping block with you."

"I think you'll find the people I've invited to be, well, unlike any you've met thus far." Copernicus responded and turned to them, making a screwed-up facial expression that Moore had no idea how to interpret.

"Uh huh. That's great," he said, not sure what to expect.

Copernicus continued manipulating the fuzzy boundary of the clear, rippling wall with his left hand, and the surface morphed around his fingers like oobleck. As the alien pulled his hands from the wall the material stuck to his fingers and stretched outward to them. There was no splatter, only ripples and waves. The clear, glowing pudding danced about his fingertips, with each movement sending trails of green light shooting through the image in the window like fireworks and skittering fireflies. Alexander couldn't get his brain around how any of that was a repeatable control function. There were no buttons, knobs, switches or displays. It was just damned confusing.

As far as he could tell there was no direct-to-mind interface either, unless it happened through the skin-to-goo contact. Otherwise there were no known detectable signals.

How the hell does he know what he's doing? he thought.

I am studying this very closely, sir. I'm not sure either, but I do believe the light patterns and the wave patterns are the key, Abigail, his artificial intelligence counterpart, or AIC, said in his head. The AIC computer was one of the smartest ever made and had been implanted in Moore's brain since long before the Martian Desert Campaigns almost two centuries prior. He trusted she would figure it out. Abigail had gotten him and his family out of many scrapes in the past. He had high confidence that once she had set her AI mind to the task she'd crack the code.

"Aha, now. We are ready," Copernicus stated. Then the exterior skyscraper large spires over the central QMT pad of the facility began to spark and glow. A circle of rippling, watery blue light appeared and then flashed like an explosion in the kilometer-wide expanse between the spires. There was no sound or shock wave and there was no damage, but the phenomenon briefly left Moore lightheaded just as it had the last time he'd seen the thing in action almost two years before—the first time that Madira and Copernicus had shown him the Chiata Horde.

Then the wall turned opaque, like a dimmer switch was being turned down. Just as quickly as the wall faded dark, it began to fade to clear again, but this time the view was different. 61 UM was no longer outside in the field of view. Instead there was a different star system, and in the background was a large ship. The ship was more than three times larger than any U.S. Navy supercarrier or any Separatist hauler. In fact, Moore was guessing it was three times larger than a supercarrier and a hauler combined. Scalewise, it was on par with the Chiata ships they had fought at the battle of Alpha Lyncis five months prior. Then the screen zoomed rapidly into the bridge, and it was as if the interior of the ship was just on the other side of the window.

Large green translucent glowing monsters stood at what Moore could only assume were bridge stations, and the largest of the monsters sat in a thronelike chair in the middle of the room. Moore had seen enough starships and battleships to know that the throne was the captain's chair and he was looking at the Ghuthlaeer in charge. If proportions were right, and Moore thought they were, the captain of the alien ship must have been at least three meters tall and a meter and a half wide at what he assumed were shoulders. He appeared bipedal with heavily armored clawed boots or feet, Alexander wasn't sure. The creature had extra-long, very beefy, heavily armored muscular biceps and forearms ending in humanoid hands. Each hand had seven very long fingers, with spiny protrusions that looked like fins or plates from the back of a stegosaurus along the back of each hand and up the forearms. And the damned things glowed and pulsated. The entirety of the creature from foot to topknot pulsed in a bright luminescent green. The glow was too bright to determine the type of skin the thing had. The creature's face looked more like a human's than Alexander had expected. That was, if a glowing green spiky foreheaded creature with glowing orange eyes looked human at all.

"I am Ghuthlaevex Uurrgan," the creature said, almost with a guttural throaty growl and rolling of the r's. Boomingly and somewhat over the top, it continued. "I am captain of this vessel. Whom am I speaking to?"

"You speak English?" Moore was shocked. But the creature did something that could only be interpreted as laughing, maybe with a side of annoyance. At least Alexander hoped it was laughter.

"Language is so primitive a concept. But yes, human, you can assume I understand your language, as I know there is no hope of you learning mine," Ghuthlaevex Uurrgan replied. "Now why am I here so far away from the battle zone?"

"Captain Ghuthlaevex," Copernicus nodded. "You have been briefed on the humans' raid on the Chiata star system Alpha Lyncis?"

"Yes. Courageous, surprising, and most probably stupid," he replied. "And, I must say, interesting tactics, even if they were very three-dimensional. The use of your Von Neumann automatons was quite impressive and with some upgrades could be useful in the future. But know this, the Horde will adapt very quickly to these primitive technologies and tactics."

"Yes." Copernicus nodded again, this time in agreement. "Nevertheless, they did manage to make a dent in the Chiata machine at that system."

"Ha ha ha." Ghuthlaevex boomed in what Moore

recognized as pure laughter. The strange alien creature was easier to understand than Copernicus in a human clone body. "A dent, you say? Not even a single hydrogen atom in a sea of stars!"

"Granted it was a small impact, but an impact, you must agree," Copernicus argued.

"Bah!" The alien grunted in dismissal. Moore wasn't sure about Copernicus, but he could tell by looking at Madira that she was getting impatient. He needed to take the bull by the horns before she stepped in. It was time to quit beating around the diplomatic bush and start being Alexander Moore—in other words, an armored bull in a china shop.

"Enough of this small talk. We made enough of an impact that you are here." Moore raised a hand. "I'm General Alexander Moore, the commanding general for the human expeditionary forces. Our attack on the Chiata system was apparently significant enough that you brought your battleship a thousand light-years from your present battle to speak with us, so stop looking down your big-assed glowing green fucking nose at us and start talking about how we can align ourselves to generate more orchestrated attacks against our common foe and how we might defend our region of space." Alexander had read the details that Copernicus had given him on the Ghuthlaeer. They had been fighting the Chiata for so long that war was all they knew anymore. Moore hoped that speaking to this alien as a soldier rather than a diplomat would make a difference.

"Ha ha ha," the alien boomed. "I like this human. He has more freazles than you amorphous leeches,

Copernicus. Although I must admit you would be much easier to kill in your present form, and I very much like that."

Copernicus made no facial expression or response. He simply waited. Moore wasn't sure what a freazle was, but he got the gist of it. The concept of courage to bull into a situation even when outgunned must be universally accepted as "having balls," he thought. A smile almost crossed his face, but he fought it back.

"So you'll help us then?" Madira asked. Ghuthlaevex Uurrgan looked at her as if he was studying her closely.

"I already have helped you. These slugs didn't invent what you call quantum membrane technology. The great scientist Ghuthlaeven Shoffire did. He discovered this technology over thirty thousand of your years ago and because of it we have kept the Horde at a stalemate on the outer arms of the galaxy. Unfortunate for you that your spur was not under our protection."

"I see." Madira smirked at Copernicus. Moore could see she was having some revelations of her own and was most likely spinning up some god-awful complicated plan within plan within plan to use that information.

"We thank you for that," Alexander said. "Now we need to move farther and we need to be able to hit the Chiata harder than our technology has allowed us."

"Yes. While you have destroyed a Chiata ship or two, you have yet to stand face to face with them and push them back," Uurrgan replied, thumping a seven-fingered fist against the armor on his chestplate. "Law prohibits me from directly giving you technology. While Copernicus is sneaky, it can still be argued that the female behind you discovered quantum membrane technology for humanity. His plan was clever for a slug."

"I cannot 'give' you new technology. But if you were to find it on your own there is nothing the courts can say about that. Not even the Chiata-controlled and -threatened ones could win such a case. The law is still the law for now." The alien captain tapped several locations in midair in front of him and then nodded to another alien sitting to his right. Moore wondered if direct-to-mind and virtual battlescape projections had also somehow been seeded into humanity or if it was coincidental development. He didn't really give a shit. He needed a way to fight the damned Chiata. They were knocking on humanity's door with a battering ram, and he couldn't care less about these aliens' laws.

"How might I find something of use?" Alexander grunted, getting tired of the ping-pong match.

"There is a system you should look at. If you can get there, stay there, and perhaps defeat the small contingent of Chiata there you might find something of use to you," Uurrgan said. "But be warned, the system will let you QMT in, but will not let you QMT out. We do not know why and are no longer attempting to take it. We lost several engagements in that system attempting to combat the Chiata. The Horde is using the system for a staging ground as they know we are no longer able to push that deep into their territory to study the phenomenon. At least, we have let them believe this. Also know that our intelligence-gathering operations have learned that there is something on that planet that scares the Horde. We are not actually clear on what. We think this is why they continue to protect the system rather than rip it apart for its resources. That, or for whatever reason, they cannot destroy it."

"Where is this system?" Moore asked.

"And what are we looking for?" Madira added.

"I am sending the system location and all intelligence we have on it to Copernicus now. It is roughly seven hundred lightyears from your Sol. It is within Chiata space, so you will have to stay away from star systems along the way. While we don't know why QMT, as you call it, will work into the system but not out of the system, we do know that the Chiata do not have this technology. Somebody else put it there."

"Who else?" Madira asked.

"Sadly, we do not know. And that suggests that the Chiata must have destroyed them all," Uurrgan replied. "But there is non-Chiata technology at work there."

"What if the Chiata reverse engineer it?" Moore almost gasped. "That would remove our one advantage."

"Yes. This is a fear the Ghuthlaeer Dominion has had for more than ten thousand years. So far, we have been lucky." Uurrgan turned and nodded to an alien to his left. "The information has been sent. Perhaps this will help you, perhaps not. The only other advice I have for you comes from my chief engineer. He says you are not putting enough power into your new point barrier shields and that you should also implement it as personal armor, like we do." Uurrgan smacked a seven-fingered fist into his chest again, this time much harder, causing a wave of green light to ripple across his body. "We must be getting back to the fight now. It will take us days to return."

"That's it?" Madira snapped.

"Yes, human, that is it. The law forbids us to do more at this point. Perhaps if you continue to impress, who knows?" The alien captain's face seemed to glow slightly brighter for an instant. "General, I wish you good luck."

"Thank you, Captain Ghuthlaevex." The wall instantly zoomed out, flashed dim, and then Moore was looking at the distant UM61 once again.

"That female is so elusive," Copernicus said. "Mutual hatred aside, she never can talk straight with me."

"The captain was female?" Moore asked. "How do you tell them apart?"

"Perhaps I forgot to put that in my briefing notes. Family names ending in -vex are female and -ven are male. The females are much larger and are dominant. And by the way her face pulsed and lit up when talking to you, General, I'd say she was somewhat fond of you."

"Ha!" Madira couldn't contain her laughter. "You better not be stepping out on my daughter for a seven-fingered orange-eyed monster!"

"Not that type of fond," Copernicus added. "More like you, Sienna, with your cats. Yes, fond in a master and pet sort of way."

"Son of a bitch," Alexander rubbed at the stubble on his chin. "This alien shit is gonna take some getting used to."

Chapter 1

February 19, 2407 AD
***U.S.S. Sienna Madira II* Expeditionary Fleet**
Deep Open Space
691 Light-years from the Sol System
Monday, 6:30 A.M. Ship Standard Time

"Up and at 'em! Quit your goldbricking, Marine! It is time to get up!" The ten-centimeter-high holographic image of General Alexander Moore shouted from the light blue sugar-cube-sized holocube projector clock on Deanna's night table. "Move it, princess! Get your ass up!"

USMC Major Deanna Moore rolled over onto her side, carefully pulling USN Major Davy Rackman's hand out from around her breast. She then smacked the alarm button on the cube, and with a grunt and an exhale, rolled out of bed naked onto the floor, catching herself in plank position at the last minute before hitting the cold metal deck plates of her cabin floor. The cold against her hands and toes sent a chill up her body, covering her in goose bumps.

One, two, three, four, she counted in her head as she completed each military style pushup. Dee forced herself all the way down until her breasts touched the deck plates with each repetition and then she exploded upward using all the muscles in her tight core and strong arms. As her body began to wake each of the pushups became a bit easier.

Good morning, Dee. Would you like me to count for you? her AIC Bree asked.

Thanks.

Seven, eight, nine, ten . . .

"Dammit, Marine, you couldn't even take time to put clothes on or turn the lights on or make coffee," Rackman said through half-open eyes.

"Didn't want to wake you. And I've told you before the key to flying mecha is in the core muscles. DeathRay always says there's no such thing as too many pushups and situps." Dee managed to grunt between breaths. "Besides, aren't you due back on the *Hillenkoetter* in thirty?"

"Shit, that means you woke me up about twenty-five minutes early." Rackman rolled back over, pulling the cover over his head.

Deanna put the SEAL out of her mind for a bit and focused on the job at hand—pushing the floor. Back, core, and buttocks tight, breasts all the way down, touch, explode up.

Thirty-seven, thirty-eight, thirty-nine . . .

"All hands, all hands," the bosun's pipe sounded

throughout the ship. "Stand by for a message from the Commanding General."

"Does anybody in your family sleep in?"

"I doubt it. Mom's probably been up for hours. And Dad, well, I don't think he's slept since the Martian Desert Campaigns like two hundred years ago." Dee grunted.

"Hell, guess I might as well get up then." Rackman grunted again. Dee ignored him as he stepped over her and into the little bathroom of the officer's-sized cabin. He looked back at her and she could tell he was eyeing her nakedness. She liked the fact that the SEAL liked looking at her. It made her feel like a woman, and, well, pretty. She was already glistening with sweat and sex from the night before with Davy—not only was she pretty, but she was also a badass marine mecha jock who would kick anybody's ass who pissed her off. She knew she looked good. She hoped deep down all the way to her soul that Rackman felt the same way.

Fifty-six, fifty-seven, fifty-eight . . .

"Like what you see?" she panted jokingly, holding her body up in plank position a few extra seconds as she turned and smiled at Rackman, her naked breasts firm and pointed at the floor and her legs tight and flexed all the way up. She made a point that her slight sideways turn gave Rackman a full frontal view of her rippled stomach and fighter-pilot muscular attributes.

She continued to push at the floor after giving him the brief smile. The coldness of the floor was wearing away, and beads of sweat were running down her body and starting to drop from her nose, forming a puddle underneath her.

"Like what I see? Damn right. What's not to like, Marine?" Rackman said with a raised eyebrow. Dee could tell that more than his eyebrow was raised and again, that made her feel good. She smiled inwardly as he turned and continued into the bathroom. Dee continued to push the floor. "Chicken shit. You should push the floor with me."

"Ha," Rackman looked down at his obvious excitement. "Not like this. Maybe with you under me?"

"Didn't get enough last night?" Dee continued the playful banter through panting for breath. It helped take her mind off the burning in her chest, shoulders, and arms.

Sixty-seven, sixty-eight . . .

"Good morning." Her father's voice and image projected above the holocube on her nightstand and on the screen on her wall. Almost in an instant the playful mood left the room. Her father had a way of making every situation serious. "We are slightly over nine light-years out from our target star. We are three jumps from the combat zone and as far as we can tell, we are deep within Chiata-controlled space and running silent. From this point in we are at full high alert and will be making last-minute preparations for engaging the Chiata once again."

Eighty-three, eighty-four, eighty-five . . .

"While we have no idea how much resistance we will meet here, we can assume that it will be alien, and if we use our previous engagement as any form of example, their technology will far exceed our own. I'm not going to lie to you because you all volunteered to be here. This could very well be a one-way trip, and anybody wishing to go home should do so now, as our intelligence suggests that QM snap-back teleportation might not function once we reach the target. We have no way of knowing how close to target it will be when the teleportation jamming becomes effective. Therefore, we have no way of knowing how long of a hyperspace jaunt will be needed to reach QMT space again. This could end up being a long trip."

"Nobody better fucking snap-back home at this point," Dee grunted as she dropped to her knees and rose up for a brief second to shake out her arms. Sweat poured down her body as she slowed her breathing and rolled her neck from side to side.

"What's that, Marine?" Rackman leaned his head around the bathroom door, toothpaste foam at the corner of his mouth. His eyes widened and she could see he wasn't looking at *her* eyes.

"Just sayin' that nobody better be flashing out now. Not this damned close. If any of the Archangels bugged out, DeathRay would kick their asses. And if he didn't . . ." She shook her arms once more and then dropped back to plank position with a big exhale.

"Oh. Roger that." Rackman agreed. "I'm sure the *Hillenkoetter* crew will stay. Hell, most of them are all AIC-controlled clones anyway and I don't think they have feelings like we do. Hell, I dunno. Maybe they do?"

"As the morning shift kicks off I want all teams reporting to battle stations and getting battle-rattle-armed and dangerous. Report in to your respective team leads and prepare to take hell to the Chiata Horde. Stick to our attack plan, and God willing, we'll come through this, and on the other side of it there will be great rewards. All of you please take one last opportunity to send messages home and assure loved ones we'll be home soon. It's time to fight the good fight, now. Good luck. Godspeed. God bless you all."

One hundred thirteen, one hundred fourteen . . .

"The old man likes to keep it short and sweet, doesn't he?" Rackman stepped out of the bathroom, pulling the shirt of the universal combat uniform, or UCU, as it was more often referred to, down over his head. The hyperdense long-chain molecular material uniform top sucked to his body like paint and then changed to navy colors per his AIC's direction. He folded the cover and put it in his back trouser pocket.

"He's never been one for beating around the bush. Not even when he was a politician." Dee replied. "You gone?"

"I'd better snap to or Captain Penzington will be ready to toss me out a goddamned air lock," he said as he melded his nametag, rank, and insignia patches to his shirt. "Hey, I won't get to see you again until, well, you know."

"Yeah. Keep your helmet on, Navy. You remember what happened to the bridge crew of the *Madira* last time." Dee looked at him with concern on her face, but didn't stop pushing the floor. "Lost too many good people that day. If only they'd been wearing their damned helmets, they'd still be with us."

"Hey, you stay on DeathRay's wing and watch your ass out there. And keep that new shield thing Buckley came up with on all the time." He looked down at her, and Dee liked the way he looked concerned for her. But at the same time it made her heart twist into knots in her chest.

They each had their jobs to do and thinking about Rackman made it both harder and easier at the same time. She figured, or at least hoped, Rackman had similar feelings. Dee paused from pushing the floor and stood in front of him, naked, glistening in sweat, her heart nearly beating out of her chest and breaking at the same time with the thought that they might not get to see each other again. She wasn't certain if she should be vulnerable or full of bravado. The only thing she knew she was full of was absolute adoration for the SEAL—unadulterated, unfettered, unconditional, unbelievably heart-wrenching adoration. She had to face the facts no matter how much she wanted to ignore them. She was ass over tits in love and there was little she or anyone else could do about it.

"Don't worry about me." She stood on her tiptoes and kissed the tall Navy officer gently on the lips. He leaned down and returned the kiss but kept his distance from her, acting as if he didn't want to get her sweat on him.

"No offense, Marine, but you're pretty damned sweaty and gross and I just got dressed." He smirked. Dee put her hands on her hips and raised an eyebrow at him. She almost pouted, then almost got angry, and then the marine in her kicked in and she completely understood. Starship bridge crews had a certain air of pomp and circumstance and required formal sharpness they had to portray even in combat situations. She understood, but she didn't have to like it.

"It's okay. We got plenty close last night," she said, flashing her big half-Martian brown eyes at him. "Just be careful, Davy."

Tell him, Dee.

Shut up.

I'm just saying, you may not get another chance for a while. Tell him.

Shut up, Bree.

Deanna turned about to drop to the floor again but felt a hand grab her by the wrist and pull her around. Davy pulled her into him, wrapped his gigantic Navy SEAL biceps around her and pulled her into a long, slow kiss that she joyfully returned. A surge of excitement rushed over her as he gripped her in his strong hands, and she wrapped herself around him in a long embrace. She could feel his excitement through the UCU pants as well. There was mutual adoration there, she just knew it.

"Come back safe, Dee. I mean it. I, uh . . ."

"You too," she said before he could finish.

Chicken shit, Bree said in her head.

Shut up, Bree.

She kissed him once again and then let him go. The SEAL smiled at her as he tapped his wristband, and her cabin was filled with a flash of light and the sound of frying bacon, and then he was gone. Dee looked around her cabin briefly and noted the sling-forward QMT countdown clock being projected on her wall. The timer showed a jump in fifty-three minutes and twenty-one seconds. "Be safe, SEAL. I love you," she almost whispered as she dropped to the floor.

One hundred forty three, one hundred forty four . . .

Chapter 2

February 19, 2407 AD
U.S.S. Sienna Madira II Expeditionary Fleet
Deep Open Space
691 Light-years from the Sol System
Monday, 6:45 A.M. Ship Standard Time

"You know, in some other life, you might be going off to a day job and I might be headed to take the kids to school." USN Captain Jack "DeathRay" Boland adjusted his UCU top, bumping into his wife as she brushed her teeth.

"Why do you get to take the kids to school and I have to work?" USN Captain Nancy Penzington responded as she spit the robotic toothbrush cube into the sink. The little bot shook itself clean under the flowing water from the faucet, then climbed up on the edge of the sink and retracted itself to about half the size of a sugar cube.

"I just figure you're the responsible one and all, and

that you are more likely to hold down a regular job," DeathRay replied.

"Why couldn't we just be independently wealthy and let the kids have private tutors from home? The two of us could just lay around the pool all day drinking fruity drinks filled with ethanol like they serve on the beach near New Tharsis. Hell, we could even live on the beach at New Tharsis."

"Now you're talking, Captain. What'd'ya say we snap-back there and call all this soldiering shit quits? It'd be the life," DeathRay kidded. "You heard the General. Now's our chance."

"While I'd love to sit on a beach half naked with you and contemplate how many children we should have and how much fun we'd have making them, I'm not so sure now is the time." Nancy smiled back at Jack. "Besides, Boland, who'd lead the Archangels boldly into overwhelming numbers of Chiata fighters and who'd command the *Hillenkoetter*? And somebody has to watch after the Moores. Who would do that if we ain't here?"

"Just half naked? Why not all naked? Aw shit, we'd get bored anyway." Jack grabbed Nancy around the waist from behind and pulled her to him. Then he turned her around and looked into her eyes. "I think I'm right where I want to be right now any damned way."

"Shut up and kiss me, idiot. I've got to get to the bridge and you've got to get back to the *Madira*," Nancy told him.

Commander Joe Buckley Junior, Chief Engineer of the *Sienna Madira II*, sat across the breakfast table from the armored environment-suit marine he'd been spending most of his free time with for the past year or more. Joe sat leaning on an elbow and playing with the eggs on his plate. He wasn't sure if he wanted to eat or not. He wasn't sure he was awake or not. He looked up at Rondi who was already wide-ass awake and in her UCUs. She leaned back in her chair and finished off her coffee.

"Having a hard time getting going this morning, CHENG?"

"Yeah. Guess so. You kept me up too late." Buckley decided he didn't want the eggs and then realized from the look on Rondi's face that he'd said something stupid. He backpedaled as quickly as he could. "Not that I'm complaining, mind you. I'd stay up all night with you any time you'd let me."

"Ha ha," Rondi slapped the table. "Good save, CHENG."

"Listen, I know you're an AEM and all and you often go traipsing into thick shit that would make the most courageous of soldiers piss themselves, but . . ." he tactically changed the subject and displayed his concern in one move.

Nice move, Joe, his AIC told him in his head.

"But what?" Rondi leaned in closer to him. The little two-person table in the CHENG's quarters was just small enough that she could almost lean nose to nose with him. Joe looked into her eyes and at her face. He'd never spent as much time with a person before as he had with Rondi. The Master Gunnery Sergeant was tough as nails, but from where Joe sat she was soft and vulnerable and squishy in just the right places.

"But, keep the shield system on and your head down." He finished. "And, uh, keep it frosty, like you marines like to say."

"That's *stay* frosty. And, well, you keep your helmet on in engineering in case the ship gets hammered by those zig-zagging blue beams, and no crazy-ass Buckley shit if things go bad down there," she said. Joe was sure she was talking about the now infamous Buckley maneuver where he had damned near sacrificed himself to save the power systems of the ship during a major battle. He could never live that particular incident down, even though he'd been decorated and promoted for it.

At the time it had been the only thing Joe could think of to save the ship and it had worked, but he'd fried his body with radiation in the process. He didn't have any plans to repeat the process. Almost all of his internal organs had to be replaced and the worst of it was the pain from the immunoboost drugs regrowing his testicles. He felt a bit of unease in the pit of his stomach just thinking about it.

"Well, stay frosty then, and keep your shields up."

"I'll be on an extremely hostile alien fucking planet fighting extremely hostile fucking aliens and breathing God only knows what type of toxic hostile fucking alien air. I'll keep my fucking shit on tight," Rondi promised. Joe wasn't exactly sure when or how the two of them had managed to become a thing. In fact, to him, even though they'd known each other only a few years it seemed like forever. He liked her. She was definitely more than just "boat cute." She was take-home-to-mom-and-dad cute. That was, if his dad were still alive, but his mom would love to meet her, he was certain. He'd just have to ask her not to be so expressive with the "F-word" in front of his mother. While his mother was plenty old enough and seasoned as a longtime military wife, she would curse Joe for cursing in front of her, very hypocritically, as often as she could manage. Joe just didn't want to throw rocket fuel on that fire.

But, he'd like to take her home nonetheless. Rondi was a bad-ass armored e-suit marine with a body that went with the title. AEMs were hard as rocks, tough, and smart, and Rondi was no exception. Joe also liked the way her glow-in-the-dark tattoo of a snake wrapping itself around her body looked when he got to see the entirety of it. That thought did something else to the pit of his stomach—and a little bit lower.

"Good. I can't eat these eggs this morning. Want 'em?" He pushed his plate back.

"I'm good. The damned things look too, uh, green almost, for me to eat," she replied.

"What?" The statement startled him more awake. He looked closer at the eggs and realized there was a slight green tint to them. "Holy shit! Why didn't you say something sooner?"

"What? About the eggs? Hell, the eggs always taste like shit. What's new?"

"CHENG to Commander Benjamin," Joe said after his AIC opened a com channel for him.

"Benjamin here. What's up, Joe?"

"Keri, why are my eggs green this morning?" he asked his second engineer.

"Uh, shit, are they? I haven't eaten yet. Hold on, Joe,"

she said, but left the channel open so he could hear her shouting expletives at one of the petty officers. "When was the last fucking time you checked the Ox mix and the carbon dioxide scrubbers? I don't give a good goddamn what else was taking place. If we can't fucking breathe we can't fucking fight. If we try to put pilots, tankheads, and AEMs in suits after breathing too much pure oxygen they're gonna get headaches or worse." There was some garbled talk and more expletives and Joe wasn't exactly sure who was getting the brunt of it, but Benjamin was giving some poor seaman hell.

"Keri?"

"I got it, Joe. Looks like we had a LOX valve freeze up on the upper tier near the tower. The O2 got too rich and the nitrogen too low. Don't have to worry about the bends, but there might be some headaches because the carbon dioxide is a bit high now. Only bigwigs like the bridge crew and CHENGs ought to be affected. Four minutes and it'll be good."

"Damn right it will," Joe ordered. "Do I need to come down there and . . ."

"Aye, sir. We've got this and I will be on top of it. Is that all?"

"That's all for now. Get that shit locked down, Keri. Buckley out."

"Minor emergency already?" Rondi looked at Buckley with a look that told Joe the same thing he was feeling but didn't want to say. The crew was on edge. Silly shit like letting the air mix getting screwed up just couldn't be happening. Not on his ship. Not nearly seven hundred light years from home in the middle of nowhere. Not on his ship.

No need to stress, Joe. Commander Benjamin is very competent, his AIC said in his mind.

Of course she is, and I trust her, he thought. *But we've gotta keep it wired tight and locked down. Silly shit like this will get us dead. I want you running nonstop diagnostics and updating me if there are any even minor changes in the flush water in the heads.*

Roger that, Joe.

This mission was crazy as hell and likely a suicide one, but somebody had to do it. If there was a chance in hell that there was a magic device or ally on the distant planetary system they were headed to that would help them stop the Chiata Horde from totally annihilating humanity then they had to go look for it. The way the Chiata had kicked their asses on the fleet's first encounter with them had rocked all of them to their core. Humanity was way behind, outnumbered, and seriously, laugh-out-loud hilariously outgunned. Somehow, the Expeditionary Fleet would have to change that. Joe had to keep his shit together.

"Do you think the QMT will work within the system?" Rondi broke his AIC conversation trance.

"Dunno." Joe thought about it for a moment. "If they are using some sort of jamming technology there it will probably suppress all QMTs once in range. Just like Elle Ahmi's trap at the planet you were stranded in space nearby, on the mission before we found UM61. You could snap in but not out. I suspect it'll be like that."

"Well, there was a backdoor there," Rondi added.

"Yeah, thank God that Captain Penzington and DeathRay found it."

"And the fleet they found, but Penzington wasn't a

captain then," Rondi corrected Joe and then looked expressionless as if she were talking to her AIC. "I don't really have to report anywhere for about an hour after the next jump. How about you?"

Debbie? He thought to his AIC.

Commander Benjamin is there and doesn't have a scheduled break until after the next jump, unless you feel the need to micromanage her some more. You are not scheduled to be active until time to relieve her, his AIC replied in his mind.

"Keri can handle engineering until I get there, I guess. Hell, I wouldn't want to be that POFC she's riding right now. But still, I've got some calibrations runs on the increased power conduits on the shield switches and I need to get on recalibrating the QMT subspace detection grids the warrant officers are working on. I plan to use them to look for whatever will be suppressing snap-backs in that system. I've really got a lot to do before we get there. Gonna be a long Navy day," Joe answered. "I long for the days of just hitting a valve with a big fucking wrench and making it work. Now it's all quantum membrane calibration sensors and hyperspace field manipulator accelerator coils and so on."

"Well, damn." Rondi stood and stretched. "I was hoping we might have time for sex."

"Like I said," Joe raised an eyebrow. "I'm not scheduled to be on duty for almost an hour."

"I'm not scheduled to be on duty for almost an hour, Top!" AEM Lance Corporal Jacob Roy pleaded with Sergeant Major Tommy Suez.

"Roy, I don't give a shit what the duty roster says. Armored environment suit marines of the *U.S.S. Sienna Madira II* are always on duty if I say they are on duty. You heard the General just now, didn't you?" Suez wasn't shouting. In fact, Tommy had more of a calm, matter-of-fact way of speaking sternly than a stereotypical drill instructor. Sergeant Major Tommy Suez looked at the new transfer into the squad. He had not yet been able to size the kid up. He was a true kid of only twenty-five years old, no rejuves yet. Tommy hated seeing kids going to fight. They hadn't even had a chance to live yet. He had felt the same way about the General's daughter, who was young, very young he thought. She had certainly seen her time in the shit, some really serious shit. And each time she had fought her way out of it like any other good marine. That was just the way it was and he didn't make the law. Anybody over twenty-one who wanted to join up could. Anybody over twenty-five could volunteer for combat duty. He didn't have to like the law. Hell, Tommy felt that you shouldn't be able to fight until after your first rejuve. But the law was the law and young marines had been going into the shit for centuries. It was up to him to see to it that his marines were best equipped and suited and trained to optimize their chance of coming home in once piece that was still alive.

"I heard the General, Top Sergeant." Lance corporal Roy responded. "But I didn't understand that meant to report to duty, Top Sergeant."

"Skip it, Roy. Get your gear together and rally in the equipment hangar in ten. And get your roomie's ass up and at 'em as well. Major Sellis wants the squad ready for pre-mission briefing on the double." Tommy softened slightly. There was plenty of hardnosed shit coming their way in a few hours, he'd bust their balls then. Tommy had fought against the Chiata at Alpha Lyncis. He knew he was one of the few lucky ones who made it home from that fight. He was pretty damned sure that their odds were way worse for coming home this go-around than they had been then.

"Right away, Top!" Lance corporal Roy tossed a pillow across the walkway to hit the curtain on his roommate's bunk. The AEM quarters were top bunks with private storage and desk space underneath, much like a college dorm room. A sliding soundproof curtain allowed for privacy. "You heard him, Jerry, get your ass up!"

Tommy continued his walk through the squad's quarters banging his metal coffee mug against the bunk walls as he walked. He didn't miss the sardine bunks the junior enlisted lived in. E fours and E fives shared an actual quarters and E sixes and above had private quarters. Tommy hadn't quartered in the sardine can for years. He didn't miss it at all.

He kept an eye out for the Master Gunnery Sergeant who was usually there before him berating the shit out of some junior, but as far as he could tell she hadn't reported in yet either. According to the duty roster she wasn't due for another fifty or so minutes.

Any word on Howser? he thought to his AIC.

Master Gunnery Sergeant Rondi Howser has not reported yet. She is not due yet either, Tommy, his AIC responded.

Where is she?

Master Gunnery Sergeant Rondi Howser is in Commander Buckley's quarters presently. Would you like me to open a channel?

Ha ha, he thought. It was no secret that Howser had been spending a lot of time with the CHENG. Tommy was glad for her and as far as he could tell, the CHENG was a good soldier for a squid. *No. Let her be. She's a pro. She'll show up ready to go.*

"Good morning, Top." One of the AEMs walked by him in his underwear with a towel draped over his shoulder.

"Ten minutes, Private Hall."

"I heard, Top. Roger that."

Tommy looked down the long corridor that was the AEM bunkroom. The dull gray diamond-grooved metal deck plating clanked beneath each boot as he walked calmly through. Even though he hadn't slept in bunks like this in years, he could still remember that first day he was getting ready for combat in the Oort back in the Sol System. He was sweating and shaking and needed a chill pill as he pulled himself from his bunk the morning of his first day in combat. To Tommy, these kids seemed to be less concerned than he had been, or they were hiding it better. Maybe they were better trained or the meds were better. Or maybe they just had no idea what the hell was about to happen to them.

"Sir, if I understood the mission videos and debriefs I don't think there is any way in hell to understand what is about to happen to us." US Army Colonel Maximillian "Dragon" Slayer, the new leader of the tankheads, stood in front of General Alexander Moore's desk in the captain's ready room.

"I agree with you, Max. There is no way anybody can fathom what fighting the Chiata is like until they've done it." Moore nodded for the man to sit down. "General Warboys was as hardcore and badass as they come. I don't think history will show a tank driver with a better, more courageous career. I knew Mason for a long long time. His loss left quite the void to fill."

"Yes, sir." Colonel Slayer replied. "I will do my damnedest, sir!"

"I know you will, Max. That's why I stole you away from the school to lead my tankheads here. Listen, you know it as well as I do, once Warboys was lost, and we lost several of the other Warlords in that fight, my tank squadron was decimated."

"Yes, sir. I had a hard time picking up the pieces. Several of the Warlords will never be the same without General Warboys," Max agreed. Alexander watched the man to gauge his response. After five months he was beginning to feel confidence in his choice for Warboys' replacement.

"Max, your new Slayers squadron scores have been through the roof on the sims, but as soon as those damned red and green blurs start attacking in massive numbers, the sims go right out the damned window. You understand that, but somehow you have to make these new tank drivers get it before they get hit like a deer in headlights. The Chiata move faster than anything we've ever encountered before and kill relentlessly and in droves. It's a helluva thing you're being asked to do."

Alexander took a sip of coffee from his favorite mug, which he had acquired while in the White House, as he sized up his new colonel one last time.

"Sir, the men can handle it. We've trained for it as best we know how. They'll either win, die in distress, or die gloriously fighting. It is what it is."

"I prefer we win, Max. Or, at least, we live to fight 'em another day. Get 'em ready and good luck."

"Yes, sir." Colonel Slayer stood and saluted. Alexander returned it in kind and held quiet until the man had exited and closed the cabin door.

Abigail, where is Sehera? He thought.

She is on her way to Deanna's quarters. Would you like me to open a channel? his AIC replied.

Negative. This, I must do in person.

Yes, sir.

"Time to face the music." Alexander stood and let out a long sigh before muttering to himself something about soldiers being easier to handle.

The walk to the elevator and down a few floors seemed like it took hours, but it had only taken Alexander about three minutes. The corridors were a flurry of activity with soldiers and crews running to and fro to put out or start some prebattle fire. Each time the crew passed by they would stop and salute, and Moore would nod or salute in return with a smile and an occasional "Carry on."

Finally, he reached his daughter's quarters. He buzzed and had Abigail announce to his daughter's AIC he was at the door. A second or two passed before the door hissed open. His daughter stood before him in her UCU, standing at attention. She was the absolute perfect spitting image of her mother.

"General Moore, sir!" Deanna said to him with a salute. Alexander could see his wife standing a few feet behind her, looking at him with a raised eyebrow.

"At ease, princess. This is a daddy visit, not a general visit," he said to his daughter, and held up his arms, waving her forward to give him a hug.

"Good morning, Daddy." Deanna hugged him like she was a little girl again. To Alexander she always would be, badass marine or not.

"Morning, princess." She dragged him in through the door and he tapped the controls, closing it behind him. "I hope you are well this morning."

"She's fine, Alexander," Sehera smiled and put an arm around their daughter's shoulder. "We should have met for breakfast this morning."

"Haven't had time to eat yet. Still can, well, we have about thirty minutes before we jump," Alexander said as he noticed the countdown clock projected on his daughter's video screen.

"There isn't time, Daddy. I have to check in with DeathRay before the jump," Dee said. "CAG is doing his 'all call' prebrief. Mecha jocks gotta be there."

"Right. I know. I just needed to see the two of you before is all." Alexander reached for his wife's hand. "Sure wish I could talk you into going home, Dee."

"Daddy, that's a hell of a thing for you to say to me!" Dee sounded almost hurt.

"I had to say it. I know you're not going anywhere else but into the shit like the mecha jock you are. I just, had to, well . . . what kind of father would I be?" Moore didn't want to show weakness but she was his little girl. She was his only little girl whom he'd somehow managed to put into harm's way over and over and over. But she was stubborn like her mother and her old man. She was not one to turn from a fight. Hell, she continuously volunteered for them.

"I know, Daddy. Now let's not talk about it anymore." Dee hugged him again.

"Alright," he said. "You just stay frosty and be safe, Marine."

"Is that an order, daddy?"

"Alexander, stop babying her. You act like we've never been through this before," Sehera Moore berated her husband. "Our daughter is a pro. She is, by God, United States Marine Corps Major Deanna 'Apple1' Moore, mecha jock extraordinaire. She will be fine. You could no more keep her away from this fight than you could me."

"Well, now that you bring that up," Alexander stammered over his words a bit, "I was kind of hoping you would snap back at least to UM61 if not home for this one."

"I have volunteered for duty in the hospital. They need me here," Sehera said. The irritation in her voice was obvious. "I'm going nowhere."

"But Sehera, listen to me. This is going to be rough and there is no guarantee that we are even going to be able to come back. It may take weeks, months, or even years to jaunt out of this place without the QMT snap-back gates working. I would feel better knowing that at least one of us was safe." Alexander hoped that made as much sense to his wife as it had to him. He'd been rehearsing that little speech in his mind for days now. He finally had said it and was sure it didn't work out nearly as well as he'd planned.

"No," is all Sehera said. Deanna looked back and forth between her parents, looking as if she were not sure if she should butt in. Alexander didn't give her the chance.

"You could go and stay with your mother while we do this. Help her plan the next attack wave."

"No."

"Just *no*?" Alexander asked. "That's all you're going to say?"

"There is nothing else to say, Alexander. Now drop it. I'm staying with my family right here. If something happens then I will be there when it does. End of story." Alexander knew when to give up. His wife could be quite formidable when she wanted to be. All those years before, when she'd rescued him from the torture camps on Mars, he had seen just how formidable she could be. He knew that when she decided on something there was no stopping her. He wasn't stopping her now, and that was clear.

"Very well then. But listen, both of you. I want you to keep those new Buckley shields on at all times. You hear me?" he said, pulling both of them to him in a family embrace. "Nothing can happen to you. You understand me!"

"We love you too, Daddy," Deanna said to her father.

"I love you, princess. You keep your fucking shields on!" Alexander kissed her on the forehead and then leaned into his wife. A tear formed in the corner of his eye but he managed to fight it and hide it from the women. "You too, Sehera. I love you both with everything I have."

"I know," she said.

Chapter 3

February 19, 2407 AD
U.S.S. Sienna Madira
Target Star System
700 Light-years from the Sol System
Monday, 1:47 P.M. Ship Standard Time

"Nav! Change the hyperspace jaunt coordinates to the ones you are receiving now!"

"Got it, sir!"

"Seven seconds, General!" the XO shouted. "Mission clock at six minutes, forty-three seconds."

"Go, Nav!" Moore gritted his teeth as the purple whirling vortex spun up in front of them just in time. The *Madira* couldn't sling-forward or snap-back because, as the Ghuthlaeer had warned, the QMT systems were nonfunctional, but the FTL hyperspace jaunt system worked just fine. Seconds later the maneuver placed them in reality space at almost the mirror-image location of where they had been facing off with the Chiata battleship. The bow of the supercarrier pointed directly at the system's bright yellowish-green star, and the tilted blue-green planet to starboard and on the port side slightly aftward was the giant, menacing Chiata behemoth that looked like a cross between a giant mechanical sea snail sans the shell and a porcupine on steroids. The giant tuning-fork weapon jutted from the top of the ship, looking almost like a caricature of the sea snail's antennae—a giant, deadly, mechanical, alien, scary-as-hell caricature. Alexander hoped and prayed they could manage the "hit and run" tactic and "chip away at the stone" until they broke the behemoth's back. And then they could worry about the next one. And the one after that. And the one after that. But first things were first.

"I've got the target acquired, General!" Lieutenant Commander Lisa Banks, the new Weapons Deck Officer, shouted through her open faceplate. All of the crew had their helmets on, Buckley reaction e-suit shields operational, and their visors up. Alexander was no different as he commanded from the oversized captain's chair on the bridge of the bot-built supercarrier. His mindview of the battlescape was filling the air about his head with red and blue dots and energy curves and battle tactics, statistics, and weapons inventories. He made mental notes on the blue dot in the aft section of the ship where Sehera was, and the one he could now see moving wildly and erratically through space in the thick of battle. Dee would take care of herself, but if he had to sway the tide of the engagement to help her odds, he most certainly would.

"Well, don't waste time telling me about it, Lisa! Fire at will, goddammit! Put energy on the target before it can hit us!" Alexander ordered. He'd been through this before with the Chiata and knew that even fractions of a second meant life and death.

"Twenty-nine seconds, General!" The XO started the jump clock over. It was the ominous thirty seconds until the damned Chiata targeting system could work out a solution and bring to bear the "zig-zagging blue beams of death from Hell," as the veterans of the Alpha Lyncis battle called them. The clock was projected throughout the ship on every display and through every AIC direct-to-mind to all crew including the mecha jocks, tankheads, and ground pounders. "Mission clock at seven minutes."

The Expeditionary Fleet had QMTed into the system only seven minutes prior, and it hadn't taken more than a matter of seconds before the Chiata had an armada of the giant beast ships engaging them. The planet that the Expeditionary Fleet materialized near on their final QMT jump was the nexus of activity in the system according to all sensor sweeps. In other words, the jump had apparently dropped them right into the middle of an alien hornets' nest. Even though they had caught the aliens unaware, the fleet had managed to poke the hornets enough to piss them off. The alien ships were on them like a swarm at their maximum FTL speeds of about seventy-five times the speed of light.

The long, misshapen dull-brown metal alien sea-snail starships were covered with spires that looked like tuning forks, stretched out into space halfway between the bow and midsection, with the largest of the tuning forks running from the middle of the ship all the way out the front, giving it the appearance of antennae. The smaller forks laid down anti-aircraft and missile-defense fire. It was the large forks jutting forward that spat the zig-zagging blue beams of death from Hell.

"General, I'm picking up a huge EM buildup around the main tuning fork spire!" the new Science and Technology Officer, USN Commander Tori Snow reported. The entire bridge crew except for Firestorm and Moore had died in the last engagement. Moore had managed to put together the best crew he could and train them in the short period of time since. "According to records it is similar to ones seen before as they malfunctioned. I think it is about to blow, sir!"

"On screen, STO!" Moore ordered. It was déjà vu all over again. The spire was cracking all about the base and upward through the center between the tines, with big blue arcs jumping from tine to tine like the alien structure was about to engage the primary weapon, but then orange and red plasma ejected out around it in all directions, just as they had seen in the past in the Alpha Lyncis battle.

The spire exploded. The space around the alien vessel was filled with a mix of blue arcs and red and orange plasmas, and with the force of a small tactical gluonium bomb, an extremely intense high-energy gamma ray burst fried systems throughout the alien ship, sparking off and spreading secondary explosions longitudinally up the ship until one final huge blast threw pieces of the multiple-supercarrier-sized alien vessel into its nearby companion swarm ships, breaking through parts of the exterior armor of its closest wingman.

"Nineteen seconds!" Firestorm shouted. "I've got fire crews being called to the lower hangars and the outer hull tubes, sir."

"Stay on it, Sally," Moore told his XO.

"Damn right, sir! Seventeen seconds!"

"Gunner! Target the damaged area of the second ship with everything!" Alexander turned to the 'Bosses.' "Air Boss, are my fighters deployed yet?"

"Aye, sir!" Commander of the Air Wing USN Captain Patrick "Nosedive" Krieger responded. "The Dawgs and Maniacs are laying down cover for the ground pounders as we speak and the Saviors and the Archangels are mixing the ball like hell! No reports of pukin' deathblossoms yet."

"Ground Boss, report!"

"Roger that, General!" Commander of the Ground Combat Mecha Group Army Brigadier General Geri "Killjoy" Ibanez replied. "The Dragon Slayers have dropped to the planet with the Juggernauts riding piggyback. The hovertanks are smashin' and trashin' and the AEMs are bringing Hell, sir. So far there has been less ground resistance than we expected."

"Damn good, keep them moving on the ground away from the population centers."

"General Moore, CDC!" the voice of the officer in command of the Combat Direction Center called in through the bridge command net.

"Go, CDC."

"Sir, all ten ships from the Fleet are in their pre-described non-Keplerian orbits about the planets over the preplanned target continents. Each ship reports drop tanks deployed and fighters in the mix. Admiral Walker is getting hit the hardest, sir! The *Thatcher* has already taken several blue beams and the forward DEG batteries are down," the CDC reported.

"Keep on it, CDC. I want the fleet moving with random jaunts and if we see it is too thick for any of our teams anywhere I want to know about it before it happens. Game clock is ticking, people. We've got to hold to the plan as long as we can."

"Aye, sir!"

Abby, you stay on top of it.

As always, sir.

Give me a Fleet view zoom-out and keep me apprised of Walker's status. I don't want to lose the Thatcher *in the first quarter of this game!*

Roger that, sir, Abigail replied in his mind.

"General, Admiral Walker is hailing us," the communications officer stated.

Shit.

Yes, sir. I think from her status readings she is sidelined.

Shit. Moore hated taking his most trusted and experienced naval officer out of the mix so quickly.

"Open the channel, lieutenant." Moore nodded in her direction.

"Aye, sir." The young comms officer turned to her console. "On screen, sir."

"Fullback, my stats tell me you're getting pounded to Hell and gone." Moore could see the very large intimidating figure of Admiral Sharon "Fulback" Walker before him. There were alarms sounding in the background, and a fire crew was diligently working on a flaming panel behind and to the left of her.

"Yes, General. I believe I've drawn the short end of the stick. My CHENG tells me that I can either jaunt or fire the DEGs, but not both. All we can do is make a decoy of ourselves and jaunt about." Walker sounded disappointed but calm.

"Casualties are starting to run up on you, Sharon. Pull your ground teams in and get out." Moore looked at the hole in the line that losing the *Thatcher* would make. He would have to make adjustments to the attack plan. An entire continent of the planet would be uncovered. But from the battle statistics, that continent looked like it would be the most troublesome anyway and would need a much larger force than a single supercarrier to hold it.

"Sir, we can still be of some use to you bouncing about to confuse the alien targeting systems." The admiral almost pleaded to stay.

"No. We'll make do. Pull your people, jaunt to QMT range, and lick your wounds. If you get yourselves back in order, feel free to come barreling ass back in. I'm sure we could use any help we can get."

"Yes, sir. I'm sounding the recall and retreat now. Without QMTs it will take several minutes to pull back my fighters and ground teams."

"Get what you can and have the rest retreat to other ships or support other ground engagements. But do not get the *Thatcher* destroyed."

"Understood, sir. Good luck, General! *Thatcher* out."

"Godspeed, Sharon."

Sir, I calculate that it will take over ten minutes to

retrieve *seventy percent of the* Thatcher's *flight and ground teams,* Abigail warned him.

Who is closest to her?

UM61 Alpha03, sir. Captain James 92601, Abigail replied in his mind.

Open a DTM link between Fullback, the clone captain, and myself.

Done, sir.

Captain James. Fullback.

Sir.

James, you are to cover Fullback's retreat and take on any of her teams that she cannot manage to evac. The two of you work out some leap-frogging FTL jumps and get it done. Sharon, I want you out of here in two minutes. Understood?

Roger that, sir, James answered.

Thank you, General, Walker's voice sounded in his head.

Admiral, don't worry about the crew you have to leave behind. As soon as the Hillenkoetter drops in I'm putting her on top of them, Moore thought to them. *Captain Penzington can help cover your retreat as well.*

Aye, sir.

The gunner continued directing the red and green beams from the DEGs of the *Madira II* across the next target. The beams tracked across into the open wound of the Chiata ship. The cannon spires on the side facing them were mostly wiped out by the explosion of the first one. It was the *Madira* versus the local swarm of three Chiata ships nearest the northern pole continent region of the planet. At Alpha Lyncis the three enemy ships would have easily been enough to overpower the *Sienna Madira II*. But that was before Moore had figured out the random FTL jumping tactic, and to top it all off, the new and improved Buckley-Freeman shields were holding solid. Whatever upgrades the CHENG had made after getting the note from the Ghuthlaeer CHENG seemed to be helping for the moment.

"Give me a missile in there and don't let up on the DEGs!" Moore ordered.

"Aye, sir!" the gunner replied. Alexander could see in his DTM battlescape the blue track of a gluonium-tipped missile as it rocketed out from the ship and corkscrewed about the DEG beams all the way to target. As he looked out the viewscreen and saw the missile visually, the DTM tracks overlaid in his mind the energy curves and probability of hitting the target. The missile vanished into the burned-through armor and then the probability of hit went to one hundred percent as it exploded on the interior of the alien ship. The Chiata vessel bulged like a bowl of instant popcorn in the center then popped at multiple orifices from the overpressure. The ship was separated into halves as secondary explosions finished it off.

"Nine seconds! Mission clock at nine seventeen."

Then a blue beam zigged from out of nowhere, it seemed, and slammed into the aft barrier shield. Moore felt the jolt but, unlike at Alpha Lyncis, this time he and his crew were fully armored and strapped in and wearing their helmets.

"That was a solid fucking wallop, Sir," Executive Officer USMC Brigadier General Sally "Firestorm" Rheims shouted. "But we were ready for the bastards this time!"

"She'll hold. She's a good solid ship," the Chief of the Boat Chuck Sowles added from his COB's chair behind the captain's chair and to the left. Alexander had lost his COB on the last mission. He'd hate to lose this one. Sowles had been in the Navy for more than a century. The man just liked to be in space. Alexander had found him on a long-haul cargo cruiser at Tau Ceti. The man was originally from Biloxi, Mississippi, which was another thing that Alexander liked about him.

"Hold or not, COB, she's getting the shit kicked out of her," the XO replied.

"Where did that one come from?" Alexander turned to the STO.

"General Moore! CDC!"

"Go, CDC!"

"We have seven more ships that just dropped out of hyperspace, sir!"

The ship rocked hard forward and vibrations rang throughout it like the inside of a bell. Alexander gripped his chair tighter and thought through the battlescape mindview. All of a sudden the *Madira*, specifically, was terribly outgunned.

The bastards know who's in charge? he thought. *Are my naval tactics that transparent to them?*

It would appear so, sir, Abigail agreed.

How long until the Hillenkoetter team arrives? he thought almost rhetorically. The mission clock highlighted in his DTM view almost as soon as he thought it.

Seven minutes and forty-one seconds, sir.

Might as well have said forever.

"Shit," Alexander Moore hissed through his gritted

teeth as the ship was thrown forward again by another zig-zagging blue beam of death from Hell. It was going to be a long seven minutes and forty-one seconds.

"CHENG to CO!"

"Go, Buckley!" Alexander held to his chair tighter as it continued to shake.

"Sir, the port side DEGs are venting coolant into the exterior hull tubes and we've lost both batteries on that section. Worst of it, sir, is that the coolant leaks have shorted out the structural integrity field generators there. If the shields go, that hull plating isn't gonna hold up to fratricide debris, not to mention one of those damned blue beams!"

"Get me those DEGs back up, CHENG!" Alexander clutched his fists and focused on the DTM battlescape view. The new influx of enemy battleships was turning the tide against his first attack wave. If more enemy reinforcements appeared they would be in serious trouble. Alexander had to rethink his strategy, but there was little time to think. He barely had time to react.

"Aye, sir! But you need to be aware, if we get a feedback pulse from the damaged DEGs, it'll blow every breaker in the hyperspace vortex projector. We'll be dead in the water, sir!" Buckley explained.

"Fix it, Joe! Fix it!" Alexander didn't have time for explanations and excuses. They were in the thick of it and he needed his guns. "COB, see if you can reroute some fire teams to the forward DEGs to help with the CHENG's team."

"On it, Captain!" The COB replied.

"More fire teams are on the way, Joe!"

"Sir!"

"Ten seconds, General!" Firestorm shouted from her station. "Looks like the bastards are trying to flank us and force us into a damned bowl on the planet!"

"Nav! Jump us now!" Alexander watched as the spin-up cycle for the vortex projector counted in his head. They were cutting it too close. Then, out across the bow zigged and then zagged a brilliant blue beam. Moore watched as the vortex of whirling purples, pinks, and blues of Cerenkov radiation flashed against the changing structure of space and time before the ship. Just as the *Madira* stretched forward into hyperspace, the blue beams of death from Hell tore into the port side. The alien horde motherfuckers knew just where to hit him!

"Shit!"

"Shit!" Deanna Moore shouted through the mouth-piece between her clenched teeth as the brilliance of the continually firing zig-zagging blue beams of death from Hell filled the ball with overwhelming irradiance. The illumination reflected off the hull of the *Madira* seemed to Deanna to be looming far too close to the planet's upper atmosphere for her liking. But that was the least of her worries presently. "DeathRay, get that motherfuckin' porcupine off my ass!" Dee grunted through the high-gee-force maneuver as her FM-12 mecha somer-saulted forward, transfiguring from fighter to bot mode, all while her AIC drove the plasma cannon targeting and tracking system to the limits trying to lock onto the Chiata porcupine-shaped fighter that was on her ass. "Guns, guns, guns."

"Fox three!" DeathRay's voice cut through the mecha tac-net. The mecha-to-mecha missile zipped past her cockpit, damned near ricocheting off it. Dee winced at the glare from the hot plasma and ion stream pouring from the missile's propulsion system. As the missile exploded against the shields of the alien fighter, fragments of the warhead housing and orange and white plasma exploded, shifting the alien craft's vector as its shield rippled and shimmered but didn't burn out. "I got 'em, Apple1. Guns, guns, guns! Just feint over and go to fighter and kick the HOTAS hard on my signal."

"Hurry it up!" Dee could see the trajectory curves of her fighter and the aliens' fighter twisting about each other with red and blue traces in her DTM battlescape view. DeathRay's Navy Ares VTF 33-T fighter jinked and juked through the trajectory plots in an almost discontinuous motion. As far as Dee could tell, DeathRay must have been holding the trigger down continuously as racquetbal-sized fireballs pounded at her pursuer's hull. The sharp gee loads DeathRay was enduring to clear her six had to be enormous on the pilot, but that was what wingmen were for. Dee continued to twist and roll her mecha like a giant mechanical Olympic gymnast squirming over a fire ant hill. She looked straight through the bottom of her fighter via her mindview and could see the porcupine's forward spires glowing blue and firing.

"Shit!" She grunted and squeezed her legs, buttocks, and abs as her neck muscles strained against the forces pulling her and pushing her apart. "Aaaaarrrr whooo uhnnn!"

"Warning, enemy targeting lock eminent. Warning,

targeting lock eminent!" Her Bitchin' Betty sounded and warning lights filled her DTM display.

"Now, Dee! Now!" DeathRay shouted. "Guns, guns, guns. Fox three! Fox three!"

Dee didn't hesitate or take time to watch whatever the hell magic flying shit Captain Jack "DeathRay" Boland did. If she'd waited that fraction of a second it would have killed her. Instead her training and proficiency as a mecha jock prevailed. Dee slammed the throttle forward with one hand and the stick forward and right with the other. With her index finger on her left hand she hit the transfigure toggle as she stomped both of the upper left pedals with a tad of lower right pedal.

"Holy shit!" she shouted, and then grunted a guttural scream as the g-suit squeezed her legs, forcing the blood back into her torso. Dee flexed her core muscles and swallowed back bile as the negative nine gravities turned over and then threw her backwards with a positive twelve gravities for a brief instant as the nose of her fighter pointed straight at the alien ship. Her own nose had a slight red trickle of blood draining from it that the seal layer of her suit would quickly absorb.

Just as the blue zig-zagging beams began to leap from the porcupine fighter, Jack's guns tore into the shields. A swirl of blues and greens flashed as the fighter's shields failed. The cannon fire continued pouring into the side plating, making a weak spot for the mecha-to-mecha missile to paint with high explosives. The blue beam seemed to backfire for a brief frozen instant and then the alien ship erupted into a blue and orange ball of shrapnel and plasma. Dee's fighter, now reversing its velocity vector, shot through the fireball and debris cloud, rocking and pinging from small impacts against the Buckley-Freeman barrier shields.

"On your six, DeathRay!" There was no time for Dee to catch her breath. She threw the HOTAS sideways and back and kicked in the throttle as she screamed past DeathRay's fighter, only missing it by meters. The red and blue energy curves spiraled and corkscrewed in her mind but there were none that would converge in time for her to help Jack. Her energy vector was in the complete wrong direction and she'd have to make a hairpin turn as she just had. It was going to hurt but Dee was not going to allow Jack to have sacrificed himself to pull her ass out of the fire.

"Hold on, Boss!" USN Commander Karen "Fish" Fisher shouted through the tac-net. Dee could see Jack's old wingman's energy curve making a U-turn around an enemy porcupine and twisting with her wingman USMC First Lieutenant Wiley "Bridge" Cruise in a ballet spiral with two other porcupines on his tail. The mish-mash of energy curves and possible combat tactical scenarios of more than forty fighting mechas and what was running at the current toll of ninety-seven enemy targets twisted into what looked like a horrific spaghetti nightmare pulsating and entangled about space in her mindview. To anyone else it would have been an incredible overload of data that could simply shut the mind down. For anyone else it would have been overwhelming. But USMC Major Deanna "Apple1" Moore wasn't just anyone.

Then, almost as soon as Dee's mind acknowledged the mix of energy curves her training, instinct, and fighting brilliance converged on a solution almost at the same instant the super-quantum computing artificial intelligence in her head highlighted it. She pulled the throttle to a full stop and rolled and yawed her fighter mode mecha, then kicked in the burners. The two maneuvers slammed her forward with seven gees and then backward with nine gees and no telling how many somersaults her stomach took from the angular accelerations.

"Fish! Stay on your target!" Dee told her. "You and Bridge dance the dance. I need the diversion, and don't worry, I've got your backside curves. DeathRay, you're gonna have to feint as soon as Fish goes hot!"

"Guns, guns, guns!" DeathRay shouted. "I got you, Apple1. But I see what you're planning and I don't like it! The only way out of what you're planning is to start pukin'! Your body is gonna be fried and out for precious seconds and we're overwhelmed!"

"If I don't, you and Bridge are toast! Just cover my ass on the back end!" Dee said. "Fox three!"

Dee loosed a mecha-to-mecha missile as she tore through the middle of Fish and Bridge's energy curves, hoping to draw off at least one of the porcupines from Bridge's tail. The enemy fighter that Fish had made the U-turn about had spun facing her and was firing the blue beams in her direction. Or at least that was the way it seemed. Those fucking zig-zagging death beams could turn on a dime so it was never clear where they were targeted. The missile spun about, juking and jinking through the enemy countermeasures until it hit home on the nearest porcupine on Bridge's six. An energy curve from the edge of the ball cut across in front of DeathRay's nose and a blue curve from one of the Utopian Saviors plowed the road behind it, zipping off her three-nine line at many kilometers per second of relative velocity. The mind-numbing data overload of the alien-paced space combat only exacerbated the physical pounding it was giving the pilots. There literally was no amount of push-ups or weight training that could prepare the human body for the toll mecha combat took. There was no more grueling a fitness program in existence, and that was why mecha jocks looked like they were chiseled from stone and harder than carbon neutronium.

As Dee rolled right, forcing the propellantless engines to the redline, she could feel a bit of tunnel vision fighting in at the corners of her field of view. But the violent rocking of her mecha as one of the blue beams rocked her forward shield snapped her out of it.

Hold on, Dee. Her AIC counted down her maneuver. *Hold. Hold. Now!*

Damn right! she thought.

"Now, DeathRay!" she shouted.

"Fox three!" Boland rolled over into the well-known Fokker's feint as his fighter transfigured into bot mode. Simultaneously, he fired missiles and guns at the porcupine on his ass. The rapid ass-over-heels maneuver distracted the enemy on Jack's six enough that Fish and Bridge spiraled about it, finishing it off and leading the enemy fighters closing on them into the perfect kill box.

"Fox three, fox three, fox three!" Dee loosed three mecha-to-mecha missiles as she twisted through the red and orange fireball that had been an enemy porcupine, keeping her fighter mode mecha pushing at top speed on the same vector, but yawing and pitching the nose of her mecha at targets that were closing on her teammates and opening up their blue beams of death. "Guns, guns, guns!"

Bree, tighten up my energy spiral on the second enemy fighter!

I've got it, Dee, her AIC replied. *Sure you want to do this?*

We're committed at this point.

"Cover my ass, DeathRay!" she shouted as she toggled her fighter over to eagle-mode, took a huge gulp of air, and then she hit the DeathBlossom algorithm. "I'm pukin'!"

DeathBlossom clock spinning. One second and counting, her AIC informed her.

Instantly, the attitude control system accelerated her eagle-mode FM-12. The mecha looked like a sleek fighter plane with two giant cannon-wielding arms underneath and two clawed feet that housed propellantless engines in each. The mecha began to spin in random directions with wings, nose, tail, arms, and feet engines akimbo. Each handheld cannon fired a stream of well-targeted, racquetball-sized, armor-piercing gluonium-tipped exploding rounds, and the directed energy weapons burst precision pointed beams in every direction. The rotational accelerations and decelerations were far too great to fire missiles.

Dee was thrown into her couch with the gee forces of the whirling madhouse. Her stomach tossed and lurched as she clenched her teeth down hard on her temporal-mandibular joint bite block, releasing stimulants and anti-nausea drugs into her system. Dee tracked the energy spirals and red and blue targets in her mind as the universe whirled around her at such a maddening pace that it was all her mind could do to track what was happening. The star field, the ball, the *Madira*, the planet below all blurred into a mosaic of red and blue traces and the targeting solutions pinged in her mind faster than the eyes could follow. The only way to keep up with the data was direct-to-mind.

Five seconds, Dee.

Even mentally, all Dee could manage was a grunt. But she did feel elation as explosions began to fill her blurred, whirling view and red targets blinked out of the battlescape. The DeathBlossom timer seemed to take forever to count down in her mindview. The longest any pilot, DeathRay of course, had ever managed to stay in the maneuver and come out on the other side of it still coherent was thirty-three and a half seconds, and that record was five seconds longer than any other challenger.

Thirteen seconds in! her AIC shouted in her mind as the guns and DEGs continued to fire at targets.

Keep firing until DeathRay, Fish, and Bridge are clear! Dee ordered her AIC.

Several times the cannons or DEGs hit targets but didn't knock out the shields. But the DeathBlossom weakened the enemy in the ball enough so that one of the Archangels or Utopian Saviors could add insult to injury and finish them off. Dee's fighting fury was helping. Whether it was working or not was unclear, but it was at least helping in the short term.

The maneuver continued to take an extreme toll on

Dee as the average random gee forces topped as much as twelve gravities with occasional instantaneous spikes as high as fifteen. Dee calmed herself as best she could and held her abdominal muscles as rigid as hull plating with the structural integrity fields at max. Her core was strong but it was already beginning to ache as it was being expected to support more than twelve thousand kilonewtons of force on her body. Dee grunted and growled, forcing and willing herself to remain conscious and alert through the maneuver. Bile began to trickle upwards into her mouth and her nose continued to bleed.

Dee focused on the red dots in the battlescape DTM and watched as her maneuver continued to pound at them. She had managed to hit more than ten of them and personally take two of them out as the timer clicked over to twenty-one seconds into the DeathBlossom.

Dee was losing her ability to focus. The energy lines of the porcupines and the mecha started to blur and her mind was beginning to lose the ability to track. The laws of general relativity and universal gravitation weighed in on her as the high-gee maneuvers caused her perception of time to slow down. There was little she could do at this point other than ride out the maneuver as each of her arms was so heavy that moving them was almost impossible even in the pilot's armored suit.

Then her ship bounced even harder than she'd ever felt in a DeathBlossom before, and her energy vector radically shifted off her planned course. The tell-tale signs of a zig-zagging beam passed in front of her maddening spin and several new red dots filed into her local battlescape view. The number of enemy fighters in the ball grew as the ball shrunk into a bowl. And the hell of it was that every one of those red dots was firing blue beams and missiles at her and her colleagues. Dee could see the rest of the Archangels scattering and doing their best to lay down cover for her as she approached the end of the maneuver. But she'd never been shot while in a DeathBlossom. Had it not been for her suit and the new Buckley-Freeman shields, she'd have been dead already.

Twenty-six seconds! Bridge is locked up, Dee and Fish can't help him! her AIC warned.

Can we get him?

You can't hold it that long!

I'll hold it! Save Bridge! That's an order.

"Dee, drop out!" DeathRay's voice sounded in slow motion and Doppler-shifted toward bass tones over the gravity-shifted tac-net. "Drop out!"

Stay on it, Bree!

Thirty point seven seconds!

Dee's abdominal muscles felt like they were on fire, exploding, and about to rip from her body from her breasts all the way to her groin, but she continued to squeeze them as best she could. Sweat, blood, and now bile poured from her. She clenched as best she could to keep from vomiting and heaving. The high-gee forces were the only thing keeping that from happening now. But Dee held on as she watched the energy curves of the enemy fighter on Bridge's tail converge.

Thirty four point three.

Dee's vision tunneled in around her and she could no longer hold her abdominal muscles tight. They felt as if they gave way. The red dot on Bridge's blue dot faded out as Dee could feel the weight of the world lift from her body and time rushed in on her as rapidly as her stomach turned upside down and she heaved vomit into her faceplate. She wished she hadn't eaten all day.

Dee choked and held her breath between heaves as best she could to keep the vomit and bile from getting sucked backwards up her nose and down her windpipe. She heaved again and was out of air. She fought back the urge to breathe. She fought hard as she lurched and heaved again. This time, nothing came out. Her stomach was empty. The organogel from the interior of her helmet filled in around her face and quickly absorbed the horrid-smelling bits. A fresh burst of oxygen and stimulants overpressured her helmet to the point that her ears popped.

Two seconds out, Dee! Major Moore! Major Moore, snap to! You've got to move, Dee!

"Apple1! Apple1! Dee!" DeathRay's voice pierced the fog in her mind.

Dee had held her breath as long as she could, and let in a huge gasp. The rush of air and stims into her mouth and nose burned her blood-raw throat like acid.

"Dee! Feint! You have to feint now!"

"Warning! Enemy targeting lock. Warning, enemy targeting lock!" the Bitchin' Betty chimed.

"Dee!"

Blue beams tore into her aft shields, tossing her spinning on a trajectory deeper into the upper atmosphere of the planet. The force of the atmosphere hitting her mecha at a relative velocity of over seven kilometers per second caused the superalloys to groan and creak from the strain. The transparent hull plating of her cockpit deformed in the middle, and spiderweb cracks scattered across it. Dee shook herself as the stims started kicking in. She toggled the bot mode switch, but nothing happened.

"Warning. Port engine failure. Warning. Port engine failure."

Bree! Keep power to the shield generators and give me full throttle on the starboard drive! she thought.

With one engine firing, the mecha was extremely sluggish, but she managed to pull the spin from the blue-beam impact to something manageable. Manageable, yes. Controllable, no.

She hit the transfigure toggle again and still didn't change to bot. Then she attempted to go to fighter mode, but she was stuck in eagle mode.

"Warning! Structural integrity fields at thirty-three percent. Propulsion system failure is imminent. Structural failure imminent. Warning reentry angle off nominal."

"DeathRay! I'm hit bad. Lost an engine and scraping the atmosphere. I've got no trajectory solutions that get me out of the gravity well. I'm going down!" she explained. "Repeat. This is Apple1. I'm going down."

"Eject, Dee!" Fish shouted. Dee thought of that for a brief instant, and just for sake of trying, hit the emergency snap-back button on her QMT wristband. Nothing happened. The quantum membrane teleportation system was nonfunctional in this system. "Eject, Apple1!"

"No good! I'm already venting plasma from reentry. I'm falling too fast at this point. I'm just gonna have to ride it out."

Bree, get me some reentry solutions now! she thought.

Roger that, her AIC replied, as multiple landing solutions started plotting in her mindview. Few of them looked good to her.

That one! It is farthest from any population centers. Might be less uglies there. She highlighted one of the curves in her mind. *Now, just keep us together long enough to crash!*

"*Sienna Madira, Sienna Madira,* Apple1." Dee called in her distress and activated her purple signal for the blue force tracker. "I'm hit and on a collision course with the planet. Projected coordinates being transmitted. I'm going down. Hope you can send an evac soon."

"Roger that, Apple1. Search and rescue will be activated as soon as possible. It's thick out there, Apple1. Lay low and we'll get to you. Good luck."

Chapter 4

February 19, 2407 AD
Alien Planet
Target Star System
700 Light-years from the Sol System
Monday, 1:55 P.M. Ship Standard Time

The drop had been no more difficult than expected. In fact it seemed all too easy. Once the Expeditionary Fleet dropped out of QMT, the ships had immediately started popping out the drop tanks. The *Sienna Madira II* was no exception there. Within seconds of rematerializing in reality space, the M3A18-T army hovertanks were shot out of their drop tubes at the blue and green world below.

Colonel Maximillian "Dragon" Slayer was first out with his squad of "Dragon Slayers." Riding atop of each of the Slayers' ten drop tanks there was at least one AEM. USMC Colonel Francis Jones and Jones' Juggernauts in their armored environment suits held onto the exterior of the hovertanks as they dropped from low orbit all the way through the atmosphere to the surface of the alien planet. For the Marines it was one hell of a ride, but that was how they liked it.

The tankheads and the AEMs dropped at full stealth and didn't engage targets as they fell through the mecha- and porcupine-filled ball. The mecha jocks covered them and engaged the enemy with full ferocity to distract the Chiata as best they could from the drop teams. Strangely enough, the Chiata didn't seem all too interested in the teams once they had penetrated through the upper atmosphere. The drop teams made it to the surface of the planet with zero casualties. But as reports came through the ground team tac-net, it became evident that geography was extremely important in their mortality rates. The *Thatcher's* teams were getting chewed up near the planet's equatorial plane on one of the central more inhabited continents. The *Madira's* ground teams saw little if no engagement—at first.

At first, the Slayers and the Juggernauts didn't see Chiata anywhere planetside. The surface of the northern continent was mostly wilderness, with occasional structures and buildings sparsely set about, not much more populated than a very rural area in old Earth farm country, but even those structures seemed to be abandoned and deteriorating. There were no Chiata military centers in the area as far as the tankheads and AEMs could determine, but that could mean they just hadn't detected them yet. Or, the Chiata hadn't been concerned with them yet. Or perhaps, there was some other strange alien reason that was too bizarre for humans to grasp at the moment. Maximilian had no idea, and more importantly, he knew he didn't really give a shit at present, as the Chiata seemed to rain down on them from the sky like red and green blurs of fire and brimstone.

Once the shooting had started full bore above the planet at less than two minutes into the mission clock time, several giant porcupine-shaped ships screamed over the tankheads and the AEMs, dropping Chiata armored multi-tentacled amorphous red and green glowing monsters on top of them. And that is when things went to shit. For cover fire, the larger alien ships laid down the zig-zagging blue beams of death from Hell.

"Watch targeting locks and the blue beams from above!" Max warned the tankheads and AEMs. "Don't bunch up!"

"Four, take cover!" was the last thing Max heard Slayer Nine say as one of the blue beams hit Nine's tank dead center. Max caught a glimpse in peripheral view of the tank as the shields appeared to hold for almost two seconds, but then, in a flash of green and blue light, they flickered and failed. And then the tank was almost instantly vaporized in a flash of blue engulfed in orange and white plasma and vapor. There was no explosion or parts being scattered about, just the tank being vaporized and the plasma disseminating into the atmosphere.

"Nine!" his wingman Slayer Four shouted as the beam tracked from the vaporized Slayer Nine to Slayer Four. Again, the hovertank only lasted seconds against the alien death beams.

Maximillian did his best to react, but could only watch as the beams tore through the tanks, scattering their formation and totally vaporizing two of his team as well as taking three AEMs with them. Gouges of scorched trees, rock, dirt, and molten mecha parts pockmarked the countryside where the beams had torn through. The two downed Slayers popped up as KIAs in his DTM battlescape view. Serendipity was the only reason his hadn't popped up in somebody else's blue force tracker. For now, Max was fine with serendipity being in his favor. But the onslaught of enemy mecha and ground troops dropping on them from above was quickly turning the probabilities against them.

The hovertank shields are no match for those beams, Colonel, his AIC James One Mike Alpha One said into his mind.

No shit. Max thought. *James, we need to find a weak spot and hit it. That, or turn tail and run like a mother.*

Should I consider retreat and evac, sir?

That was a joke, James. Hell no, let's show these alien bastards how the Army goes rolling along right up their alien asses.

Yes, sir, the AIC replied.

"Slayer One, you see that shit!" Colonel Jones said through the ground systems tac-net. Max adjusted the sensors on his longer-range scanners to give him a larger mindview of the battle so he could get a mental fix on just how outnumbered they were and would be in the next couple of minutes as two more alien dropships lowered from orbit. He kicked the hoverfield into full ahead and toggled his tank over to bot mode. The giant metal vehicle shifted upward into its menacing mechanical bipedal form just as one of the blurs screamed by and stretched out a glowing green tentacle that encompassed his bot-mode tank.

"Shit!" Dragon grunted and kicked the boot thrusters to full. He struggled like a safari hunter wrestling a giant anaconda, clutching the alien beast with the metal hands of his mecha. The mecha strained against the tendrils that continued to force themselves into cracks of the Buckley-Freeman shields, but the shields held. As ripples of blues and greens scattered across the energy barrier, Colonel Slayer managed to squeeze and pull at the Chiata until it burst like a water balloon filled with red and green phosphorescent paints. The thing let out a squeal that was as much eerie as it was earsplitting, but Max continued ripping the thing apart until the writhing and squealing stopped.

"Slayer Two to One! You've got one taking up your three-nine line!"

"I see him, Two." Dragon released the dying Chiata and leaped up high and backwards, firing his main cannons and DEGs as he somersaulted over the blur beneath him. The creature followed at mind-numbing velocity upward into the air after him, and the weapons firing at it didn't seem to give it much concern. "Fox three!"

But the damned thing should've been concerned because the DEGs and cannons were doing their jobs. As the beams and rounds tore into the creature, it weakened the armored and shielded exoskeleton of the amorphous alien, creating a soft spot for his missile to drive home. The mecha-to-mecha missile twisted and turned around countermeasures and then exploded, splitting the creature in half and slinging orange, red, and green plasma in every direction.

"Dragon, you seeing the cloud of targets moving in from the west?" Colonel Jones pinged him over the commander's net. "That's a shitload of bad news."

"Roger that, Colonel. I see 'em and am already working out targeting solutions. Guns, guns, guns." Max fired at another of the strange armored blurs cutting in between him and the AEMs as he sent out a sensor ping at high resolution and repainted the red and blue dots in the direct-to-mind battlescape view in his head. His guns tracked along behind the blur, sending fiery armor-piercing high-order explosive rounds that just missed the alien and passed through several large trees in their path. The trees exploded on impact and fell forward as the trunks scattered in splinters. The amorphous tentacled red and green blur bounced off the ground and began to tear through the atmosphere, leaving a blue ion trail as it disappeared into the trees. But it wasn't fast enough as Slayer Two U.S. Army Major Jackson Applegate bounced across the clearing catching one of the large falling trees by the trunk and slamming it into the fleeing Chiata baseball-bat style. The alien blur squished and morphed around the tree trunk, sticking to it just long enough that USMC Master Gunnery Sergeant Rondi Howser kicked her jumpboots at full thrust upward, rolled over the swinging tree, and popped grenades into the mix. As the grenades detonated, the tree and the alien burst into a fiery ball of splinters and alien goo.

"Good shot, Marine!" Slayer Two noted.

"Behind you, Slayer Two!" Howser shouted as she

fired her hyper-velocity automatic rifle nonstop into the oncoming alien blur. The rounds tore through the planet's atmosphere, leaving a bright purple ion trail as they tracked the amorphous alien attacker. Then Slayer Two turned his bot-mode tank just in time to fire his larger cannon into the creature's midsection. The large plasma rounds exploded against the alien on impact, punching through the shields and then into and through it, splattering red and green viscous liquid in all directions.

"Guns, guns, guns!" Colonel Slayer saw the alien trying to take up position on Slayer Two's six in time and let loose his guns, driving it backwards. "Keep it together, Slayers, and we need to keep pressing through that oncoming line."

"Great shooting, Dragon! Thanks."

So many of the alien blurs had dropped on them, filling the battlescape, that their wild, rapid motions created eerie screeching sounds and sonic booms that thundered across the mountainous forest before the *Madira* ground team. At least for the moment, the area of operations was so crowded that the blue beams of death from Hell weren't zig-zagging about them as often, most likely for fear of friendly-fire kills on their own troops.

"Maximilian, this shit is pretty damned thick," Colonel Jones said over the private command channel. "Our best bet is to run a phalanx up the gut and find some natural cover."

There is a ravine several klicks to the east, sir. His AIC painted the planet's geography in his mindview. *It might make a decent killbox.*

Damned right, he thought.

"Roger that, Colonel," he replied.

Okay, James, plot me some battle solutions and let's start leading the bastards in there.

Yes, sir.

"Listen up, Slayers! We are vastly outnumbered, but remember our training. We are better if we stay together and not spread out too thin. We need to pull these things into the fray here on the ground and keep the pressure off of the mecha jocks as best we can manage. The jarheads will hit them from the top and keep them jumping and hopefully soften them up. And keep the alien bastards close enough to discourage the dropships from firing those fucking death beams."

"Roger that, Slayer One!" resounded from the eight remaining Slayers. Max made a mental note that Slayers Four and Nine, who were now showing on the KIA list in his mindview, would require letters written for them at some point. He just hoped to survive long enough to write them.

"I've got more targeting solutions than I have ammo, Slayer One!" Slayer Three exclaimed. "There's more than a shitload of them!"

"Fire at will, Slayers. We've got to find a way to mix 'em up and make a crease in their attack plan so the AEMs can penetrate in and raise hell. I'm passing along a modified battle plan to your AICs. Let's stack the sonsabitches up and start burning them like cord wood," Slayer One ordered. "Fox three!"

Colonel Slayer let go another mecha-to-mecha missile across the bright green landscape as the radar locked onto a blurred target. The sensors would lock on briefly and then would lose track for a microsecond. That microsecond was enough advantage to the Chiata ground trooper that it morphed its body away from the missile. The missile passed through the alien blur like it wasn't even there, and then a tentacle jutted out from the creature, wrapping itself around the missile. The alien then spun the missile about like an Olympic hammer thrower, letting it go at just the right moment and sending it back at him. Maximilian fired the thrusters on the tank's feet and leaped upward into a forward roll, all the while firing his guns at the missile he'd just fired.

Max's bot-mode tank pounded through the giant fir trees at a pace of nearly one hundred kilometers per hour, all while the single cannon at the bot's nose fired volleyball-sized incendiary rounds that ripped through the tree canopy at targets of opportunity. The first and foremost target was the mecha-to-mecha missile he'd fired only seconds before. His guns struck home on the tip of the warhead, setting it off and blasting him backwards just as the Chiata ground trooper closed in on him, stretching out amorphous tentacles. In a red-and-green oscillating blur it spun about him as if trying to put him in a straitjacket.

"Not this fucking time!" he said as he shoved the barrel of his giant cannon into the thing's front orifice and fired several rounds. The close proximity to the alien's shield armor was enough advantage to the guns that after several rounds the barriers failed. Amor-piercing rounds tore through the back of the creature, scattering its internal bits across the battlescape with a splash of green glowing goop. Colonel Slayer thought for a brief second that he was getting better at killing these alien bastards, and then as his targeting locator pinged wildly, he thought again that he was going to have to get a hell of a lot better.

Chapter 5

February 19, 2407 AD
U.S.S. Sienna Madira
Target Star System
700 Light-years from the Sol System
Monday, 2:01 P.M. Ship Standard Time

"Holy fucking hell! What just happened?" Joe Buckley pulled himself up off the deck plating, doing his best to shake the ringing in his ears away. The helmet of his armored suit automatically started pumping fresh oxygen and stimulants at his face. He took a deep breath, hoping to take some of them in before he was coherent enough to assess the situation in Engineering.

As far as Joe could tell, things were in a hell of a mess. A jet of white-hot plasma streamed from the hyperspace projector tube overhead, cutting through the wall like butter. Molten slag metal popped and skittered across the floor in sticky, glowing red embers.

"Benjamin, I need a report on the projector tube ASAP!" Joe shouted but got no response.

"Benjamin? Report?"

Joe, check your blue force tracker, his AIC thought to him with a solemn tone. *Her suit shows complete failure, and she and her AIC are listed as KIA.*

What? No!

"Benjamin?" Joe could see, out of his peripheral vision to his right, his second in command. Her armored suit was melded to the metal plating in the wall with almost all of her right shoulder, and most of her head from her mouth up was burned away. Commander Keri Benjamin and her AIC were dead.

We need medics and firecrews in here now! he shouted in his mindvoice.

I've already called for them, Joe, his AIC replied.

"CHENG! What the hell is going on! Status report!" He could hear General Moore's voice shouting over the command net.

Joe thought a DTM view of the FTL projector up in front of him and expanded it. He swiped his hands in the air, pulling back layer after layer of complexity until he got to the root of the problem. They had managed to jaunt through hyperspace, but just as they had slipped into the vortex's event horizon, one of the blue beams of death from Hell had hit the overloading DEG generators on the front of the ship. The Buckley-Freeman barrier shield protecting the area held against the blue beam's energy, but for whatever reason had caused the failing DEG generators to lock into an energy-absorption mode rather than transmission mode as directed energy weapons were supposed to do. The alien beam somehow managed to convince the DEG generators to absorb as much of the blue beam's energy as it could until the overload breakers blew, dumping that energy into the vortex projector conduits. Joe wasn't sure if the aliens had meant to do that or if it was a freak accident of engineering components. Either way, it had killed his second engineer, and according to the blue force tracker view in his mind, three other enlisted sailors were dead as well. There were many wounded. And to top it off, the hyperspace system was down, which was bad. Very. Bad.

"Hyperspace is out, General!" Joe shook himself to get his thoughts straight. "I need a minute to figure out what to do."

"We don't have a minute, CHENG!" Moore shouted. "We'll be taking on blue beams in half that time!"

"Understood, General! We've got casualties, fires, and plasma explosions all over down here. I'm working it as best I can. The shields are holding. I can tell you that. But I don't want to see if they can take many more of those blue beams, sir!" Joe turned as a fire crew rushed into the room near another large hole burned through in the wall on the opposite side of the engine room. Several firemen and firemen's apprentices in armored suits were ducking through the hole, beneath the white-hot plasma jet that was now streaming out in two opposite directions, welding whatever it hit into a chunk of molten slag.

"How do we put that out, CHENG?" one of the firemen shouted over the noise of alarms and the secondary and tertiary pops, sizzles, arcs, fires, and explosions that were scattered about engineering. Gases were venting from everywhere they could vent from, and Joe wasn't sure if some of the coolant leaks weren't coming from places that had nothing to leak.

"We've got to cut the power to the conduit and it'll burn itself out quickly. Then we'll have to replace that power conduit section or repair it before we can cycle up the FTL system. That's a several-hour job. We've got minutes at best before the Chiata blast us into oblivion."

The breakers will not cycle, Joe. I've attempted to reset them several times. If we can't recycle the breakers we can't shut off that plasma fire in the energy conduit.

We'll have to do it manually then, he thought.

"The control software is hung up. We'll have to shut it down manually!" he shouted over the noise to the fire crew. Joe turned toward the wall where Benjamin's body was welded upright against it in what was left of her suit. He could see that Chief Petty Officer Sarala Amari was coming around and pulling herself up from the floor. There was a gash in her nose but her suit had sprayed organogel on it. Joe checked her vitals in his DTM and she was fine. He was relieved. He sure as shit didn't want to lose another of his team. Joe could tell that once she caught a glimpse of the remains of Commander Benjamin though, her olive skin nearly turned green. Her heart rate increased dramatically and he thought for a minute that she was going to lose her breakfast, but the seasoned sailor got herself under control.

"Somehow, we've got to get through that bulkhead right there right now." He pointed just to the right of Benjamin's body. "There are three breaker boxes in there that have to be shut off. But with that shit burning right there, the only way into the utility closet is, well, welded shut!"

The white-hot plasma continued to burn hot like a solar flare against the metal bulkhead, melting Benjamin's body even further into the wall and suit as it blasted away. The metal several tens of centimeters away from where the plasma jet impacted the bulkhead glowed red hot. The door on the starboard side of the breaker room had been melted and welded together. There was no way of getting through easily. The other door, the one on the port side of the breaker room, well, there was no door there anymore, but nobody was getting through that opening either, as it was filled with star hot plasma.

The manual circuit control room was the only way Joe could figure out how to shut off the plasma flow, and it was on the other side of a welded door and the white hot jet, and might as well have been on the other side of the galaxy. The clock was ticking fast and Joe knew he had to figure out how to get there from here, shut the breakers off, fix the energy conduit, and then recycle the hyperspace vortex projector. He thought about releasing the repair bots, but they wouldn't make it through the plasma either, and he didn't want to waste the bots. He was going to need them to fix all the broken shit on his boat once they got it somewhere safer.

That's too many things at once and no fucking time, he thought. *There is just no way to fix that energy conduit in time, even with a swarm of bots.*

First things first, Joe. Just keep moving. We have to vent that plasma tube first, his AIC suggested.

So, how do I cycle those breakers open? he thought.

I'm not sure.

We can't do these one at a time. It is a bigger fix than that, and somehow it all has to get accomplished right now, he continued hopelessly.

There is no time to replace the energy conduit even if you recycle the breakers and put the plasma fire out.

Right, I know that. We're going to have to find a way to do it all at once. He didn't like where this line of reasoning was taking him.

My thoughts exactly, Joe. You have to blow the breakers, vent the plasma, and power the vortex projector all at once. Only been done one other time that I know of, his AIC replied. *So, we both know there's only one thing to do.*

Shit. Shit. Shit. Joe knew exactly what his AIC was talking about. He'd been there and done that, bought the fucking tee-shirt, spent several weeks in the hospital, and swore he'd never ever do *that* again. Not ever again. Ever. And it looked like he was going to have to do it again.

Yes, shit, his AIC agreed.

Buckley maneuver.

I cannot see any other solution, Joe. I'm sorry.

Me either. Fuck me.

"CHENG! Do you have anything that will redirect that plasma just long enough for one of us to get through that door?" Fireman's Apprentice Clark Rogers looked as if he were looking for a piece of bulkhead to use.

"That plasma would vaporize any material in nanoseconds. We'd need a damned barrier shield generator the size of a hovertank. Won't work." Joe would have scratched his head if he hadn't been wearing an armored suit. Instead, he shrugged his armored shoulders.

"Joe!" CPO Amari turned away from the gruesome sight that she'd been mesmerized by. "We don't need the breakers!"

"What are you talking about, Sarala? We have to throw those damned switches so the tube's plasma will dump overboard through the aux prop vents." Joe wasn't sure if the Chief Petty Officer hadn't been hit harder than it appeared. He knew that she completely understood that as the energy fields flowed through the ship's various conduits they would vaporize air, metal, dust, you name it and would create dirty plasmas. So, to keep the plasmas from getting out of hand and actually eating away the insides of the conduits, a noble gas was flowed and cycled through them. The energy ionized the gas into a very hot plasma, which created a stable current flow path for the billions of amps of current flowing there. Amari knew that. Joe checked her vitals again in his DTM.

"Yes, I know that, Commander. But all that means is that we have to open the switches!" she replied. Joe looked at her, puzzled for a brief second. Then he looked at the bewildered fireman's apprentice. Then he looked back at the plasma venting at the bulkhead. Then he looked at the wall where the breakers were on the other side.

"Son of a bitch, Amari! You're right. We don't need those fucking things." Joe turned to the fireman's apprentice. "Rogers, all we have to do is destroy those breaker boxes and the circuits will be thrown open. Somehow we've got to blast that wall. How quick can we get some dets and explosives down here?"

"Minutes, probably, sir," the young E2 replied. "Too bad that damned plasma just didn't vent a meter and half to the right and it would've burned 'em out for us."

"Joe, we could weaken the structural integrity field around the holes in the conduit and let it get bigger," Amari suggested. "The SIFs around that pipe are the only thing keeping that piece of conduit from splitting like a potato that's been in the microwave too long anyway."

"Wait, let the plasma get bigger!?" the fireman's apprentice was startled. Joe ignored him for the moment because he knew where Amari was going with her line of reasoning. She was a good engineer.

"Yes! Great idea, Chief. But that'll be a one-shot deal, so we better time it right with fixing the conduit," Joe said. Joe turned to the fireman's apprentice. "Rogers, get to the tool room and get me the biggest fucking wrench in the cabinet and twenty meters of number zero stranded power cable. That cable will be heavy. Take help. Move it now! You have twenty seconds."

"CPO Amari, get on those SIF calculations and be ready to toggle them on my command as fast as you can!" Joe ran through past events in his life to make certain he was going about this the right way. He'd better alert the General because they could go into hyperspace once, and then they'd be down for several hours. It was the best he could do under the circumstances. It'd better be enough.

"One time!" General Alexander Moore shouted over the alarm klaxons and damage reports. He held tight and gritted his teeth each time the ship rocked from impacts with Chiata weapons fire. Things weren't going great and he sure as hell didn't need to lose hyperspace propulsion too. Needless to say, he didn't like what he was hearing. "CHENG, that is unacceptable. We are outnumbered and have soldiers deployed everywhere. We can't just leave them here. Fix the damned hyperdrive!"

"I'm sorry, sir! That is the only solution we have. And worse, sir, when we come out of hyperspace there will be a five-hour fix at top repair pace before we'll be able to jaunt FTL again," Buckley assured him. "And to top it off, it is one of those fixes we can't start on until we turn the thing off. So I recommend we stay in hyperspace as long as we can, sir."

"Alright then, Joe. Get to work on it, but do not engage it until I give the word," Moore ordered the engineer.

"Aye, sir. We will be ready in less than five minutes. I'll notify you when we are ready here. CHENG out!"

"Nav! Take us right up belly to belly with that ship to starboard!" Moore shouted. "Keep it between us and the rest of the alien fleet. I don't care if we swap paint colors. I mean close!"

"Aye, sir!" The navigation officer replied without looking up from his station.

"Seven seconds to next enemy firing solution!" the XO said. "Get us there fucking quick, Nav!"

"Air Boss! Recall every pilot now!" Moore ordered.

"Yes, sir!"

"Ground Boss! Tell the tankheads and AEMs to dig in and hold on."

"Yes, General."

"Sir, the Maniacs have been pushed into the planet's atmosphere covering the Slayers. There is no way they can pull out now. It would leave the tankheads and AEMs vulnerable from the top," the Air Boss reported.

"Tell them to dig in with the Slayers and Juggernauts then." Moore replied.

Sir, search and rescue reports that the starlifter sent to evac Deanna was destroyed, Abigail said in his mind. *There were no survivors.*

Damnit! Deploy another one. He slammed his right armored fist into his chair arm. The metal creaked against the impact.

Sorry, sir, they are either all loaded and bringing in downed crew or have been destroyed.

Show me where she is, he thought. As soon as he did so the planet view popped up in his mindview and zoomed into the continent below, very close to to the north pole, more than eight hundred kilometers from other members of the fleet. That part of the planet was almost completely tilted toward the sun and looked like lush jungle, probably not all that different from the Congo on Earth or the southern equatorial regions south of New Tharsis on Ares. It would be thick, uncomfortable wilderness, with no telling what type of wild creatures inhabiting it. At least there weren't any red forces in that region that sensors could detect. Dee was either lucky or she had managed her crash smartly. *How did she get so far away?*

Her mecha engines failed on reentry and she had one drive stuck on full throttle. She performed a miracle being able to crash-land and survive with the engine stuck the way it was. She managed to navigate to that low probability of engagement region as well. The apple didn't fall far from the tree, sir. She knew what she was doing and managed it under extreme duress. Her sensors show she had a broken ankle but has injected immunoboost and will be fine very soon.

We've got to get to her somehow. I can't just leave her there.

"Blue beams, General!" the XO alerted him.

"Brace!" Moore grabbed the edge of his chair and held on for dear life as the beams stretched out in front of them then turned straight down and to the right twice. The *Madira* was close enough to the enemy ship that Alexander hoped the beams couldn't successfully target them. But he had hoped wrong.

"Jesus H. F'n Christ!" Joe fell backwards onto the deck, flailing like a turtle that had been flipped upside down. "Amari, I want every bit of excess energy we're not gonna need for this jump put into the barrier shields! I mean every last microjoule!"

"I'm on it, CHENG!" Joe could see her location behind the Engine Room control board in his DTM, but he couldn't turn his body that way in his current position and actually see her. He finally managed to roll himself up and over into plank position, then crawled to his feet.

"Joe! The SIFs are down to twenty-one percent and the barrier field generators are single digit!" Amari told him. "One more hit like that and we're done for."

"Then we better get us the hell out of here fast. All of you start antiradiation drugs and immunoboost now. And for God's sake everybody pay attention because it's gonna start getting hairy in here!" Joe shouted. "Faceplates down. And watch out for random high voltage jumping about."

Just as Joe finished his warning, a high voltage crackle of electricity broke free from the hyperspace-lensing system and reached out across the gas vapors in the air, arcing through the streaming plasma fire and throwing dendritic fractal tendrils of electricity in several directions. One of the tendrils found a path to electrical ground through the outer layer of Buckley's armored suit. The Buckley barrier flickered and dumped the energy in a flash of green. The last time Joe had been in his present situation he wasn't wearing a suit and the high-voltage shock knocked him a good six meters into the bulkhead on the aft side of the engine room. As far as he was concerned he wasn't much for déjà vu. But here he was again and it couldn't be anymore déjà vu-esque if he'd planned it. At least this time he was wearing an armored suit.

Debbie, start cycling stims, immunoboost, and anti-radiation drugs into my system.

Roger that, Joe, the AIC replied. *The suit and barrier shield should mostly protect you this time around.*

God, I hope so. Thoughts of the pain he'd gone through the last time he had to do a Buckley maneuver sent chills down his spine.

"Fireman's Apprentice Rogers."

"Yes, sir?"

"You see this coolant flow valve right here?"

"Yes, sir."

"Alright then, I want you to hit that motherfucker right there with that BFW until I tell you to stop!" Buckley shouted over the whistling and crackling of the raging fires, electric arcs, and hissing flow-system leaks as the sailor hefted the *big fucking wrench*. Joe thought about it and had the brief notion of a Buckley Maneuver Manual starting with hitting the valve with a BFW.

Rogers didn't hesitate or ask questions. There was nobody in the entire fleet who hadn't read about the Buckley maneuver. Rogers took the meter-long tool and clanked the thing against the valve assembly. Being in an armored suit certainly made the task easier than it looked. The wrench itself massed at over forty kilograms but Rogers managed it one-handed with ease.

"Amari! Have you got that SIF generator calculation done yet?"

"Completed, Joe! We're ready when you are," the Chief Petty Officer replied.

Joe understood the hyperspace propulsion system probably better than anyone alive. He was the man for this job. Hell, he'd done it before. But this time around it was a little different. There was an advanced alien horde outside with super crazy weapons that couldn't be explained, and they were hell bent on using them to kill all of humanity. Joe had to get it right this time, and do it without putting himself and the engineering crew out of commission. Last time he'd done the Buckley maneuver, he had fried himself with high-energy X-rays and put himself in the hospital for weeks. This time around he needed to be there to fix the damage he was about to do, and the only other engineer on the ship he would have trusted with the job was now dead.

The power couplings between the vacuum fluctuation energy collectors and storage system and the hyperspace projector and fluctuation field shields were intact, but the lensing tube was not swirling a perfect pink and purple hue as it normally did. The power conduit that immediately fed into the projector was barely holding together and venting two large jets of plasma that was hotter than Sol, and those leaks were acting as a switch that was keeping the energy from flowing into the projector. Without that energy the vortex projector couldn't manipulate the fabric of spacetime creating the Krasnikov Tube's event horizon, and therefore no hyperspace jaunt.

Joe was pretty damned certain that if they attempted to pull power through that damaged conduit on the order needed to create a hyperspace vortex while it was venting plasma, the thing would go off like a bomb that would ripple all the way down the energy conduits throughout the ship and would take out almost every system while igniting plasma fires along the way. In order to minimize the damage from going into hyperspace, Joe had to first put out the plasma fire, reboot the projector, and give the energy flow a temporary pathway that would last long enough to jaunt them to a safe distance from the Chiata.

"The valve is crushed to hell, CHENG!" Fireman's Apprentice Rogers said, dropping the BFW to the floor. Just as he did, the crushed and mangled valve atop the coolant flow tube popped, spewing superheated ethylene glycol. The liquid cooled almost immediately from rapid expansion as it sprayed about. The system quickly drained and covered the floor on the port and aft side of the Engine Room about three centimeters deep. The smell of the coolant brought memories to the forefront of his mind—bad memories.

"Okay. Grab that power cable and wrap it at least twice around the power input to the vortex projector here and weld it to that thing there. Quickly!" Joe traced the power flow loop in his mindview backwards from the power input of the projector through the damaged tube and to where he hoped the plasma was burning normally, not superheated, and was well maintained by the conduit and the structural integrity fields. "There. Right there."

Joe bounced across the floor, slopping in the coolant with each armored step. He stopped on the far side of the engine room where the power conduit protruded through the bulkhead. The quantum fluctuation energy collectors would be on the other side of that wall. That was where he needed to tie off the other end of the cable.

"Tie this end off right here and weld it down!" he shouted. "Amari, thirty seconds."

Joe grabbed hold of the cable and helped Rogers and two other firemen drag the heavy ten-centimeter-diameter cable across the room. They threw it over the conduit and then pulled it tight. The plasma welder made short work of the insulation layer on the outside of the cable and melded the stranded steel wire right to the metal conduit.

"Now we have to time this just right." Joe transmitted his mindview display to all of the team so they could see what was about to happen. "Amari, when you throw the SIFs, hopefully the tube will fail at the right place, burn through the wall, and take out those circuit breakers. When that happens the plasma flow will shut off at the junction on either end of the damaged tube, the vortex will spin down, and the plasma fire will burn out. Then everyone immediately evacuates the Engine Room! I'll throw the restart sequence on the vortex, cycle a SIF around this cable, and then open the energy flow. The combination of the cable and the SIFs should allow us to spin the vortex projector for several hours before it burns out. It'll be a hell of a mess and a radiation funhouse in here while that thing is going. Everyone understand their tasks?"

"Aye, sir!"

Debbie, you got the software patch for the cable's SIF ready?

I'll watchdog it myself, Joe.

Good. Then I guess we're good to go.

I think so.

"Everyone take their places and stand by." Joe looked around the Engine Room once more to make sure he wasn't forgetting anything. "CHENG to CO!"

Chapter 6

February 19, 2407 AD
Alien Planet
Target Star System
700 Light-years from the Sol System
Monday, 2:03 P.M. Ship Standard Time

"Roger that, Dragon," USMC Colonel Delilah "Jawbone" Strong replied to the tankhead's leader as she weaved her FM-12 about the mix of horrifically blinding blue beams from the porcupines mixing up with her and the rest of the Maniacs, the even more horrific and larger blue beams coming from the dropships above, and the alien AA fire coming from the surface of the planet. And at the same time she was doing her level best to cover her wingman's ass and give top cover to the ground pounders below. She had high expectations, very high expectations, that her squadron, her wingman, and the groundpounders were likewise covering her ass in return.

"We can't last like this, Jawbone!" Colonel Jones, the AEM leader, added to the conversation. Delilah could see in her DTM battlescape view that the ground teams were getting the shit kicked out of them. Casualties were racking up quickly. "We have to make it to cover!"

"There's no way evac is getting through this fucking murder factory!" Dragon added while grunting through maneuvers. That was all too familiar to Delilah as she was currently grunting and biting her TMJ bite block because of her own high-gee flying. "We're stuck here to fight this out."

"Don't worry, the Maniacs ain't going nowhere! The mission clock shows the *Hillenkoetter* wave should be here soon. Reinforcements are on the way. We have to make it that long and we hold out for evac then. But I agree we need to find cover until the reinforcements arrive."

"Reinforcements, hell! By the time they get here they'll be replacement forces," Colonel Slayer replied.

"Shit!" Delilah blinked and winced as the continuous purple plasma balls of AA fire from the ground rippled her shields and jostled her pretty damned hard. Had she not had her bite block in her mouth she might have bitten her tongue off. Jawbone stomped the upper right pedal and pulled back on the HOTAS, yawing and pitching at the same time. The maneuver put her under spine-crushing pressure, but she breathed through it and then toggled her fighter mode mecha over to bot. "Fox two!"

Delilah's mecha transfigured to bot as the missile screamed across the top of the tankheads into the AA gun escarpment. The infrared guided missile locked onto the heated bores of the alien anti-aircraft systems and drove home. The warhead exploded, scattering the guns to bits of rubble, and several red and green blurs careened from the explosion in several directions at once. The disruption in the entrenched weapons fire gave several of the AEMs on the ground all the opening they needed to rush through the line and lay waste to the remaining enemy within by popping grenades and spraying hyper-velocity rounds about.

Delilah bounced the mecha's armored feet against the surface as she serpentined through the tankheads, firing her guns and blasting away at any ground targets of opportunity. As the mecha bled off speed, a rooster tail of dirt and debris was flung high behind her, arching across the surface. Along her path she practically clipped an alien ground troop from behind, enabling the tank it was taking position on to take it out. Delilah continued to roll through and back up to her feet in a flurry of motion, still with way too much forward momentum to come to a controlled stop. But she didn't want to stop anyway.

"Warning! Enemy radar targeting lock detected! Warning! Enemy radar targeting lock detected!" her Bitchin' Betty chimed.

"Shit!" Delilah threw the HOTAS full forward and stomped her thrusters against the ground, rolling forward in a judo roll and then leaping over one of the Slayers' hovertanks parkour style. The bot-mode tank tracked in behind her, firing its mammoth nose-mounted gun and the shoulder mount DEGs at the porcupines that were closing in on Delilah's six. The lead alien porcupine closed in and managed to avoid the tankhead's cover fire. Delilah didn't have time to reconfigure her mecha, so she fired her thrusters at full, pushing the bot-mode fighter up and straight at the porcupine and firing her guns. "Guns, guns, guns!"

"Fox three!" her wingman, First Lieutenant Sara "Coffee" Ames pounded the alien fighter with an air-to-air missile that tore through it, causing it to spin out of control into the battlefield just short of several more AEMs. The groundpounders finished it off.

"Great shot, Coffee!" she shouted through her bite block as she gasped for breath, very relieved.

"Colonel, I'd sure appreciate it if you'd quit using yourself as bait like that, ma'am."

"You just be there to catch the fish and it won't matter. I owe you one, Coffee!" Delilah replied.

"Yes, ma'am! Watch your three-nine line!"

"I've got 'em." Jawbone had time and speed now so she toggled back to fighter mode. The bot flipped upside down, rolling through the transfiguration to a fighter plane, causing her stomach to somersault.

You've got plenty of energy to match trajectories. Her AIC posted red and blue flight paths in her mindview.

Right there. I'm too close for missiles but perfect to close on guns. She highlighted one of the combat solutions playing out in her mind. *Optimize me for that engagement!*

Roger that, going to wide area targeting and guns.

"Guns, guns, guns!" Delilah fired the mecha's larger cannons and continued to hold the trigger down as orange racquetball-sized plasma incendiary rounds plowed into the porcupine's shields, overpowering them, and then into and through the alien fighter's structure.

"What's our play, Colonel!" USMC Captain Yariv "Blue" Sandeep asked over the Maniacs' channel on the tac-net. "The *Madira* is pulling out all the ships from the first wave and we can't make it back up through the ball in time."

"I say we do what the CAG always does," one of the other Maniacs added.

"Yeah, we go in there and kill all those fuckers!" another one grunted. "Works for DeathRay."

"Yeah, well, Blue Force Tracker shows the Angels loaded on the bus." The banter on the tac-net continued through high-gee maneuver grunts and shouts.

"All right, Maniacs, knock that shit off and listen up! We're stuck here for now, but the second wave is coming. Until that time we stay here and we keep killing the alien bastards 'til there're no more to fucking kill. You don't have permission to die until all the killing is done!" Delilah responded, her Florida accent ever present in her speech. "The tankheads and AEMs are sitting ducks without us. We ain't leaving them. Track all your energy curves toward the ravine at the location I'm forwarding to you. We cover the ground teams, keep the porcupines in a low top bowl, and bring hell with maximum ferocity at maximum velocity!"

"Roger that!" Blue responded.

"Ooh-fuckin' rah! Ma'am!" one of the other Maniacs replied.

"Major Sellis, our right rear stack is getting spread too far apart!" Sergeant Major Tommy Suez alerted the ranking officer on the right side of the phalanx the

Juggernauts were doing their level best to push through the Chiata ground troops that had dropped to the surface between them and the ravine ahead and about four more klicks away.

"Roger that, Top. See what you can do to help with that, will ya?" Sellis replied. "I'm in the middle of some serious shit right now."

Aren't we all, he thought.

You sad that right, Tommy, his AIC replied to him.

"Yes, sir! Do you need help, sir?" Tommy asked. His DTM battlefield view showed the AEM major's blue dot surrounded by several red ones, but the major was moving like a blur in the DTM view. He was holding his own and then some, but Tommy had enough experience in combat to see what was going on. The horde was doing its best to lead the major and whoever would follow him into a makeshift killbox. A dropped AA escarpment and several alien tankships were just behind them, and in the general direction the major was being drawn, blue beams were tearing through the large conifer-like alien trees. Their phalanx was getting spread too far out on the right, and near the point of the spear, the Major was in danger of drawing the right half of the AEMs into some really bad shit.

DTM this to Colonel Jones, Jackie, Tommy thought to his AIC.

Done. What are we going to do, Tommy?

First things first, he thought while firing on the move. Several of the Chiata amorphous red-and-green-blur ground troops whizzed about and between the separation in the V-shape the AEMs were pushing. But Tommy wasn't about to let them get through their formation and then come knocking on the backdoor. No, he wasn't going to let that happen.

"Oh, hell no," he muttered to himself.

Tommy kicked his jumpboots hard, firing the thrusters, jumping him up and over the line just ahead of Colonel Jones at the spear's point and slightly left of Major Sellis and several others further back on the stack.

"Top! What the hell are you doing?" Colonel Jones shouted over the groundpounder tac-net.

"I'm killing two birds with one stone, sir," he replied. Then he popped several of the shoulder-mounted grenades into the fray a few tens of meters in front of him and dropped to a knee as he laid down several bursts from his rifle. The hypervelocity rounds ripped through the grenade explosions leaving tunnels of blue ionized trails in the orange and white fire and debris cloud. Tommy had chosen his targets precisely and each of the grenades hit home on large trees, bursting them into splinters at their trunks and causing them to fall across their path to the right. This cut the Chiata's path to the killbox off, or at least made it more cumbersome to travel through. As a side effect of the trees falling, the AEM's phalanx formation was forced to slow on the right side and to turn their vector left into the point of the spear. This tightened the V-shape and closed the ranks in tighter.

"Major Sellis, watch your backside!" Top heard Rondi Howser's voice over the net, and turned in time to see the master gunnery sergeant in mid-leap over one of the Chiata and onto the top of another one taking up position on the major. Howser applied incendiary rounds liberally to the situation, popping one of the red and green blurs like a water balloon. Tommy looked at the overall formation of the team and at the aliens' killbox. And he got an even bolder idea.

"Colonel Jones! Is there any chance we could get the tankheads to lay down a line of fire behind the AA guns up ahead?" he asked his superior.

"Why's that, Top?"

"Look at the landscape, sir!" Tommy quickly transmitted his DTM view to the Colonel. "A line of fire there would drive a wedge between the first drop wave and the second, cutting them off from each other. Then they'd only have two choices. One, move parallel to that line and parallel to us or, two, they'd have to turn and come through us."

"Okay, Tommy. I see that. Then what?" Tommy wasn't sure why the Colonel couldn't see what he was driving at, but he was busy at the point of the spear. So he'd just have to lay it out for him.

"Well, sir, either way they'll have to go where we want them to. If they decided to turn on us and they get through, the tankheads are right behind us and the Maniacs are atop them. We'd have them surrounded. If they go along the line of fire then they are headed right toward the edge of the ravine and there the Maniacs can shoot them like fish in a barrel!" Tommy ducked and winced as the green blur of a tentacle or pod or whatever the hell it was wrapped around his helmet. Instinctively he grabbed at it, but when he did, another amorphous shape twisted around his left gauntlet and up his arm.

"Top, look out!" Both Master Gunnery Sergeant

Howser and Major Sellis bounced on top of his position, firing rounds on full auto into the alien creature. Tommy fell backwards from the impact and instinctively did a back handspring kick-over that failed because the alien had itself wrapped around his legs. But where the alien had gone wrong was leaving Top's hands free.

Tommy popped his shoulder-mounted grenade tube open and fired one at point blank into the Chiata ground troop. The spiny, amorphous armored blur wrapped itself around the grenade and spit it out its backside just as it detonated. The creature's barrier shields flickered against the explosion and failed. At that point, Tommy gripped it with his armored hands and strained with all the might of the powered armor. The alien screamed and writhed in what could only be described as pain.

"Hold on, Top!" Howser bounced just beside him, slamming her HVAR into the side of the creature as she popped off several hypervelocity rounds into what might or might not have been the thing's head.

"Damn." Tommy felt the thing go limp in his hands and continued to tear it apart and throw it off of himself. "Thanks."

"No time for that. We've got to keep moving." Major Sellis bounced between the two of them onto a knee, never ceasing fire the entire time. The automatic hypervelocity rounds zipped from the rifle with the tell-tale *spittap, spittap* sounds of the rounds breaking the sound barrier as they were accelerated down the bore of the weapon. The major rose to his feet, firing behind Tommy, and then bounced over backwards, firing into what was left of the tree canopy above them. One of the

Maniacs screamed overhead in fighter mode, firing missiles just ahead of them, and several of the Slayers were closing around their position. The remainder of the AEMs were filling in as well, staying in their phalanx formation as best they could.

"Right. Sir, we need to push these bastards against that hill line there as the tankheads start dropping fire on them." Tommy explained his plan.

"Yeah, I agree, Top. Colonel Jones is ahead of us on it!" Sellis replied and pointed at their squad commander. The USMC Colonel was riding atop a hovertank that was cutting through the enemy line at over one hundred kilometers per hour.

"Follow me, Juggernauts!" Colonel Jones ordered them.

"Ooh-fuckin'-rah!" Howser shouted.

"Damn right, sir!" Tommy almost smiled.

Chapter 7

February 19, 2407 AD
The "Ball" nearest the *U.S.S. Sienna Madira II*
Target Star System
700 Light-years from the Sol System
Monday, 2:05 P.M. Ship Standard Time

"Spandex! Spandex! Watch your North Pole! You've got two porcupines gonna lock you up!" DeathRay shouted at the young Navy Lieutenant Junior Grade Gregorio "Spandex" Muniz. The kid was known for taking a beating but staying on his wingman tight, like Spandex running tights. Unfortunately, his wingman, USN Commander Sondra "Brains" Edwards had been killed in action only moments before while trying to cover Spandex's approach on the hangar just after the General had recalled them. Spandex had to abort, and had it not been for DeathRay mixing it up in the ball as a floating partner, both of them would have been lost.

"I've got 'em, DeathRay!" DeathRay could see the young pilot attempting to roll over into a Fokker's feint, but he didn't have the angular momentum needed on the pitch axis. Jack knew he'd have to cover the kid's mistake or he'd be meat for the grinder. "Fox Three!"

"Guns, guns, guns!" DeathRay shouted over his guttural grunts as he kicked the HOTAS full throttle and forward upwards through the ball, jinking and juking about debris, enemy AA fire, and porcupines trying to lock him up. At maximum acceleration he was being pushed into the seat at over nine bone-crushing, lung-collapsing gravities. A porcupine was doing its level best to match Jack's energy vector just off his five o'clock and slightly beneath his flight path, but DeathRay wasn't going to let that alien bastard stop him from saving the youngest member of the Archangels from impending death from alien assholes. He'd already managed to let Dee get herself shot down and had lost Brains as well. Two other Archangels were showing up as casualties in his DTM, but they were alive and already on the *Madira*. Jack hadn't seen this much loss in his own squadron since the Separatist War and he sure as shit didn't like it.

"Warning! Enemy targeting lock imminent! Warning! Enemy targeting lock imminent!" the Bitchin' Betty chimed in his cockpit.

You have less than seven seconds, Jack! his AIC warned as energy vectors and trajectory alternatives popped up in his mindview. Red enemy trajectories spiraled and corkscrewed about his blue trajectory up to his current position in spacetime. Branching out from the "now" was a bifurcation of possible courses of action. Jack quickly found one he liked and adjusted the foot pedals, switches, and HOTAS to match it.

Countermeasures, Candis! he ordered. *Pop flares and jammers!*

"Aaaarrrrrrr, wooooot!" DeathRay grunted and rocked and rolled with the HOTAS, slamming it from side to side and from stop to stop. The lateral forces on his body were nearing intolerable and his internal organs jostled around with each extreme jerk, leaving internal bruises. His brain moved about in his skull, slamming into the brainpan with such force that he was lucky not to be concussed. He did see stars briefly though. "Spandex! Kick your boot thrusters full now! Toggle to fighter and get the fuck out of there! And drop some chaff!"

"Warning! Enemy targeting lock! Warning, enemy targeting lock!"

Three seconds, Jack!

"Guns, guns, guns," he screamed.

Spandex's mecha seemed to move sluggishly, as it had taken on multiple hits already. The two porcupines ripped down from the top of the ball head-to-head with Jack, and poor Spandex was the caught monkey in the middle. The porcupine setting up on Jack's ass-end was closing and would fire before any normal human could do anything. But USN Captain Jack "DeathRay" Boland was anything but normal and was really fucking tired of his squadron taking losses.

"Not. Fucking. Today!" he grunted against the acceleration.

DeathRay threw his fighter into an orbiting spiral about the vector that the porcupine on his rear was taking, then he bit hard on the TMJ bite block, taking in a burst of oxygen and stimulants. That gave him the rush of strength he needed to reverse yaw so that his nose was facing the alien that had been on his six. Now Jack was corkscrewing backwards, upwards through the ball at full throttle and locked up by three porcupines at once. Spandex was almost clear at this point.

"Fox Three! Fox Three! Fox Three!" Jack let loose three mecha-to-mecha missiles that he knew wouldn't hit home, but it would buy him a fraction of a second and that was all he needed. Fractions of a second were small bits of eternity in a dogfight.

Start pukin', Candis! he shouted in his mindvoice to his AIC. He took in a deep breath, clenching his jaws around the bite block and his asshole on the seat. There wasn't a muscle in his body that he didn't squeeze as hard as a rock and hold.

All guns and DEGs on auto target! Hang on, Jack! his AIC said. *DeathBlossom clock at zero seconds and counting!*

The three missiles twisted out in opposite directions towards the Chiata fighters. The first one hit nose-on the fighter on Jack's rear trajectory vector, now the direction his fighter's nose was pointing. The missile exploded against the shields of the porcupine, slowing its pursuit only minimally. The other two missiles twisted about the alien countermeasures, but were taken out before they hit their targets.

Jack's Ares fighter started the madhouse whirl of the puking DeathBlossom while at the same time following the corkscrew spiral vector he was previously on. With each spin around, his plasma cannons or the directed energy guns would target one of the three porcupines. The ball spun madly outside Jack's cockpit and there was no way humanly possible to focus on anything outside the cockpit from his actual vision.

He breathed in the stims and closed his eyes, using only his DTM battlescape. Rather than having the mindview spin wildly with him at the origin, Jack used a trick that only a few pilots could stand. He had his mind view sit stationary at the origin of the DeathBlossom and let his fighter spin around him. He used space as his frame of reference, not his fighter. The targeting Xs stayed in a stationary ball while his fighter spun and twisted rapidly around him, targeting the enemy fighters. It took great focus and an intense grip on his abdominal and leg muscles to keep blood in his brain. The running joke was that DeathRay's retirement plan was to stick a lump of charcoal up his ass before each mission, because he had to squeeze his sphincter so hard and for so long he brought back a diamond each time. This time was no different.

The mind's view of the lack of motion was at complete odds with his body's sensing of the horrific stress and pressure being placed on him as he was physically tortured by the wild accelerations of the DeathBlossom's whirling madness.

Four seconds, Jack.

Target the two on Spandex first!

Understood.

"DeathRay is laying down the cover for us Archangels! Now shag ass to the *Madira*!" Commander Fisher ordered over the squadron's tac-net. "Move it! If you can lay down cover on your way in, do it."

Jack listened to Fish's voice and could see the formation of the Archangels breaking as best they could from the ball. They were going to make it. The rest of the squadron was going to make it. He turned his view to Spandex, who had managed to toggle to fighter mode and was driving full throttle toward the supercarrier. Jack's gamble to save the kid looked like it was going to work. The young pilot's mecha screamed past Jack at only a few meters distant, on guns full trigger. He was taking some of the pressure off for Jack.

Good job, kid, he thought.

"I got the one on your six, DeathRay!" Spandex grunted. Jack would have smiled if the forces of the spin didn't have his lips pinned against his teeth. He knew, though, that he owed the kid a beer.

Twelve seconds.

DeathRay's DEGs tore through the ship advancing on him from his forward vector on the left. The beams pounded the alien porcupine and the shields on it began to fail, but not before blue beams shot outward from the ship and turned several ninety-degree turns tracking Jack. But as his fighter spun, plasma balls from the cannons hit the alien fighter's weakened shields and then tore into the craft's armor plating, causing it to explode in an orange and green fireball. But the zig-zagging blue beams of death from Hell had already been fired, and hit the underside of DeathRay's mecha's empennage. His shields flickered but they held; however, the added momentum tossed his fighter sideways and into the oncoming porcupine on his right. The impact was so hard that Jack was certain he'd bitten through his bite block. Stars shot across his vision and it felt to Jack like several of his ribs had to have been cracked or separated.

The two ships stuck together like two balls of clay and continued to spin through the ball on a resultant vector of the two ships' original trajectories. A red and green tendril stretched out from the alien fighter, wrapped itself around Jack's fighter plane, and squeezed the shields to the bursting point.

Jack recentered his mindview to actual and swallowed back bile, doing his best not to vomit in his helmet. Now just wasn't the time. He hit the bot-mode toggle, and the sound and feel of straining gears and motors reverberated throughout the mecha but it didn't transfigure. The ship was too wrapped up by the alien to transform to full bot-mode.

"Shit! Guns, guns, guns!" he said hoarsely and fired the guns, hoping they would help, and they did. Sort of. The plasma balls tore through one of the spines on the porcupine and caused it to crash against the tendril wrapping around Jack. "You flinched, asshole!"

The alien flinched just long enough for the mecha to toggle to bot mode, ripping loose the appendage that was holding him. Jack fired his boot and back thrusters to give him control of the spin as he bear-hugged the alien craft. More tendrils shot out to encapsulate Jack, like a constrictor eating a mouse, but DeathRay was no mouse. He pushed off from his bear hug and unslung the cannon, gripping it with his left mechanized hand and firing it into the alien tendrils as they closed on him.

"Guns, guns, guns!" he continued to shout as he grabbed a tendril in his right hand and blasted it into pieces with his left. Jack stomped at the pedals and worked the HOTAS with both hands, all fingers on a switch. The bot mode mecha twisted, ducked, jumped, slung elbows, head butted, kicked, and punched like a mixed martial arts champion in close range. "Get the hell off me, you alien son of a bitch!"

"Warning! Enemy targeting lock! Warning! Enemy targeting lock!" the Bitchin' Betty chimed.

Behind us, Jack! his AIC warned.

Jack could see the targeting system showing a red X directly behind him and moving fast in his DTM. Then he could see the flash of the blue beams coming off the tines in the midsection of the porcupine. As the enemy from behind closed and fired the zig-zagging beams DeathRay gripped his cannon with both hands and fired the guns on full auto as he slammed it into the belly of the porcupine he was currently entangled with.

The plasma rounds tore through the alien's outer armor plating and squished red and green viscous fluids as it boiled off into space. Jack kicked his thrusters at full throttle, spinning himself and the porcupine over just as the blue beams tore through the backside of the alien fighter, vaporizing through the hull and reducing Jack's shields to zero. His mecha was flung backwards head over heels, arms flailing akimbo. As the approaching alien fighter passed by, a tendril reached out and wrapped around Jack's waist, yanking him so hard in the other direction that he nearly lost consciousness from the overwhelming deceleration.

He bit onto his TMJ bite block, releasing more stimulants. And he noted that the suit had administered immunoboost for several cracked vertebrae in his neck. But that was the least of his worries. If he didn't get loose from this alien bastard, a broken neck would be the least of his worries. Jack forced himself to work the HOTAS and pull the cannon back into toggle position.

"Guns, guns, guns," he said faintly. The plasma rounds cut through the tendril, giving Jack the second he needed to kick off from the alien fighter. "Fox Three!"

Jack fired the missile at point-blank range. It had no sooner rocketed out of the canister than it exploded against the porcupine's shields. The warhead rippled energy across the alien craft with green flickers of light as the orange fireball engulfed both of them. Jack hit the fighter-mode toggle and slammed the HOTAS all the way down, hoping to pull out of the blast.

Great flying, Jack! You made it, Candis told him.

I don't feel so fucking great, he thought.

Just as the alien fighter's shields failed, a tendril shot through Jack's cockpit like an amorphous green spear. With no shields left, the alien appendage penetrated the fighter's armor plating, broke through his suit's shields with ease and pierced through his abdomen, then out the back of DeathRay's armored suit. Jack hit the rear DEGs, cutting into the unshielded alien craft until it gave way. The tendril went limp and retracted from his fighter.

"Oh, my God!" Jack screamed in pain as red blood squirted from the hole across the control panel in front of him. Quickly his suit sealed the wound with organogel and seal layer, and immunoboost, pain meds, and stims were pumped into his system. Jack needed to get onboard the supercarrier. He knew he couldn't stay and fight any longer. "Fly the plane, Jack."

Fly the plane, Jack! Candis told him.

"Fly the plane," he told himself. He looked at vectors in his mind to get him landed as quickly as possible and to avoid targeting locks as best he could. He slammed the HOTAS full throttle at the hangar bay. AA fire from the *Madira* cut in all around him, clearing his path.

"DeathRay to *Madira* tower starboard aft bay. I'm hit and coming in hot. I'm calling the ball!"

"Roger that, DeathRay, you are clear to land. You have the ball. DeathRay, throttle back! You are coming in too hot! Start your decel protocols!" the tower control officer ordered him.

Jack, I can take it. Your heart rate is fading quickly, his AIC said. *Increasing stims.*

I think you're going to have to, Candis. I can't feel the stick anymore, Jack thought hesitantly. Then the tunnel vision in his eyes was too much. The last thing he could see at the end of the tunnel was the bright lights of the interior of the hangar bay rushing in at him. Then the tunnel collapsed inward to blackness and Jack was gone. His suit's defibrillator engaged.

Captain! Jack Boland! DeathRay!

Chapter 8

February 19, 2407 AD
U.S.S. Sienna Madira
Target Star System
700 Light-years from the Sol System
Monday, 2:07 P.M. Ship Standard Time

"Roger that, CHENG! Stand by for my command." Alexander clutched his captain's chair so hard that grooves the shape of his armored suit's gauntlet fingers were forming. With each impact of an alien missile or blue beam the *Madira* would rock, lurch, and list wildly.

"General! We just lost UM61 Alpha Zero One and Alpha Zero Seven at the same time!" the XO grunted. The tally in Moore's DTM view had begun with ten ships and they were now down to seven. "We're getting chewed up. Three other clone ships are in pretty bad shape and I'm not sure how much longer they'll last. Hell, sir, I'm not sure how much longer we'll last."

"CO, CDC!"

"Moore here. Go, CDC!" Alexander was searching his mind for some tactic to push the fight in his favor but they were spent. Without reinforcements, hell, even with them, the first attack wave was on the mat and almost down for the count. It was usually at this point in a battle that Alexander would decide that the enemy had him right where they wanted him. And it was at this point where he had historically become the most dangerous. How he was going to become dangerous was completely and utterly lost to him at the moment.

"The *Hillenkoetter* and the other thirty clone ships just QMTed in, sir!"

"About fucking time," the XO said with a hint of relief in her voice. "Sir, we can't take any more big hits. Our shield generators are spent."

"I agree with the XO on that, sir," the STO added.

"The casualty list keeps piling up, sir," the COB added. "We're gonna have to stop and lick our wounds soon. Every fire crew and repair bot is working beyond capacity at this point, sir."

"Understood, CDC. Firestorm, COB, STO, I agree." Alexander looked at the status of the initial attack wave. They were in deeper trouble than he'd expected to be at this point. They were only about thirteen minutes into the fight and taking on serious losses. The Chiata were able to respond to the surprise attack much quicker than he'd imagined. The intelligence they'd gotten from the Ghuthlaeer was damned near useless. There were way more Chiata megaships in the system than expected.

The *Thatcher* had already had to bail. Two of the clone

ships had just been lost and three others were in very bad shape. There were ground teams scattered across the alien planet and almost every attempt at evac or support to them was destroyed as soon as they were started. The casualty list continued to grow and grow. The Chiata continued to flood toward them like a dam that was about to burst, and he had all his fingers and toes plugging holes while the flood gushed over the top at him. It was time to do something else. What else, he wasn't sure. But he had to get out of the system while he could and rethink the battle plan. And the problem with that was, he would be, at least for some amount of time, leaving some of his soldiers behind. And that grated on his very being. He'd been left behind back during the Martian Desert Campaigns and wouldn't wish it on any soldier. But he realized now that sometimes the man in the captain's chair had to make decisions that left young soldiers in very bad situations.

What is it the Navy pukes say? he thought to his AIC. *Do something even if it is wrong?*

Yes, sir. That is the gist of it. And I agree. If we keep doing what we're doing, we are doomed, Abigail agreed. *By the way, your wife knows of Deanna's situation and is making inquiries with the SARs teams as to how to get to her.*

Keep me in the loop on that. Dee is in an uninhabited area. She is safe for now. He'd have to deal with his wife later, and he was keeping an eye on Dee. He was always keeping an eye on Dee. But right now he was at risk of losing thousands of souls instantly, and that had to take priority whether he liked it or not. It was just one of the things about command that he hated. He WOULD come back for his princess. He WOULD.

Yes, sir.

In fact, to Alexander, the absolute worst thing of all was the fact that his daughter was down there stranded and extremely isolated from any help. And there was nothing he could do about it. While every fiber of his being was telling him to go to his little girl he knew he couldn't. His daughter was a Marine and she was doing her duty. He had to do his. And that meant optimizing the results of the big picture. Since with one more hit the *Madira* would be dead, he had to make the tough decision—greater good or his little girl. To exacerbate the decision, the hyperspace systems were fried and he could only jump once more, and it would be hours and hours before they could return. But he WOULD return.

DTM me to Dee, he thought.

"General, Captain Penzington is hailing us," the communications officer almost shouted with excitement.

"On screen." Alexander had never been happier to see the spy turned captain in all his life. "Just in time, Captain. We need you to block our evac for us as best you can."

Daddy? I'm okay. Dee's mindvoice filled his head.

"With all due respect, sir, the *Madira* looks like shit from out here. What can we do to help?" Penzington asked.

Princess, we're getting the shit kicked out of us up here, Alexander replied, his heart torn with what to tell her next.

"We've got to go now, Nancy. I mean now. We can't retrieve everyone and we sure as hell can't hold this AO.

Take the fight to the Chiata and get our people out. Make
sure the recon teams are in place then get yourselves out
in one piece. I'm ordering the jaunt to the first rendezvous
immediately." Alexander hated to leave his daughter and
the ground teams, but they had no choice. They either left
now or there would be no ship for them to come back to.

You have to get out of here, Daddy!

*But, princess, I can't just leave you stranded on an
alien planet.*

*I'm a by-God-Marine! I'll take care of myself and
continue the mission,* Dee said defiantly. *I'll be fine.*

I know you will. Alexander wasn't exactly sure what to
say.

*Don't worry about me. It's a great day to be a fucking
Marine,* Deanna replied with what Alexander was certain
was false bravado.

"I understand, sir." Penzington said while DeathRay's
and Deanna's blue force dots were simultaneously
highlighted in his mindview. DeathRay's dot was actually
purple, which was a bad sign, but he was alive and landing
in the aft hangar. His little girl was on the planet below,
alive. Then Dee's blue dot transferred from the *Madira*
roster to the *Hillenkoetter*. Alexander wasn't exactly sure
how Penzington had managed that, but he was glad she
had. "We WILL get them back, sir. All of them."

*You lay low and escape and evade until Nancy can get
you out of there. That's an order, young lady,* Alexander
thought.

"Thank you, Captain. We'll return as soon as we can.
Hold out as long as possible and then head to the
secondary jaunt point."

"Aye, sir!"

Yes, General! Dee's mindvoice replied.

"Good luck, Captain."

"You too, General."

And, princess, Moore hesitated. *I love you. You be safe.*

"Moore to CHENG!"

I love you too, Daddy!

"Buckley here."

"Now, CHENG! Get us the hell out of here."

"Blue beams, sir!" the XO exclaimed.

"Now, CHENG! Now!"

Chapter 9

February 19, 2407 AD
U.S.S. Sienna Madira II
Target Star System
700 Light-years from the Sol System
Monday, 2:07 P.M. Ship Standard Time

"Now, Amari! Drop the SIFs!" Commander Joe Buckley ordered his now second engineer Chief Petty Officer Sarala Amari. The structural integrity field dropped around the failing plasma conduit that was already spewing white-hot plasma in two jets across the engine room. As the SIFs cut out at precisely calculated locations along the conduit, the metal erupted like a volcano, throwing molten red bits of metal across the room at deadly speeds, followed by an even deadlier spew of plasma.

The plasma jet cut across the room and into the precise location where the unreachable circuit breakers were on the other side of the bulkhead. The metal glowed red hot as it was blown away from the bulkhead and then the plasma poked through.

"It's working!" Fireman's Apprentice Rogers shouted with excitement. "It's working!"

"It hasn't worked yet!" Joe said as he turned to the super-thick power cable still lying across the floor in the green ethylene glycol coolant that had leaked everywhere.

Debbie be ready to throw the aux prop vent coolant switch as soon as those breakers let go, he thought. *Then we restart the vortex and we'll be ready to go on the projector.*

Roger that, Joe, his AIC replied in his mind. *I've checked Chief Petty Officer Amari's calculations for reinforcing the cable with a SIF and it should work well. However, I will need to continuously update the field tensor calculations based on variations in the power flow and the ambient electromagnetic fields within the room. I should be able to squeeze the cable with enough pressure from the SIFs to keep it from liquefying and vaporizing for at least several hours, maybe more.*

That was my plan all along, Debbie, Joe agreed. *Stand by.*

All at once there were three loud, thunderous booms from the other side of the bulkhead. Alerts and power system failure notices popped up in Joe's mindview on the ship's status page. Instantaneously, the pink and purple whirling within the vortex tube stopped and it grew dark. It had worked. The plasma jet had burned through the bulkhead and incinerated the three main conduit breakers on the other side.

The plasma jets spraying across the engine room like a solar flare didn't fade the way Joe had expected. He'd sort of thought they'd act like a water hose once it is turned off. Instead, the streamers burned out like a combustion rocket engine running out of propellant, coughing and burping. As the plasma vented from the conduit, the spraying jets made a final *puff*ing and *chugg*ing sound and blew out.

"It worked, Joe!" Amari cheered. "Now what?"

"Alright, everyone evacuate the engine room. But I do need one volunteer to stay behind and help if I need it. And it can't be Amari." Joe ordered. If things went bad, he at least wanted somebody that knew engineering to survive. He'd already lost Commander Benjamin and he didn't want to lose Amari too. "Amari, I want you to report immediately to the alternate engineering section of the ship and monitor from there. Double time. Go!"

"Aye aye, Joe."

"I'll stay with you, CHENG!" Rogers said. "I know all about the Buckley Maneuver, and I ain't afraid of it, especially in a suit with shields."

"Thanks, Rogers. We'll make an engineer out of you yet." Joe turned to the control panel along the wall where Amari had been as she shagged tail across the wet floor and out of the room. Rogers followed and stood a few steps behind Joe. "CHENG to CO!"

"Hope you're ready, Buckley!" General Moore's voice replied.

"Ready to engage when you are, General!" Buckley replied as he toggled the vortex power grid.

Alright, Debbie, start the show, he thought.

"Nav has already set the coordinates, Joe. Get us the hell out of here!" Moore ordered.

"Aye, sir." Joe nodded at Rogers. "Fireman's Apprentice, we're about to do some serious cooking down here. Hold on to your ass."

The cable that had been stretched from the vortex input coupler across the room to the conduit flange at the bulkhead appeared to get even stiffer than it already was as the structural integrity fields engaged around it. There was an eerie sizzling and crackling noise coming from it, and Joe noticed the occasional flicker of light from ionization of air molecules at the surface of the fields around the cable.

SIF is in place, Joe. Vortex tube restart initiated. His AIC stated as the blues, purples, and pinks of Cerenkov radiation began to flash about within it. The lights inside the vortex grew brighter and swirled faster and faster.

"Hyperspace vortex is spinning." Joe said to nobody in particular. "Alright, now for some power to the projector." Krasnikov hyperspace tube calculations appeared in his mindview along with power graphs, bar charts, and curves.

A bolt of electricity stronger than any lightning crackled and arced in multiple directions out from the busted valve stem of the coolant flow loop and across the room to ground through Fireman's Apprentice Roger's armored suit. His shields flashed green as he was slammed backwards against the deckplate underneath the broken conduit that ran across the engine room overhead.

"Rogers, get out of there!" Joe turned and kicked his jumpboots toward him landing beside him in a sloshing clank against the deck. He knelt to get a handhold on Rogers and used all the strength in his suit to throw the sailor out from underneath the conduit. He then set his kickboots, about to bounce out from underneath the power cable, but he hadn't been fast or lucky enough.

At that instant the electric flow found the path it was looking for, or the SIFs forced it through and into the cable. Either way it was bad news for Joe. As the energy flowed into and through the large power cable and across the gap to the projector power coupling it danced around, at first wildly like a poorly thrown jump rope, as the SIFs strained against the millions of volts, billions of amps, and the ten times ten to the fifteen watts of power, the random motion from the crazy electromagnetic field variations whipped the cable about the room like an unstoppable force. Unfortunately for Joe, he wasn't an immovable object.

Joe's armored suit and shields were no match for it. The SIF reinforced cable slammed into his torso with the force of a hovertank at full hover speed, and then somehow his barrier shield intertwined with the cable's SIF, briefly wrapping his left arm around the cable as the field strained and flickered out. Then, just as quickly as he'd been hit and the cable's mad dance had begun it, was over as the cable was locked still with a *snap* by the extreme electromagnetic bottle created from the field lines of the system. The cable jerked itself free from Joe in a microsecond with a whip-cracking sonic boom that made his ears ring. Joe was dazed, but he looked to make sure the SIF, on the cable was holding. The last time without the SIF, the cable sheathing had melted away, and the metal strands glowed bright like the filament of an incandescent light bulb. Then the cable had vaporized into a plasma of metal gases, and the electric arc lasted just long enough to give the ship a short jump in hyperspace. But this time the SIF was holding and the cable hadn't vaporized. Instead it vibrated only millimeters against the SIF, causing it to shake the air like a speaker. The cable hummed and filled the gap between the conduit and the projector power coupler. Joe watched as the vortex tube whirled into the projector, which, in turn, began to whirl up. It whirled faster and faster as the gamma particles tried to breach the massive gravitational boundary of the event horizon within it. The exotic energy flow pulsed through the spacetime bubble created within the field projector.

"Sir!"

It's working, Joe!

Yeah, let's hope and pray it holds! Joe felt elated but sick to his stomach at the same time. And for whatever reason his blue dot in his mindview turned casualty purple.

You did well, Commander, his AIC reassured him. *I've administered more stims and immunoboost.*

For what?

"Sir," Rogers repeated to him again. "Sir! We need to get you to sick bay."

"What are you talking about, Rogers?" Joe felt the queasiness in his stomach again. He hoped he hadn't gotten fried again. The queasiness in his stomach was making him nervous that he had.

"Sir, you shouldn't have done that." Rogers said. "But

thank you, sir. Come on now, sir. We have to get you some help."

"I have to stay here and make sure the hyperspace system continues to function." Joe said.

"But sir, look!" Rogers pointed at Joe's left side. Joe finally looked down at himself to where the fireman's apprentice was pointing. Rogers looked quite pale. As he realized there were alarms going off in his DTM and his mindview for his suit diagnostics, the awareness to check himself finally set in. His suit diagnostic three-dimensional view in his mindview showed no communication with the left arm in his suit from the shoulder down. Joe turned his neck and looked down.

"Shit!"

His left arm was gone from the shoulder socket. The cable had yanked it clean out of his body armor and all. A large ball of organogel and seal layer had formed over the hole where his arm and shoulder had been. He didn't feel like he was going to pass out. He just did.

Chapter 10

February 19, 2407 AD
U.S.S. Roscoe Hillenkoetter
Target Star System
700 Light-years from the Sol System
Monday, 2:07 P.M. Ship Standard Time

"Air Boss, I want a full roster of pilots from the first wave who are still in system. And I want them transferred to the closest ship that can take them in. ASAP!" Captain Penzington ordered. "They've been through hell, let's get them in."

"Yes, ma'am," the clone Air Boss replied. "According to the blue force tracker there are still seventy-three fighter mecha strewn about the system from the previous attack wave."

"Ground Boss, how many tankheads, AEMs, or downed pilots?"

"Ma'am, the casualties were severe. All ground

contingents were lost except for the Slayers and the Juggernauts. And they are down to eight tanks and six AEMs. There is only one downed pilot presently still alive on the planet," the Ground Boss said in a monotone voice. Nancy wasn't sure if the clone/AIC was being somber or just emotionless. The AIC-driven clones either overexpressed their emotions or showed none at all. Nancy had been commanding the mixed human-and-clone crew for almost a year, but she was still not quite comfortable around the clones yet.

I have them tagged for you, Nancy. Her AIC highlighted their locations in the mindview battlescape. *I'll start a running tally counter on those we retrieve on your mindview.*

Good. Thanks, Allison, she thought. *Nine of the ten ground teams dropped were lost. That's ninety tankheads and over a hundred armored e-suit Marines. Clones or not, we didn't need to lose them. If I didn't know General Moore better, I'd start to think this mission wasn't worth it.*

Hopefully, it will be worth it, Allison replied in her mind. *And don't forget the one downed pilot.*

We're not leaving without her, Nancy reassured her AIC and longtime friend.

"One downed pilot." She whispered under her breath.

"What's that, ma'am?" her XO asked. Nancy looked at the Navy SEAL and knew it must be hard on him, knowing how close he was to Dee. "I want a running tally counter on the main screen for the first wave soldiers in need of rescue and one for all the second wave soldiers deployed. We're not leaving them behind."

"Yes, ma'am." Rackman nodded his armored head.

"Gunner, if we're not shooting we're not fighting. I want to see the DEGs, AA cannons, and missile tubes firing nonstop at targets of opportunity, do you understand?"

"Yes, ma'am," the clone weapons officer said.

"Commander Rackman, it is your job to keep the mission clock in synchronicity with the jump clock." Nancy looked at the battlescape in her DTM mindview and could see the thirty new expeditionary fleet ships in the system and that the entire first attack wave had managed to hyperspace jaunt out—all of them minus eighty eight soldiers, that was.

There were twenty-two Chiata ships in local space engaging her attack wave. Long-range sensors were not detecting any other Chiata ships but that didn't really mean anything. Space was big. They could be hiding on a planet, or in an asteroid field, or they might be using some sort of alien stealth technology that they hadn't encountered yet. There was just no way to know how many Chiata were actually in the system.

Allison, keep working on detecting the source of the QMT dampening field, she thought to her super AIC. *We need to narrow down where to send the recon teams before we jaunt out of the system. And it would be damned nice to find a backdoor we could QMT through.*

I'm pinging away with every sensor we have. So far I've yet to find a transmitter or any backdoors. But that doesn't mean they are not there, her AIC replied. *By the way, I have Dee's location correlated with enemy activity. It looks like a small team of Chiata vehicles are flying in her general direction. It looks like they are in search pattern mode, so I don't believe they know exactly where she is.*

Can we get a SARs team to her? Nancy asked in her mindvoice.

It would tip them off because there is no other fighting activity in the northern continent, so I would suggest heavy fighter support for it or get her to move to a different extraction point. It appears she crashed in an abandoned area of the planet. Her vitals show she is recovering from a broken ankle and two metatarsal bones in her left foot.

Alright, update her, keep her safe, and keep me updated.

Yes, Captain.

"Fourteen seconds to alien targeting," Commander Rackman said. "Nav, prepare jump coordinates."

"Hold out to the last second, Nav, and jump on two seconds remaining. We don't want to get hit during spin up," Nancy ordered. Her AIC and the General's AIC had swapped notes as soon as they had entered the system and she had already learned the mistakes of the first attack wave. She didn't want to make the same ones.

"We have two megaships preparing to engage to starboard, Captain!" the STO noted.

"Well, let's engage them back. Gunner, let's start burning some holes in these two ships. Nav, when we jump, let's jump right between them and launch a couple gluonium-tipped surprises for them." Nancy turned to the air boss. "Air Boss, I want SARs with fighter-squadron cover to the planet for rescue and extraction of our ground troops. I want them all onboard ships a minute ago. Understood?"

"Aye, ma'am."

"Ground Boss, tell the tankheads if there isn't time to lift out their mecha to leave it. We don't plan to stay long," Nancy said.

"Roger that, ma'am. Not sure the tankheads are gonna like that a whole lot."

"Like or leave it, Ground Boss," Nancy grunted in response. There was nothing she could do about it, and the plan was never to hold the system anyway. The plan was to hold the system long enough to insert recon teams to search for whatever was doing the QMT dampening and either turn it off, steal it, or destroy it. The Chiata could not get their grubby glowing amorphous tendrils on a technology that would mitigate the only advantage the human forces had over them. She was pretty sure the Ghuthlaeers felt the same way about it.

"CO! CDC!"

"Go, CDC!" Nancy replied, but even before the CDC could respond, her super AIC had already alerted her to the bad news in her DTM battlescape. Several blobs of red dots suddenly appeared from hyperspace and were painted about the planet in various orbits.

"Ma'am, we've just detected more than thirty new enemy ships dropping into local space about the planet," the AIC-controlled clone down in CDC said almost deadpan. "The numbers just shifted in the enemy's favor."

"Understood, CDC. Get better resolution on the actual number of ships." Nancy never liked uncertainties.

A number of "more than" anything didn't really mean much to her. She needed better detail. She turned to the clone science and technology officer. "STO, what are you reading on the new threats?"

"Ma'am, using multiple sensor suits and various refinement algorithms an estimate with a mean of thirty-four ships with an error bar of six is the best I can do," the STO replied.

"That'll have to do, STO." Nancy would have smiled if she weren't in the middle of a large space naval battle where her troops were now vastly outnumbered and outgunned.

"Time to jump, Nav!" Commander Rackman ordered. "Now!"

"Aye, sir." The Nav replied emotionlessly. "Engaging hyperspace jaunt."

The swirling hyperspace vortex spun out in front of the ship and pulled them through the event horizon into FTL travel. The crew didn't have time to breathe or relax because almost as soon as the jump started it was over, and they were smack dab between two very large alien warships. The two giant, menacing hybrid porcupine-like snails were faced in opposite directions and on opposite sides of the *Hillenkoetter*. Nancy was hopeful that this would put the *Hillenkoetter* too close for the zig-zagging blue beams of death from Hell to be targeted.

"Twenty-nine seconds on the jump clock!" Rackman announced.

"Gunner, start hitting some targets. Missiles and DEGs! Now!" Nancy was barely able to get the command out before the ship to the starboard vanished into

hyperspace. Simultaneously, a blue beam zigged parallel
to where it had been, and then zagged ninety degrees to
hit home on the starboard and aft exterior of the
Hillenkoetter.

The blue beam pounded the shields and rocked the
ship with the force of a several hundred megaton nuclear
blast. Alarms started to sound, both audibly throughout
the ship and DTM to almost all the crewmembers. Nancy
blinked hard to quiet the stars zooming about in front of
her eyes, caused by the abrupt sideways rocking from the
jackhammer pounding the ship had just taken.

"Shit! That wasn't thirty seconds. They're changing
tactics on us! Alert the fleet!" Nancy shouted, just as a
second blue beam zig-zagged into the same spot. The ship
felt as if it had run into an asteroid. "Random hyperspace
jaunt now!"

Nancy gripped the arms of the Captain's chair,
anticipating a third hit. The vortex spun up out in front of
the ship and the *Hillenkoetter* managed to slip through
before being targeted by another beam.

They changed their tactics on us. We need a new plan,
she thought. *Any suggestions, Allison?*

*Nonstop random jumps from all the fleet might work.
It took only nine seconds after the last jump, so I would
theorize it is possible that they are predicting where we
are jumping.*

*Or, maybe they are targeting us before they jaunt into
engagement range?* Nancy suggested.

*That is an interesting thought. It might be a bit of both.
Let me work on that one,* the AIC replied.

"XO, are the recon teams deployed yet?"

"All six teams are currently inbound, ma'am. ETA ranges from two to six minutes," Rackman replied.

"CO! CDC!"

"Go, CDC!"

"We just lost three of the Fleet, ma'am." Nancy could have sworn she had heard some sort of emotion from the clone that time. "Understood, CDC!"

"Ma'am, we don't need to take another direct hit like that," the STO informed her. "The barrier shields are down to forty-seven percent."

"Keep us jumping into and out of engagements with other ships, Nav. Coordinates are at your discretion unless I tell you otherwise. Jumps on a ten-second clock now!"

"Yes, ma'am."

"Communications officer disseminate that tactic as a standing order to all remaining Fleet ships."

"Yes, ma'am."

The vortex spun up in front of the ship again, and they were in hyperspace almost immediately. Seconds later they were in a completely different part of the battle in slightly deeper space. The planet now only filled ten degrees of the horizon, as they were over seventy thousand kilometers from the planet's surface in a non-Keplerian orbit. Almost immediately, Chiata battleships converged on their position with hyperspace jaunts and maximum standard propulsion. Nancy needed to think. It was all happening so fast she had merely been able to react rather than plan.

"Captain! We just lost recon teams three and five!" Rackman announced. "Teams two, four, and six are taking on extreme resistance. Team one is on the ground."

Then *UM61 Beta 23* and *UM61 Beta 29* vanished from her battlescape view. More than ten thousand souls or AICs, or whatever the clones were considered, per supercarrier had just been taken out. Then the blue beams zigged and zagged out before the bridge viewport and made contact at the forward shield generators.

"Shields at seventeen percent, ma'am," the STO reported so stoically that it was almost unnerving to Nancy. She could barely hang onto her chair and keep up with the excitement and stressful details of the engagement, while her clone crew seemed unfettered.

"Nav, time to jump!" Rackman ordered. "We lost Team six. Teams two and four are still fighting their way down."

Nancy, UM61 Beta 4 and Beta 12 can either fire DEGs a few times or jaunt. They've taken on heavy fire and are damaged considerably.

Are they through loading troops?

At ninety percent, Allison replied.

Have them jaunt out and we'll jaunt there next. Transfer coordinates to the Nav. Also have five other ships jaunt there. We have to hold long enough to load troops.

Yes, ma'am, the AIC said. *Also note that from battle analysis it is clear that the equatorial continents and the southernmost continent are heavily populated by the Chiata and where the most casualties have occurred. The northern continent where the Slayers, Maniacs, and Juggernauts are seems to be much less protected. Also, nearest the northern pole, where Dee is, seems practically uninhabited.*

That means something.

But what?

"XO, we just lost two more ships. We're jaunting in to those locations and loading. We need to start cycling into AOs and loading with a plan of getting the hell out of this system before we all get killed in it," Nancy said to the Navy SEAL turned XO.

"We need to do something to slow them down," Rackman thought out loud. Nancy could see him waving his hands about his head as if he were moving icons around in his DTM mindview.

"I'm open to suggestions, XO. But make them fast."

"Well, ma'am, we have no killbox set up, but there is an asteroid field seventeen light minutes from here. That's a thirteen or fourteen-second jump at standard jaunt speed. It'd sure give us something to use for cover and it'd beat the hell out of this fighting out here in wide-open space." As Rackman explained his idea, Nancy could tell he was looking to her for some sort of reassurance that she knew what was going on and what to do. Nancy had been in a lot of sticky situations in her long career as a spy, but her short career as a ship's captain hadn't come close to preparing her for this. But she was a quick study. She knew she'd have to be if they planned to survive for much longer. And now there were over a hundred thousand troops looking to her for answers.

"Yes. But it would leave our troops in need of extraction in the lurch." Nancy thought for a second. Rackman was right though. What they were doing wasn't working worth a damn, and it was getting a lot of people killed very quickly. They needed a new play. Hell, anything would be better than what they were presently doing. She thought of the Navy saying that Admiral Walker had once told her at the battle of Alpha Lyncis. "Alright. We're going to do something different even if it turns out to be the wrong thing. We jaunt in waves to the asteroid belt and send four ships at a time back and forth for pickups. Also, let's release some damned bots on that asteroid field when we get there. They might come in handy when we come back for the recon teams."

"Yes, ma'am. But we are getting no response from any of the recon teams. They're all gone, Captain," Rackman said.

"CO. CDC."

"Go, CDC."

"Seventeen Chiata megaships just materialized from hyperspace over the equatorial continents."

"Understood, CDC."

"Blue beams!" Rackman shouted just as several of the beams from the new ships started tearing through the fleet. Then a giant porcupine snail materialized just off the port bow of the *Hillenkoetter* and fired the blue beams almost as soon as it appeared in reality space. "Nav! Get us out of here now! Send the order to all ships to jaunt to the asteroid field!"

Chapter 11

February 19, 2407 AD
Alien Planet, North Pole Region
Target Star System
700 Light-years from the Sol System
Monday, 2:05 P.M. Ship Standard Time

There was a small clearing ahead in the mostly green canopy of large trees, but Dee couldn't manage to get the controls of her fighter mode FM-12 to react more than about half of the time, and they did react, they were sluggish. One of the thrusters was stuck wide open, and the roll control was malfunctioning so badly that she would see sky one second and trees the next. She was screaming across the sky, spinning wildly like a missile and streaming smoke and plasma and debris on a dangerous path about to auger into the surface of the planet.

Following the puking DeathBlossom up with a

random rolling semi-controlled crash was a living hell on her inner ears and stomach. Every muscle in her body ached, and Dee was on the verge of total-body exhaustion. She did everything she could to focus her mind off of how bad her body felt and on the job of flying the plane. Since her very first day in flight school the instructors had drilled into her that the number one job of any mecha pilot is to fly the plane. Everything else in the cockpit came second. When all else failed, a pilot was supposed to just fly the plane.

Fly the plane! she thought.

The trees rushed up at her quicker than she wanted as she did her best to stall the forward vector and time it so that the cockpit would at least be pointed up when the mecha hit the ground. She was rolling too wildly to eject, so there was only one thing to do, and that was ride it out. She had no choice but to stay in the cockpit and fly the plane.

You've got to level out the vector as best you can, Dee!

If I can yaw at just the right time, I might be able to use the stuck drive to stall out. She thought. *Give me some vectors on that!*

That might work!

"Mayday! Mayday! Apple1 going down!" Deanna repeated into the tac-net but that wouldn't do much good, she was pretty certain. As bad as things were up top, she didn't expect help anytime soon. She was hoping there'd still be a supercarrier to get back to once all was said and done and she had figured a way out of her current predicament.

"Crash warning! Pull up! Crash warning! Pull up!" the

Bitchin' Betty chimed, as if Dee didn't already know she was about to crash.

Bree! I can't get the landing cycle to start. See if you can do anything with it.

I'm sorry, Dee. The power couplers to the servos are completely blown out. That last blue beam we took fried or overloaded every system on the plane. Stay with your current energy curve. I think it will work.

Shit. Hold on!

"Oh God. Oh shit. Oh God! Oh ssshhhiiiitttt!" she shouted as the mecha rolled and snapped through the canopy, shaking violently as it tore through giant tree limbs. A large *thwack* sounded against the cockpit and rang throughout the fighter as a large tree trunk snapped against it, causing spiderweb cracks to form. "Shiiittt! This is so going to fucking hurt!"

Pitch and yaw now, Dee! Now!

The mecha pounded through one last tree as Dee stomped the left upper and lower pedals and yanked the HOTAS full back to the stop. The plane rolled and almost somersaulted nose over tail, and the thruster that was stuck on flashed against the ground for fractions of a second. That fractional thrust was just enough to push the vector of the mecha closer to parallel with the ground.

Hold on! she thought. Her teeth clenched against her mouthpiece so tightly she couldn't have spoken at this point if she had to. Sparks and smoke started to spray about the inside of the cockpit. *Bree! Fire protocols!*

Fire protocols initiated! her AIC responded. The cabin was quickly evacuated and flooded with an inert gas that extinguished any possible fires. With no oxygen or other "oxidizer," a fire couldn't burn. Any sparks that flew about made strange neon-blue hues in the noble gas environment.

The fighter hit the ground tail first and skipped, almost like a flat rock on a pond, then bounced over, rolling with the cockpit down against the surface for another bounce. The second time it rolled over nose first as one of the wings of the fighter dug into dirt and tore through the trunk of a tree. The drag and sudden impact on that side sent the fighter spinning like a discus, making it bounce off the ground with the underside of the empennage facing down, and then the beat-up fighter plane dug deeper into the surface nose first.

As the mecha bored into the surface, an overbearing metal scraping sound mixed with the sound of a stampede of bulls shook Dee to the bone. Her teeth rattled against the TMJ bite block. With one final jerk forward, the propellantless thruster that was stuck in the *on* position at full throttle pushed the nose through the dirt like a plow, throwing debris, vegetation, and dirt over the empennage and onto the fractured cockpit. Something finally ruptured in the thruster system and there was a very loud *bang bang bang,* and then the tail of the fighter fell against the surface with a metallic *thud* as the harrowing crash finally came to an end.

"Holy shit! We did it! We're still alive, Bree!" she shouted as the plane creaked, groaned, hissed, and popped. "I don't like all those noises."

Diagnostics show the plane is completely destroyed with no systems functional. You are hearing leaks and fires. Fire protocols are offline and the cabin is flooding with atmosphere. It is mostly oxygen and carbon dioxide. We should evacuate the mecha, Dee, Bree warned her.

Roger that, Dee replied and immediately started the egress checklist.

"Fire warning! Evacuate craft! Fire warning! Evacuate craft!" The Bitchin' Betty sounded muffled and like her audio was dragging.

"Oh. Shut. Up! Like I don't already fucking know that!" Dee shouted angrily. "It's fucked up that you're the only thing that still works in this plane."

Deanna, your father is calling you DTM, Bree informed her.

Okay, patch him through, she thought. *Daddy? I'm okay.*

Princess, we're getting the shit kicked out of us up here. Her father's mindvoice filled her head. He sounded more worried than she could remember him ever sounding. Dee knew he didn't need the extra stress of worrying about her. But, she also knew that it came with the job. She pulled up the wide field of view in her virtual battlescape. Things didn't look good.

You have to get out of here, Daddy! Dee could see the blue dots in the battlescape mindview turning purple or black faster than she could count. The ball was flooded with porcupines, and the supercarriers were no match for the alien porcu-snail megaships. It was an all-around shit sandwich.

But, princess, I can't just leave you stranded on an alien planet. Dee hated putting her father in a situation where he had to choose her or do the right thing, because there was no winning scenario to it. If he lost more lives to save her she'd feel guilty, and if he saved those lives and sacrificed her he'd feel guilty. Again, it came with the job, but that didn't mean it still didn't suck.

"This is just a hell of an all-around shit sandwich," she muttered to herself, but she knew she had to paint a better picture for her father and do her best to make it easier for him to do the right thing. She could take care of herself. After all, she was Alexander Moore's daughter. He'd taught her well.

I'm a by-God-Marine! I'll take care of myself and continue the mission, Dee said with her mindvoice defiantly as she toggled switches and depressed activators, hoping to get some system to function on the mecha, but it wasn't happening. The mecha was dead and she was stranded on an alien planet seven hundred light years from home that was eaten up with Chiata. Dee was sure she'd been in worse situations, but she couldn't think of when. *I'll be fine.*

I know you will. Her father sounded as if he wasn't exactly sure what to say and Dee was pretty certain he didn't believe her when she'd said she'd be fine.

Don't worry about me. It's a great day to be a fucking Marine, Deanna replied with as much false bravado as she could muster. "I'll survive. It'll be fun," she whispered to herself.

You lay low and escape and evade until Nancy can get you out of there. That's an order, young lady, Alexander told her boomingly with his mindvoice. It was clear that he was giving her an order as General Moore, not as her father. Or was he? Dee could never really tell the difference between the two.

Yes, General! she mindvoice-replied, hoping to give her father the image of her snapping a salute at him.

And princess, her father hesitated. *I love you. You be safe.*

I love you too, Daddy! And then he was gone that quickly. The USS *Sienna Madira II* vanished from her battlescape blue force tracker. She was okay. Her parents were safe and Nancy was coming to get her. She'd be okay.

First things first, she had to get out of the damned plane. Dee toggled the cockpit release but the damned thing didn't rise as it was supposed to. She depressed the toggle again and heard an actuator click but nothing moved. She raised her arms up and disconnected the safety harnesses from her armored suit, and then she placed her hands against the top of the cracked cockpit. With all the might of her suit she pushed upward until the cockpit started to creak at the hinges and then something popped like a piano string that had been wound too tight. Then the cockpit rose with ease.

Dee dragged herself upwards so she could stand on the seat with her left foot as she had done thousands of times. But this time when she put pressure on her left side to stand up, pain rushed over almost to the point of making her sick.

"Ouch, fuck, shit. That hurt." Deanna quickly took the pressure off her left foot and reoriented herself on the seat. After a few seconds of shifting her weight onto her right leg she managed to pull herself from the pilot's couch and over the edge of the control panel of her downed mecha. She sat on the edge of the hatch and threw her right leg over to the outside of the plane, then went to sling her left leg out, but one of the safety harness straps hung on her left jumpboot. The sudden stopping of her left leg caused her to lose balance and fall backwards over the edge of the plane. She was stuck momentarily upside down and hanging from the boot. Pain coursed through her like fire burning through her bones and muscles. Her stomach turned and Dee had to fight hard not to throw up in her helmet.

"Son of a fucking bitch!" She bit at the bite block in her helmet to help her cope with the pain. With the bite, a shot of stimulants and oxygen was flushed into her face. That helped her gain her composure and start to figure out how to get out of her predicament. She looked around at the world from an upside-down viewpoint and let the beautiful greens and blues of the alien world mesmerize her briefly. The giant red and brown tree trunks were larger than any trees she'd seen on any planet before, even the giant redwoods she'd seen on Earth as a kid. Several trees were splintered and laying about her path and Dee could see a rip in the green canopy that led back upwards to the sky. Dee thought to herself that she'd made quite an impact on the planet already. The bad pun entangled in that thought snapped her wandering mind back, and the pain in her left leg brought reality crashing back to her quickly. She realized that first things were first. She had to get herself upright to remove whatever it was that had her entangled.

"Here we go. Uhhnnn!" She grunted as she used her core muscles and the suit's power to pull herself back up sit-up style, enabling her to see what had her caught. As she'd guessed, it was the damned safety harness wrapped up in the fasteners of her jumpboots. She began to tug at the safety harness while twisting her boot as best she could. Dee tugged and yanked, and with each pull, pain shot upward through her left leg almost all the way to the knee and downward across the top of her foot all the way to her toes, causing her to have to swallow back the pain and bile that was creeping upward and threatening to escape. She swallowed it back again.

Dee instinctively reached for the blade in the right chest compartment of her suit but quickly thought better of it. The safety harnesses of the mecha were made of a hybrid composite metal matrix fabric that could damn near take on a plasma cannon round. With the mass of an armored suit and pilot, and the ridiculous gee forces the straps had to maintain to hold the pilot in place, the things were damned near indestructible. The mecha pilots had often joked that they should make the mecha out of whatever those straps were made of. There was no way she would cut the straps loose. Because the material was so strong, there were several redundant failsafe release mechanisms. There were electromagnetic releases at the top and bottom and at the center hasp of each strap. Dee reached for the release nearest to her but it was just beyond her fingertips. She stretched with all her might and pulled herself closer and closer, grunting through the pain that caused in her leg.

"Goddamnit! Come. The. Fuck. Loose!" She grunted again and lunged her upper body a millimeter more forward and was able to wrap her fingers about the release, snapping the mechanism free. Instantly the straps popped loose and recoiled away back into the seat. As the safety harness gave way Dee toppled backwards off the plane, doing a complete backflip and then some, bouncing off the wing of her fighter, and then landing face down in the grass and dirt beneath the crashed FM-12 mecha fighter. FM-12s had been the love of her life since she'd been a little girl. There was never any situation in which she could perceive them as anything other than pure art, a thing of beauty, a masterpiece of firepower, might, and strength. But as it was at the moment, her FM-12 was nothing more than a pile of banged-up metal. In other words, it looked like shit.

There was still white steam and gray smoke and various other coolant and hydraulic fluids seeping from the space fighter's armored joints. Dee was certain if she had her mask open that she'd smell burning plastics, lubricants, and other pungent odors of a downed plane. Dee pushed herself up to plank position and then rested on her knees. Dee inhaled deeply and took a second to steady her mind and collect her thoughts.

Suit inventory, she thought. A three-dimensional translucent image of her suit popped up in her mindview with diagnostics and lists scrolling beside it. Arrows highlighted minor dings and damage, but there were no major malfunctions. The suit was functioning in proper order but there was a blatantly obvious missing item.

"Forgot my fucking gun," she grunted as she managed to raise herself to her feet and jump one-legged back up onto the right wing of the mecha. The canopy was cracked and open and there were very few useful systems still functioning. She reached over into the weapons compartment in the ejection seat and pulled out the M-blaster stored there, and then pulled a handle that had been hidden behind a closed panel marked "EMERGENCY." There was a metal-releasing-from-metal grinding sound and that gave her at least some comfort. Dee turned from the cockpit and dropped to the surface of the planet, her jumpboots crunching against the tall, thick-bladed grass and into the dirt as she landed. Dee's situational awareness rose as she began scanning quickly with the M-blaster in her right hand, brandishing it about looking for potential targets. She didn't see any at the moment and the adrenaline rush she'd had from crashing was wearing off. She paused for a second to get her breath and to allow the immunoboost, stims, and pain meds to kick in.

What's the damage, Bree?

Your left ankle is broken and you have two metatarsal bones fractured pretty severely. Her AIC brought up an image of her injuries in her mindview. *It will be maybe as much as thirty minutes before you can run top speed and probably an hour before you should be using the jumpboots on the suit.*

Any uglies around?

Not as best I can tell so far. Your position is being monitored by the Hillenkoetter.

Are you in contact with it?

Yes. I am in contact with Allison. She is monitoring your situation closely.

Good. Dee was hoping they could send a SARs team down for her. But she wasn't keeping her hopes up for it to come anytime soon.

Dee! We need to get out of here. Bree's mindvoice sounded alarmed. *Allison has just informed me that a Chiata search vehicle is heading this way.*

"Shit! We'd better find a place to lay low," Dee said audibly, jumping to her good foot and bracing with her elbow against the side of her trashed mecha. She did a quick inventory of what she could get to within the plane. There was the compartment that she had popped loose. It was time to see what was in it. The compartment was on the lower aft right end of the mecha, was about seventy percent covered in dirt, and was bent inward pretty badly, but it was open at one corner where the hasp had been. That hasp must have been the metal-on-metal noise she'd heard letting go when she pulled the emergency handle.

Although the panel was bent inward pretty badly and was almost buried in the dirt, Dee managed to use the suit's strength to tear it open and get at the survival gear within. There was a hypervelocity automatic rifle, extra ammo for the HVAR, reloads for the med kit in her suit, one food and water refill, and an inflatable one-man shelter. All of the kit other than the rifle fit in a small pack about ten by twenty by thirty centimeters. She slung the pack over her back and it melded quickly in place to the armor. Then she snapped the rifle across her chest plate where AEMs wore their weapons until they needed to fire them.

We have to hurry. Allison is tracking them with the ship's sensors. They are getting closer, Bree warned her. *They are approaching in a pushbroom sweeping pattern from the south.*

Which way do we go? We should take the easiest

terrain for now until my foot heals. Dee scanned about looking for any signs of Chiata. *I don't see anything yet.*

They're not in visual range yet but I've added them to the battlescape view using the Hillenkoetter's *data and passive-only suit sensors. We should go further north for now. The terrain that way looks mostly flat and covered with forest and jungle.*

Dee looked around to get her bearings. The planet was tilted and was almost pointing at the star, with the axis of rotation tilted at about thirty degrees off the ecliptic. The northern axial pole of the planet at its present season was pointing toward the star. It was summertime and the region she'd gone down in was green, very green. There was thick-bladed grass standing almost waist high, with giant trees spread about every ten or twenty meters. The canopy was thick and much like the jungles of the Amazon on Earth. Or at least that is what Dee thought the Amazon would look like—she'd never actually been there.

Dee's armored environment suit was of the standard issue USMC mecha pilot variety. While it had the new Buckley shields and was a tough system, pilot suits were slimmer and slightly less bulky than the standard AEM suits. Being less bulky also meant less armored. While Dee was proficient in her suit and with her weapons, her hopes were that she wouldn't be getting into any hand-to-hand situations with the Chiata anyway.

Dee put weight on her left foot, and it felt weak and gave her only the slightest hint of pain. The pain meds had kicked in and the immunoboost was beginning to do its job. Her suit realized she was moving on the injury and overfilled the area with organogel and pressurized the armored boot to form a temporary compression cast. That made her walk with a stiff ankle joint on the left side but it completely removed the pain. The suit would know when to ease up on it.

Dee moved as swiftly as she could through the alien jungle, wading through the high thick green blades of grass and doing her best to stay covered by the tree canopy and out of sight. The canopy was filled with motion and infrared signatures, and around every tree, bush, and blade of grass the yellow and green hues from the star's light cast strange shadows about. Every sound and every flicker of motion triggered her startle factor, and she had to focus her mind and breathing to overcome the fight-or-flight adrenaline.

After she'd limped several kilometers northward, the trees led her to a clearing at the edge of what looked like a swamp marsh. There was an outcropping of rocks at the bank of the swamp, and something that appeared to be a large termite or ant mound. She steered clear of it just in case it wasn't friendly. Sounds of rushing water grew louder as she snaked her way around the marsh at the edge of the treeline.

Wonder if there are any creatures in there on top of the food chain?

Looks like a good place for snakes or crocodiles if they have them here, Bree agreed. *But, I'd bet none of them are higher up the chain than a well-trained United States Marine in an armored suit.*

Ooh-fuckin'-rah. Dee smiled inwardly.

I'm detecting incoming on passive sensors. Suit stealth is fully operational and functioning as expected. But who knows if their sensors can detect it or not. Would you like me to go to active stealth?

No, Dee replied. *We don't want to take a chance that going active might alert them to where we are instead of spoofing their sensors. For that matter, who the hell knows if our active spoofers can actually engage the Chiata shit anyway?*

Commander Buckley or the STO might.

Well, they ain't here. Feel free to ask them next time we see them. Dee almost thought it catty.

The suit blended into the environment and was for all intents and purposes invisible to the human eye and most sensors in the electromagnetic spectrum. Her DTM battlescape view activated and a red dot appeared almost on top of the blue dot that was her downed mecha. Dee was lucky in that there were still Fleet ships in the system and all their sensors were creating a system-wide battlescape view. The red force and blue force tracking systems were still transmitting data to her suit. The suit also had its own sensors but not with enough range to detect red force signatures at more than four or five kilometers. The best the suit could do was a few hundred meters when pinging active with electromagnetics and a few tens of meters on passive. If the QMs were functioning the suit would do another factor of ten better, but none of the quantum membrane technologies seemed to function well in the region except for the barrier shields. Dee didn't understand why they'd work and none of the other quantum-based systems would, but again, that'd be something to bother Buckley with the next time she saw him.

Dee decided her best bet was good old fashioned recon, escape, and evade techniques. So, in order not to leave tracks, she took to the swamp. Carefully, she stepped out into the edge of the swamp water, using her imaging and polarization sensors to peer through the murky brown goop that spread out into something that looked like mangrove trees and lily pads that were much larger than they should have been.

Give me the best resolution maps we have of the place, Bree, she thought.

The Fleet ship's sensors mapped the planet in great detail as soon as we jumped in. You are here, Bree said. *And the Chiata search party is here.*

A map appeared before her eyes in her mindview with her blue dot on it and nine red images a few klicks away that were the aliens pursuing her. The edge of the trees and the marsh banks were clearly visible. The canopy did a lot to cover the imagery data in the visible, but the combination of all the electromagnetic spectrum, active radar and lidar, magnetic imagery, and the active particle scattering data gave her high-resolution detail down to the type of surface at better resolution than the unaided eye could ascertain. The maps could even give a general idea of the geological epochs the planet had gone through and would give mineral hunters most of the information needed to find whatever materials they were looking for.

Looks like they found my mecha, Dee thought. *This party is just about to get started. All we need now are streamers and noisemakers.*

Would you like me to release the present we left for them?

By all means. Fox! Fox! Fox! Deanna said in her mindvoice.

The red dots in her mindview scattered abruptly in several directions. Two of the nine dots turned black and vanished almost instantly. Three more of them didn't appear to be moving any longer. About fifteen seconds later she could hear three very loud *booms* in the distance. Dee watched her mindview closely, hoping that the detonation of the missiles that were left on the mecha was enough to take out all the aliens that were searching for her, but apparently not. Four of the red dots clustered together very briefly and then began moving much faster than they had been previously. And they were headed northward.

Shit! They've picked up my trail, Deanna thought. *Deeper into the swamp.*

They're moving fast, Dee. Very fast.

Dee humped as fast as she could with one stiff suit ankle joint and a leg numbed from mid-shin to the tips of her toes. The bottom of the swamp wasn't helping much either. Almost with each step she had to engage her jumpboots just to pull free from the muck. And to top that off the water was getting deeper. Dee pulled an imagery view of the area up in her mind and could see that the swamp spread eastward into a big outcropping of boulders that then dropped off as a fairly large waterfall splashing down several tens of meters into a broad river. The river was nearly a kilometer wide in places and it was only a few kilometers away. According to the map, the river died out into a stream at the base of a large ravine almost the size of the Grand Canyon nearly a thousand kilometers to her southeast. To the west, the swamp dried up, the vegetation started looking more and more sparse, and the terrain appeared to be very desolate and rocky.

The images from the western direction sort of reminded her of the Cydonian region on Mars. The pole of the planet was very arid and dry, or at least that was the way it looked on the map in Dee's head. The Marslike region made her think of her father and how he'd evaded enemy troops in his suit for more than thirty days a century earlier. And the suits back then were primitive compared to hers. She used that thought for reassurance and strength. She also wished her daddy were there to kill the monsters chasing her, get her off the planet, and take her home, but Dee was a Marine. She'd be fine. She'd escape and evade as long as it took. She'd just have to kill the monsters herself.

We'll head north until we hit that river and then we will see if we can take it eastward. Dee chose to stick with the cover of the trees and the swamp. *Maybe we can use the water for cover.*

We must move faster, Dee. The search team is closing on us. Bree highlighted the alien squad's location and zoomed out. A blue line snaked across the map showing Dee's path. A red line tracked out and around the area where her plane had crashed and then turned to follow hers. *They'll be on our ass in less than five minutes at their current pace. It's like they can smell us. Their path precisely overlays yours. I can only assume they have access to imagery data as good as or better than ours. If they can't see you through the suit's stealth they can certainly see your path.*

Hmmm, Dee thought. *That might be worthy of note. And, we'll have to cover our tracks better.*

Dee bit down on the bite block in her helmet for another shot of stimulants. It had been a very long day already and it was just getting started. She felt up the HVAR strapped across her chest unconsciously with her left hand and held the M-blaster in her right. Her stomach was beginning to tighten and churn like it always did just before being slung out of a supercarrier into "the shit" as it was often referred to. Well, she was in some shit now. The only problem was that she wasn't sure exactly what type of shit and how deep it was. But that was always the way it was with "the shit," it didn't matter if it was the same or different. It was still bad shit and it was coming her way.

Chapter 12

February 19, 2407 AD
Alien Planet, Northern Continent Southern Region.
Target Star System
700 Light-years from the Sol System
Monday, 2:15 P.M. Ship Standard Time

"Why the shit didn't they just follow us in here?" Master Gunnery Sergeant Rondi Howser asked, almost rhetorically, because she knew nobody else had the answer either, especially not the only two junior surviving members of the AEM drop team. "I mean, they were all over us like stink on shit and as soon as we dropped over the edge of this ravine they just stopped. I'm sure they're still up there."

"I don't like this shit at all, Gunny." Lance Corporal Jacob Roy was clearly shaken up. Rondi realized that she'd better do something to get the kid frosty or he was going to pop a gasket. "They were chewing us up and spitting us out. We lost almost all of the team, for fuck's sake. They could blast us from above with the fucking blue beams any time they wanted to, even. What are they waiting for?"

"Don't give them any ideas. Besides, I don't think they're waiting at all, Mr. Roy." Rondi nodded at the strange ruins they'd taken shelter in. The large granite structures were ornate and looked very similar to a hybrid mix of ancient Egyptian, Roman and Greek, and something extremely weird and alien-looking that she'd never seen before. There were large columns and arches but there were also buttresses and structures hanging out into midair that almost seemed to defy physics. They certainly defied ancient or primitive architectural knowledge. "Maybe there's something in here they don't like."

"Well, that's just really fucking reassuring, Gunny!" Lance Corporal Roy was clearly shaking and Rondi was afraid the kid was going to lose control any second. It was possible he was getting suit jitters and needed to take a "chill pill," which wasn't a pill at all any longer. The "chill pill" had evolved into antianxiety medication that would be released into the body through the organogel layer.

"I don't have another explanation for it," Rondi added. "Something in here is either valuable, rare, or scares the Chiata. The main reason for coming here was to find out why the horde hasn't built another homeworld or just eaten this planet like they do everywhere else."

"Those fucking things out there are nightmares from Hell, boogeymen if there ever was one, and they're *afraid* to come in here? Fuck that."

"Maybe they smelled that you shit your suit, Roy," Lance Corporal Constance Weems grunted almost laughing, but Rondi could tell that she was scared witless as well. Cut-down humor was her coping mechanism. In fact, Rondi had noticed over her years in the Marines that machismo and superego humor seemed to be a standard feature with most soldiers. Highlighting that other kick-ass heart breakers and life takers had flaws and got scared probably was reassuring that everybody got scared, even Marines.

"Knock that shit off, you two," Rondi scolded them. The situation was bad enough as it was. While a little locker-room goading was sometimes useful for coping with nervousness, she didn't need the two remaining members of her team at each other's throats. "Keep your shit frosty and eyeballs peeled. If there are some other uglies in here we want to find them before they find us. Is that straight?"

"Yes, Gunny," The two AEMs said in unison. But neither of them sounded too happy about it. Rondi didn't blame them. If she was being honest with herself, she wasn't that happy either. She really wasn't happy that the *Madira* had been shot up and had to leave them there. For an instant the thought of Buckley's quirky-assed smile popped in her head. She hoped he hadn't done anything too stupid when things got bad up top. And now they were gone in hyperspace to who knew where. Hopefully, the *Hillenkoetter* would do better in system, but from the battlescape mindview she wasn't putting any real money on it.

"Howser!" Major Sellis' voice snapped in her helmet,

catching her off guard and startling the shit out of her almost literally. She realized that she was far too jumpy and needed to settle the fuck down.

Stay frosty, Marine, her AIC reinforced the thought for her. *The kids don't need to see you jumping like that.*

Damned right.

"Major?" Rondi turned from the two corporals and moved closer to the edge of the giant column that was carved out of the granite wall of the ravine. The yellow and green light from the star peeked over the edge of the cliff wall across from them, casting an eerie brightness against the ruins and a faint shimmering over the small river that ran through the basin. The light shimmered and reflected off the ripples of the flowing water and illuminated the strange glyphs on the ruins. Patterns of the star system covered the wall, and there were indentations spread about the surface of the granite that looked like some sort of insect, about the size of a twenty millimeter armor-piercing HVAR round with eight legs. The spiderlike things appeared to be a central theme in the artwork, but Rondi wasn't an artist or an exo-archaeologist. She turned her mind to what she did know, and that was being an AEM.

"What can I do for you, sir?" Rondi asked Major Sellis.

"Colonels Jones, Slayer, and Strong have set up a bit of a TOC behind the tank perimeter in a large antechamber we found. Shag ass up here for a minute," the Major ordered her.

"Yes, sir. Do I bring the corporals or leave them at rear guard?" she asked.

"Bring them. Not sure we want to leave any stragglers

about until we know what the hell all this place is," Sellis told her. "Double-time."

"Roger that, sir. We're on the bounce." Rondi turned back to Roy and Weems. "Alright, you two, on my ass and stay there."

The three of them bounced their jumpboots along the ravine staying as close to the gray and beige granite wall as possible and away from the center of the basin near the running water. Just in case the Chiata decided to start lobbing those blue beams down at them, Rondi wanted to at least make themselves more difficult targets. And while the river looked docile enough, this was an alien planet and Rondi's imagination was doing its level best to fill every dark nook, cranny, and other unknown with monsters that Chiata were afraid of. For the meantime it just seemed smart to steer clear of potential unknown threats until she had a better grip on their overall situation.

The ruins or temples or whatever they were filled the northwestern wall on a continuous path as far as the eye could see. Had Rondi not known better she'd say the ravine was the entrance to a giant underground city, but as far she could tell there weren't any passageways leading inward. They had just found stone walls with all those glyphs scattered about them.

"Look at those." Weems pointed at several concrete-looking three-meter-tall spires along the river that seemed to be spaced every ten or twenty meters. "What the hell are those things supposed to be?"

"They look like termite mounds from Africa or the giant blue ants that live on Ares about seven hundred klicks south of New Tharsis. Those things will eat you alive in seconds," Rondi replied. "Never seen 'em myself, but I've seen video that will make you puke."

"Shit." Roy sounded like a frightened kid who had just been told a campfire horror story. "Like the Chiata aren't bad enough, and then these fucking ruins, and now giant ant hills with no telling what kind of bad shit lives in them. I am liking this planet more and more every minute."

"Just don't touch any of that shit. Who knows if they are still in there or not?" Rondi warned them. "Besides, it might just be some cute fluffy creature or a weird geological thing."

"You don't believe any of that shit you just said, do you, Gunny?" Roy asked rhetorically.

"Fuck no. Let's keep moving," Rondi replied. She wasn't sure, but she could have sworn she saw something skitter across the riverbank and up one of those mounds.

Settle down, Marine! I'm letting my mind play tricks on me, she thought.

Did you see something, Rondi? I have not detected anything on sensors, her AIC asked with a concerned tone in her mindvoice.

Uh, well, no. No. I didn't see anything.

About a klick upriver the tankheads and the mecha jocks from the Maniacs had managed to find a much larger archway and had formed up a perimeter underneath that. The arch was cut into the granite ravine wall and had a peak height of more than thirty meters. The width of the archway at its base was at least fifty meters. The stonework on the ground had been intentionally laid out like a cobblestone roadway leading out of the archway and then vanishing into the river.

There were no unusual colors or shapes, but the construction was made with laser-precise cut square granite blocks with dovetails set precisely into each other with less than a hair's width of error where they mated together. Rondi was pretty certain that whoever built this place weren't primitives.

The eight hovertanks that were left were strategically blocking the entrance with their guns pointed upward. There were seven Marine FM-12s also. Four of them were in bot mode standing guard with their large plasma cannons at the ready. The other three were in fighter mode and were sitting inside the large-hangar-sized cavernous room with their canopies up.

Rondi could see the three colonels, Major Sellis, and Major Dana Miller standing just inside and out of the sunlight, waving their hands about. They were clearly doing some sort of battle planning in their collective mindviews. Rondi recognized Major Miller without the blue force tracker. The mecha jocks all had their handles painted across their helmets, and hers read "Popstar." Colonel Strong's read "Jawbone."

"What's going down, Top?" Howser bounced in beside Sergeant Major Tommy Suez. Major Sellis was involved in the DTM conversation and she didn't want to interrupt him. Besides, his blue force tracker would alert him to their arrival.

"The *Hillenkoetter* and the rest of the second attack wave were just overwhelmed by Chiata megaships. They've all bugged out to an asteroid field farther out in this system and it appears that most of the Chiata followed them in pursuit. The colonels are working a plan with

Captain Penzington to zip in and extract us without getting everyone blown to hell," Suez explained.

"Jesus. There were thirty supercarriers in the second attack wave," Rondi gasped.

"Well, there are twenty-four of them now," Top replied. "Maybe they all just need to come down here and hang out with us."

"Pretty fucking eerie, ain't it." Rondi nodded. "I mean, I'm not complaining, but what the fuck?"

"More than eerie. Whatever this place is the Chiata are leaving it alone," Top said, motioning to the ruins with his armored hands. "Maybe this is why we're here. I've been scanning for signs of Chiata tracks, garbage, hell, anything, and I've found nothing. If they have been down here there's no sign of it."

"You think whatever is blocking the QMTs is in these ruins?"

"I overheard Colonel Strong say that. Not my idea," Tommy said.

"We need some techs down here then. Or Buckley, or Captain Penzington." Rondi thought about it and was pretty sure the fact that the Chiata wouldn't come down into the ruins meant something important.

"The colonels and Penzington are working on it, but there's more. Even if we could all load up right now, I don't think we'd leave. Or, well, at least not Captain Penzington."

"More what?" Rondi couldn't think of what in the universe could keep the Captain in the system a second longer than she needed to be there. "There's no way we can hold this planet until we can get scientists in here."

"I agree, and I'm sure even General Moore does. But I'll guarantee that he'll be back as soon as he can, and that Captain Penzington isn't leaving just yet."

"Why?"

"Major Moore was shot down and is running escape and evade near the northern pole," Top explained to her. Rondi almost gasped. She was friends with Deanna and if she needed help, Rondi would be one of the first in line to volunteer to go to her.

"How far away? Can we get to her?" Rondi asked Top.

Give me Major Deanna Moore's current location, she thought to her AIC. A blue dot near the northern pole region popped up in her mindview, and only a few hundred meters from her dot four red dots appeared to be closing in on her position and one of them was trying to flank her.

She is outnumbered. From the lack of motion she is presenting, it would appear she is dug in and hiding.

Shit. She is really far away. There is no way to get to her in any time that would help. Hang in there, Dee, she thought.

Chapter 13

February 19, 2407 AD
Northern Region
Alien Planet, Target Star System
700 Light-years from the Sol System
Monday, 2:25 P.M. Ship Standard Time

While Deanna had ripped the alien creatures from within enemy fighting mecha with her own armored mecha's giant robotic hands during space dogfights, she hadn't truly seen one up close and personal—at least not until now. As far as her AIC and Dee could tell, it appeared that the stealth mode of her suit did hide her from the Chiata's sensors and eyeballs. Once Dee had realized that she was not going to outrun the search party, she had decided to dig herself into the mud at the bank of the now rapidly flowing swamp waters to add to her camouflage. Her hopes were that she could either lay low until they gave up the search and moved on or that she could at least manage to maintain the advantage of a surprise ambush.

Three of the four Chiata were spread out about the bank of the fairly fast-flowing murkiness, and the fourth was somewhere behind her and beyond her visual field of view. Were it not for her suit's red force tracker, the alien would clearly be in the perfect position for an ambush. The alien closest to her was only about six meters away and Dee was getting a very close look at the thing. It was a monster if she'd ever seen one.

Until that instant, she'd thought of the Chiata as purely amorphous blobs stuffed into armor and shields, but Dee realized that wasn't the case at all. In fact, she was beginning to think the amorphous blobs were actually part of the armor and less a part of the creatures. The alien things were a mix of red and green fluorescent colors, from the tip of their heads to the end of their toes and, as far as Dee could tell, they were bipedal with two arms. The alien's legs were a meter and a half long and bent at the knee just like a human's. The boots of the thing's armor were much larger at the toe box than at the heel, which suggested to Dee that the creatures had something radically different about their feet. Perhaps they were like primates or even birds, but there was know way to know from her hidden viewpoint several tens of centimeters buried upright in the mud on the banks of the swampy tributary. Dee left her suit's audio sensors up as she detected the sounds of the search team slightly louder than the sounds of the swamp waters rushing out, into, and across the boulders nearing the main channel of the flowing river. Water swirled about the rocks, creating swiftly moving eddies and upwardly churning whitewater that Dee could barely make out just beyond the tree line.

The marshy soil appeared to be turning more rocky and the trees were thinned along the high muddy bank she'd managed to bury herself into.

The Chiata closest to her, now only about four meters away, searched for her as it pressed through the water and pushed back vegetation, thorns, and downed tree branches. One of the branches extended like a catapult and recoiled as the alien pushed passed it. The branch slapped against the alien behind it and Dee could see ripples of reds and greens swim across the alien's torso. The personal armor was also a personal barrier shield.

The arms of the creature were longer than those of humans, again, possibly primate-like, but there was something different about the hands. As far as Dee could tell the thing had five fingers, and one long, slender double-jointed thumb. The Chiata's hands were not in gauntlets. Dee noted that instead of gloves there were tendrils extending from the backs of its hands and up its forearm from within the creature's skin that led into the weapon it was carrying in its left hand. Dee wasn't sure if the tendrils were part of the alien's body or if they were some sort of interfaces to what appeared to be its body armor. In fact, Dee wasn't truly certain where the alien's body stopped and the armor started. It was possible that they were somehow connected or even fused, but she wasn't sure.

More of the tendrils reached out from the creature's torso and touched leaves, limbs, and the water as the Chiata *schlurp*ed and *splash*ed and stomped about in the mud, rocks, and knee-deep water. The amorphously growing appendages ranged from a centimeter to upwards of five or six centimeters in diameter and sometimes stretched out as long as a meter or more. Each time one of the tendrils stretched, out a ripple of light would wash over the armored suit. Dee could see the similarities in the alien's armor and the Buckley barrier shields of her own.

The torso of the creature had no particularly interesting features other than the tendrils that would appear and disappear from within the outermost armored layer. At the waist the creature was only about seventy-five centimeters around, but at the shoulders, about a meter above the waist, it was at least one hundred twenty centimeters around. Front-to-back width of the torso was no more than its waist width most of the way up, widening slightly at the chest. Just above the chest area there was a V-shaped ridge in the body armor suggesting something like a collarbone and maybe a ribcage that had a long thin neck protruding from it.

The Chiata's neck was no more than thirty or so centimeters wide and was maybe as long as it was around. There were ridged overlapping green plates or bands protecting the neck and that led to a head that, to Dee's surprise, did not have a helmet on it. The back of its head was covered in spiky tendrils almost five centimeters long each that waved about continuously as if they were sensors testing the air for something. Dee thought for a brief moment that the tendrils could be confused for hair if she hadn't gotten a really close look. All in all, the creature stood more than two and three-quarters meters tall. That was a good head taller than a Marine in a fully armored environment suit.

Don't move a muscle, Dee, Bree warned her while keeping a very resolved three-dimensional map of the local area out to a few tens of meters away in her mindview. Several possible courses of action plotted about the image in Dee's mind. *Maybe they will not detect you.*

Which one do I hit first and then in what order, Bree? Give me some scenario options here. Dee worked through how she was going to fight if they found her. *And unlock my ankle. I'll need full range of motion, ready or not.*

Done, Bree noted. *I suggest rushing past the one closest to you and hitting the third target. This will put the other two between you and the one behind us. Perhaps some grenades along the way will help.*

Right. Dee almost gulped once the creature closest to her turned and almost looked right at her. At first she thought that it had detected her because it seemed to look right through the mud at her. The hair-like tendrils on its head stopped moving and pointed in her direction as well.

The eyes were pointed upward in the middle of the thing's face near the bridge of its flat, ridged nose. The eyes were menacing and yellow with dark, vertically slitted pupils. Dee thought that if she had ever imagined a scary monster in her closet as a little girl, this one would certainly fit the job description. The nose was larger than she'd expected and was much flatter. The four horizontal ridges gave the appearance of reptilian or insect exoskeletal plates. The nostrils were almost as big as twenty millimeter hypervelocity automatic rifle rounds and were more holes than nostrils. The alien's face had scars and age lines across it and looked like it had seen its share of rough times. There was a continuous snarl that led from its extra-wide, toothy mouth up to its smaller-than-looked-natural ears. The ears had no lobes, only holes. Instead of lobes they were simply ridges external to the skin on the sides of the head that matched the exoskeletal ridges on the nose. There were also ridges at what might be considered the alien's hairline.

The Chiata's skin looked green and like worn leather from an ages-old sofa, with freckles of bright reds strewn about. The freckles appeared so bright against the green skin that Dee believed them to be bioluminescent. The alien closest to her had one long scar that stretched from its forehead across its right eye and down to its understated chin. And when it would turn, tendrils would jut out from its body and wave at the other members of the search team as if it were commanding them with tendril signals. Dee thought of how whitetail deer back in Mississippi would signal each other by flashing their tails. And that concerned her. Clearly, they were nonverbally communicating with each other, but what they were saying eluded her.

Certainly, they have DTM comms, right? she thought.

Who knows? Bree replied in her mind.

Dee held herself perfectly still and did her best to remain calm and at the ready. The Chiata continued to fan out about her location, with the closest to her within spitting distance. Had she not been wearing an armored suit she could have felt the thing breathing on her.

Steady, Major Moore! Steady!

I'm frosty. I'm frosty. I'm frosty, Dee repeated to herself. She'd had been through escape and evade training before, many many times, but she'd only ever trained to fight humans. Nobody really knew for sure if fighting styles would translate to hand-to-hand with aliens. But Marines were trained to adapt, improvise, and overcome, and Dee was as good a jarhead as any.

The Chiata that appeared to be the leader made several hand and tendril motions and then turned his back to Dee's location. As he appeared to be stepping away Dee almost sighed with relief. But then, three red and green glowing tendrils shot out from the alien's back armor and into the mud, just missing her torso enough that they glanced off the shields. The shields of the tendrils and the shields of Dee's suit clashed, sending flashes and ripples of light through the mud like electric arcs. The alien's tendrils then wrapped around Dee's waist and yanked her out of the mud, tossing her head over heels past the alien, her arms and legs twisting from the mud as she was yanked up like a rag doll.

Fire, Dee! Fire!

Dee was flung through the air with neck-jarring force, but somehow she managed to have the presence of mind to bring her HVAR up with her left hand and fire into the alien's tendril grasp. The rounds *spittapp*ed out fast, leaving blue ionized plasma vortexes behind as they tore into the tendrils, cutting Dee free from the alien' s grip as she came crashing across the water against a tree that was half fallen over into the river. The alien screeched as if in pain and turned toward her, tracking across the swiftly moving water with some sort of automatic plasma weapon. The blue bolts of energy hummed and splashed into the water around her, throwing up vapor and steam and debris as they hit. One of the bolts hit the tree she had crashed into, and bits of charred wood splintered just above her helmet. She ducked and instinctively fired her M-blaster with her right hand while twisting around the tree trunk for cover in a backwards handspring. She splashed down hard behind the fallen tree immediately bringing the HVAR up with her left and firing hundreds of hypervelocity rounds at the nearest alien. The rounds lit the Chiata's shields up for a brief instant, but in a blur it moved and was firing back at her.

Dee kicked her jumpboots against the bottom of the muck, and fortunately they homed on what must have been a boulder at the bottom. Unexpectedly to both her and the aliens, Dee was shot upward out of the water and more than five meters into the air, somersaulting almost out of control. Dee tightened her core muscles and pulled her knees in to control her vault.

Don't fail me now, Buckley! Dee prayed that her armored suit shields would hold as the other nearest two Chiata tracked their weapons at her across her vault's trajectory. Fortunately, the aliens were surprised enough that they missed.

Deanna bounded back and forth across the water from rock outcropping to tree trunk and back again with her HVAR in her left hand and her M-blaster in her right, all the while firing both two-gun mojo style on full automatic. Her suit enabled her to hold the weapons steady and fire them both precisely and simultaneously. The blaster bolts caught the lead Chiata in the chest, knocking it off balance, with a ripple of light from its armor, forcing it to stagger backwards and lose its balance in the water. But her advantage didn't last long as suddenly the creature moved so quickly that all Dee could see was a red and green blur.

Fuck, they're fast! Dee thought. *Find a way to track their motion and predict their paths.*

Working it! Bree replied, and just as quickly ran billions and billions of calculations in the blink of an eye. One aspect of the AICs was that they were quantum bit-based processors and could perform quantum superposition based reduction of data, which meant trillions of instructions per fractions of a second. *Your best option is, fire at the energy curve predicted locations, Dee. Fast or not, they still must follow the laws of physics. Their trajectories will still follow ballistic paths. Lead the paths instead of tracking behind them.*

Roger that! Dee fired both weapons as fast as she could, leading the aliens' motion based on predictions appearing in her DTM mindview. Several times she shot into empty air with the rounds or blaster bolts zipping off into the trees or into the water. But, at least about thirty percent of the time Bree's calculations were correct and she hit home against one of the aliens' body armor and shielding.

The fourth Chiata had joined in almost as instantly as the action had started. As soon as Dee splashed down from her jumpboots' powered leap, the fourth alien landed on top of her feet-first, pulling his weapon up to her face and knocking the M-blaster free. The magnetic tether-holster pulled at the blaster and it affixed itself to her right thigh. Deanna managed to sideswipe the barrel of the alien's weapon with the barrel of her HVAR as they both fell backwards beneath the water. Dee grasped one of the tendrils with her right hand as the thing twisted about her wrist like a snake. She squeezed the squishy, amorphous structure with all the might of her gauntleted and power-assisted hand until it popped and went limp. The alien flinched just long enough for her to punch it in the gut with her right hand while she fired several rounds at point blank against the thing's chest armor with the HVAR in her left. Red and green barrier shields flickered, and then the alien moved away so fast that she couldn't track it. And almost as soon as that one had moved out of the way, one of the others shot a tendril into her leg armor. The shields held for the moment but that tendril wrapped about her leg and began to squeeze, straining the suit's barrier field generator.

"I'm. Getting. Tired. Of. This. Fucking. Shit!" she shouted gutturally at the alien, and fought it back with a flurry of splashing punches, kicks, and shots from the rifle and blaster. The Chiata moved as fast or faster than the AEM suit enabled Dee to move, so she had to anticipate the creature's movements to keep up. That proved very difficult. Very difficult.

Dee squirmed and kicked against the alien with all the might of her armored suit and only barely managed to duck the barrel of the alien plasma rifle as it lunged at her face. She twisted her armored torso and palm-heel struck the midsection of the weapon just as blue bolts of energy buzzed past her faceplate. The bright beam caused the autodim feature of the visor to kick in just in time to prevent her from being blinded. Holding on to the alien weapon, she spun backwards toward the alien, smashing it in the nose with her left elbow, and then with all the speed and strength in the suit, drew her blaster and shoved the barrel through the creature's left eye, and at the same time, she pulled the trigger. The back of the alien's head exploded with a splatter resembling a bursting water balloon.

Dee didn't have time to admire her handiwork as the other three continued after her. Without removing the barrel of the blaster from the alien's well-ventilated skull, she tilted the heavy, limp body while continuing to fire at the other attackers. Using the alien's dead body for a shield, she ducked as blue bolts snapped against its backside. Dee fired several more rounds through the red and green glowing muck that was oozing out of the alien's skull all over her, and then she withdrew the blaster, pulling with it alien gray matter.

She kicked her boots again, tossing her upward against one of the large trees along the marsh bank, and then she kicked them against the tree, jumping to over forty meters out into the deeper and much faster-flowing water. She tucked and rolled into a dive, splashing loudly into the raging water. For whatever reason the Chiata didn't follow her out; instead, they stood near the edge of the water firing at her. Dee ducked her head under the water and kicked out deeper as best she could. The weight of the suit was pulled to the bottom by the planet's near-Earthlike gravity. Each time Dee reached the bottom she bounced with the current. Blue blasts of alien plasma fire tore through the water around her, vaporizing the water and causing steam bubble explosions. One of the rounds hit her in the back, pounding her face first into the deeper water and stunning her, but while the Buckley shields flickered, they still held.

Shields generators at forty-seven percent, Dee. We can't keep taking hits, Bree warned, all while more of the blue bolts peppered the water around her. Another one hit her on the shoulder, tossing her into a forward roll into an underwater rock outcropping. The vortex of whitewater whirling about it caught her and rolled her up to the surface feet first. Dee managed to land her left foot against the rock and triggered her jumpboots, rocketing her back downward into the water's depths.

Deeper, Dee! her AIC told her. *It is twenty meters deep here. Go deep.*

Right.

Then the AIC highlighted a path underneath the water toward faster-flowing vectors. Arrows appeared in Dee's mindview, showing her the flow fields of the now roaring waters. Dee did her best to kick off the mucky bottom and into one of the underwater currents highlighted in her mindview. The blue bolts of energy continued to tear through the water all around her. Another bolt hit her on the left thigh plate, spinning her about under the water and causing her to lose her bearings.

Shields at twenty-seven percent!

Dee finally hit the currents that were so swift the flowing force was enough to grab her and take her away. Although she was being tossed head over heels and tumbled about by tons and tons of rushing water that was bottlenecking and speeding up and rapidly approaching the falls, which seemed bad, the distance between her and the Chiata search party continued to grow. Dee could see through her multi-sensor amalgamated image that the aliens were taking to the trees, hoping to get a high-ground shot at her. Dee did her best to right her tumbling motion and hug the bottom of the river.

We're going over, Dee said. *Maybe we can get some distance between us and them.*

That's a forty meter fall, Dee! I hope the water is deep enough at the bottom. Bree sounded concerned. *I don't have enough data to know.*

Well, we're dead if we stay here! Dee replied as she continued to tumble. She did her best to stretch out her arms and legs to control her tumble, but the currents were too strong. Another wave of blue bolts ripped the water up all about her but she was deep enough that their energy was dissipated before it managed to make it to her armor. With one last foothold on the bottom, she kicked her jumpboots at full power, launching her up and out of the water into a long arching ballistic trajectory over the edge of the waterfall. The view was amazing. The large lake of swamp behind her had to be kilometers across and was being bottlenecked by the natural terrain and forced to flow to the falls. Large boulders lined the cliff, and downed and washed-up giant trees dammed and constricted the flow even more. Water rushed over the edge of the natural dam with the raging sound of a thousand hovertanks. Blue beams tore about the sky around Dee as she reached the apogee of her dive. A bolt pounded into her abdomen armor plate causing the shields to flicker and flash and inducing a spin and a roll into her dive. And then Dee felt the weightlessness of falling over a cliff.

Chapter 14

February 19, 2407 AD
U.S.S. Sienna Madira II
Hyperspace, 47.5 Light Hours from
  Target Star System
700 Light-years from the Sol System
Monday, 2:45 P.M. Ship Standard Time

"He won't leave, sir. I've tried everything I can to convince him that we have things under control here." Chief Petty Officer Sarala Amari stood behind the control panel displays for the hyperspace projector. Alexander could see from the look on her face through the visor in transparent mode that the CPO was truly concerned for the CHENG's wellbeing. Looking across the mangled structures, bulkheads, wires, and conduits that could only be described as the mess that the Engine Room had become, he could see Buckley several meters away, standing near the vortex projector. Buckley's suit looked like hell. Most of the right shoulder was missing and his arm was gone. There was a

blob of organogel and seal-layer material that had formed
a scab over the suit's wound. Moore double checked the
blue force tracker in his mindview and the CHENG's vitals
were stable. The suit was functioning properly and keeping
Joe alive and well.

"He ain't going anywhere as long as we're in hyperspace, sir! I can't budge him," Fireman's Apprentice
Rogers added. "To tell the truth, I'm not sure if I should
without a med team."

Moore nodded and surveyed the engine room again
from end to end and top to bottom. It was more a
shambles and torn to hell and gone than he'd seen it in
some time. There was a giant melted hole in one wall and
the projector energy conduit was blown out. What was left
of an armor suit looked to have been welded to a bulkhead
and incinerated in place.

What happened there? Moore asked his AIC.

*Commander Keri Benjamin, second CHENG, was hit
by the conduit plasma leak and killed instantly there. The
medical teams have had a difficult time removing all the
remains as they are fused to the bulkhead wall. It was
quite gruesome, sir,* Abigail replied.

Alexander turned away from the sight and focused on
Buckley's current situation. Nearest Joe, there was a giant
cable vibrating in midair, connecting a conduit coupler to
the projector input. The cable was flashing ionized sparks
and was humming like a lawnmower. Firecrews were
scrambling madly about and repair bots were skittering to
and fro with various and sundry tasks that Alexander likely
wouldn't understand anyway without Abigail explaining
them.

"Thank you, Ms. Amari. Thank you, Mr. Rogers. I appreciate you looking after him. We need to figure out our plan of attack for getting engineering back up to speed," Alexander said solemnly and clanked into the room. There were occasional puddles of green coolant liquids and other blobs of molten materials that he couldn't identify. Automatic radiation sensors in the suit pulled his visor down and the barrier shields were brought up to full.

Sir, the cable humming about in midair is acting as a small particle accelerator and the whirling aurora about it is putting off dangerous levels of gamma radiation, his AIC warned him.

Are we safe? Moore brought up his suit health image in his mindview.

Oh, yes, sir. The suit and the shields are more than enough protection, but the visor must remain down while in the engine room or you'll need antiradiation treatments.

Understood.

He walked cautiously over to Commander Joe Buckley Jr. who was standing before the hyperspace projector, waving his one remaining arm about in the air. He was clearly running some sort of simulation or performing some other engineering task. The blue force tracker view of him was still up in the forefront of Alexander's mindview right beside his own suit health page.

His vitals are stable, sir, Abigail told him. *Although he will need several days of recovery to get his arm replaced and to come off the stims and painkillers.*

I'm not sure we have several hours, much less several days.

"I've seen engineering in much worse shape, Commander. But I'm not sure when." Alexander placed a glove on his remaining shoulder. "Joe. Thank you. You saved the ship and her crew with it."

"At what cost, sir? I hope this mission was worth it," Buckley replied. "Hope we got what we came for."

"It'll be okay, Joe. We can get you to medical and get you fixed up," Alexander started, but the CHENG interrupted.

"Sorry, sir, I'm not going anywhere until we get the drive up and running. And with all due respect, General, I wasn't talking about losses I suffered. I'll be fine, hell, I've been a lot worse. We lost a lot of people. My second down here was killed instantly when the conduit failed. She was damned near irreplaceable and I don't look forward to writing the letter to her family. She had seven great-grandchildren, you know." Buckley seemed to zone out for a second and reached up into the air and moved an imaginary object. Alexander could see that the CHENG was very distracted or perhaps in shock. "And who is still back there? How are we going to get them out?"

"I assume you know the answer to that question, CHENG, so I won't answer it. We've yet to determine if we got what we came for on this mission. That was always the second wave's mission, not ours. Ours was to soften and distract. I do have to admit that they responded with more numbers than the Ghuthlaeer intel suggested they had there." Alexander sighed. Normally, he would be more aggressive at answering such questions and showing anyone doubting his decisions who exactly they were talking to. But, Alexander could see the CHENG was likely in shock from his injuries and losses as well as being preoccupied with whatever it was he was doing.

"Uh, yes, sir." Joe continued to move objects about in his mindview. Then Alexander was certain he stopped to talk with his AIC briefly. He wasn't sure if the CHENG was being insubordinate in not paying him full attention, or if Alexander himself was distracting the CHENG from keeping something on the ship from exploding or flying apart, or if the CHENG had just lost it altogether.

What is he doing, Abby?

I'm not sure, sir, Abigail replied in his mind. *Do you want me to inquire with his AIC?*

No. I'll just take the direct approach.

"CHENG. What are you doing?" Alexander motioned to the distracting movements, doing his best to sound genuinely curious rather than overly stern. He wasn't sure he'd gotten the inflection he was going for, but the CHENG didn't seemed to notice.

"I'm orchestrating the bots on emergency repairs and keeping that damned cable from popping sooner than we need it to." Joe turned to the General briefly. "By the way, sir, how long do we need it to last? I mean how long do we need to stay in hyperspace?"

"Uh, well, to the first rendezvous point at two light hours out. That would give us at least four hours before the Chiata could detect us and then get to us, assuming the intel of their top speed is seventy-five times lightspeed." Moore hesitated a bit then asked, "Will that be enough time for repairs to the drive?"

"No, sir. It will not." Joe continued his thousand-yard

stare into his DTM mindview and waved pages in and out and moved invisible objects. Alexander wasn't annoyed, but it was damned distracting. "It will take on the order of seven hours minimum to replace that conduit and then another three to realign the projector once we bring it down. Add in an hour or so for general contingencies and you're talking about eleven or twelve hours, sir. And I'm being very optimistic."

"Even with the bots, Joe?"

"Even with the bots, sir. Well, unless . . ." Joe seemed to drift off again into his DTM and it looked to Alexander like he filtered through several pages until he found what he was looking for. "Unless, well, maybe . . ."

"Unless what, CHENG?" Alexander did his best to hold his patience. He'd never seen Buckley this way before. He was pretty sure the engineer was in shock and needed medical attention.

"Unless what I'm building in virtualscape will work."

"So you are doing more than just repairs?" Alexander's gut instinct was right. Buckley was up to something as usual.

"Well, sir, uh, I'm building, well, uh, designing actually right now, a new projector system that won't blow out like this again and we'll never have to do a Buckley Maneuver ever. Ever Goddamned fucking ever a-damned-gain, uh, sorry, sir," the CHENG answered.

"I see. Maybe on the next ship we'll implement it." Alexander understood. Buckley had damned near been killed twice because of the ship's engine design. That was certainly enough motivation to warrant a redesign as well as colorful expletives. But he wanted the CHENG focused on getting the ship up and running and getting to medical. "But we need to take care of you first, Joe. The team can finish up the repairs. I think you need to see a doctor."

"You don't understand, sir." Buckley turned toward Alexander and finally stopped playing around in his virtual world briefly. "I plan to fix the ship now using the bots. We will, rather the bots will, build the system and then we'll drop out of hyperspace for a brief moment and switch it over. We could be back to the AO in a couple hours rather than several hours to a day."

"Wait, you mean you are fixing the ship now?"

"Well, I'm figuring out how to fix it using parts and materials we have. We'll build the secondary system and just turn it on. It should actually work better and be a much quicker plan. See, look." With that Joe shared his blueprints DTM to the engineering team and the General.

Abby?

Yes, sir. It is brilliant actually, sir, and would have multiple redundancies. The AIC ran billions of simulations and analyses almost instantly. *I believe it will work. Otherwise, I agree with the CHENG that we might be at least a day from repairing the system.*

Keep checking it. The CHENG is, well, quite distressed.

Yes, sir.

Any change in his condition and we need to get him to medical, understood?

Of course, sir. I'll keep a watch on his suit's monitoring systems.

Good girl.

"Joe. Why didn't you tell us? We can help with this," Amari said after viewing the DTM blueprints. "The bots will have no trouble building this. But, where are you going to get the extra SIF generators needed for the secondary conduits?"

"For now we build those conduits into the armored hull and use the structural integrity fields there. Eventually, I'd like to add more field generators though."

"Very well, CHENG. I see you have work to do." Moore nodded to the Chief Engineer and to the rest of the team that had filtered about him. There was nothing more he could do there. Besides, he had to figure out their next move against the Chiata and to get his people back—to get Dee back. "Keep me posted."

"Yes, sir. The cable is going to fail in about an hour anyway. We'll have to come out of hyperspace then no matter what. I was never sure we were going to make it to the rendezvous to start with," Buckley said while nodding toward the buzzing and humming cable that was carrying the power of thousands of lightning bolts through it continuously. "Without the SIFs that Amari put on it, the thing would have exploded in milliseconds."

"Keep us in hyperspace as long as you can while building the replacement system," Alexander said. "I don't want us to be sitting ducks any longer than we have to be."

"Understood, General." Joe replied.

"Joe. Any changes in your condition, I'm issuing a direct standing order to have you immediately removed and taken to medical."

"Aye, sir."

✦ ✦ ✦

"Stop squirming, Jack!" Sehera Moore told DeathRay, but he either didn't listen or simply couldn't hold still. She had the pilot lying flat on an aft hangar emergency triage table with a brace around his neck and chest. According to the log he'd gone into cardiac arrest three times in the last thirty or so minutes. Fortunately, Jack's suit had kept his heart beating and his body in stable condition, but his wounds were so severe that he was going to need extensive body part replacement. They just weren't severe enough to warrant the ship's surgical staff at the moment. There were much worse-off soldiers taking their attention. That fact alone gave Sehera a bad feeling in the bottom of her gut. Jack wasn't even ranked in the top hundred on the casualty priority list. But that was why Sehera was there. She had been a field rated emergency medical technician for almost a century and she was picking candidates from the list that she could heal without the need of the surgical staff.

"Well, I'm telling you it fucking hurts, uh, ma'am," he told her as Sehera adjusted the three-dimensional printer over his open abdominal wound. The organogel from his suit had sealed it and stopped the bleeding and hemorrhaging long since and had already been dissolved away, but it was still a horrific wound even if it wasn't a priority one wound. Those wounds were really horrific and life threatening and in many cases the suits were all that were holding the patients together and alive. Honestly, that's the way it was with Jack too, but his suit could keep him alive for days, probably, without proper medical attention. The others were in the minutes to hours category.

"If you don't stop moving I'll have to strap you down or put you in a stasis field, Jack. Besides, the vertebrae in your neck aren't fully healed yet and you could rebreak them with sudden movements." Sehera looked at the full body scan in her mindview and zoomed in on his neck. The vertebrae were still sticky and showed multiple fractures still healing. Two discs were bulging and had yet to reduce back to normal. The immunoboost was still working and would take a while for the nanomachines in the serum to completely repair the damage. "I could up the meds, but they won't give you the complete pain shunt that the stasis field will."

"Shit. Just do that. It hurts too goddamned much to stand. The pain meds ain't helping at all and I don't see how more would make a difference," Jack complained. Sehera knew the pilot and had known him for years now. He was as tough as they came. If he was hurting then he must really be hurting. The preprinting wound prep required that the organongel scab be removed by a solvent mix filled with nanorobots designed to eat dead organogel. The solvent cleansed and sterilized as it flushed into the open wound. Bright red blood covered the table but was almost immediately absorbed by the organogel layer of the tabletop. His wound was almost purely open and cleaned. Sehera could see completely through the pilot. It was a scene she'd seen many times over the last thirty or so minutes and expected she would see more wounds of similar nature throughout the rest of the day.

"Okay then, hold on." Sehera tapped the controls on the side of the medical bed and it started to whine softly in the background. Almost immediately the grimace on

Jack's face went away and he breathed a sigh of relief. The field paralyzed him for the rest of the procedure and would allow him to withstand it without any pain. "That better?"

"Oh my God. Night and day. But, now I can't move anything." Jack let out another deep breath and coughed, this time gurgling up blood as he did so. The blood drooled down his cheek, leaving a red stream that stained his lips and then dripped to the table. The petroleum jelly-like organogel reached up off the table, sensing it, and *schlurped* against his face, removing the rest of the blood. "Don't I need a doctor on this?"

"The three-D bots will have this fixed in no time. I've been doing this procedure since before the stasis field was invented. You wouldn't believe what I had to do to Alexander so many years ago in a survival tent in the Martian desert. Alexander never saw a doctor for it until after he'd gone in and killed about a hundred Separatist terrorists with his bare hands. I'll never forget what he told me then."

"What was that?"

"I'd never seen a man so driven and angry and certain of purpose all at once. He looked up at me as he grimaced in pain. Like I said, there were no stasis fields then. I told him not to die on me. He just grunted and between his screams of pain and anger he said that he had too many, and I quote, 'evil motherfuckers to kill before dying.' I'll never forget the look on his face."

"I, uh, well, I don't know what to say to that," Jack said. "Though I wouldn't mind killing a few million more of the Chiata."

"The point is, Mr. Boland, you will be fine even if you don't see the doc. But don't worry. I'll finish you up here and when there is time, if you still feel you need it, the doctor will be by for rounds. Then she can to check you out. But obviously, she has other priority patients right now." Sehera looked at the open wound. Seeing all the way through him continued to remind her of Alexander and how they had met. It also gave her worry about her daughter. From hyperspace they had no way of knowing how things were going and if Dee was alright or not. Even if they broke out of hyperspace, without the QMT communicators they were speed of light and hyperspace speeds limited. Communications would be nonexistent. She'd have no way of finding out about Dee from deep space. If she got a break from the wounded soon enough she'd make a point to talk with her husband about their plan to rescue her.

"Doctor or not, I've been in good hands. I'm sure I'll live." DeathRay said quietly and sighed. "Mrs. Moore, I'm sorry."

"Don't worry about it, Jack. I'd be complaining to see the doctor if I was in your situation too. When Alexander was in the White House I'd see a world-class doctor for a hangnail. There is nothing to apologize for. Besides, what would the Fleet do without the CAG in top working order?" Sehera did her best to offer a bedside manner smile, but her mind was elsewhere at the moment and she was sure Jack's was too. After all, his wife was still back there fighting the horde the same way her daughter was.

"I don't mean that, ma'am. Uh, I know I'll be fine. I mean . . ." Jack hesitated. "I'm sorry I couldn't save Dee."

"Dee will be fine. That is the only way I can see it in my head. And from what I understand she didn't need saving at all. We just need to get back to her and get her to safety." Sehera could see that DeathRay felt guilty about her daughter getting shot down. "It wasn't your fault, Jack. You damned near got yourself killed trying to save your entire squadron. You can't fight the Chiata all by yourself. Dee is a mecha pilot and a Marine. She knew what she was getting herself into. Alexander and I have been dealing with this for some time now. We can't protect her forever, but at the same time we hate seeing her in harm's way. No. For now, we just pray that Nancy can get to her."

"Yeah, well, she is my wingman. *It was my job to watch her*. And she ended up having to save my ass because I got in too deep." Jack's eyes glazed over briefly as if he were talking to his AIC. Sehera figured he was checking on the battle statistics and survivors. She decided it wasn't her business and let him be to his thoughts.

"Stop thinking on it. You need a couple hours to heal. Would you like me to turn on the sleep field or do you want to stay awake?"

"All the same to you, I'll sleep." Jack replied.

"Very well. Sleep well then, Jack. When you wake you'll feel brand new," she told him and tapped the sleep control. Boland immediately was out like a light after flipping the switch off.

Sehera watched as the printer began laying down the first layer of internal organ material to replace what was missing. The system didn't miss a cell or vein or tissue as it matched what was already there exactly. She noted to herself how much more advanced it was from what she'd used on Mars so long ago. Had Sehera not been watching it closely to make sure nothing went wrong, there would have been no way she could tell the difference from where the old organ material ended and where the new material began. After a few seconds of blood flowing through the new tissues she couldn't tell the difference anyway. She set the system to perform the operation and repair as well as perform as much rejuvenation as the portable machine could offer. It wouldn't completely reverse Jack back to a twenty-five-year old's body, but it would make him feel like he was in perfect health and peaking physically and mentally once he was fully healed. The partial rejuv was always standard procedure because it aided in recovery from post-traumatic stress syndrome.

She looked about triage at more than seventy tables set up and the bloody and sometimes screaming soldiers waiting for help. She had spent too much time on DeathRay already, but he was family. She knew she had to move on to the next patient.

"Sweet dreams, Jack." She patted his head lightly. "You'll be fine."

Chapter 15

February 19, 2407 AD
U.S.S. Roscoe Hillenkoetter
Asteroid Belt, Target Star System
700 Light-years from the Sol System
Monday, 2:45 P.M. Ship Standard Time

USN Captain Nancy Penzington looked out of the forward viewport from the main bridge at the now nineteen ships the second wave of the Expeditionary Fleet attack force had remaining. They were scattered about and hugging rocks or alien ships as closely as they could. There just was no tactic that seemed to be of much use against the alien bastards.

They had lost eleven ships already. As best they could manage, the clone-commanded ships were using the asteroid field for cover, but the damned alien blue beams could zig around obstacles and zag around corners and bring death from an alien Hell. Nancy was glad she had decided to keep all the pilots in the supercarriers because they would have just been thrown out into the grinder and the ships wouldn't have time to pull them back in before the Chiata were on top of them blasting them to oblivion.

"All the buzzsaw bots have been deployed, ma'am," the Air Boss stated. "But it will be some time before they can self-replicate to any critical mass that would help our effectiveness against the Chiata."

"Understood, Zander." Nancy had to keep their names on a pull-down list in her mindview. The clones only had a few hundred names because the names represented their host. The Commander of the Air Wing for the *Hillenkoetter* was actually Zander4364. His number having four digits meant he was from the fourth generation of clones generated from the original source material. More detail than that, Nancy didn't really care. In cases where she had multiple clones of the same source material she called them by title or had thought of nicknames. She had three Teena clones. Her CHENG was Teena597431, a sixth generation clone, while her STO and Nav were eighth generation Teenas. Dealing with all the similar faces hurt her head. At least her Chief of the Boat was the only Franklin clone and her Ground Boss was the only Alexia clone she had on the bridge crew. She wished there had been more humans available trained for bridge duty. She hoped she lived to remedy that situation.

As it stood presently, the bridge was a chaos of fire and sparks erupting from panels, the smells of burned plastic and metal, and the constant communication of yet more losses from the alien armada within the system and communications from engineering about yet another system that was failing. Nancy turned up her nose as the searing hot plastic smell burned at her nostrils. She could easily activate the faceplate of her suit but she liked having the actual sensory data of her environment. It kept her more alert and attuned to just how bad things might have gotten. Besides, Allison would activate the suit functions instantly if there were any imminent threat.

"CHENG to CO."

"Go, CHENG." Nancy used her mind to click the engineering channel open.

"Ma'am, there is no way to get the forward DEGs back up without an extensive EVA. The conduits are blown and I have no way to reroute the coolant. And the SIFs are going to fail on the starboard hull in minutes. Sooner if we take on another blue beam hit," the CHENG explained.

"Understood, CHENG. Keep the ship flying and keep the shields and drive up," Nancy ordered.

"Working on it, ma'am."

"Work harder."

Nancy pulled up the ship's engineering diagnostic diagram in her mindview. The forward DEGs were down and the SIF generators were overloading the power conduits on the starboard false hull. There were multiple breaches in the armor plating of the upper decks of the ship, and several of the secondary ship's systems were offline. Main propulsion was still functional, but only barely. One or two more hits from one of the blue beams and the *Hillenkoetter* would be stuck dead in space and surrounded by the Chiata horde.

Nancy held the complete battlescape virtual view

about her head and played with probabilities and possible outcomes, but between her and the super AIC living within her skull, neither of them could develop any strategy that was going to see them hold in orbit long enough to extract the Maniacs, Slayers, and Juggernauts. And she could find no way to move further northward to extract Dee without major losses. Her first attempt at dropping a ship in on top of the ground team's location planetside had resulted in the complete loss of the supercarrier UM61 Beta Seven. As far as she could tell there were no survivors.

It was possible she could throw several of the supercarriers at the problem of extracting the downed teams. That would mean risking the lives of thousands of clones, but Nancy wasn't certain if it was moral to sacrifice so many clones and AICs, or were they one and the same, for a much smaller number of normally born humans. Nancy wasn't really certain that there was any difference other than the fact they were born in a different process. They were lives nonetheless and Nancy couldn't justify the meat grinder. Clones or not. Dee or not. It was time to make the tough decision.

"Rackman!"

"Aye, ma'am?" her XO responded over the klaxons and din of activity as a mix of clone and human firemen and techs rushed about the bridge tending to fires and repairs. Nancy turned and focused on Rackman for a moment. She preferred hearing his voice over the clones. At least Rackman's carried the vocal inflections of emotions that matched the present situation. The clones of the crew sounded too deadpan, or when they did display emotional inflections, they always seemed to be the wrong one for the moment or way too much or too little to be situation-appropriate.

"I can't find any way that we can extract those on the planet without losing most of the fleet." Nancy hesitated for a second. "All recon teams are KIA. The ground teams and pilots seem to be safe for the moment. They'll have to stay put. This party is a bust."

"You're not thinking of leaving them?" Nancy could almost see the SEAL's dislike of the idea on what little facial expression she could see through his faceplate. "Uh, ma'am, with all due respect, we can't just leave them there."

"I don't like it any more than anybody else does. But there are seven Maniacs, eight Slayers, six AEMs, and Dee. Twenty-two people for thousands is not a good battle plan. The Chiata have responded with far more numbers here than we had anticipated. Our fleet is overwhelmed. We need to regroup and lick our wounds and come up with a better plan. At our current rate of loss, we'll not survive much longer ourselves." Nancy didn't hesitate to look at Rackman further. He didn't have to like her order. He just had to carry it out. "Comm! Send retreat order to all ships. Hyperspace immediately to rendezvous location."

"Aye, ma'am," the clone communications officer, a Malcolm clone like the gunner, replied.

"We have to tell them." Rackman pleaded. Nancy turned to her XO and nodded her head subtly up and down. "Yes. I already have."

Chapter 16

February 19, 2407 AD
Northern Region
Target Star System
700 Light-years from the Sol System
Monday, 2:45 P.M. Ship Standard Time

The river was much deeper than Dee had expected, which had been fortunate for her. The blue bolts from the alien rifles had pounded her armor during her mad leap over the cliff, causing her barrier shield generator to fizzle out. Her shields were gone. She fell in a gymnastic twirl, spinning wildly over the waterfall, doing her best to gain control of her body, but the angular momentum was too great. Dee hit hard against the water with a loud *slap*ping sound that echoed about the jungle cavern. The noise scattered alien birds and other creatures scampering off in every direction.

She pierced into the water, doing a backflop that

jerked her so hard it made her see stars. The armor had protected her but the impact concussed her enough that she was knocked silly for several seconds. Still punch drunk, Dee finally came to being tossed about by tons of rushing water that pushed her deeper and deeper and further out into the rapidly flowing and churning river that was over thirty meters deep at her current location. The water flowed so swiftly that it swept her into the deepest and fastest currents. Dee had no choice but to simply let herself go limp and let the waters wash her away to wherever the river wanted to take her. At least, she hoped, it would take her away from her Chiata attackers.

She had flowed with the water for some time, ten or so minutes maybe, with her suit banging against rocks and trees at the bottom. Dee was afraid to turn on her active sensors from fear of detection, and that made avoiding obstacles all the more difficult. There were a few times that she would have sworn she saw artificial structures under the water near her, and others she thought some type of creatures had swum by her on several occasions, but she was moving too swiftly and doing her best not get too beat up along the way to pay them much mind.

Bree! Any idea where we are and where the Chiata are? she thought. A map of the river illuminated in her mindview almost instantly with her blue dot on it. The red dots of the Chiata search team were still moving about the waterfall region almost three kilometers behind her. They appeared to be searching the waterfall and the nearby area thinking Dee would have crawled out of the river nearby. As far as Dee could tell they had yet to push the search farther along the river. That suggested that they could no longer detect her trail.

I recommend you stay in the currents and let them take you as far away from the alien search party as we can get, the AIC suggested.

I'm with you on that. Any chance we can get my shield system working again? Dee was hopeful, but wasn't betting on it.

Unlikely, Bree told her, and then an image of her suit popped up in her mind, rotated, and then zoomed in on a spot on her back, lower left side. A small metallic box blinked and highlighted. Layers of the armor covering it peeled away and led to several circuit components and some sort of coil wound about a crystalline rod. The rod was fractured and chips of it were spread about and embedded in the circuit boards, giving the appearance that the rod had exploded. *The generator was completely overloaded and we do not have replacement components. The field initiating substrate has been destroyed.*

Shit. I was afraid of that. What is it made of?

Yes. Shit. I agree. The rod is made of degenerate matter and built by nanomachines from the atom up in such a way that it can trap strange matter in small pockets.

What the hell is strange matter?

Strange matter is a degenerate collection, cloud, or gas of quarks that usually contains strange quarks in addition to the usual up and down quarks. The only place in nature it is found to my knowledge is in quark stars or the core of neutron stars formed by the collapse of objects above the Tolman–Oppenheimer–Volkoff mass limit for neutron-degenerate objects. We actually don't know how to acquire natural samples from within a star. The strange matter is generated inside an accelerator event, like inside a hyperspace projector during initiation of the Krasnikov tube. The rod itself is there to hold the very sparse distribution of this matter in place. The physics of the rod is what enables the quantum field fluctuations and probability bending that causes the barrier effect. It is known as a Buckley-Freeman Initiator.

Okay, so you are telling me we can't make one out of stuff we find lying about on this planet.

Yes. That is exactly what I am telling you.

You could have just said that and spared me the fucking physics class.

Sorry.

Any other good news? Dee asked sarcastically as she did her best to negotiate through the water. The river still moved swiftly but had spread out and the bottom felt more and more like stone and gravel. Objects in her path seemed to be fewer in number and the river's depth seemed to be steady at twenty-six point four meters. It was a very big river. Dee thought inwardly that in Marine vernacular it was a BFR—big fucking river.

Well, I believe we are in an artificial channel within this river now. Perhaps it will be easier to negotiate, Bree said. *That is, perhaps, good news.*

Hmm. Artificial? A barge channel like on the Mississippi? Dee thought of home briefly.

Probably. Or at least it would appear so, although this channel itself is as big as the Mississippi at its largest point. There was a pause and then the AIC changed the subject. *Dee. Captain Penzington is making an announcement.*

Put it through in audio.

Roger that.

"This is Captain Penzington of the *U.S.S. Roscoe Hillenkoetter*. I am sounding the systemwide retreat order. The Chiata have overwhelmed us at the current time. We have already lost eleven supercarriers with hopes of retrieving all of our downed soldiers and ground teams. For the moment that appears to be an impossible task, which we cannot afford more losses against. We are currently evacuating this system to our predetermined rendezvous coordinates at which point we will, and I emphasize the word WILL, make plans to return for you. Find a place to dig in or a way to avoid engagement with the enemy if possible. Stay alive. We will return for you as soon as we can." There was a brief pause and Dee could almost see Nancy swallowing and gulping down her loathing of this situation. Dee knew that there was no way that Nancy would leave her if she didn't have to.

"To all of you, good luck. God bless. And we will see you soon."

She is requesting a channel with you, Dee.

Open it.

"Dee, are you okay?" Nancy sounded both nervous and sad at the same time. She had always been like a big sister to Dee. And now, her big sister couldn't come to her rescue. DeathRay hadn't been able to help her, her father hadn't been able to get to her, and now Nancy couldn't get to her. Dee had a feeling of being on her own.

"Yes. For now. I'm playing cat and mouse with some pretty big fucking cats," Dee grunted. "I'll be fine, but who knows for how long."

"I'm so sorry I can't get to you. The Chiata have blockaded the planet from us completely. See if you can make it toward the Maniacs and the groundpounders."

"That would take days, Nancy. They are over six hundred kilometers away and I'm on foot."

"I can't tell you honestly that we will be back before then. We've been hit very hard and we have to go now," Nancy told her. "I'm sorry. Stay alive."

"I will. You too."

Jarhead? Davy Rackman's mindvoice sounded in her head.

Squid boy? Are you okay?

Just banged up all to hell. We're jaunting in ten seconds. I just had to tell you . . . I love you.

You too. Davy, I love you too. Dee finally said it or at least thought it to the SEAL, but she hoped it wasn't too little too late.

You stay alive. Come Hell or high waters we'll get back here and rescue you. Rackman's mindvoice sounded ready to leap from space down to the planet to fight off the Chiata barehanded. Dee loved him even more for that.

I will be here when you get back. And with that, the channel was dead and the dots for the Fleet ships above the planet vanished from the battlescape.

Dee used the flow of the river for another twenty minutes until the currents died down to the point that the water was no longer enough to move her in her suit by itself. She took long bouncing strides off the bottom like she would if she were on a low-gravity planetoid. The water made her movements easier to control than if she were on an airless rock in space with little to no gravity to speak of. This was easy stuff for a Marine in an e-suit.

Dee studied the map of the region and of the river while she bounced, and at the same time realized that without the fleet there she no longer had access to the system-wide red force tracker. That made her life much harder. She had no idea where her pursuers were. They might be kilometers away or they might be right on top of her. She'd just have to play this game alert and ready for anything. She considered releasing a couple of nanodroid skyball cameras but wasn't sure if it would tip off her location when the cameras came back to her or when they uploaded the video to her over the spread spectrum communications tac-net. Once she was certain she had lost the Chiata search party she might reconsider the skyballs.

The tac-net was the one thing she did have access to. The spread spectrum communications network with the other teams on planet was still available with all other tanks, mecha, suits, and AIC-to-AIC. Dee could barely fathom that of all the droptanks and mecha and AEMs that hit the planet, all of them but twenty-two were dead. Why the others were still alive was a complete mystery, but at least they were alive. She needed to keep in contact with them but was a bit apprehensive to transmit. As far as she knew the spread spectrum below the noise floor algorithms the communications devices used were untrackable. But that was as far as she knew. She had no idea if the Chiata had technology that could track a signal below the noise floor and spread across the entire electromagnetic spectrum on randomly encrypted frequency hopping patterns. There was also the quantum entangled network that didn't function the same as the quantum membrane teleportation technologies. The entanglement based systems were functioning but the QMT based systems were not.

Dee studied where the rest of the *Madira's* forces were in relation to herself and realized that they were in a tributary of the river she was currently in, but the river looked much smaller there.

Bree, show me the complete path from me to them, she thought to her AIC.

Roger that. The path twists and turns a bit and covers a distance of seven hundred and six kilometers, give or take.

Then the map zoomed out with a light blue line tracing a path downriver, through what looked like more jungle and marshlands, and then down one more set of rolling older mountains and into a much more arid region that looked sort of like New Mexico or Arizona. Currently, Dee was on the largest part of the river chain and it branched in three directions a few klicks ahead. She had to take the easternmost branch to stay on a path leading to the others. And from the looks of it, that would be the most jungle-like region of the planet. Deepest and darkest African Congo sprang to mind. At her current pace she'd reach the three-way split in the river in less than a half hour and then she'd have to negotiate a couple more waterfalls into the jungle swamps region. At least she was wearing her e-suit and wouldn't have to worry about snakes and bugs. Tough as hell Marine or not, Dee hated spiders and snakes.

✢ ✢ ✢

As she approached the triple branch in the river the currents picked up and were becoming unmanageable. For more than a kilometer she had no longer needed to bounce off the bottom to continue to move forward and she had to force herself downward to control her direction. While the suits were designed for almost any environment they had not been designed for swimming. Dee decided it best to bounce to the banks and take to dry land. Her plan was to follow the river for a while, and then she came to the waterfalls.

She was fortunate that the waterfalls were a shorter drop and had multiple ledges that she could use for landing points with her jumpboots, and there were several of the giant mangrove trees towering nearby and overhanging the falls. As it turned out for Dee, negotiating the two waterfalls hadn't proven as difficult as the previous one since they weren't as high and she managed to make covert leaps to the rocks, through the trees, and along indigent animal paths to the bottom of each. Dee noted to her AIC as she dropped through the trees and down the rocky moss-covered slopes without incident how much like any jungle on Earth the place seemed to be. She also noted that there was something unexpected and beautiful about it.

You have to admit, the place is a pretty green, she thought. Given other circumstances Dee would have thought the place to be absolutely beautiful, but those circumstances would certainly not include any scenario where the Chiata were involved.

And from appearances must be untouched by the Chiata. There must be a reason for that, Bree added to the sentiment.

Maybe there's nothing here that interests them? It made zero sense to Dee why other parts of the planet were fairly densely populated by the Chiata and had become alien construction and manufacturing and dwelling sites, but the Northern continent along the river was deserted.

From all we've seen the Chiata horde devours and uses everything in their path. There must be an important reason as to why they are not here, Bree said. *Maybe there is something here they are afraid of.*

That is a chilling thought. Something that scares the Chiata. The thought frightened Dee.

Nevertheless, they are not here. There is something important here.

I agree. I'm not sure how but perhaps we need to think on investigating this a little deeper. It could be why we're here in the first place. Dee began to roll recon procedures in her mind. If she was going to do more than escape and evade then she needed to have a plan.

Agreed.

After passing the second waterfall the terrain became mostly flat along the river. The ground was covered with greener than green vegetation and the riverbank was covered with thick vines and mangrove-like trees. The canopy was thicker and the sounds and heat signatures of creatures scurrying about became more and more prevalent. Dee had been on the bounce and slinking through water and jungle alike for the better part of three hours. As far as the sensors and the maps in her suit and that her AIC had access to, she had traveled almost fifty kilometers, evaded the Chiata search party, not to mention killed three or four of them, dropped down three waterfalls, and more recently been pushing though some pretty nasty vegetation and underbrush. It was likely that the Chiata would have found her by then if they were tracking her. At least that was Dee's hope at the moment.

"Screw it," she said quietly to herself. "I'm taking a break."

Dee surveyed the riverbank and the canopy for a well-covered spot and found just the place underneath a giant tree several meters from where the river appeared to have receded, leaving the large root system of the tree exposed. The trunk of the tree was at least two meters in diameter as it spread at the base, leading into hundreds of smaller roots that reached into the soft, moist soil. The base of the circle where the roots met the ground was more than four meters in diameter. The roots kept the large tree elevated above the ground by about three meters or so, leaving Dee to the conclusion that in the rainy season the water was much higher and covered the roots. She looked about and could see trees with similar root systems as far as she could see. Various types of foliage of bright greens and yellows that matched the star's light yellow-green spectrum covered the jungle floor. Vines appeared as fibrous sinewy tissues that spiraled upward and twisted about the trees in slightly darker greens and browns. Dee noted that she saw almost no reds or blues in the jungle fauna. She also noticed several more cone-shaped mounds that she had seen along the way for the past couple of hours. The mounds were almost two meters tall from the ground to the tip and were a beige, almost concrete color.

What are these things? Anthills?

Something similar most likely, Dee. They could also be like the termite mounds in Africa.

Well, they seem to be everywhere along the river basin. Are they active? she thought as she tapped her knuckles against one. It was hard as granite. *There is something almost artificial about them.*

They were built by some sort of creature, that is for certain. Perhaps like the bullet ants in Central America.

Let's not find out. Dee backed away from the mound and returned to the base of her giant tree. She began kicking at the roots on one side. The extremely dense wood made cracking and clanging sounds against her jumpboots.

Dee managed to kick away enough of the vines to make an opening large enough for her to crawl through. She scanned the small cavern underneath the tree and found nothing fearsome, so she sat down opposite the opening and rested the back of her suit against the roots.

Has anybody tested this air yet? she thought.

Yes. The AEMs have. It is breathable with no known pathogens. However, the carbon dioxide content is about seven point five percent in the local air. That is high enough that it will start causing headaches and potentially more severe effects after about ten minutes. Breathing the air for more than fifteen minutes at a time will cause blackouts and could possibly be fatal.

Alright then, start a clock. Dee smiled to herself and popped her faceplate. She hesitated for a moment and then took a deep breath.

"Doesn't seem so bad," she whispered. A clock started

ticking in her mindview and a blood gas carbon dioxide measurement in millimeters of mercury showed her real-time toxin level.

If the CO2 goes above forty millimeters it is time to put the visor down, Bree warned her. *You can make it a bit higher but let's not push it.*

Roger that.

Dee searched through the front compartments in her suit and opened up the rations kit. She pulled a meal bar out and started to unwrap it, but the gauntlets made that very difficult. If she concentrated and focused her motor controls she could easily unwrap the bar. Hell, she flew a space fighter mecha that had over a hundred levers, buttons, toggles, and switches with the gloves on, she could certainly unwrap a meal bar. But in a breathable atmosphere there was no need. So, she sat the meal bar on her lap and cycled the glove retraction, and the armor peeled back to her wrists, exposing her hands and fingers. A cool chill ran up her spine as the organogel vaporized off her skin. She briefly considered peeling back her helmet and giving her head a good scratching, but she was hungrier than she was stir crazy.

She cracked the seal on the meal bar and it heated itself to body temperature. She let out a long sigh and then bit into the bar, savoring the sweet and salty flavor of the peanut butter, almond, and granola bits that were mixed throughout the chocolate-covered meal. The bar had been bioengineered to provide a complete day's worth of calories in the right ratios of macronutrients and yet still tasted good. It also had appetite and hunger pain suppressants mixed in so the solder would have the feeling of being satiated after eating it. Dee continued to chew the bar. As it was, she was hungry enough to eat the ass end out of a bull.

"Just like momma used to make," she grunted through a mouthful and then hit the water tube in front of her face in her helmet.

You know this is dumb, right? Dee thought to her AIC.

What is dumb, Dee? the AIC asked.

Me walking all the way to the Maniacs and the groundpounders. That's what. Dee continued to chew as she carried on the mind conversation. *If the aliens don't know where I am, then I should be doing the recon we came all this way to do. There is some reason the Chiata are not overwhelming my position right now. What is that reason?*

I suspect you are on to something. What would you suggest we do?

Well, to start with, start tracking any overhead flights and activity. Use audio, IR, UV, RF, multi-spectral, quantum, I don't know, if the suit has it use it. That's a start. Let's see if the alien bastards are going anywhere specific up here. Dee paused for a minute to think. *Hell, we have three skyballs. I say we launch them and use them for recon.*

The Chiata might be able to detect and track them, Bree said.

Yeah, well, they might not, or might not care. Dee finished off the super-dense chocolate peanut butter bar and drank more water, thinking briefly that at least water wasn't going to be a problem on this planet. It was humid and covered with it. The suit could filter out any pathogens and toxins.

We could just send them out and bring them back and not transmit the imagery if you are that concerned about it, Bree suggested.

Yes. Let's do that to start with. Then we might test the com relay with one of them later if we need to. Dee brought up the shoulder launch tubes and popped open the one holding the skyballs. She increased the pressure in the tube slightly until three small gray balls about the size of ping pong balls popped out and hovered in front of her face. The operator's window opened in her mindview, telling her that they were ready for instructions.

How would you like them configured? Bree asked as a pull-down page for each one opened in Dee's mind.

Send one along the river southeasterly. Dee thought about the other two for a moment. She reached in through her open visor and rubbed her nose and her eyes as she thought. *Send the other two in opposite directions, one east and one west, and do standard reconnaissance sweep patterns. If they get hits on any artificial structures they are to dwell and then collect as much data as possible. Then they fly back to me. Oh, and any signs of the horde they should report back also.*

Understood. No sooner than Bree had said that, the skyballs zoomed out from under the tree and were out of sight. The little camera bots made no noise from their propellantless propulsion drives and left without leaving any trail behind them.

Keep the sensors on max and as soon as we get any

idea of something that needs investigating we'll head that way. Dee dropped the visor back down over her face and redeployed the gauntlets over her hands. *Until then, I'm taking a nap. You're on sentry duty, Bree.*

Affirmative.

Chapter 17

February 19, 2407 AD
Northern Region
Target Star System
700 Light-years from the Sol System
Monday, 5:06 P.M. Ship Standard Time

Colonel Delilah "Jawbone" Strong hit the toggle to transfigure her FM-12 mecha from fighter mode to bot mode. Several of the other Maniacs stood guard and all of the tankheads were ready for action. But, as it appeared so far, as long as her squadron and other soldiers stayed in the canyon basin and within the ruins the Chiata were leaving them alone. The blue force tracker showed that every other drop team across the planet was dead.

The only other person still alive on the planet other than the Chiata or local fauna was Major Deanna Moore. Delilah had known Ms. Moore since she was a child and in fact had been partly instrumental in rescuing her and her father, who never really needed rescuing because he was such a badass, at the battle of Orlando on the day of Tau Ceti secession in the Separatist war. She had become friends with the Moore family since that time and hated to see Dee shot down and on her own on an alien-infested planet.

Delilah wanted to get to the Major but for the moment there was nothing she could do to help her. In fact, as far as she could tell, she was just as screwed. She was stuck where she was until somebody came up with a better idea for getting them out of there. Good or bad, the alien forces were above them in overwhelming numbers, but as long as they stayed put there were no blue beams, no red and green blurs, no porcupines, no AA fire, nothing. The aliens simply didn't attack.

So, as any good Marine would do, Delilah decided to do something rather than sitting around with her thumbs up her ass waiting for someone else to save her. They were stranded with the ruins. Where there were ruins there were no Chiata. That meant something. What exactly, Delilah had no fucking clue. But she did know that if the Chiata didn't like it, whatever "it" was she was going to find "it" and use "it" to kill a whole bunch of the red and green blurs and porcupines. She hoped.

"Alright, Popstar, the two of us will move this thing together once we're in place." Delilah told her second in command. They *clank*ed across the large artificial chamber floor tossing small puffs of chalky gray limestone dust with each mecha step. Delilah brought the view of the large granite wall up in her sensor view and scanned it across all frequencies and with active particle scans. Her sensors gave her no reading whatsoever. As far as the mecha's sensors and computer were concerned there was no wall on the back side of the large cavern. But she could see it. She could touch it. It was there.

"Jawbone, I'm reading nothing on my sensors. Are we being jammed?" Major Dana "Popstar" Miller said over the pilot's tac-net. "I can see it with Mark I eyeballs, but nothing else."

"Roger that, Popstar. I've got the same thing here. Stay with eyeballs and let's see if we can find a doorknob." Delilah wasn't sure the back end of the cavern was a doorway, but the floor looked like a roadway that rose up out of the river and tracked right into the wall. There were markings on the floor that suggested movement of large objects toward that wall and onward, but to where?

The "doorway" itself was covered with wild ellipses and circles and fractal patterns that looked like somebody on a cocktail mixture of alcohol, pain meds, acid, and immunoboost went apeshit with a spirograph. Scattered about the wild curves were little insect-like drawings about the size of ping pong balls. The curves twisted about each other, and there were several star systems drawn about and along them as well. Every location where there was a drawing of one of the insect things, there was a star system. If Jawbone didn't know better she'd swear the drawings looked like the energy curves that mecha pilots trace in their mindview to engage with enemy craft during dogfights. But the things seemed to look like they were on planetary scales rather than dogfight scales. The damned thing was perplexing to say the least.

Several of the Juggernauts bounced about the feet of

the bot mode mecha and were looking about the wall for handholds, buttons, secret levers, even magic words, but nobody was having any luck. So, they had decided to use a more direct approach—pound the shit out of it with mecha. After all, they had seven FM-12s and eight M3A18-T hovertanks at their disposal just sitting there collecting dust.

"Alright, everybody stand back," Strong said over her external speakers and the tac-net. As soon as the AEMs had cleared out she balled up her right mecha hand into a fist and drew it back. "Here goes nothing."

The giant armored fist pounded into the wall with the force of the largest battering ram ever built. Dust flew out from around the fist and the ground shook. The impact reverberated backwards through the hand and up the mecha's arm. The entire bot mode mecha rang like a bell, jarring Delilah's teeth and bones. She bit down against the bite block. She hit the same spot again, but this time harder. The cavern didn't falter and the stone before her didn't budge. There was no indentation in the granite. There was no crack. There wasn't even a scratch on it.

"What the fuck?" one of the AEMs said over the net. Delilah noted it was Master Gunnery Sergeant Howser. While she had met the AEM, she didn't really know her. All she knew was that the Marine was very close to Deanna Moore and to CHENG Buckley.

"Hit it again, Colonel," Colonel Francis Jones, leader of the AEMs added.

Delilah bit down hard on her bite block and tightened every muscle in her body to prepare for the reverberation, and then she let her entire mecha torso twist into the punch. The large mechanized fist slammed against the stone with such force that the thunderous crack of impact was nearly deafening. Delilah's body was shaken to the bone and the mecha rang even louder than the previous times.

"Warning! Structural Integrity Field collapse imminent! Warning! Structural Integrity Field collapse imminent!" The Bitchin' Betty chimed.

A flicker of blue light washed across the wall and then reduced itself to a circle only slightly larger than the mecha's fist and directly over the spot that Delilah had just hit. The blue light rippled from the outer circumference to a single point in the middle and then it flashed again. This time light seemed to rush from within the circle and jumped off the wall with a burst of white light, tossing the many-ton mass of the mecha like a rag doll across the cavern floor.

The mecha skittered and tumbled with earsplitting screeches of metal against stone as Delilah fought against the controls. She did all she could to keep the mecha upright, but her efforts were to no avail. She tumbled over out of control and came careening down against the stone floor on her back, sprawled out like a tortoise upside down on its shell.

"Holy shit!" Delilah shouted. She squinted her eyes and fought the urge to shake her head until her suit diagnostics said she had no broken bones. Her ears rang, her teeth ached, her body felt like ants were crawling on it, and she was in pain from head to toe. "Nobody, I repeat, NOBODY, hits that fucking wall."

"Yes, ma'am," resounded from the other pilots, tankheads, and AEMs.

"Major Miller, did your sensors get that?" Delilah asked as she picked herself up off the rock floor.

"Uh, no, ma'am. Sensor systems replay shows that nothing happened other than you flying across the room and landing on your ass, uh, ma'am," Popstar replied. "Colonel, if you don't mind my saying so, this is some weird shit."

"Goddamned right it is," Delilah said as she dragged her mecha back to its feet. She took a deep breath then pounded over to the spot where she'd previously been standing and zoomed her optical sensors in close on the spot she'd been hitting. "Not a fucking nanoscratch on this thing!"

"My guess is it has some sort of structural integrity field and clearly a point barrier shield," Colonel Slayer said. "I don't even think a tank would scratch it."

"I wouldn't want you to try it, Colonel. This wall has something behind it. Why else would it be protected like this?" Delilah added. It was the damnedest thing she'd ever seen.

"Looks a lot like that underwater wall that we found back at Epsilon Ursae Majoris that Captain Penzington and DeathRay vanished through," Howser said.

"How so, Gunny?" Colonel Francis bounced beside the AEM standing beneath Delilah's mecha.

"Well, sirs, it was a solid wall to us. We could see it, but water was flowing through it. Captain Penzington, who wasn't a captain then, figured out that it was some sort of oscillating SIF or some such damned thing. She said she'd seen Elle Ahmi use something like it before on Ares. I don't know. She did say something about cloaking algorithms. Since then I've heard the CHENG call it a backdoor."

"And that right there is why you're here with us, Gunny!" Major Sellis bounced beside her and pounded her on the back with his armored hand. "A backdoor is just what we're looking for."

"Yes, sir, but . . ." Delilah noted the hesitation in the gunny's voice, and she had already figured out what the "but" was about. So she interrupted.

"But," Delilah tilted her mecha head down toward them. "We don't know how to open it and we don't have Captain Penzington or the CHENG here with us. So, somebody else is going to have to be clever."

"Anyone here got a science background?" Delilah pulled up the personnel roster in her mindview. There were history majors, logisticians, and strategists. One of the team was even a grandmaster at chess, but none of them were scientists or engineers. They were all smart and well trained soldiers, but their careers had not led them to engineering or science. "We'll just have to get on-the-job training, I guess."

Chapter 18

February 19, 2407 AD
U.S.S. Sienna Madira II
Hyperspace, 10.5 Light Days from
  Target Star System
700 Light-years from the Sol System
Monday, 6:06 P.M. Ship Standard Time

Alexander's mind raced with the events of the day as he walked down the corridor with his Chief of the Boat Chuck Sowles. Occasionally, they found themselves stepping aside as repair bots skittered by or to let repair crews through with equipment. The two men had made most of the rounds through the medical bay and triages where they talked to as many of the wounded as they could. The COB made a point to direct Alexander to every sailor, tankhead, groundpounder, and mecha jock there that wasn't being operated on. That was part of the COB's job and Alexander appreciated it.

A few times during the process Alexander had caught his wife's eye across the aft hangar bay triage but they didn't have time to speak. Sehera had her hands full tending to wounded that didn't require immediate care from a doctor. He loved his wife dearly and was moved by how selflessly and tirelessly she worked with the casualties. She had done the same for him on many different occasions and seeing her brought back those memories. Some of them were really very bad but some of them were very good. His wife had a strong demeanor and a big heart, but she was also a force to be reckoned with that even gave the big bad Marine pause at times. This just happened to be one of those times.

Alexander's heart and soul were torn and he was both glad and sad at the same time. His heart was truly breaking because he simply had no idea what to say to Sehera at the moment and he was tormented by his decisions of the day, the loss of his people, and the fear of losing his daughter. He had only three hours and twenty one minutes earlier just given the order to leave their only little girl, his princess, on an alien planet in an alien-controlled star system, not knowing when he could get back to her. He prayed that Nancy Penzington came through for her. But with the overwhelming odds looming against the Fleet when he had jaunted out of the system, he was very concerned for his daughter's life. He could think of nothing but blame for himself and wished he'd never let his daughter get into her current situation so far from his ability to come to the rescue.

Alexander checked his casualty list update menu to see how many had come off the triage and surgery list and made the recovery list. Of the nearly three hundred listed as casualties all but four were on the recovery list. The other four were now moved to the killed in action list. While the names were faces he could recall, they were not people he knew well. But they *were* crew. They were *his* crew. And *he'd* led them to their deaths. Alexander's stomach churned. Again he thought about his daughter and prayed he hadn't led her to her doom. Somehow, he knew, this mission would have to mean something more than just casualties, but for now there was nothing else to show for it. The second wave had to come through. If not the second, he wasn't sure how to muster up a third. But, again, somehow, he knew he had to. The direness of the situation reminded him of the thirty-some odd days he'd spent in his armor suit wounded and hiding out in the deserts of Mars so long ago. Back then vengeance drove him to stay alive and to keep pressing forward. Now, vengeance would help, but saving his little girl was plenty motivation.

"Cup of coffee for your thoughts, sir?" Sowles asked.

"Just reviewing the casualty list again. We lost four more sailors," Alexander replied. "What the hell have we got to show for it?"

"Well, Captain," Sowles started. Chuck being an old Navy sailor, Moore had noted that it was difficult for COB to address the captain of the boat by anything other than "captain." While some called him General Moore at times and some Captain at times, Chuck always referred to him as Captain. It was a Navy tradition, not a Marine one. Alexander had often gotten a kick out of that. "If you ask me, and I know you didn't, each time we face the Chiata, the more prepared our soldiers get to face them. Which is something, sir."

"I don't know, Chuck." Alexander thought about it very briefly. "Is it something enough for the cost?"

He has a good point, Alexander, Abigail thought to him.

I know. I know. But, very costly, he thought. What is the casualty total now? Fifteen thousand and growing?

Not sure about that, sir. It is possible that the AIC-imprinted clones could be reimplanted into a new clone if they survived. I'm just not sure how that works and what their procedures are in such cases. I'm not sure they have such procedures in place yet. Even so, more than fourteen thousand were completely lost, AIC and all, Abigail explained. Alexander let his attention drift back to the COB.

"Well, Captain, I don't truly believe you believe that. But if you don't think you know, I'm going to tell you that I do know. This engagement is very critically important. We're going to face these bastards someday soon in an all-out winner-take-all fight for our homeworld. I'd like to face them with a battle-hardened and pissed-off crew when that day comes, sir." The COB made sense, Alexander thought. Perhaps, at least, that was something.

"Let's hope we can find a way to keep the bastards from ever getting to Earth." Alexander grunted and bolstered himself up a bit, even if it was for appearances only. "I mean, that was the whole point of coming out here."

"Roger that, Captain." Sowles agreed. "Roger that. If I may, sir . . ."

"Speak your mind, Chuck. You haven't been with me

long enough to know that I'd rather have it straight in the face than blown up my ass." Alexander could tell the Chief was nervous about whatever it was he was about to say. "You'll never get a reprisal from me for telling it like it is, COB."

"Okay then, sir." The man hesitated only slightly as he seemed to be sizing Alexander up. "Well, I know we just got our asses handed to us, Captain. And coming into that place at all was brash and bold and took hundred-millimeter armor-piercing balls. But this here, sir, this what you're saying right here, *this*, isn't the man I've read about in the history books. *This* isn't the man that according to legend went barrel-assing and screaming like a demon from hell into an enemy camp of over a hundred Separatists after being stranded in an e-suit and wounded for more than a month and killed them all with his bare hands. *This* isn't that guy. Or *this* isn't the man who during the Exodus fought a Seppy tank to a standstill on the Martian desert while unarmored and using just an HVAR. Or who fought off an army of crazed terrorist robots at Disney World. Or, from what I hear, singlehandedly defeated an entire swarm of maniacal buzz-saw bots to save a squad of AEMs including one younger Moore, the CAG, and one of our Fleet captains. This right here, sir, *this*, isn't that man."

"Are you getting to a point, COB?"

"With all due respect, Captain, I just made my point. The crew is banged to hell and gone, but they'd go through it a hundred times over as long as they know that the great man of history, the great United States by God Marine Corps General Alexander Badass Monster Killing

Motherfucking Moore is leading them into it. Pardon my French, but Captain, we're all volunteers and could resign whenever we'd like, but we choose to follow you, sir, into whatever shit you want to take us into, death be damned. And it is a disservice to that fine Marine mecha jock stranded on that God-forsaken planet to be anything less even for the briefest of seconds that it takes to walk from the elevator to the Captain's Ready."

Ooh-fuckin'-rah, General! his AIC cheered in his head. *I like this new COB.*

Alright, enough of that shit, he thought.

The two of them turned the corner to the Captain's ready room and Alexander stopped and held out an armored gauntlet to shake the COB's hand. Alexander's days as a politician still ran deep within him. The COB shook his hand and then stepped a half step back and saluted.

"If that is all, Captain, I have a boat to get back in order," Chuck said proudly and all businesslike.

"Chief. I think you just did that." Alexander returned the salute with clenched jaw and steeled eyes and a fire behind them that was starting to grow. "That'll be all for now, thank you. I've got some shit to figure out."

The COB snapped his hand down and turned on his heels back down the corridor. Alexander stood silent for several seconds and watched almost catatonically at the flurry of activity throughout the hallway of the ship. His ready room was off the bridge to the starboard side but on the same floor at the top of the command spire. Any activity happening here would be somehow related to fixing problems between the bridge and the Combat

Direction Center, which was a few decks down. The COB was right, the ship and crew were battered and beat, but they weren't beaten. They were absolutely not fucking beaten.

Alexander shook his head and turned to his office. The door slipped open with a hiss and he stepped through, letting it close behind him. He fell back against the door and fought the urge to weep. Even though it was an overwhelming urge and single tears formed at the corners of his eyes, General Alexander Moore gritted his teeth, clenched his jaw, drew his fists tight, and then he managed to blink them back.

"Princess, I'm coming," he snarled inwardly. "You Chiata bastards get ready to meet whatever fucking maker you pray to."

Abigail, get me a line to my wife.

Yes, sir!

"Joe, how are you feeling?" Fireman's Apprentice Clark Rogers wouldn't leave his side. No matter what errand Joe sent the kid on, he finished with vigor, and, like a puppy, crawled right back under his feet.

Or maybe that was the wrong metaphor, Joe pondered briefly. The kid was more like an overprotective mother hen. He was constantly asking if he was okay and if there was anything else he could do for him. Joe appreciated the effort and the concern, but enough was enough.

"Rogers, you see that BFW over there hanging on the tool rack?" Buckley pointed it out.

"The red one, CHENG? You need it?"

"Yes. I want you to go over there and pick the thing

up and then come over here and bash me in the fucking head with it until my brains splatter all over the fucking floor and I quit flopping like a goddamned fish."

"CHENG? Are you okay, sir?"

"Fuck no, I'm not okay, Rogers!" Joe shouted. "I got my Goddamned arm ripped right out of the fucking socket and now I'm sitting here with a gob of dried up fucking organogel and e-suit seal layer goop as a replacement while I've got my one good thumb up my ass waiting for the hyperdrive to explode and kill us fucking all. And all the fucking while you and Amari and every other sailor on this ship keeps asking me every two goddamned seconds if I'm fucking alright!"

"CHENG?" Rogers was startled and Joe could see the rest of the engineering team peeking around the corners, turning their heads in his direction, or in Amari's case, taking several steps towards him.

Joe, his AIC started to interject.

Don't you fucking start on me too! he thought in the harshest mindvoice he'd ever used.

"So, let us just get one thing fucking straight right motherfucking now! For fuck's sake!" Joe raised his voice even louder. "I am NOT fucking O motherfucking kay! Got it? Good. So don't fucking ask me again. Nobody ask me that shit ever again."

Joe could see that Amari was considering saying something, but he gave her a look that warned her to just back the hell off. Then he turned and motioned at the dancing cable with trillions of watts of power surging through it that was flashing with Cerenkov radiation, ionizing the air around it into a plasma, and buzzing like a tweeter that aspired to be a woofer, or was it the other way around.

"Now that we got that shit out of the way, this fucking thing right here is going to explode in about three minutes, which is a damned good thing that we are approaching the rendezvous coordinates in about thirty seconds. It is time to bring it down before it brings itself down and us with it. Then, we back out and turn the repair bots on full with the new conduit designs and parts. They can derad the place and work the replacement. We'll be down for an hour. Anybody wants to get something else done, grab a snack, and maybe wash off some of the blood, soot, and radioactive charred carbon shit off, or hell, I dunno, go see about getting a new fucking arm, then would be the time."

Joe, I'm concerned you might be going into shock, Debbie warned.

Oh, shut up. I'm not in fucking shock, he thought. Then a page opened up in his mindview with his vital signs and a definition of being in shock appeared there.

> *Acute stress disorder—sometimes referred to as acute stress reaction, mental shock, psychological shock, and sometimes just shock, is a psychological condition arising in response to a terrifying or traumatic event and in many cases events following serious bodily injury or threat thereof. The condition is not to be confused with circulatory shock which is a different life threatening condition.*

Would you stop that shit, Debbie? he thought, and the hyperdrive counter clock in his mind approached zero.

Several tens of seconds had passed and still nobody had said a word. But Amari did step back behind the control panel and throw a circuit breaker. The cable stopped dancing and humming and fell with a great thud to the floor. The power flowing through it had stopped. Seconds later the vortex projector started to dim and the event horizon it was projecting ahead of the ship collapsed, and just like that, they were stranded in space. Countdown clock was at zero and position calculations showed they came out of hyperspace into reality space accurate to within a tenth of a light second from where they had wanted to be.

"We'd better leave the SIFs on it for a while or it will explosively vaporize. The damned thing is hot." Sarala Amari pointed at the cable and warned the rest of the team. "Now, I'll take care of the bots, Joe. Fireman's Apprentice Rogers, why don't you take the CHENG down to medical for a cup of coffee. He likes it black and thick as fucking mud with two sugar packs and no cream. You might see if you can find him a fucking chill pill to go with it."

"Roger that, Chief." Roger looked at Joe and then looked back at the big fucking wrench attached to the tool wall. "You coming, CHENG, or do I get the BFW?"

Chapter 19

February 19, 2407 AD
U.S.S. Sienna Madira II
Rendezvous Point, 10.5 Light Days from
  Target Star System
700 Light-years from the Sol System
Monday, 6:15 P.M. Ship Standard Time

"What do you see out there, STO?" USMC Brigadier General Sally "Firestorm" Rheims sat in the captain's chair while General Moore was taking care of other business elsewhere on the ship. She wasn't sure what the General was doing exactly, but it wasn't her job to ask, either. Firestorm had her visor open and could smell the remains of the long since chemically extinguished fires. There was a mix of air freshener and burned metal and plastic aroma that reminded her of worse battles, if there was such a thing.

"The remains of the first attack wave are twenty seven hundred kilometers to port. All DTM battlescape views and blue force tracks should be updated now, XO," the Science and Technology Officer USN Commander Tori Snow replied while looking up from her console. "Long-range sensors report no other vessels or signs of artificial machinations within several light years, but the way things have gone so far today, there is really no way to be certain, ma'am."

"Thank you, Commander Snow." The XO raised an eyebrow to the new STO but wasn't sure she could see it through her helmet. "COB, now would be a good time for one of your famous pots of really bad coffee."

"I can send the quartermaster's apprentice to get you some of that uppity stuff they sell in the mess, or if you seriously think you can handle it, XO, I'll get some started?" The COB smiled at her. "But, be warned, as long in the tooth as this day is, you'll need an elephant tranq to get any shuteye later."

"Just happen to have an elephant tranq in my room, COB." Firestorm laughed a bit. "If you don't mind making some, I'd love a cup."

"Sounds great, ma'am," Chuck said. "My AIC has already got it brewing for you."

"I don't know about you, XO, but I for one am glad to be in reality space for a minute," the Air Boss said. "Without the QMTs I realize how much I hate hyperspace."

"Uh huh," Firestorm grunted. Then she checked her DTM blue force systems and they had indeed been updated. There were five supercarriers sitting in formation. And with the addition of the *Madira* there were now six. Firestorm knew two had been destroyed, but two were unaccounted for. She pulled up the list in her mindview before her eyes.

U.S.S. Sienna Madira II—significant damage, repairs initiated

U.S.S. Margaret Thatcher II—significant damage, repairs ongoing

UM61 Alpha02—fully functional, minor repairs ongoing

UM61 Alpha 03—significant damage, major fire alarms, atmosphere loss in forty percent of the ship.

UM61 Alpha 05—significant damage, repairs ongoing

UM61 Alpha 08—moderate damage, repairs ongoing

"Jeeesus! Talk about a shit sandwich." Firestorm said. "What the hell happened to Four and Six?"

"Comm, get on the horn and call around and see if we can get some info on that."

"Aye, sir." The Nav replied.

"Sir! Look!"

At that moment UM61 Alpha Zero Three erupted in blue and purple plasma from the forward hyperspace projector structure. A partial event horizon opened and sucked the bow of the ship forward almost as instantly as the horizon had formed it, then collapsed, squeezing the front quarter of the supercarrier into nothingness. Orange and white plasma vented from what was left of the ship's front half and then it erupted from within from bow to stern. The ship poured open like a disemboweled pig, throwing parts in every direction. The explosion raced up the command spire, and then what was left of the ship vanished into a field of flying debris and death that was now impinging upon the rest of the fleet ships.

"Nav! Get us fucking clear of that!" Firestorm shouted. But they were too close and there was little they could do but ride it out. "All aux power to forward barrier shields and SIFs! Standard prop all back full!"

"Sorry, XO, all propulsion is down for the drive replacement," the STO said.

"Well then, hold on to your shit, cause this is gonna be violent." Sally grabbed the edge of the captain's chair and gritted her teeth while at the same time mentally triggering the ship-wide warning klaxons.

"Warning! All hands brace for impact! Warning! All hands brace for impact!"

There was nothing left to do but sit tight and ride it out. Sally popped her visor in place and bit down on her bite block with anticipation, and then common sense took hold and she calmed slightly.

"STO! Get me Doppler on that debris field and ETA to impact! Now!" Firestorm ordered.

"Aye!"

The debris from the exploding supercarrier spread out fast in a three-dimensional spherical wavefront. Almost instantaneously with the explosion, three other hyperspace tubes appeared and the *Thatcher*, UM61 Alpha Zero Two, and UM61 Alpha Zero Five vanished, leaving just the *Madira* and the remains of the exploded Three in local reality space. The *Madira* had no hyperdrive capability at present. She was dead in the water and going nowhere.

Klaxons sounded throughout the ship as the debris field approached. Large chunks of the supercarrier the size of hovertanks and even larger filled space in front of it. Firestorm watched for what seemed like an eternity, but her AIC had put a clock in her head that said nine seconds and ticking.

"Commander Snow!?"

"Yes, ma'am. Got it. The centroid of the blast was two thousand seven hundred and one kilometers distant and the radar tracks show the blast front at seventeen kilometers per second. Impact is estimated in two minutes and twenty-eight seconds and counting. Clock is transmitting DTM."

"Two minutes and a half to figure this shit out." Firestorm punched the com. "XO to CHENG."

"Acting CHENG, CPO Amari here, XO. CHENG is in medical."

"I need Aux Prop now, Amari!"

"Sorry sir, there is no way. We are sitting still for at least an hour."

"Not the fucking answer I need, Acting CHENG! We've got a debris field closing on us fast!"

"Understood, XO. All we can do is route as much power to the shields and SIFs."

"Do that then. XO out." Sally shook her right knee up and down a few times impatiently trying her best to think. She pounded her fist against the arm of the chair and let out a sigh.

Give me trajectory curves of the largest debris that are going to hit us, she thought to her AIC.

Right away, her AIC responded by displaying the field in her mindview and then showing the large chunks headed their way. Several pieces the size of hovertanks, in fact, a few of the pieces actually were hovertanks and other mecha, were headed right for the bridge and other parts of the port side of the ship.

"We've got to do something, XO," the Ground Boss shouted over the alarm. "Fast!"

"I know." Sally grunted gutturally. Then it hit her. "Fight fire with fire! Gunner! Target and fire the DEGs at the largest pieces of debris! Wide dispersal."

"Sorry, XO! The DEGs are offline!" the weapons deck gunnery officer replied.

"Is nothing on this ship fucking working?" Firestorm pursed her lips and exhaled hard through them. "Okay then. Missiles still fucking work, don't they? Put a nuke in front of that blast wave now!"

"Yes, ma'am!" The gunner turned and worked at her controls, and then Firestorm gritted her teeth and watched as the missile rocketed out in front and twisted and turned as it righted itself on course. The missile tracked across the space between the oncoming debris field and the *Madira*, and as it did, the entire bridge crew's anal sphincter pucker factor shot through the ceiling bulkhead.

"Captain on the bridge!" the COB announced as the door opened and General Moore stepped through.

"Talk to me, Firestorm!" Moore nodded to her. Sally was glad to hand over the reins.

"Bridge is yours, General." She bounced up from his chair. "UM61 Alpha Zero Three exploded and what's left of her is going to hit us in one minute and forty nine seconds. DEGs are offline, Aux Prop is offline, hell, about all we have is missiles and shields."

"Understood." Moore looked at her and then sat

down. Sally could tell from the thousand-yard stare he gave her that he was conversing with his legendary AIC. She felt better knowing that the General was on the case.

"STO? Have the other Fleet ships reappeared from their jaunts yet?"

"Yes, sir! Off Starboard by several light seconds."

Firestorm watched as the General continued to have the thousand-yard stare but at the same time was working commands from his chair console and in his mindview. As he waved his left hand about in front of him it was clear he was having a detailed conversation with at least his AIC if not several others.

"UM61 Alpha Zero Two just went into hyperspace," the STO reported, but no sooner than she had said it, the supercarrier reappeared on the bow before them. "Woah."

"Everyone hold the fuck on." Moore growled. "CO to CHENG! Keep the barrier shields at max on the bow docking moors."

"Understood, CO!"

"Warning! All hands brace for impact! Warning! All hands brace for impact!"

Firestorm watched in awe as the clone-driven supercarrier gently nudged into the bow of the *Madira* and began pushing it backwards. As the momentum of the two ships built up, Alpha Two was then able to make very slow steering maneuvers, much like a tugboat pushes a barge up a river. Firestorm thought for a moment that she'd bet the General had seen that happen on the Mississippi River where he was from, or he was just fucking brilliant, or both.

"Damn, sir, I wish I'd thought of that," Firestorm said. "Do we deactivate the missile?"

"Yes," Moore replied.

"You heard the man, Gunner Banks. Deactivate the warhead and bring that missile back home," Firestorm ordered.

"Aye sir."

"The missile would have worked, XO, but we might have taken on more damage still," Moore said to her. "And from the looks of it, we don't need to take on any more damage." Moore gave her a sincere smile.

"Yes, sir. I'm just glad you were able to get up here in time, sir."

"XO, as soon as this crisis is over, I want you to rally up the senior officers and advisors and the captains we have left through virtual conference in my conference room. I want to get a complete assessment of what did and didn't work on our attack wave."

"Aye, sir." Firestorm turned to her console and started putting together the list of attendees. Over her shoulder she heard the General's armor mechanisms rubbing against his chair and assumed he was settling in.

"COB, we need to get our minds right here. How about some of that nasty shit you call coffee? You got any of that secret recipe of yours made?"

"Just so happens, sir . . ."

Chapter 20

February 19, 2407 AD
Alien Planet, Northern Region
Target Star System
700 Light-years from the Sol System
Monday, 6:15 P.M. Ship Standard Time

"Up and at 'em! Quit your goldbricking, Marine! It is time to get up!" The life-sized direct-to-mind virtual image of General Alexander Moore stood in front of Dee shouting at her. "Move it, princess! Get your ass up!"

Dee. Wake up. The skyballs have returned and downloaded. I've sent them back out, Bree said in her mind. Her father's image still stood over her repeating her morning alarm sound.

"Up and at 'em! Quit your goldbricking, Marine! It is time to get up!" The life-sized direct-to-mind virtual image of General Alexander Moore stood in front of Dee shouting at her. "Move it, princess! Get your ass up!"

✧ ✧ ✧

Funny, Bree. Turn off the alarm. Dee scanned about her and after seeing no immediate threats about, she stretched and popped her visor open. Immediately, a timer started and her carbon dioxide blood gas level indicator lit up in her mindview. *How long was I out?*

A bit more than an hour, Bree replied.

Any more Chiata movement? Dee straightened up against the tree roots she was leaning upright on and bit down on her water tube for a fresh drink. Her hidey-hole underneath the giant mangrove tree had turned out to be a good place for refuge, or at least she had a good vantage point across the river and through the trees. As far as she could tell nothing could sneak up on her without her knowing it.

From the skyballs it would appear that they are still searching for you but only with a very small team of six ground troops. They have no idea where you ended up and we are a good two hundred kilometers from them. Your suit stealth systems must be working. Still, I think it is strange that they do not search with more resources.

Well, that is good news. I wonder if it is really the suit's stealth or the foliage cover? Dee checked her blue force tracker and there was no change in it. The others stuck on the planet with her were all still in the same place and there were no Fleet ships in the system.

The yellow and green star was almost completely over the horizon and was turning orange. With no external lighting from her suit on it was growing too dark underneath the tree to see more than a couple of decimeters in front of her face. Dee looked out across the river through the trees and could see orange and pink rays barely peeking over the mountains in the distance, casting beautiful hues of color against the sky. In another ten minutes it would be completely dark.

"So the question is, do we just sit tight for the evening or keep moving?" she said quietly. She realized she hadn't relieved her bladder all day and considered briefly popping out of the suit rather than just doing it in the suit and letting the organogel absorb and recycle it. She'd been in the suit for the better part of a day and would appreciate a moment or two not in it. Common sense prevailed, though.

"The General stayed in one for over a month, guess I can handle a half of a day," she mumbled to herself and let her bladder go. She concentrated on that task for a few long seconds and sighed with relief as the warm liquid left her body rapidly giving her a quick "pee chill." She shivered twice due to the laws of thermodynamics and then was done. "That feels better."

Dee reminisced briefly of survival school as a cadet. For final AEM rating they spent seventy-two hours in the suit on maneuvers. Then in pilot training the escape and evade course required a full week in the suit. Dee had been there and done that and got the rating. That didn't mean she liked it. Even though the organogel kept a person from itching or chafing or a myriad of other things that would make a person want to touch themselves, there was still an aspect about being a human being whereas an exoskeleton was still a prison of sorts. There were times when feeling your skin unencumbered by super-alloy body armor and integrity fields and barrier fields and gel layers and sealant layers and one's own body waste materials was much more preferred.

There were many AEMs who preferred sleeping nude, hanging out and relaxing nude, and various other versions of being uncovered by anything. Others were the opposite and preferred to always be enclosed in clothing but also in tight spaces. Military psychologists had studied the phenomenon for as long as there had been exosuits and it turned out that there were two groups within the AEMs that were on the extreme sides of the behavioral norm. The first group were the pure nudists and the others were more along the lines of Christian nuns or Muslim women wearing clothing that covered them completely. But those were the extremes. Most of the AEMs fit somewhere in between. Dee was pragmatic. If it was hot and in a safe environment and she didn't need the gear for whatever reason, it was coming off. If it was cold, she'd put gear on. If she was about to go on a mission where she'd be in a suit for a while she preferred to be unencumbered. And there was a bit of vanity aspect with mecha jocks to show off their superhuman core muscles. Dee's were indeed that and she was not afraid to show them off. It was a badge of honor in the FM-12 squadrons.

In public, she mostly wore sporty clothing or her duty clothes. While her modesty profile was right down the middle of the normal average for Marines, her performance as one was in the top one percentile. That was part of the reason why her mecha jock handle was Apple1. Her flight instructor had discovered on many different occasions that the apple hadn't fallen very from the Alexander Moore tree. Median psychological profile or not, she would have loved to get the hell out of the suit rather than peeing on herself even if it meant standing naked in downtown New Tharsis.

Deanna peeled back her right gauntlet just long enough to rub the sleepiness from her eyes. Then she redeployed the armored glove and used Mark I eyeballs to scan the local area for any motion or signs of trouble. She saw none. She then brought up infrared, radio, microwave, ultraviolet, and particles, and as far as she could tell there were a few small heat signatures indicative of small animals scurrying about, but there was nothing scary at least within three hundred meters of where she sat. She also noted that all the quantum membrane sensors were still dead.

She rolled over to her hands and knees and crawled through her makeshift door and out from underneath the giant tree. Rising to her feet, she rolled her shoulders back a few times and rocked her neck from side to side, generally stretching herself awake.

What now? She thought. *Have a look around maybe?*

Perhaps we continue to move south along the river and continue to push closer to the Maniacs? Bree suggested. *But, before you decide, I think we should discuss the findings from the skyballs. I have had time to analyze the imagery data and it is interesting.*

Oh, by all means, let's hear it. Dee rested her left hand against her HVAR on her chest and took comfort noting that it was completely full of rounds. She cautiously took steps through the underbrush toward the edge of the water. *Keep sensors open for any not-so-nice local pets.*

Roger that. Bree almost laughed. *So, there is Chiata*

air traffic here. In the last hour two different vessels traveled slightly south of here and to the west about thirty klicks. It looks like one flew in to a location and then immediately a second one left the same location and returned along the same path as the previous. And I don't mean roughly the same path. I mean they flew the exact same path to within centimeters of variation up, down, left, and right. And the fact that they swapped out positions, well, I think that suggests a shift change. As far as the skyballs could tell there were only three Chiata in the incoming vessel and two in the one leaving.

What are they doing?

There is some sort of ruin there. The skyball lingered long enough to see that two of the aliens stood sentry while the third entered the construct, Bree explained and put the image of the ruin up in her mindview. The image was a reconstructed three-dimensional model of the actual construction. *As far as I can tell, other than your search party, there are no other Chiata in this region of the planet. That is very odd.*

Damn right it is. And the Chiata are interested in this ruin. We need to know why. Dee thought about that for a second and asked herself what her father would do. Then she thought about it a little more and realized he'd go over there and kill all of the alien motherfuckers he could. Then she wondered what DeathRay would do, but she knew his standing generic plan was to go in there in kill all those motherfuckers. Perhaps more finesse was required, she thought, which led her to thinking of Penzington. Nancy, the superspy, would handle things differently. While she might very well go over there and

kill all those motherfuckers, she'd probably observe them
first and figure out just what in the hell they were up to.
Then she'd kill the shit out of them. Dee liked that
approach.

Dee? Bree prodded. *What are you thinking?*

*Plot me a path of least resistance to the ruins. We're
gonna go and check them out.*

Roger that. Then the map appeared in her mindview
with a route highlighted. The place was downriver a bit
and then to the west through the jungle on the other side
of the river. It was not all the way over to the middle
tributary of the river, but it was closer to it than it was to
the branch of the river she was on. Dee paused and
zoomed in on the path Bree had laid out for her, not sure
just where she wanted to cross the river. In the suit it
didn't really matter, but she knew she didn't want to get
wrapped up in a swift overbearing current again.

*Bring up the river and do a current analysis. Or, is
there a stretch that would be within jumping width?* From
the looks of it Dee could tell that the river was moving
very swiftly where she was, but perhaps not so swiftly that
she would have trouble managing it. She wasn't quite sure
and was hesitant to test it.

*Roger that, Dee. You could jump it down about ten
klicks from here, but that would put you further off path.
The current isn't so bad here that you couldn't cross and
maintain control with the strength of the suit and the
jumpboots. The bottom of the river here appears to be
bedrock in the barge channel so you would have a solid
surface beneath you if you jumped to there. Outside the
channel is mostly mud. I'd steer clear of that. If you*

jumped just right you'd cover more than half the distance across anyway and land perfectly at the edge of the channel. I calculate you could then do a big jump and the underwater trajectory would bring you down just a few meters short of the bank on the other side. You would get some mud on you, but you wouldn't get stuck.

*Okay, that is what we'll—*Dee started to think a reply, but then something grabbed her by the leg and yanked her off her feet. Her face hit the ground and whatever had her drug her backwards several meters, causing her open helmet to dig into the ground and sling dirt and leaves into her face. A thorny vine zipped across her face like a saw blade, cutting deep into her nose, barely missing her left eye and causing her to wince in pain. Then whatever had her put an enormous pressure on her right leg at the shin and tossed her into the air upside down. Suit diagnostic alarms started lighting up in her mindview.

"What the fuck!" she shouted. As she rolled over in the air she could see something beneath her in the waning light of the now almost completely set star. There was barely a silhouette of the creature that had her and all she could tell was that the thing was very large.

There's nothing on most sensors and optical can barely perceive it! Bree said urgently in her mind. *All I can tell is that it is much larger than a hovertank!*

What the fuck is it? Dee reached for her HVAR as she fell but the alien creature leaped upward and opened its mouth. Dee could see an orifice of teeth like something out of a bad monster movie, and to top that off, there were four large mandibles spread out more than twice her height. In an instant the darkening canopy vanished and the sounds and pressure of large teeth biting against her suit armor became overwhelming. Suit alarms continued to flash in her mindview.

Dee slung her elbows about as best she could, trying to get her left hand around her rifle. As she continued to punch, grab, kick and wildly squirm for her life she could feel teeth or bone crushing against the super-hard alloys of her suit armor with intense pressure.

Visor! she thought and the visor activated, covering her face, and the suit pressurized, making it even stronger. Organogel rushed in about her face to clean out the dirt and blood. Suit self-healing protocols were initiated.

The tunnel of inward-pointed teeth continued to drag her downward into the gullet of the creature, and at one point she thought she felt something solid to kick her jumpboots against. Not knowing when that opportunity would arise again, she did just that. The jumpboots hit briefly against what was most likely a ribcage or sternum within the beast, and Dee released the thrusters. When she did, the creature let out an earsplitting sound and spat her up. As she almost cleared the creature's grasp, it chomped back down on her midsection with its mandibles and dragged her back downward into its throat with a long snaking tongue or tentacle—it was hard to tell what it was in the poor lighting and flurry of action. Dee continued to kick and squirm and could feel the creature, making larger movements now. She grabbed frantically for a handhold or anything to rip out, but found no purchase. The wild bouncing movements threw her about inside the creature and with each bounce it seemed to squeeze her even tighter. The wild jarring movements told Dee that the creature must have been running.

The teeth lining the creature's bony throat continued to work like barbs against Dee's suit making screeching and scratching stone-against-metal sounds. The teeth hung onto her left gauntlet hasp and crunched and sawed back and forth, trapping Dee's hand.

"This fucking thing has teeth all the way out its ass!" she exclaimed while managing to squirm her right hand free and finally grasp the M-blaster on her right thigh. She pulled the weapon upward as best she could and as soon as it cleared the built-in holster something wrapped around her hand, constricting it from further movement and pulling at her downward into the creature's stomach. It was almost as if the thing knew she was going for a weapon.

Her right hand was quickly bound to her leg and her blaster in such a way that if she squeezed the trigger she was going to hit herself as well. And with her suit's shields down, that was something she was hoping to avoid. The suit diagnostic window continued to complain. The three-dimensional image of the suit popped up in her mindview showing warning lights and damaged systems all around it. There were extreme pressure differentials where the creature's teeth clamped down on her. Some of the pressure readings were on the order of three and four hundred atmospheres, and mechanisms and plates on her suit were starting to fail.

She kicked her jumpboots against anything she could push them into, but she found very little to push against. The beast had her trapped longways within it, keeping her away from rib cages and such. She was so constricted by the creature's gullet and the weird tentacles that with every move the thing seemed to find a way to tighten its grip and clamp down even harder. She couldn't reach her knife, or her rifle, but she had her blaster in her hand. The bad thing was that it was pointing slightly toward her right thigh.

The suit cannot take much more of this pressure! Bree warned her. *Emergency seal layer has been activated.*

Shit! Shit! Shit! Dee thought. *Administer immuno-boost and pain meds now!*

With that, Dee worked the controls of the M-blaster, doing her best to push the muzzle upward and away from her leg. Her best wasn't good enough. The blaster released an electric plasma bolt that evaporated a strip of armor on the side of her thigh and all the way down the back of her calf. The energy bolt dug through the armor, past the seal layer and organogel, and then through several centimeters deep of flesh and skin, but at least it kept on going.

"Jesus Christ!" she shouted, wincing at the pain. The bolt of energy skittered out the back side of her armored calf muscle and into the stomach of the alien monster. The creature must have had methane forming in the bottom of its stomach, because once the energy bolt hit home at the bottom of the creature's belly there was a rapid release of heat and light energy and a clap of thunder that left Dee's eardrums ringing.

The inner wall of the creature's stomach exploded, and it burst open like a piñata, spilling Dee and other fairly sticky and gross contents out underneath it onto the mud of the river bank. It howled and lurched up onto its hind legs, but Dee was quick on the draw and let loose three more blasts into it. Red and orange bits of heated flesh exploded with each bolt. The creature howled one last time and then fell over on top of Dee. Strands of muscle and inner workings of the creature's innards stuck to her and squished into the joints of her suit under the weight of the hovertank-sized beast. Dee managed to squirm her body face down to the mud and then she pulled herself out from underneath it as best she could.

"You bit off more than you could chew, didn't you, beasty," she said, and then instantly dropping to a knee, she pulled her HVAR, looking about for other danger. Another one of the creatures came rushing out of the underbrush at her, but this time she was ready for it. She jumped high into a somersault over the beast, firing several hypervelocity rounds into the back of the creature. The rounds tore through the beast like it was paper. It screeched and then slid to its final resting spot only a few meters from the other one.

I hope there aren't more of these things! Dee spun about, aiming her rifle in various directions, looking for movement. There wasn't any at the moment. At least not that she could see anyway.

We need to get a closer look at these things with the sensors to determine why we couldn't see them, her AIC said. *It would make avoiding them easier.*

Okay. Crank up the mics though and let's keep a supersensitive ear out for giant footfalls.

I'll do that. No need in you worrying about it. If I detect them I'll bring up the sound and track it for you.

Great. Thanks, Bree. Deanna knelt next to the first creature and waited as her suit conducted detailed close-range scans of it. *Well?*

This creature, while it was alive, didn't look like any creature nature would create, Bree began. *I think it is artificial.*

How so? Dee was confused. Were the Chiata making new creatures, she wondered?

The outer layer armored scales and skin have synthetic materials in them that are practically identical to the stealth micromaterials in your armored e-suit, Bree explained.

That's why we couldn't see it?

Precisely.

This planet is just fucking weird, Dee replied. Then a suit diagnostic popped up in her mind showing the large burn down her right thigh, through the suit's seal layer, into her calf muscle and then out just above the Achilles tendon. *Shit, that's gonna hurt I bet.*

Hopefully not. There is now enough immunoboost in your system to heal you rather quickly. The self-annealing and healing process for the suit has also begun.

Dee noticed for the first time that she wasn't anywhere near where she had been. The creature had run with her for several hundred meters. The thing just didn't know what it had gotten itself into and had probably been scared to death. Either that or it had known exactly what it had gotten itself into and was following whatever purpose the thing was built for.

She brought the map page up in her mindview and zoomed in on her blue dot, and had it reroute her to the path toward the alien ruins. She slowly turned to her right and realized that she was on the opposite side of the river now. Somehow while she was inside the beast it had dragged, jumped, run, swum, or flew as far as she knew, but whatever it had done, it had carried her to the other side of the river in only a few tens of seconds.

Maybe that thing is a hovertank, she thought jokingly and turned toward the ruins and started moving, cautiously.

You might not be wrong about that, her AIC told her. *Perhaps the creatures are some sort of autonomous weapon system.*

Still fucking weird if you ask me.

Then she was distracted as one of the skyballs whipped down in front of her face and stopped. The little floating ball blinked an infrared light at her and quickly downloaded what information it was carrying. Instantly, the red force tracker lit up in her mindview, showing that her six pursuers were moving as a group fairly quickly upriver in her direction. Imagery data overlaid upon the tracker data showed some sort of vehicle flying just above the treetops.

Shit! They must have heard all the ruckus.

Or saw it from space platforms is more likely.

We need to move fast! Dee said, turning into the dark jungle in a full suit speed trot. *Low level IR floods on and let's stay under the canopy.*

They are ten minutes away at their current speed. We need to move! Bree said with urgency.

Send the skyball to watch them and let it ping an active download every minute. Use only the quantum entanglement transceivers, Dee ordered.

Roger that. Now pick up the pace! Bree had sounded urgent, angry, sad, and even excited on many instances as long as Dee had known her, but at the moment, Dee was pretty sure that her artificial intelligence counterpart was just as scared as she was.

Chapter 21

February 19, 2407 AD
U.S.S. Roscoe Hillenkoetter
Rendezvous Point, 10.5 Light Days from
  Target Star System
700 Light-years from the Sol System
Monday, 6:53 P.M. Ship Standard Time

"Coming out of hyperspace, Captain." The STO, one of the Teena clones, said without looking up from her console. "There is a long list of repairs the CHENG wants to do, but it will put our hyperdrive offline for some time."

"I'll approve that once I know our situation," Nancy replied to the STO.

"Yes, ma'am."

"Nav, get me an updated position and make sure we're where we are supposed to be," Captain Penzington ordered. "Comm, ping friendly to the rest of the Fleet if they are here."

"Captain, we pulled through with nineteen ships left," Rackman noted, and he didn't sound too thrilled about it either. Nancy wasn't thrilled herself. In fact, she was appalled at the outcome of the first mission and couldn't understand why their intelligence on the system was so bad.

"COB, you should take a walk around the boat and look out for any personnel requests that need my personal attention."

"Yes, ma'am." The COB, a Franklin clone, replied and then efficiently closed down his console and was out the hatch.

"While all of our Beta wave have reappeared in reality space, reports show they've begun licking their wounds." Rackman continued. "I might add that there are a few with some very significant wounds that's gonna take a lot of licking. Ma'am, if you don't mind my saying it, we got our asses kicked."

"Thanks, XO." Nancy pulled up the local space of the rendezvous point in her mindview and noted that there was a large debris field and only five supercarriers from the Alpha attack wave, the *Thatcher* and the *Madira* among them. Between the two attack waves they had started with forty ships and were now down to twenty-four. From the status readouts she was getting in her mindview, she could tell that at least half of those ships were in piss-poor shape and wouldn't really count as a supercarrier in a real fight. They'd barely be good enough to use as something to duck behind once the shooting started.

Nancy couldn't help but question the mission and the

plan. The expeditionary fleet ships that had gone on this search for a pot of gold at the end of some unseen rainbow that was a long damned way from home and very well protected were damned near cut in half and were battered and bruised. And that was just the ones that had survived. There was something about the mission that reminded Nancy of King Arthur's Quest for the Holy Grail, whereas the search was for a prize of infinite reward but never to be obtained. Nancy thought about those promised rewards that only led to the downfall of the noble knights and their king. But in her former life as a spy, Nancy understood that sometimes the long shot is the one that would win the day. She just hoped the day wasn't over and there was still a long shot that could be taken. And on her next attempt, she would have a much better fucking plan.

She scrolled by the casualty lists in her direct-to-mind view and could see that the day had truly gone against them. They had taken on some really serious casualties. The number of lives lost in the engagement was mind numbing to Nancy and made her feel knots in the pit of her stomach as if she were going to be sick. Her attack wave alone had been decimated. The first attack wave hit even worse and was cut completely cut in half. She pulled up the *Madira's* casualty list and had Allison run a quick search algorithm.

Captain Jack Boland is listed on the Madira's wounded and his current status is "recovering," Allison alerted her. *His condition was only ever critical for a few brief moments during and immediately following his ingress and landing procedure. I'll get you the full report.*

Thank you, Allison. Let me know if there is any

change. And start working our work schedules to figure out the soonest I can get to him or him to me.

I will. I'm in contact with Candis now. Would you like to speak with Captain Boland?

Uh, I—she didn't have time to finish the thought before Allison interrupted her.

General Moore is pinging you, DTM. He wants to speak with you now, Allison told her.

Shit. Didn't take him long. I haven't even had a chance to talk to Jack yet. Just keep an eye on him for me and tell Jack I can't talk right now.

Done.

Nancy felt the knots in her stomach twist up even tighter. She wanted to get to Dee and the rest of the ground teams just as bad as anyone did and that included the General. But there had just been nothing she could do about the overwhelming situation. The planet had simply been cut off by the Chiata and that was that. She continued to tell herself that there was nothing she could do. Every attempt at getting to them led to the loss of ships and thousands of more lives. She knew that she had made the right decision, even if it did suck shit.

Open the channel, Nancy thought.

Captain Jack Boland says he will be fine, by the way. Channel with General Moore is open.

General Moore, Captain Penzington here.

Nancy, from the blue force tracker I see you've taken on serious casualties. I'm glad you made it through. At the risk of sounding selfish and putting personal needs above the mission, what of Dee? Alexander Moore asked about his daughter. *I can see that she's not with you.*

Sir, we pressed and pressed but couldn't get to the planet. There were so many ships that we were overwhelmed and the planet was cut off to us completely. We started taking on heavy losses very quickly. I have to tell you that recovering Dee was personal for me as well. I was afraid I was letting my personal feelings put more of the Fleet at risk trying to get to her. I couldn't continue in good conscience to risk hundreds and maybe thousands of lives for a handful. Nancy stopped and collected her thoughts for a second. She was telling the truth. She hadn't realized until she had just thought it that she was playing the situation differently based on it being about someone she cared for rather than just the next mission. Her life had changed to the point that she barely recognized herself. She liked her reflection, but barely recognized it.

I'm sure what you did was justified, Captain. Moore's thought was deadpan.

No sir, I didn't mean it that way at all. My actions as a Captain were justified, certainly, but me personally, sir, I wasn't even close to done. I'll go back in there right now to get her, but not with more crew to send to the graveyard. I'd just take a small team with a smaller shuttle. You could drop us out of hyperspace and go. Give us time to get down and back up then drop back in. I'm pretty sure I already have another volunteer ready to go, General. You just give us the word.

I'll take that plan under advisement, Nancy.

Sir, feel some better in knowing that Dee was fine and evading any pursuits when we left. Her first group of pursuers she handled like a true Marine. She's strong, sir.

She will survive until we can get back to her. I will get back to her. I promised you I'd take care of her, sir, and I failed for now, but I won't next time.

You said it yourself, Nancy. Alexander hesitated. *The Chiata have the planet cut off. We need a better plan of attack to get our people back.*

Yes, sir. I'm sorry, sir. Dee is like a little sister to me.

I appreciate that. Have your senior officers ready for a Fleet-wide virtual conference in fifteen minutes.

Yes, sir.

Moore out.

I'm not sure how that went, Allison said in her mind. *Are you?*

No. No, I'm not.

"You talking to the General, ma'am?" Rackman looked at her through his open visor. He had a good intuition about situational matters and Nancy could see the concern and worry on his face. She nodded an affirmative to him. Nancy knew about Rackman and Dee's relationship and was sure it was tearing at the SEAL. But the job came with its woes and there was nothing to do about it now but to figure out what to do about it. And now. The longer Dee had to stay on that planet the worse her odds for survival got. She figured General Moore was having similar thoughts.

"Assemble the senior staff in the conference room in fifteen minutes for a Fleet-wide virtual con. Alert the rest of the Beta attack wave to do the same," Nancy told him.

"Yes, ma'am." Rackman turned to his console and started initiating her commands and then he paused and turned back to her. "Ma'am, if we're going to drop a team down there, I'm much better at close-up wet work than all this big ship stuff."

"Duly noted, Commander. Honestly, me too," Nancy replied while smiling inwardly. She'd already counted on him volunteering in her conversation with the General.

Allison, get the full story on Jack for me. Get me data on his mission, injury, surgery, status, images, whatever. You know the drill.

Yes, Captain, her superspy AIC replied. *Do I ping him directly?*

Not yet. I want to know what I'm dealing with before I talk to him. He's alive according to the blue force tracker, but I want to know if he needs coddling or scolding or both.

Understood.

"Captain," the STO clone interrupted. "If you don't mind, I could use a moment of your time."

"Of course, STO." Nancy looked at the clone. She had been working with the clone crews for a good while now and was beginning to appreciate their work ethic, abilities, and intelligence. Each one of them was like a digital library with superhuman intelligence and a damned near inexhaustible level of deadpan enthusiasm which came in very handy at times, but she still couldn't get used to not being able to size up a person by their body language. She thought that the AIC quantum computational abilities were so advanced and fast that they'd be able to mimic facial expressions, vocal inflections, and body language better. But for whatever reason, all the clones were horrible at it. It was both amusing and disturbing at the same time.

"Ma'am, if you don't mind, this would be easiest explained in the mindview," the STO said.

"Very well." Nancy nodded.

Allison, let her in.

Roger that.

"Ma'am, I have been studying the blue beams hoping to determine how they are guided and how they can hold so much energy within each shot. And it is curious how they managed to penetrate the shields with only a few hits." A virtual image of a blue beam incident on one of the Fleet ships appeared in Nancy's mind. At first there was little to see other than the blue beam being dispersed across the shield's surface area.

"Go on." Nancy was curious where the STO was going with this. To date, nobody had a damned clue how those fucking blue beams of death from Hell worked, and any insight might prove to be a tactical advantage. Nancy was all for a tactical advantage right now. Any good news to report right then would be, well, good news.

"Watch as the beam interplays with the quantum barrier shield. At first the interaction is what we'd expect to see. The beam is spread out across the barrier. But then something else happens," she said, highlighting an area just in front of the beam. The point in the image zoomed in quickly enough that it took Nancy off guard, and she would have lost her balance had she not already been sitting down.

Nancy took a breath and focused her mind on the image and could see the that blue beam was only dispersing across the barrier shield at its outer periphery. It wasn't being completely redirected as any other kinetic or directed energy weapon would. The interior of the beam seemed to stop millimeters before the barrier and do something else. The brightness of the image was so far beyond saturation it was difficult to see in great detail and on such a small scale what was actually happening. But something unusual was happening at the beam's point of incidence. Then the barrier shield flickered about that point and a wave of blue light pulsed in ripples like dropping a pebble in a pond—the pebble being the blue beam and the pond the ship's Buckley-Freeman quantum barrier shield. As the circular wavefront rippled, the waves crested and spread from the center. Then the centroid opened and the blue beam passed through, hitting the super alloy of the hull plating on the ship.

"Son of a bitch." Nancy tilted her head sideways as if it would help her change her viewpoint in the virtual world. "Play that back."

"Yes, ma'am. I thought you'd find that interesting. I'm not exactly sure what to make of it just yet," the STO replied and ran the sensor loop again.

Allison? What the hell is that?

The quantum barrier field has been negated, rerouted, or simply opened, the AIC responded. *I'm not sure that is a possibility within physics we know of. The actual spacetime would have to change in that local region.*

My thoughts as well. We need some bigger brains on this.

"What are your thoughts, STO?" She asked.

"Well, there's more, ma'am."

"More?"

"Yes, ma'am. Watch this file now." The Teena clone

appeared to be pleased with herself. Nancy wasn't sure. But what she was sure of was that the next video was just as perplexing and interesting.

The tines of the tuning-fork spires on one of the alien porcupine-snail megaships lit up with a blue beam. The sensors tracked it and the video froze just as the beam made a hard left turn. Then it zoomed in and was highlighted. Nancy watched patiently as the motion in the video was slowed to almost a stop. The time sampling rate was labeled in her mind as one frame per femtosecond and the video frames were clicking by about once every two seconds to give Nancy time to take it all in.

"Now watch just before the beam turns." The STO grabbed the spot and spread it out to expand it more, and then pointed with her armored pointer finger. "Right here."

Just as the image cycled to the next frame, the same ripple that appeared in the shields appeared just in front of the beam. As the beam passed through the ripples its direction was diverted, just as if the beam had passed through a lens or hit a mirror.

"Holy shit. What is that?" Nancy asked. She was very intrigued now. If she had to guess she'd say that the ripples were miniature hyperspace fields or warped regions of spacetime that were being used to steer the beam. They almost looked like the ripples a QMT jump made at the larger teleportation facilities when the gate was opened or closed. But had it been QMT technology it wouldn't have functioned because whatever was dampening the Fleet's jump systems and snap-back wrist bands would have shut those down too.

"I'm not completely certain, ma'am, but I can tell you that I have been checking all sensors across the fleet and there is one anomaly. The gravimetric sensors from each of the Fleet ships' data logs show that there is a very small gravitational disturbance that coincides with every turning blue beam," the STO told her. Nancy knew this was important and good work. She needed to percolate on it and so did Allison, but she also knew that people like Buckley and Snow and the other STOs and CHENGs and all the AICs of what was left of the Fleet needed to see this. Somebody would know how to use this to an advantage.

"So, it is gravimetric." Nancy reached up to rub her chin but remembered she had her helmet and gloves on. "Hmm. Miniature gravitational lenses. How do they project them?"

"I don't know, ma'am, but with your permission I'd like to make this my priority right now."

"Absolutely, uh," Nancy hesitated just long enough to read her full name in her mindview. It was Teena84119832. "Teena. That is great work. I'd like you to contact Commander Buckley and Commander Snow on the *Madira* immediately and discuss this with them."

"Yes, ma'am."

Nancy sat in her chair of the captain's conference room. She looked around the table at her staff. The only two humans were Commander Rackman, her XO, and herself. She had to keep telling herself that the clones were human too, at least biologically they were. Just because the sentience within them was an AIC didn't make them less alive. Or did it? The philosophical and metaphysical aspects of what Sienna Madira had done by creating tens of billions of AIC driven clones was new ground. Was she playing like a god or was it a justifiable necessity? Nancy had to admit that without the clones there certainly wouldn't be enough soldiers to defend against what was coming. Even with them she wasn't sure if there would be enough. So, for now, she gave the brilliantly mad schemer Madira a pass. For now. That crazy bitch was the Moores' albatross to bear and to take responsibility for. But Nancy would be glad to help out if the woman started overstepping and the Moores weren't able to contain her.

Nancy fell back on years of training and quickly caught her wandering mind and focused it on the task at hand. She had to put first things first. And the first thing was to come up with a plan. She needed to figure out why they were there at that star system, hopefully gain some advantage to use against the Chiata. And she had to save the downed teams stranded on that damned planet. She closed her eyes just long enough to let her mind wrap around all the information and tasks. Then as she heard more motion she let out a sigh and straightened herself up in her chair. She watched as her senior staff all took their seats and the STO rushed in at the last minute and sat in her assigned place. Nancy nodded to her. She was beginning to like the STO, clone or not.

"Sorry, ma'am, I was doing some last-minute analysis and discussion with Commander Buckley's AIC. The Commander is presently unavailable," the clone Teena84119832 told her. Nancy thought about their names. They were too long and confusing to normal people. AICs understood them. The name was the original DNA donor's file name, not the actual donor person's name, and the number was the number clone created from that genetic material. Her STO was an eighth-generation clone, which meant she was fairly young by clone standards. Her COB was Franklin 773, which meant he was much older as a third generation clone.

"Any good news, STO?" Nancy thought that she definitely needed to start assigning nicknames to the clones.

"Maybe, it is still too soon to say," Teena replied. "Uh, Captain. Perhaps with more time."

"Ladies and gentlemen, the Commander of the Expeditionary Fleet, General Alexander Moore," the voice of the General's Chief of Staff said as his virtual form appeared in the middle of the conference room. The senior crews from all the other ships were there sitting at virtual spaces around a much bigger virtual conference table than would fit in any of the ships' conference rooms.

All of the virtual personas stood at attention as Moore clanked into the virtual mindview room. Behind the General was his XO, COB, Air Boss, Ground Boss, and his CAG. Nancy had never been so happy to see DeathRay in her life. He didn't look much worse for wear than he ever had. Nancy raised a mindview avatar eyebrow at her husband and his, likewise, in return winked at her. Nancy couldn't help but notice that CHENG Buckley was missing from the meeting as well as Mrs. Moore. She did a quick blue force tracker view and saw that Buckley was still in medical and Sehera was there as well. Their dots were practically on top of each other. That meant she must be helping in whatever procedure Joe was getting. That in turn led her to think about the AEM that Joe had been seeing who was among the survivors stranded on the planet with Dee.

"Please, be seated, all of you." General Moore's mindview avatar told them all. "This is an informal staff call and planning session to determine what our next move must be. We have people still behind on that planet and I want to know how we are going to get them back. Also, we need to figure out why this planet is important to the Chiata. Captain Penzington, you were in system longer than any of us from the first wave, we'd love to hear what your analysis of the situation is."

You're up, slugger, Allison joked with her. *I'm uploading all of the STO's data now.*

I won't have time to assimilate it, she thought. *You go through it and tell me the high points if they are relevant.*

I'm on it. Give me a moment.

"Well, sir, it is a mess. You should thank your Ghuthlaeer buddies for shit intel on the size of the alien force in system. As soon as attack wave Alpha jaunted out, Chiata megaships came popping out of hyperspace like a swarm of angry hornets. They were everywhere. We fell back to the system's asteroid field and deployed the bots and played cat and mouse as long as we could. We managed to pull in fifty-four of the seventy-three fighting mecha jocks left behind by Alpha, but we lost many supercarriers in the process. The remaining pilots were lost. We made two attempts at pushing through the ball to get to the teams pinned down on the ground and could not. By the time this had transpired, all of the ground teams except for those in the Northern Region continent had been totally wiped out. I should also note that none of our attempts to emplace recon teams were successful. None of the teams even made it to the surface. Our only hope for ground intel is from either the seven Maniacs, eight Slayers, or six Juggernauts that remain there. Again the only survivors on the ground, with one exception, are of those teams. They are a mix of mecha and AEMs alike, and are pinned down in ruins along a river at the basin of the Northern Region canyon systems. For whatever reason, the Chiata will not enter the canyon basin. But, any attempts the teams have made to fly out have been met with overwhelming resistance, forcing them to take refuge back in the canyon. I ordered them to stay put, dig in, and investigate why the Chiata will not engage them there. It is very possible that the reason for us coming to this planet has something to do with these ruins, which our imagery data shows are scattered about the Northern Region along the rivers." Nancy paused to wet her lips and take a breath and to judge the reaction of the General. He hadn't made any motion at all and he had one helluva poker face. Either that or his mindview avatar was programmed to be that way. But she knew the man fairly well, in real life he was just as perplexing.

"The other intelligence-gathering possibility will come from the one exception I mentioned earlier, Major Moore from the Archangels. She was shot down and crashed very far north in the Northern Region, almost near the planet's axial pole, too far from the other teams for them to join up. For whatever reasons again, the Chiata have only responded to her presence with a minimal ground team. The first ground team, Dee, uh, Major Moore, managed to take mostly out and evade the rest. This is pretty much the limit of our surface level intel, sir, I wish we had more. Imagery and sensor analysis of the ruins taken by the AEMs, tankheads, and mecha jocks are on the net and available for analysis."

"I see." Moore didn't linger on her before he turned to Admiral Walker. "Fullback, what have you figured out? You've had longer to lick your wounds than the rest of us. Have any of your looney bin folks come up with anything from the imagery data in system?"

"Well, General," Fullback started, "our assessment isn't much different than Captain Penzington's. Although we have generated a map system of all the ruins found in the imagery and scanner data that will be highly complemented by the new data from Beta wave. All of the ruins are in the Northern Region Continent only and they are mostly along the rivers, as noted already. While the losses were staggering and horrific, it *is* quite interesting that the ground teams over that region are the only ones to survive at all. This does suggest that there is something that keeps the Chiata from inhabiting that continent. And it cannot be just a coincidence that this is the only continent that has these ruins on it."

"I agree," Moore replied while rubbing his chin. "I think we need to focus on a plan that takes us to this region of the planet, but from the data we have thus far I don't believe we have enough forces to penetrate and hold cover long enough to extract our teams and to investigate this anomaly. Perhaps this is why the Ghuthlaeer haven't cracked this nut themselves."

"If I may, sir," Fullback interrupted. "I have some analysis and a thought on that."

"Go ahead, Sharon."

"Yes, sir." The Admiral appeared to be discussing something very briefly with her AIC, and then a virtual battlescape appeared over the conference table. "As you can see from our initial engagement here, our standard naval battle tactics are antiquated for such a large number of forces spread out into an attack structure that mimics what the mecha jocks refer to as 'the ball,' sir. And, if you look at our supercarrier movement tracks, each of the individual ships fought very similar to fighters but without wingmen to cover their six. A supercarrier will tend to choose a target and stay with that target until it defeats it. Even as the blue beams began to target that ship the supercarrier jaunts to a new location and continues to engage that same target. This is a somewhat sound tactic in that it allows the supercarrier to keep hitting the same alien ship until its shields and armor weaken and can be destroyed. But this tactic also leads to the supercarrier taking on severe damage and casualties. And this is the tactic widely used by all of the supercarriers during our attack."

"Any questions so far?" Fullback scanned around the room but got nothing but affirmative looks from the senior officers. Nancy watched and did her best to size up the clones in the process. The clone captains and senior staff were all completely deadpan with no facial expressions at all. Nancy percolated on the Admiral's report a bit and realized that they had been fighting the Chiata all wrong, and she suspected this was what the Admiral was about to tell them.

"Good." The Admiral continued. "I have modeled and simulated this attack several different ways to find an optimal outcome. The one thing I have noted here is that the Chiata ships, even at the megaship level, all follow a swarm-like attack strategy. An attacking ship will attack the closest threat and several will follow suit. They do not leave that ship until it is done for. Our spreading out of the fleet and attacking one ship per ship has helped to mitigate the swarm defensive posture the Chiata take, but their numbers advantage has been enough to remove our tactical advantage. We need a new tactic."

"Would a phalanx type attack work?" Moore asked once Admiral Walker paused for a breath. "If we used every ship to attack a single megaship and then move on to the next one and so on, that might reduce the engagement time per ship."

"Well, sir, it takes us on average over one hundred seconds of engagement time to cause an alien megaship to weaken and then another twenty or more to deliver a lethal blow. During this time that ship alone has been able to target and fire their blue beams many times."

"And, excuse me, Admiral," one of the clone captains interrupted. "As we just saw today, they are doing something different in their targeting, and our old rule of thirty seconds and jump was no longer working. We had to cut that to ten seconds per engagement and then jump."

"Yes?" The Admiral raised her eyebrows as if she wasn't aware of that outcome. "That is something they hadn't done before the *Thatcher* had to evac. That is, uh, unsettling. And we will need to adjust our models to that. But to answer your original question about the phalanx approach, General Moore, all I can say conclusively is, perhaps. I actually thought of that and simulated it. While initially the phalanx approach will enable many more hits per single enemy target leading to destruction of it sooner, it at the same time makes it easier for the Chiata to target and use the blue beam weapon. The tradeoffs were almost equal."

"Make sense to me." Alexander shook his head in a gesture that appeared to Nancy to be of frustration. "We need something better, more powerful, more out of whatever box the Chiata are in. I'm open for any suggestions here."

Do I interrupt and tell him about the STO's findings or wait? Nancy thought through what proper protocols would be. *Is it a good idea to interrupt the general officers while they are talking?*

Give it a minute. If they devolve to only speaking about drivel then I'd say what you have is more important, Allison added. *Otherwise, I believe I'd wait and tell him offline.*

I agree. So, now is a good time to brief me on her findings.

Okay then.

But keep an ear out for what the General and the Admiral are talking about in case it is pertinent to any of this. Besides, we need to brainstorm this tactical approach as well. I'm thinking on an out-of-the-box idea we can discuss later.

Roger that. Allison shifted gears and placed several pages of images and charts in front of her mindview. The most interesting to her was the chart showing energy requirements needed to create the miniature warps or ripples in the spacetime structure so precisely and at will. There was more energy there than in the entire remaining Expeditionary Fleet ships combined. Each of the Chiata porcusnail megaships had some sort of power source or capability to apply power at random points about the local space around them at energy density levels of a small neutron star. Allison, or maybe it was the STO, believed that they might be projecting virtual quantum black holes. Once she assimilated that information, her mind wasn't sure what it had assimilated and just what in the hell any of it meant.

What is the difference between a virtual quantum black hole and a regular one? Nancy asked.

Well, Allison began. *The virtual quantum black hole is a theoretical concept that Commander Snow developed suggesting that the Chiata are using a projector similar to a vortex projector to create an event horizon the size that would exist about a quantum black hole. Quantum black holes are permanent and were created in the very early local known universe, possibly after collisions of universal quantum membranes, what used to be thought of as the Big Bang. But the virtual ones would evaporate almost as soon as they are formed. Our STO has used the sensor data to determine how long they last, and from that she has been able to calculate the Chandrasekhar limit for the mass-energy density needed to create them.*

Okay. I think I get it. Nancy thought about it for a

minute and double-checked the virtual conference conversation to keep up and make the appearance that she was paying attention. *The big question is, how do we exploit this new information?*

That is the big question, Nancy. Allison agreed. *And honestly, I have no idea for now.*

Okay, I think we need to disseminate this across the Fleet and hopefully somebody else will come up with more. But that isn't my call. First, transmit all this information to Abigail and give her a crack at it and give her time to brief the General. Let him make the decision on where to go from here. And at the same time, you keep digging on this. Get anybody or anything involved that you need.

Understood.

Nancy relaxed her real body but maintained an attentive-looking avatar in the mindview conference room. She wasn't exactly sure what else, if anything, she needed to say. One thing she knew was that she wanted to talk with Jack and get his feel for the day. She trusted his council, but mostly she just wanted to feel his arms around her and feel safe with him briefly. She also knew in no uncertain terms that she was going to volunteer to go back into the system and extract Dee and the rest, Chiata be damned. She just needed to think of a clever plan. Perhaps DeathRay could help her with that. She had also had time to assimilate the data that Allison had gathered on her husband's mental, physical, and emotional status. He was Captain Jack "DeathRay" Boland, larger than life, full of piss and vinegar, and ate his own puke for breakfast more times than most would ever dare. What she had seen from a discussion with the General's wife was that Jack was taking Dee's being shot down as his fault. After all, she was his wingman and an integral part of his squadron, the Archangels. Jack had always taken it as his fault anytime one of his pilots was shot down. She'd have to deal with that.

Nancy understood where he was coming from in that regard because, in fact, she felt guilty herself for not rescuing Deanna. It was painful for her to have to brief the General on the fact that she couldn't retrieve her. She wasn't looking forward to conversing with Mrs. Moore either. Sometimes Sehera was more frightening than the badass Marine. Jack had managed the conversation with Sehera and she seemed to forgive and actually not even lay blame. It didn't matter, though, because Jack and Nancy were both going to feel the guilt whether the Moores wanted them to or not. The two of them would just have to come up with a plan to assuage that guilt and save her, and perhaps get a little payback on the Chiata bastards to boot. Nancy thought about how Jack was so famous for telling his pilots what the battle plan of the day would be. He always kept it simple.

"We're gonna go in there and we're gonna kill those motherfuckers," he would say. At the moment, Nancy couldn't see much wrong with that plan. She just needed to figure out how to implement it.

She wondered why he had hesitated to contact her. After all, she'd been in system for more than fifteen minutes and he hadn't called. Perhaps he was still recovering from his injuries or he had been overwhelmed with duties, but neither of those would be so time consuming that he couldn't have DTMed her. But she hadn't DTMed him, either. Granted she had been busy running a supercarrier, but that was just an excuse and she knew it. She needed to get that ice broken between them quickly now, before whatever they were hesitating about grew into something bigger.

Allison, get me a channel to Jack.

Channel is open. Candis warns that his mood is a bit random, even for Captain Boland.

Your avatar looks great, Boland, Nancy thought gruffly. *But the images I've had Allison pull up of you from medical say otherwise. How are you?*

I am so glad you are okay! Jack's mindvoice sounded sad yet relieved. *As soon as you can, come see me. Medical has me grounded and won't let me fly. I could do it anyway, but now's not the time to be insubordinate to orders.*

It's harder without the QMTs. The distance from ship to ship even seems like a lot, she said to her husband. *I was scared when I saw your name on the recovery list. Don't do that to me again.*

I know. It hurt. Bad. Worse pain than I've ever felt. Mrs. Moore had to put me in a stasis field to shunt the pain.

Sorry.

Over now. Have you got a plan to get to Dee yet?

Not yet, but I'm thinking on it, Nancy replied. *You?*

No.

You think the General has one?

If he does, he's not sharing it yet. Jack hesitated for a moment. *She better be fucking okay.*

It's not your fault, Jack, Nancy coddled him a bit. *But I agree. She better be fucking okay!*

Chapter 22

February 19, 2407 AD
U.S.S. Sienna Madira
Rendezvous Point, 10.5 Light Days from
  Target Star System
700 Light-years from the Sol System
Monday, 7:04 P.M. Ship Standard Time

Joe looked at the new arm and clutched his fingers around his favorite coffee mug. There was no pain, no discomfort, and there was no scar. He looked at himself in the mirror at where the new shoulder had been attached, and if he hadn't seen the original wound himself, he'd have never been able to tell the arm from the shoulder down had just been printed and attached. He sat the mug down and slid the shirt of his UCU over his head.

"Looks as good as new," he mumbled as he finished dressing. "Debbie, give me a complete bow-to-stern repair status image of the ship."

"Okay, Joe. Here it is," she said, over his audio speakers since he was speaking audibly. "The repairs are almost complete as far as functional systems are concerned. The repair bots are doing amazing jobs. The new hyperspace projection system is completely installed and ready for online testing. It would have been great to have the bots all along, wouldn't it."

"I don't know, kinda scares me of my job security." He laughed and picked his coffee mug back up and finished it off. He turned and looked at his new suit sitting in the corner. One of his crew must have had it requisitioned and delivered already. It had both arms and no scratches or dings. "I'm not in the mood to get in that thing yet."

"You are not required to be on duty yet, Joe, but standing order from the General is, while we are in Chiata-occupied territory, everyone wears their suits. Helmets must be on during engagements. Other than showering, repairs, or medical, there are no exceptions without being in direct violation of that order," Debbie again spoke through the audio system in his room.

"I know, I know. Just, well, not just yet." Joe sat down at his desk and looked out the little window at the stars. "Call it medical, then. I'm not ready to jump back in with both feet after such a traumatic injury. That's my story and I'm sticking to it. Besides, the Chiata aren't coming out here after two dozen ships that they could vaporize anytime they wanted to. And, none of their sensors are within ten light days of us. They have no clue where we are. We're safe for now."

"Run down the details of the General's meeting that I missed," he said.

"Missing. They are still in the virtual conference. Would you like to join in?"

"No. Just, well, what is the status of the Juggernauts?" Joe was concerned about one of them in particular.

"Master Gunnery Sergeant Rondi Howser is among the survivors stranded on the planet, Joe. She is fine for now. According to Captain Penzington, she is taking refuge in some sort of ruins where the Chiata will not engage them," Debbie informed him.

"What? I mean, I'm damned glad she's okay, but ruins?" By missing out on the meeting while in medical, he was apparently missing out on a lot of information. Joe realized he needed to play catch-up for a bit.

"Yes, it would appear that there are ruins in the Northern Region of the planet, scattered along the main river branches there. As far as the Beta attack wave could tell, the Chiata would only engage the ground teams on the surface but would not follow them into the canyon basin along the river."

"What do the ruins look like?" Joe asked. Instantly, imagery data from the sensors of the Fleet ships started filing through his mindview. There were also mecha and suit-camera snapshots of the interior of one of the ruins. One of the snapshots was labeled "USMC Master Gunnery Sergeant Rondi Howser." Joe stopped on one of Rondi's and looked at it.

"What the heck is that?" He stopped on an image of a large wall that had all sorts of curves, circles, and ellipses spread out across it, and at various points there were little indentations of what looked like a bug-shaped hole. The hole reminded Joe of an old-fashioned keyhole. Each one of the "keyholes," as he thought of them now, corresponded with a curve that also had what looked like a star system on it.

"Debbie, can you take all the imagery data of this location and make a composite virtual model of it?" Joe asked.

"Yes, Joe, in fact, Captain Penzington's AIC has already done so. Would you like to see it?"

"By all means!" Joe continued to sit in the chair and finger the handle of the coffee mug, but his interest was now beginning to be teased away from the morbidity and potential mortality of injury, trauma, and recovery. He did like the sensation of the cup against his new finger though.

Joe immersed himself in the virtual world of the ruins and looked carefully at each curve as they traced along walls and ceilings from one curve to another, oftentimes passing through several of the little bug-like marks.

"Has anybody deciphered these things yet?" He asked. "I mean, we need to take these seriously if the Chiata will not go in there."

"Nobody has figured them out just yet," Debbie told him.

"I've seen something like this before," he said. "Bring up the diagram for all the QMT jumps we've made over the last two decades for me."

"Joe?"

"Just humor me," he said.

A virtual diagram of locations across the local part of the galaxy showing where large ships had jumped from QMT gate-to-gate, snap-back, and sling-forward jumps were also shown. To start with, it was just a map with a bunch of dots on it. Joe thought about it for a few long seconds as he stroked his chin with his new hand. The stubble there gave his new fingers an even more interesting sensation than the cup handle that was, to Joe, both something he'd felt a million times and something he'd never felt at the same time.

"Okay, let's see here. Draw a line for each gate's spacetime position over a complete orbital period of all in-system motions as well as their relative galactic positions," Joe told his AIC. To make certain it looked like he thought it would, Joe picked out the QMT facility in the Kuiper Belt around Sol and watched it. The facility's position was a slightly eccentric orbit about Sol, and it had a bit of wobble to it due to other Oort Cloud and Kuiper Belt objects tugging on it with their low gravity. There were also the occasional times when the orbit took it close enough to Neptune and Uranus to see a gravitational tug from them. The resultant graphic was an ellipse about the star, but the line drawn corkscrewed about the main elliptical path because of that slight position wobble.

Joe watched as all of the lines filled in and the local region of spacetime started looking like a spirograph gone mad. With the galactic motion added in, the curves drifted about an even larger curve set that made the graphic that much more convoluted.

"Now, where there are QMT facilities, place a supercarrier icon there. Where we engaged buzz-saw bots, put an enemy bot icon there." Joe looked at his handiwork. The graph looked perfectly confusing and not unlike the virtual one of the ruins. "You see where I'm going with this, Debbie?"

"Yes Joe, I do," his AIC replied. "What would you like me to do with it?"

"I don't have time to spend on this and keep the ship running too. Pass this to the STO, Captain Penzington's AIC, and the General's AIC. They should be able to extrapolate this and figure it out. But I'm pretty certain this is a map of gate traffic or jumps, or maybe whoever left it behind left it to show us their evacuation route. I don't know."

"The data has been passed along with a brief description of your hypothesis as ordered, Joe. The STO has sent you a priority file. Would you like to open it now?"

"Sure." Joe stood up and stretched his legs, all the while looking out the window at the stars and thinking how quiet his place was when Howser wasn't there. And how dark it was without her glowing tattoos. He brought the lights up just a bit and quit staring out at the stars. He hoped she was alright. Then the file that Commander Snow had sent him during his medical procedure opened and he was consumed by it. It was an analysis of data taken by the STO of the *Hillenkoetter* on the blue beams. Almost instantly, as Buckley assimilated the data into his mind, the wheels started turning.

"This is amazing data," Joe muttered. "There are these gravimetric spikes with each turn of the beams. These little virtual quantum black holes, if that's what she wants to call them, are being projected from somewhere that can manipulate an immense amount of energy."

"Yes, perhaps they are being projected from the spires about the megaship's surface?" Debbie pondered with Joe.

"Maybe, but to precisely place these virtual gravity lenses about space randomly and ahead of a beam means they are transmitting it using quantum entanglement. Nothing else other than membrane tech does that instantaneously in violation of Einstein." Joe thought about what he'd just said.

Somehow the Chiata ships were transmitting enormous amounts of energy into regions of spacetime instantaneously and precisely. Possibly the blue beam itself could be the source for the quantum connection with the black hole projector, and then a device back onboard the alien megaship would still be in connection through entanglement of quantum wavefunctions with the end of the blue beam. Simply decohering information from the shipboard end would allow the cohering of information at the blue beam end. In this case, that information was enough energy to create a miniature gravitational lens in spacetime with the precise spacetime structure that would gravitationally steer the beam in the direction it needed to go.

To Joe, this meant many things. The first thing was that the aliens had one helluva power source somewhere in the belly of their ships. One hell of a power source. Joe knew immediately that he needed to pin down where that was. Secondly, Joe realized that there was an amazing sensor system that, in turn, was driving a control algorithm that could follow the beam and targets, update the beam's targeting path, calculate the energy projection required for placement of the black holes, and then somehow place those black holes. The latency factor here was less than the order of femtoseconds. To do all that in such a small amount of time meant the Chiata had computational powers far superior to anything Joe knew about.

Then something that the Ghuthlaeer had told them popped into his mind. The Ghuthlaeer's chief engineer had sent word to him that the barrier shields could use more power. Joe had managed to siphon off as much power from every other system on the ship to max them out, but they still couldn't hold off the Chiata blue beams for long. And Joe now realized that the small black hole was simply sucking off all the power of the shields down through the event horizon. As far as energy was concerned, the little black holes were essentially a bottomless pit into which the entire store of a ship's energy could be drained. The amount of energy required to make those things go supernova had to be outrageous.

"Debbie, calculate the energy required to fill up one of these black holes for me. How can we make them go supernova? Or would we want too?" Joe asked his AIC.

"If a quantum black hole went supernova, it would likely produce so much energy as to sterilize a complete star system of any life. The explosion would be too much for the shields to withstand, for certain. I wouldn't recommend it, Joe," Debbie replied.

"What if we pumped more energy through the shield generators?"

"We'd need all the energy from one of those megaships to drive them. We do not have anything that can produce that kind of power," Debbie explained.

"Run a simulation and show me what happens if we pumped that much energy through the *Madira's* shields."

Joe sat back in his desk chair and waited for a second for the simulation to be complete.

The supercarrier's shields flickered as the graph of energy input rose. The shield bubble expanded from the ship and looked as if they would continue to expand in a blast wave, but then the generators exploded and the ship flew apart.

"What happened?"

"The energy transfer was too much for the shield generators to handle. We'd need at least four times as many shield generators to run that much energy through them."

"Hmmm. Okay, assume we have that many shield generators, then what? Rerun the sim that way."

"Okay, Joe. Hold on one minute."

This time the simulation was much more interesting. As the energy curve increased, the shield strength increased nonlinearly, and therefore it had to expand in a spherical wavefront with the ship at the origin. Once the energy input reached a certain level, where the *Madira* had exploded in the previous one, all of the energy immediately dumped through the system like a capacitor discharging through a short circuit. The spherical wavefront exploded like a supernova from the ship and tore away anything in its path. The blast radius covered a sphere over thirty thousand kilometers in radius.

"What the?!" Joe looked startled. "What happened there?"

"I'm not certain, Joe, but there would appear to have been some sort of quantum bounce phenomenon predicted by the simulation. I wouldn't have expected that," Debbie said.

"Quantum bounce? You mean like at the bottom of a black hole where quantum gravity prevents further compaction of spacetime quantum loops and then quantum loop compaction itself forces the black hole to reverse and explode?" Joe remembered the concept vaguely from his undergraduate spacetime engineering classes.

"Yes, that is exactly what the model shows. As the blast wave pushes energy against spacetime faster than it can get out of the way, the spacetime itself reacts by releasing energy with it. In this case the shield looks like the bottom of the black hole at maximum allowed quantum loop pressure and so the quantum bounce is occurring all across the spherical shield's surface. We have in essence the creation of a white hole radiating outward in all directions from the spherical surface of the shield."

"No shit?" Joe slumped and propped his chin in his new hand. Joe pulled up schematics of a supercarrier and of the megaships. He looked at the schematics energy transfer systems of the supercarrier and then back at the incomplete diagram of the alien megaship. They could only guess at what was inside the porcusnail things, but physics was physics and Joe had a good idea at least of where the energy plants were. "Debbie, run the sims again and make certain four times the generators is enough with ample margin for safety."

"Okay, Joe." She reran the simulations, and again, just past the failure point of one supercarrier's worth of shield generators the quantum bounce occurred, sending out the massive blast front with a total destruct spherical radius of over thirty thousand kilometers. The phenomenon was almost too much to believe, but the physics was what the physics was. It was just one of the first times that humanity had created a phenomenon that was almost stellar in scale even in simulation.

"This could really happen? No shit?" Joe didn't question the physics, it was just a whole new level of play.

"No shit, Joe," Debbie said. "Too bad we don't have four times the shield generators on this ship."

"We have them, alright." Joe was beginning to have one of his crazy ideas. "If people thought the Buckley maneuver was crazy, wait 'til they hear about this."

"Joe? What are you planning?"

Chapter 23

February 19, 2407 AD
U.S.S. Sienna Madira
Rendezvous Point, 10.5 Light Days from
   Target Star System
700 Light-years from the Sol System
Monday, 7:44 P.M. Ship Standard Time

"So, let me get this straight, Mr. Buckley." General Moore looked at his chief engineer, not quite certain if the man was losing it or not. He understood that Joe had been through a very traumatic injury within the past few hours, and sometimes those things had some unusual and adverse side effects. The immunoboost and pain meds alone were enough to make a person hyper and bouncing off the walls. "You want to take one of the Fleet ships that we are already limited on and you want to let the repair bots strip it down?"

"Uh, well, not exactly strip it down, General," Joe

replied. "What I want to do is use the Von Neumann probe self-replication code that President Madira implemented in her builder bots, inject those bots into the most damaged ship, and have them generate as many specifically programmed repair bots as we can in the next two hours."

"Okay, to what end exactly? I'm still not sure I'm following you." Moore listened to the CHENG patiently. He had known the man for some time now and knew that if he was asking for something so wild that he had a crazy plan or maneuver up his sleeve that just might save the day or end up killing them all. Moore needed something Buckley-crazy. Hell, he'd just about settle for batshit crazy if it would help him save his daughter.

"Uh, sorry sir. I haven't explained myself well. Let me start over." Buckley paused for a second and then looked to Alexander as if he were talking to his AIC. "Sir, let me DTM this to you."

"Okay. Go ahead."

Abby.

Got it, sir.

"As you can see from this image of the Chiata megaship, or uh, porcusnail, I think the CDC is calling them, there are four main shield generators, as far as we can tell anyway, here and here and here and over here." Joe pointed at the virtual image, and the shield generators highlighted in Alexander's mindview. "Two in the front and two in the back and each on opposite outer sides of the vessel. We need to hit the Chiata ships right there with a supercarrier per generator and release the repair bots into each of the four breaches created."

Alexander at first thought Joe was talking about firing the weapons at weak points on the enemy ship, until the simulation Joe was running showed four Fleet ships, aft hangar ends toward the Chiata ship, colliding with it at the generator locations.

"Wait, you mean you want our ships to *ram* the Chiata ship?" Alexander was now seriously considering that Joe had lost his marbles. "What type of damage would we take on?"

"Well, that is negligible considering the possible outcome, sir. Please stay with me on this for just a bit longer and you'll see. The risk is high, but the rewards might be, well, unbelievable, sir." Joe reached up and zoomed in on one of the impact points. "Now the shields will be reinforced on the aft hangar section to protect it as best we can but we want to penetrate into the megaship all the way into the interior hull. That will be the, well, hairiest part."

"No shit." Alexander raised an eyebrow at Buckley's description.

Hairiest part, my ass, Moore thought. *Can the ship take that kind of stress?*

I'll start running numbers and discussing it with the other engineering AICs, sir, Abigail assured him while the CHENG continued explaining his plan.

"Uh, yes sir, no shit." Buckley paused to agree. "At that point we release ground teams, mecha teams, tank teams, buzz-saw bots, I dunno, whatever is the right way and we start tearing the place to hell and gone and killing every Chiata along the way. But before the attacking wave arrives, the repair bots flood into the ship in mass quantities with one mission: attach the alien power source to the aft barrier shield conduit of the supercarrier. Now these bots from all four ships are flooding the Chiata ship, which now has no shield generators, and they are connecting our shield generators to the alien's unbelievably deep power well."

"So, you want us to board the alien ship and hold it? For how long?" Alexander was beginning to see that the idea was possible, but he wasn't sure to what end. "I guess if we could take one of the ships we could take over and use the blue beams ourselves. Now that would be an advantage. Not bad, Joe."

"Uh, well, no sir, that isn't my plan, but yes, having our own blue beams would be useful." Buckley hesitated. Moore hated when the CHENG did that.

"Well then, what the hell is the plan, Joe? Come on, we haven't got all day." Moore was getting a bit frustrated. The clock continued to tick away and his daughter was stranded on an alien planet being pursued by aliens, and with every second that ticked by, her odds for survival diminished.

"Yes, sir. This is better than the blue beams. Your Ghuthlaeer friend suggested we pump more power into the shields, and I've been racking my brain on how to do that. Now, sir, you won't believe what happens when we put *enough* energy in." Joe smiled. "Just watch the simulation."

Alexander watched as the image of the megaship zoomed way out. The four ships from the Fleet were now attached to the megaship, making the porcusnail look as if it had alligator-like legs protruding from it. As the simulation ticked at a time-lapse pace, the clock time showed thirteen minutes into the simulation when all of a sudden the barrier-shield generators extended the shields from each of the Fleet ship's stern sections. The shields expanded until they met and rippled together, forming a complete oval around the entire combination of Fleet and Chiata ships. Ten seconds more and the oval spread to a spherical barrier, which then erupted like a gluonium bomb, sending out a blast wave that exploded at nearly eighty percent the speed of light. The wave continued to grow until it was finally spread too thin and it dissipated and vanished.

"Holy . . ." Alexander backed up the sim and ran the last part again. "And this is real? I mean, it isn't just some simulation that might work? This is real physics and will work?"

"Yes, sir. This isn't based on theory, this is a simulation based on absolute measurements and experimental data and knowledge of the physical phenomena," Joe replied, smiling almost maniacally. "This is what happens sometimes at the bottom of a black hole when it quantum bounces and becomes a white hole."

Abigail? What was that blast radius?

If the CHENG's calculations are correct, sir, the radius extended at least thirty thousand kilometers. Maybe more.

Have you checked his numbers?

Of course I have, sir.

And?

This is one hell of a Buckley Maneuver, sir. It will work if we can manage to hold the ship long enough for the repair bots to make the right connections.

Son of a bitch! Alexander started to smile for the first time in days. Before this he'd only been hoping of a daring suicide attempt to get in and get his people out. But now. Now, there was a hope for more. Maybe a lot more.

"You have my full approval, Joe. My AIC is now working with full attention with yours and the XO's and anyone else you need. Make this happen faster than ASAP."

"Aye, sir." Buckley turned enthusiastically and was out the Captain's ready room door as fast as he'd come in.

Alexander turned his chair to the window and looked out at the remainder of the Fleet and the star background. He thought about what would have to happen to prepare an attack to hold a damned Chiata ship. That would be no small task. And how the hell would he keep the other Chiata ships off their ass while they were making the attack? Would they turn on their own or come to their defense? Alexander suspected the former, but only time would tell. He had a lot to figure out in a very short time, and with a beat-up and battered Fleet.

Abigail, get me the XO, CAG, and the Ground Boss in here five minutes ago. We have an attack to plan, Alexander thought. He leaned back in his chair, and violating his own rule, stowed his helmet to the shoulder containment location on his suit. He popped the gloves back and reached out for his coffee mug. The White House mug had been his favorite and had somehow managed to survive for decades of crazy events. The mug itself had led him to promoting at least three staffers and reprimanding one. He drank the nasty stuff the COB had made him in one final big gulp. It was so much better gulping it rather than drinking it from a spout through the open visor on a suit helmet.

Abby, better get the COB to send me another pot of that stuff. We've got a lot to get done in the next two hours.

Yes, sir.

Chapter 24

February 19, 2407 AD
Northern Region
Alien Planet, Target Star System
700 Light-years from the Sol System
Monday, 8:44 P.M. Ship Standard Time

Dee used the zoom on her visor to get the lay of the land as best she could. The starlight sensor combined with infrared, ultraviolet, and microwave was enough on passive to give her almost a daytime-like view even though the star had been set for hours. Dee kept as sniper-quiet and still as she possibly could underneath one of the giant trees that was bent half over and cracked at the bottom. The crack was almost large enough she could have flown her mecha up in it. It was a big damned tree.

Dee was doing her best to be patient, but knowing that there was another team of Chiata searching for her that several times over the last two hours had gotten danger-close to her, she was understandably on edge. The last shift change had just happened, and from the timing of the alien shuttles coming and going, it looked like they were on four-hour shifts. That seemed very short to Dee, but her grandmother had once warned her about trying to understand alien motivations.

"They are alien, sweetheart, and so their motivations will be just that, alien," Sienna Madira had told her. Dee had long since come to grips with the fact that she likely would never understand the motivations of her twisted grandmother either, but that didn't mean she wasn't very smart and very right. So, rather than apply meaning to what the Chiata were doing and why they were doing it, Dee just decided to accept the observation and expect another shift change in about three and a half hours from her present time.

The trees were spread farther apart in this area and the undergrowth was more like the high grass of a hay field. There were various flowering plants in reds and blues scattered about on some all-encompassing and landscape-smothering vines that reminded Dee of kudzu. As she scanned about she could see that the kudzu-like vine spanned across the ground almost as far as she could see to the west and north as if it were chasing the star. There were several of the termite-like mounds that spired upwards out of the undergrowth by as much as three meters. The mounds seemed to be lining a pathway toward where the shuttles had been landing right next to an opening in an artificial granite structure that looked more like a cross between the Capitol Building architecture on Earth and ancient Roman constructions with columns, arches and large blocks of granite. There might even have been a hint of Egyptian architecture, but Dee wasn't sure, she wasn't an exo-archaeologist. Again, she was putting human extrapolations onto alien artifices.

It was a large granite structure with glyphs and symbols cut in it and there was, as far as she could surmise, one very large entryway, large enough that three hovertanks standing fingertips apart couldn't touch the sides of it. There was a pounded-out path in the alien kudzu that led straight toward the middle tributary of the river system. The path was pounded out from where the Chiata had been landing shuttles on it. But a few tens of meters away the kudzu was unbothered. The path was lined on either side with the strange termite-like mounds that gave it the appearance of a very large road with huge traffic cones on either side. The infrared view from her visor showed a different heat signature for the pathway leading from the entrance to the river. Dee realized that there was a stone or paved road underneath the vines.

Two of the Chiata ground troops stood sentry at the passageway, and that led her to believe the third was inside, because as far as her sensors could tell there were no heat signatures in the shuttle. She had been just moments behind the shift change or she'd have been able to know for certain where the third Chiata was. At least she knew there was not a third heat signature within range of her suit's sensors.

Dee also was pretty certain that she needed to know what was inside the building, and if these things were always on guard, well, that meant there was only one way she was going to get to look. They had to be taken out. But that led her to a conundrum. There were six Chiata ground troops that had been on her tail for the past couple of hours, and those bastards had a flying vehicle that was fast. She'd managed to avoid them for a couple hours now and hated the prospect of having to grapple with them up close and personal. While there had been a couple of close calls along the way, she had given them the slip and managed to keep several kilometers between herself and them. Dee knew that as soon as she engaged the Chiata standing sentry, it would only be a matter of minutes before the search party would be on top of her. That was just something she'd have to be prepared for. How she was going to prepare for it was another question entirely.

After thinking on a plan for a couple seconds longer, she decided it was time to make her move. She armed the grenade launcher just in case, but she hoped to be as quiet as she possibly could. Dee rested her left thumb against the safety on her HVAR, and her right pointer finger played at the trigger guard of her M-blaster. There was little left to do, but do something and to do it quietly and deadly.

What are your plans, Dee? Bree asked her in her mindview.

Open for suggestions, but we need to be quick and quiet, she thought. *What about if I work around the path behind the ruins and see if I can get the drop on them from over the top and behind them? Thoughts?*

I don't know if that'll work, Dee. I'm sure they have motion trackers. We are at the edge of estimated sensor range now. Not sure there is a quiet assault path, Bree told her. *The direct approach might be better.*

Yeah, I was afraid of that. Okay, then, let me see if I

can reach out and touch one of them. Dee holstered the M-blaster and brought the HVAR up to her right side. She thumbed the targeting system and her DTM mindview became her rifle bore's sight. She waited for the yellow targeting X to turn red on the Chiata standing guard on the left of the doorway. She zoomed in and placed the X right between the alien's eye holes and then released the trigger. There was the familiar *spittapp* sound and the hypervelocity round burst out across the two hundred meters between herself and the alien, leaving a pale blue and violet trail of ions as it tore through the atmosphere. The round hit the alien's head at a velocity of over Mach seven. The alien's personal body-armor shields flickered as Dee pumped two more rounds right at the same point microseconds behind the first one. The impact of the rounds knocked the alien off its feet and backwards. The creature's shields must have burned out because Dee could see a green liquid spurt out of his forehead as he fell.

"That's one," she whispered to herself with a smile.

Great shot, Dee, now don't get cocky, and keep moving! Bree warned.

She quickly turned to the other alien, who was reacting by dropping to the ground in prone position and firing back in her general direction. Dee ducked down behind the tree roots and rolled to one of the termite mounds nearest her, closing the distance to the alien by a few meters. She then bear-crawled another twenty or so meters to a smaller mangrove tree about a meter in diameter. Dee leaned out from behind the tree and let go of a handful of HVAR rounds. The rounds pitted up earth in front of the alien and a couple of them skittered off the creature's shielded armor. As dust, ion trails, and enemy fire flashed about Dee, she took only brief pauses to breathe and to assess her situation.

Well, hell, that didn't work so well, she thought. *We can't get pinned down.*

The pursuit team must have been alerted to your whereabouts. Dee, they have turned to this direction and will be here in less than four minutes.

Then we need to get on with this! Dee grunted as she rolled up to her feet and kicked her jumpboots against the tree, accelerating her and tossing her more than thirty meters to the next nearest tree. *You know what Daddy and DeathRay would say!*

Damn right. Get in there and kill those motherfuckers, Marine!

Upon each bound into a tree or behind a termite mound, alien tracer fire tracked her path. Dirt and splinters of wood skittered in tiny blast waves, pinging against her armor. Dee really wished her damned shields were functioning. She felt vulnerable now without them, but she couldn't let that feeling slow her down. She continued to lay down the HVAR fire sometimes hitting the alien, she thought, but the targeting X would only flicker from yellow to red briefly because the damned thing was so fast. It was hard to tell if she was hitting it or not.

Jesus, they're fast, she thought as she fired on semi-auto as the targeting X flickered between yellow and red.

Just keep firing, Marine!

Ooh-fuckin'-rah!

Once she dropped to a knee just behind a tree and

thought she had the thing dead to rights as she pumped out several tens of rounds. The rounds tracked across and into where the alien had been only milliseconds earlier. Then the firing stopped and there was a red and green blur that appeared in front of her and tossed her hard against the ground. Dee used the momentum of the toss to roll over into a back handspring and used the strength of the suit's arms to toss her all the way up to her feet while kicking the advancing alien where the thing's chin should be.

But the damned alien was fast and had moved out of the way, and the blur appeared behind her. Dee spun as soon as her jumpboots hit the ground and kicked the thrusters. The momentum of the jumpboots added to her spin made the force of the elbow she was now swinging smash into the alien's jaw with a *crack* that sounded like a grenade bursting behind her. The alien's personal armor shield flickered as Dee continued to slam her left elbow into the side of its jaw three more times, each blow creating a thunderous cracking sound as the super alloy of the suit clashed with the alien's barrier shield.

Then an amorphous tendril snaked out from the creature's torso and wrapped around her midsection and upward around the throat of her suit, and started squeezing her so hard that the suit diagnostics icon popped up in her mindview, showing dangerous pressure points marked in yellow dots that were in danger of turning red. Her left hand was constricted against her chest just short of her rifle and her right was pinned to her side. It was déjà vu all over again. At least this time she wasn't being eaten alive.

Dee had been in this situation all too recently and didn't like it. She struggled with her left hand to pull at the tendril and wiggled her right downward toward her M-blaster. Quickly, she did several backwards headbutts until she felt a change in the impact. After a few more blows it no longer felt as though she was headbutting an impenetrable barrier, but instead, her helmet squished against skin and bone as it pounded into the alien's face. With all the strength in her amazing core and the suit's artificial musculature, she crunched her abs downward until she could wrap her left leg around the outside of the alien's left leg and pounded her right jumpboot against its right knee. The alien squealed and Dee could feel its knee give way. She tucked her chin and fell with all her weight in a forward roll, throwing the creature off balance over her right shoulder, and to the ground.

But the damned thing wouldn't let go of her and the tendril wrapped up on her even tighter. They were now on the ground, with the Chiata on the bottom lying on its back struggling to maintain its death-gripping bear hug around Dee. She did her best to roll from side to side and squirm with elbows and the heels of her boots, but the damned thing had her wrapped up fairly tightly.

Dee finally managed to land a solid kick with her boots somewhere akin to mid-thigh on the Chiata and it loosened its grip just enough so that she could lean backwards and headbutt the shit out of it. Between the kick and the headbutt the alien was stunned just enough to give her some advantage, and she managed to rock her body left and right gaining enough momentum to roll over and pulling the Chiata over onto her back. Using sheer will, strength, and all the power in her suit she pushed up onto her hands and knees. Finding the grip of her blaster finally, she squeezed the trigger, hitting the alien's leg. The Chiata let out a howl that was more eerie than anything she'd ever heard before, so she fired her blaster again and this time the tendril went a little slack, giving her enough movement with her left hand to grab her HVAR and fire it. The rounds burst the tendril into pieces that loosened and unwrapped, and Dee was free. She turned quickly to fire at the alien but the damned thing zipped by her in a blur and grabbed her left arm, knocking the rifle to the ground and pressing the attack.

The Chiata tossed her sideways and Dee could feel her back slam into one of the termite mounds. It felt to her like she'd been pounded against a concrete structure—it was a lot harder than she'd expected. Before she could get up two more tendrils snaked out from the alien and penetrated her suit armor in the left leg on the outer thigh and on the right shoulder. The centimeter-diameter tendrils pierced all the way through her like harpoons and out the back side, forming barbs, and then yanked her forward.

"Oh, Jesus! Fuck!" Dee shouted in pain. "Goddamn you, motherfucker!"

She raised the blaster as best she could with the right hand, but a third tendril grabbed her hand, knocking the weapon free. Dee stomped her jumpboots against the ground, throwing her upward in an arc over the Chiata. She quickly extended the knife blade from her left wrist and cut through the tendrils as she somersaulted over and came down on her hands and knees behind it.

Immunoboost, stims, and pain meds initiated, Bree said. *Don't stop Marine! Press the advantage!*

"Die, you motherfucker!" Dee jumped up from her kneeling position with a right-leg back kick into the alien's back. The creature was flung forward by the motion of the kick, all the while red and green gunk squirted from the tendrils Dee had cut loose.

The Chiata fell face first against the termite mound, immediately looked as if it were frightened, and started scrambling backwards as best it could. But it was too late. The red and green blood of the creature had covered the mound and had awoken whatever was inside it. Dee wasn't sure what was happening at first, but then she could see what looked like beetles or ants the size of two-hundred-millimeter AA rounds pouring out from the mound and over the Chiata. It looked to Dee like the Chiata couldn't move. She'd seen the aliens run so fast that they were blurs, but as soon as the first of the beetle things jumped on the alien, it was paralyzed. Her first thoughts were that the beetles were injecting the Chiata with some sort of neurotoxin. Within seconds the mound poured thousands of the beetles over the alien, and it was devoured to nothing. There was nothing left of the alien except the technology bits and some skeletal structure.

Dee backed up just to make certain that the beetles didn't get a whiff of her and like what they smelled. But as far as she could tell they weren't interested. She focused her visor on the skeleton and noted that there were weapon implants grafted to the alien's bones. The shield system appeared to be connected via conduits that were woven throughout the alien's skeleton. The bugs didn't stop, though. They continued to crawl over the alien's skeleton, picking at the bones and chipping them apart. Dee was pretty sure that in a few moments there would be no biological evidence that the Chiata was ever there.

There were three of them, Dee, and we have more on the way, Bree reminded her.

Right. Keep moving. Too bad I can't take an armload of those beetle things with me.

They might decide that you are tasty, too. I wouldn't gamble on it.

Right.

The pain medication and stimulants had knocked the pain down to a level such that Dee just felt an uncomfortable nagging ache in her thigh and shoulder. The organogel layer of her suit had filled the wounds and was keeping her from bleeding, and the immunoboost was initiating the healing process. All that didn't mean that she wasn't weaker than normal, though. Dee had to depend on her suit to help her walk and to make certain movements with her right arm. Anything overhead was all suit and none of her strength. Those muscles were shot for the time being. Her thigh was pretty messed up as well, and squatting strength on the left side would be all suit; therefore, her reaction time would be slower than normal. She'd seen worse. She was alive. She had to keep moving forward.

Dee picked up her HVAR and her blaster and sluggishly bounced to the edge of the entryway, stopping with her back against the outside wall with both weapons up and at the ready. She took three deep breaths and pumped herself up and then turned the corner moving fast. Her HVAR was in her left hand and her M-blaster in her right, the way she preferred to attack, with the two-gun mojo. Her sensors laid out a cone of visible area before her as she turned her head from left to right. The glyphs on the walls were more twisted and tangled and Dee was sure she passed several markings representing the beetles along the way. The first thing that came to her mind was that the scale of the ruin's interior was bigger than she'd expected. The hallways and entryways were all more than large enough to load mecha through. If she had to guess, she would have said that the ruins were hangars or forward operating bases for some ancient military. She dropped down one level and reached a corridor with only one way to turn. She turned left, and there she stood face to face with the third Chiata.

Startled, Dee dropped back, firing both weapons. The hypervelocity rounds pinged against the alien's body armor and pierced through it to the other side, hitting the stone wall behind it. The alien's barrier shield wasn't functioning. The rifle round slapped into the stone and didn't have the effect that Dee was expecting. Rather than slinging stone chips and debris about, there was no damage to the wall, and a ripple of blue and white light flashed starting from the impact point and travelling all the way across the walls of the corridor. It happened too fast for her to stop herself from firing her blaster as well. The M-blaster bolt hit the Chiata square in the face, exploding the creature's head and throwing red and green viscous fluids across the wall behind it. Dee paused and checked the room for other threats. There were several other Chiata forms standing against the walls, but they were not moving. Even after she had beheaded the alien in front of her its body was still motionlessly stuck to the wall.

Dee jumped backwards and dropped to her knee with her HVAR at the ready to go full auto, but the creatures didn't attack or move. They were all motionlessly stuck.

"What the hell is going on here?" Dee stood cautiously, never lowering her rifle and waving her blaster about with her right hand, searching for possible targets. A few times she had to lower it to let her shoulder rest or to let the suit lock out the joint for the same purpose. The wound was healing but it would still be a while before she was back to normal.

She closed the distance to the nearest alien and examined it closer, but very cautiously. There was no trace of infrared left in it. It had been dead for many hours if not days. Examination of the other bodies revealed multiple aliens, each having died at successive four-hour intervals of each other. They appeared to be stuck to the wall with some sort of force field. Dee guessed it was whatever field had flickered like a barrier shield when her rifle round hit the wall.

Okay, Bree, I need some answers, Dee thought to her AIC. *What the hell, the aliens know I'm here, so use full-up active sensors, pings, particles, radar, everything. Try the QMTs, but I doubt you'll get anything from them.*

Understood. And note that the search team is two minutes out.

Then hurry it up. We need answers quickly.

I got nothing from scanning sensors. We are completely jammed here. Other than the optical sensors and your Mark I eyeballs, there is nothing to see. That in itself is interesting. It is certainly technology beyond a simple primitive race of people.

Interesting, but it ain't answers. I need to have a better look. Dee thought quickly, not exactly sure what to do next. The Chiata search team was coming hot on her heels. She needed to shit or get off the pot. *They're coming anyway, so light this fucking place up and let's have a better look.*

Done, Bree replied.

The floodlights from the suit illuminated the cavernous room. There were several alien bodies pinned to the wall and rotting. Whatever was in here, the Chiata had been sacrificing themselves for a long time to figure it out. Dee figured that if she'd opened her visor, the air would have smelled putrefied and been toxic. So, she kept her visor closed.

In the corner there were several dead Chiata strapped to mobile gurneys with partial dismemberments. And next to those bodies were what looked like containers with the remains of several of the beetles in them. Dee looked closer and noticed that there was a pattern in the aliens' death. Most of the bodies were pinned to the wall near a singular beetle marking on the biggest glyph, on the center of a larger spiral with a star-system picture that looked a lot like the star system they were in. There were a few bodies pinned to the wall at other locations but the majority were nearest that marking. Right in the center of the planet in the glyphs, which Dee could only surmise represented the planet she was on, was an indentation or hole that looked just like the little beetles.

Looks like a keyhole, she thought.

It looks like the Chiata thought it was, too.

We need to open this lock. Dee looked about the room hoping to figure out what the Chiata were doing wrong. *Why didn't it work for them?*

Perhaps because they are Chiata, Bree said.

What? Chiata? Dee hesitated and then realized that Bree was onto the answer. *Bree, that is it exactly! The reason the beetles ate the Chiata and not me. They are some sort of defense system or maybe worse, a doomsday weapon. It doesn't matter. I know what to do.*

Dee turned and backtracked down the corridor and up the stairwell, back into the passageway, coming face to face with six Chiata ground troops standing at the edge of the landing zone. The six aliens and Dee froze for a microsecond and then they all reacted at the same time and in exactly the same way. Instantly, their weapons rose and they started firing towards each other's general directions respectively. Dee dove to the wall and behind a column for cover. Bolts of plasma energy bounced off the walls, causing barrier shields along the walls to flicker and ripple with energy. The blue and white flashes of light mixed with muzzle flashes and blaster rounds created a multicolor strobe effect in the cavern that made the motion look choppy and disjointed to Dee.

Filter out some of this light flickering! I can't see shit, she told her AIC.

Roger that, Dee. The two on the right are trying to work around and flank you.

I see it. Keep the radars up for full resolution on red force tracker!

Yes, ma'am!

Dee popped the grenade launcher tube controls. The tube deployed from her shoulder, and then two balls boomed out across the room with a *thwoomp thwoomp* sound from the compressed air in the electromagnetic rail-cannon launcher, and then they exploded at where the Chiata should have been standing. But the damned things were too fast and she missed them. The red and green blurs regrouped at the other side of the entranceway of the ruin, giving them a good line of fire directly at her. Dee had to bear-crawl forward to adjust her cover position, but it was no good. Alien plasma bolts resounded into the wall behind her and just over her head, creating more and more ripples from the barrier shield.

She was pinned down. The only thing she could do was sit still until the aliens finally got the drop on her, or do what Marines do when they are pinned down by overwhelming numbers of enemy forces. They attack!

Chapter 25

February 19, 2407 AD
Northern Region
Alien Planet, Target Star System
700 Light-years from the Sol System
Monday, 9:01 P.M. Ship Standard Time

"There are six Chiata against one injured Marine." Dee spat blood from her mouth into the organogel layer of her helmet. Her initial attack hadn't gone as well as she'd planned. The Chiata tendril piercing her abdomen had worked itself out her back before she could manage to slice it free and yank it out. The organogel filled the wound and she was running on pure adrenaline and hyperstimulants.

I've administered more pain meds and immunoboost, Bree said. The diagnostics of her suit were going nuts also. *Stay focused and keep fighting!*

"You sorry alien motherfuckers are outnumbered!" She screamed through the pain and fear and drove herself

to pure rage and survival mode. As she swept the knife
blade extended from her left arm across the tendrils from
the nearest alien, she reached with her right hand and
caught it as it detached and extracted. She clenched it as
tightly as she could in her fist and yanked the alien
towards her while at the same time kicking her jumpboots
against the ground, throwing and pulling herself at the
Chiata. With all the weight and force of her suit she forced
the knife blade just beneath what should have been a chin.
The alien's shields had already failed and this time she
drove home the knife all the way through and out the back
of the creature's neck. Dee spun away from it slicing the
knife outward and severing the head almost free, leaving
it dangling from bloody tissues and alien vasculature from
the torso as the Chiata fell to the ground.

With her spinning motion, she rolled across the
ground, managed to get her left hand onto her rifle, and
fired several rounds as the targeting X blinked red to her
left and slightly behind her. She kicked her jumpboots at
maximum against the stone underneath the kudzu vines
and threw herself twenty meters into the air, twisting like
an Olympic gymnast doing a floor routine, dodging plasma
rounds from the other Chiata attackers.

*They seem to attack in twos with the backup playing
sniper,* Bree noticed.

*Good, keep the snipers marked and let's go at them
two at a time.* Dee bounced sideways from the trunk of a
tree over the top of the beetle mounds lining the stone
and skittered onto her backside back into the doorway of
the ruin. She popped four grenades and ducked behind
the stone corner for cover.

The grenades popped and scattered the remaining five aliens a bit further out. The wingman of the one she'd just killed was closest, and the blast was close enough to it that it seemed to have lost its balance and was rolled over face first. Dee took the advantage and leaped forward and bounced at full sprint of the suit. The pain, even though she was pumped full of medication, was still almost unbearable. But she pushed through it.

Dee came down with a knee into the back of the alien and fired the HVAR on full auto until its shields flickered out and red and green goo exploded from the back of its ugly head. A plasma bolt caught her on the back of her right shoulder, throwing her head over heels into the vines. The armor plating of her suit turned molten hot and boiled away from the outside. The organogel on the inside reached dangerously high temperatures, broiling the already damaged shoulder with third degree burns or worse.

"Aahhh! Fucking son of a fucking goddamn alien fucks!" She screamed in pain but couldn't stop moving or screaming. Through rage and pain she dragged herself as fast as she could across the stone road underneath the vines and took up cover behind the nearest beetle mound as the plasma bolts continued to pound into the foliage around her. Small fires in the grass were starting to smolder and catch up.

Where are those bastards when I need them? Dee looked at the beetle mound and thought, all the while grimacing and doing her best to fight through the ever-growing level of pain. She bit on her bite block for a quick burst of water and more stims. A burst of pure oxygen hit her in the face as well, and the result was a brief moment of clarity and false bravado.

You need to throw some Chiata blood on them, maybe, Bree suggested.

I'll keep that in mind.

The mound snapped and chips of stone vaporized as the Chiata plasma bolts bounced off them. The material they were made of was tough, but there was no barrier shield on them and the enemy plasma bolts would eventually chip away her cover. Dee hoped the damned bugs would wake up and lend her a hand, but she wasn't sure she wanted that to happen while she was leaning against one.

Battlescape view, Bree!

Battlescape on.

Dee looked for the active sensor pings and other tracking scanners to show her where the Chiata were. They were close enough that the active sensors in the red force tracker gave her good readings. Two of the Chiata had moved to high ground on top of the ruin entrance and the other two were working themselves around behind the stone road to the river and flanking Dee to her three o'clock.

"Shit. I wish I had my mecha right now." Dee started to turn away from the mound and move towards her nine o'clock position, but the two snipers hanging back cut her off quickly with plasma-round fire. She rolled from left to right in prone position, firing her rifle the entire time on full automatic. At least twice she'd have sworn that the targeting X was red, and she saw shield flickers in the distance.

Two grenades left and I'm getting low on ammo. Give me a location on the blaster and keep it marked in the battlescape view.

Roger that, Dee. The blaster is more than twenty meters away in the vines nearest the entrance.

Yeah, thought that's where I dropped it. Dee checked the mindview and could see the two Chiata from her three o'clock were now almost on top of her. She had to make a move or it was going to be the end of her right there.

Dee popped one of the last two grenades at the two Chiata trying to flank her and decided a full-on attack at the snipers was her best plan of action. She bounced and serpentined across the stone road, behind the mounds, off of several trees, all the while dodging, ducking, rolling, somersaulting and whatever else it took not to get blasted by the Chiata snipers. With a final leap as she approached the entrance she bounced her kickboots, hard and up she flew, firing her HVAR on full auto into both of the aliens standing atop the ruin. They became blurs and moved to avoid her gunfire as she bounced to a stop on top of the vine- and grass-covered ruin.

One of the vines caught her left boot with enough force that she fell face first against the stone and scraped across it, making a screeching noise and throwing sparks that ignited the vines with the red flowers on them. Apparently, they were extremely flammable. Fire raged up around her, distorting her targeting system, and fortunately doing the same for the Chiata. Dee pushed herself up to her feet, turned her torso, and ducked just in time to miss an alien tendril shooting through the flames at her head. She deployed the knife from her left wrist again and fired several rounds in the general direction from where the tendril had come. A second tendril shot in at her from the right, hitting her in the leg. But before it could push through and harpoon her she swiped down with the blade quickly, severing the amorphous line from her.

Dee turned and ran in the direction of the sliced tendril and dove forward, catching it with her right hand. As the tendril was retracted it pulled her forward through the flames toward the Chiata. The vines continued to burn like rocket fuel, bursting all around her and crackling and engulfing the top of the ruin and spreading up the vines into the nearest trees. As the alien dragged Dee to it, she pulled up the HVAR and fired it until it clicked empty. The alien's shields dropped out with a flicker and one of the rounds hit it mid-torso, penetrating its body armor. She rolled to her back and spun her legs break-dancing style up onto her hands, and capoeira-style kicking the Chiata on the side of the head with her jumpboots. Pushing herself in the direction of the Chiata and over backwards crotch first into its throat, her bodyweight, and that of the suit, forced the alien onto its back with a *thud* against the stone. As Dee landed she drove her blade through its chest, splitting it from sternum to balls, if the thing had them. She wasn't sure and she didn't really give a fuck. It was dead. Time to move on to the next one.

The battlescape view in her mind collapsed on her rapidly as the three remaining red dots landed almost instantly on top of her within the engulfing flames. Dee jumped as hard as she could and fell over the edge of the ruin's top into the burning grass and vines at the edge of the road twenty meters below. Her wounds were taking a toll on her and landing hard against the ground knocked the wind out of her. Atop that, one of the Chiata landed feet first into her chest, knocking her completely off her feet and making a cracking noise in her back that was followed by spasm pains the likes of which she'd never felt before. All Dee could see was the alien's weapon being raised to her face. Time slowed for her just like in a pukin' deathblossom, and she turned her head and spun her left hand into the weapon, driving the knife blade through the wrist of the Chiata and severing its hand free.

The Chiata screeched and pounded her with its other hand, and several tendrils jutted out from the amorphous torso armor into her armor. But Dee wasn't stopping there. She popped the remaining grenade, caught it with her right hand, and punched it into the alien's neck, and lodged it into the seal where a helmet should be. She retracted her hand and pulled away as best she could.

Detonate it now, Bree!

The grenade blew out the alien's back and front, vaporizing the head in a fireball and throwing red and green molten bits against Dee at hypersonic speeds. Her suit mostly protected her but several fragments managed to tear through her armor into her body. She gasped for air and choked back blood as she coughed and wheezed and cried bloody tears. Suit alarms continued to ring in her ears and the diagnostic image showed catastrophic damage.

Shit, Bree. I think I'm done. Dee coughed again. *I can't feel my legs right now.*

Get up, Marine! her AIC shouted into her mind and

pumped more chemicals and immunoboost nanomachines into Dee's body, hoping to keep her moving. *Major Deanna Moore! Get up and fucking fight! Fight, Dee! Goddammit! Fight, Dee!*

Dee started to tunnel out, but the drugs were holding their own against her wounds. The organogel flowed into the open tears in her circulatory system, replacing missing plasma and blood with the specially developed organic fluids that coagulated rapidly over open wounds and flowed freely within her veins. The immunoboost machines raced through her body to repair critical lifesaving bits and the stimulants coursed through her like battery acid. But there was just too much damage to her body. Her will had been pushed beyond even superhuman breaking points and she was spent. The world spun for a microsecond and the thought of dying crossed her mind. Then an image of her father flashed before her.

"Up and at 'em! Quit your goldbricking, Marine! It is time to get up!" The image of General Alexander Moore filled her mindview at over three meters tall looming over her. "Move it, princess! Get your ass up!"

"Up and at 'em! Quit your goldbricking, Marine! It is time to get up!" The image of General Alexander Moore continued at a higher volume. "Move it, princess! Get your ass up!"

Dee could see the red dots of the two remaining Chiata moving toward her and in the mindview she realized that she had made her last jump off the top of the ruin with purpose. The icon for her blaster lay in the burning grass only a meter from her. It might as well have been a kilometer. She couldn't move her legs at all. She was stuck in place and those two Chiata were coming for her. She was going to die.

"Up and at 'em! Quit your goldbricking, Marine! It is time to get up!" The image of her father continued. "Move it, princess! Get your ass up!"

"Move it, princess! Get your ass up!"

"Move it, princess! Get your ass up!"

"Move it, princess! Get your ass up!"

Dee couldn't let her father down. She couldn't give up, but she couldn't move either. She searched the mindview for anything that would help. If she could just reach that damned blaster. She reached out with her left hand but felt something against her chest and instantly her mindview filled with an image of herself from above. Dee could see one of the little skyballs at the top of the burning tree canopy. The image from it zoomed in on her. The Chiata she had just blown in half was laid out across her legs, covering her in blood and putting off bright pinks and blues in the burning flames. As the image zoomed closer on her chest, Dee smiled inwardly.

"I'm not going to fucking die right now!" She bit the bite block for another burst of stims and air and with one last push of all that she had left, Dee grabbed the alien plasma rifle with the severed hand that was lying and drooling green fluid across her chest still attached to it. She raised the muzzle upwards and looked for a red targeting X to appear in her mind. There were two. She squeezed the alien's trigger finger against the trigger mechanism. Blue plasma bolts shot out from the weapon into the first Chiata, taking it by surprise and dropping it.

She quickly tracked the last one and dropped it as well. The alien bolts were apparently better at shutting down the barrier shields than the HVARs were. She fired several more rounds at the downed bodies just to make sure, and then she was spent.

Bree, are we clear? Dee asked as she laid the alien weapon across her chest.

Yes, Dee, for now. The skyball download doesn't show any traffic this way, right now, and we are still more than three hours from the shift change here. Even if they deployed another search team we are hours from any Chiata locations.

Dee looked around her as best she could, but could barely move her head. So, she cycled back to the skyball view to get a better view of the area and the damage done. The fire was burning away from her as the vines were being cleared away. She was in no immediate danger other than possibly dying from her injuries. A hole burned away from the canopy of trees above her and Dee could see the night sky above her. The stars were bright enough that she could see them even in the firelight. She cycled the red filter and removed the flames from her view, and the stars stood out even better. She could see the Milky Way and her visor illuminated the locations of Sol, UM61, and the rendezvous point.

Dee wondered if the Fleet was there and if her family was alright. She wondered if she'd ever get off this fucking planet and be safe again. She wanted to go home even if home meant the inside of a starship. She wanted to hug her mother and cry on her shoulder and have her mother tell her that everything was going to be alright. She wanted to hug her father and thank him for willing her to stay alive. She wanted the pain to stop and wanted her body to feel strong again. She wanted the feeling back in her lower body, but for now, at least her legs weren't hurting.

For all of that to happen, Dee knew that somehow, some way, no matter what it took, that she'd have to stay alive and get home. She had to get home because she knew she wanted to see Davy Rackman at least once more. She knew she had to see him so she could tell him how she felt about him. She meant to really tell him and not pussyfoot around the issue and chicken out this time. She had to tell him she loved him. She just had to stay alive. She'd come all that way to do something that might help save humanity and all she'd done was get herself shot down and shot up. Just maybe, she thought, if she could stay alive, there was still more she could do. Maybe there was more, but she had to stay alive. Dee brought the suit health monitor page up and looked at the damage. The suit was barely holding her together and many of its systems were offline.

"If it's all the same to you, Bree," she gurgled audibly through blood in her throat. "I'm just gonna lay here a while and look at the stars."

Chapter 26

February 19, 2407 AD
U.S.S. Roscoe Hillenkoetter
Hyperspace, 7.25 Light Days from
  Target Star System
700 Light-years from the Sol System
Monday, 10:47 P.M. Ship Standard Time

"At our current speed we should be back in system within two hours, ma'am." Commander Davy Rackman stood beside his console on the bridge of the *Hillenkoetter* debating what his next move should be. He'd already volunteered to lead the ground team to rescue Dee, but the General had nixed that idea. They were going to drop search-and-rescue crews with no other mecha support to minimize the risk of losing more pilots. Rackman didn't like the decision, but he was a soldier, he'd deal with it.

"Commander, I'd like a word with you in my ready

room," Captain Penzington told him, and turned to the Air Boss clone. "Zander, you have the bridge."

"Yes, ma'am," the clone replied. Davy turned as the Captain stood and clanked her way to the exit. He followed her, not sure what all this was about.

Out the exit and down two doors to the right they entered the Captian's ready room, or office. Davy liked how the bot-built ships that Sienna Madira had designed were all built upscaled to accommodate everyone wearing body armor suits. Supercarriers of the Separatist Wars were gigantic to start with, but the new ones that the bots were building had been scaled by at least fifteen percent in every dimension to accommodate for three-meter-tall armored soldiers running about as if they were in UCUs. The lady, whether or not she was crazy, had a flare for being prepared. Captian Penzington clanked in behind the oversized desk and sat back in the big, beefy chair. Davy stood at ease but remained silent. This was her show.

"Commander, I'm going to take you up on an offer you made me to lead some wet work," Captain Penzington told him.

"Ma'am. I'd be pleased and more than honored."

"There are plenty of clones that can jump in and do the X.O. job in your stead right now. Don't take that the wrong way," Penzington started, but looked to make sure she hadn't insulted him. Davy wasn't insulted and understood exactly what she meant. "But I really need a seasoned combat veteran who can lead the attack into the Chiata ship once we ram it. I'd prefer that person be a combat veteran I trust. I've seen you in action for more than two years now and I'd prefer you lead that team."

"Yes, ma'am." Davy's heart fluttered a beat or two. He'd be much happier leading a strike team into the belly of the beast rather than sitting up on the bridge moving icons around on a virtual battlescape getting bounced around like a monkey strapped into a carnival ride.

"I'm uploading the team roster and battle plan as designed by the General's team and the various ship captains. If you want to make any changes or additions you'll have to hurry. As you know, we're only a couple hours out." Captain Penzington raised her chin in a slight nod to the Navy SEAL and then sighed. "Davy, you and I both would prefer to go down there and save her. I'd like nothing more. But I think this is how we contribute to that rescue."

"Yes, ma'am. I understand." Rackman thought about what the Captain was telling him and agreed. "Major Moore can take care of herself, ma'am. I'm sure you believe that too. I've seen it firsthand. We just need to give her the opportunity to make a move and she'll come through. She comes from good stock."

"I hope you're right," Captain Penzington said through a forced and very subdued smile. "Okay then, get your team ready. We take the parts of the ship mapped out by the CHENG and protect the builder and repair bots at all costs. Damage to the other parts of the ship and Chiata are of no concern provided said damage is not in conflict with the missions of the other teams. Is that understood, Mr. Rackman?"

"Yes, ma'am," he replied with a salute. Captain Penzington returned the salute, and with that, Davy was dismissed to his new mission to kill alien monsters and protect robots. It was one hell of a Navy day in space.

Chapter 27

February 19, 2407 AD
U.S.S. Sienna Madira
Hyperspace, 7.25 Light Days from
  Target Star System
700 Light-years from the Sol System
Monday, 10:47 P.M. Ship Standard Time

"Just stop it right now, Alexander," Sehera Moore told him. Alexander looked at his wife and knew that there was no use. Besides, it was too late to send her back now anyway. "I'm not having the same conversation twice in one day, especially while our daughter is stranded out there and needing our help."

"Sehera, I'm not having the same conversation." Alexander turned from her and looked out the window of their quarters at the hyperspace vortex. The brilliant purples and pinks from the Cerenkov radiation were always calming to him. He let out a long sigh. Sehera was right. It was moot to argue with her. "I just hate the idea of us both going right back into a mess of trouble when at least one of us could have stayed back in safety and returned with the remainder of the Fleet. This attack, well, it is crazy even by my standards."

"If it were truly crazy, Alexander, you wouldn't be doing it." Sehera carefully stepped in behind her husband and placed an armored gauntlet on his shoulder. "While what you do may seem crazy to others or to history or to most sane people, they don't have the benefit of knowing just how precise, concise, and calculated each of your crazy actions is. You and my mother are so much alike in that regard. No, this is just what we have to do or you would have thought of something else. We are doing what we must and there is no way I would be anywhere else than by your side as always."

"As always," he said, thin-lipped, not trying to give away how much his heart was aching in fear of losing either of the women in his life. He knew he couldn't hide his emotions from her, so he just looked at her with nothing more to say.

"You'll need me anyway. The medical staff is so overwhelmed, as half of them had to go with the critical wounded in the returning ships. I hope the hyperspace jaunt isn't too far before the teleportations start working."

"Buckley and Snow are guessing a month at least in hyperspace." Alexander said dismissively. "That's a long month. We have that to look forward to after all this."

"We will make it through this." Sehera pulled at his shoulder, turning him to her. "Look at me, Alexander."

"Yes." He turned and looked at what he could see of his wife's face through the open visor. Her helmet retracted and stowed over her shoulder taking him off guard slightly. "You should keep your helmet on just in case. The General's orders."

"I will, General," she said. "But not just yet."

"I see, insubordination." Alexander smiled at his wife.

"I'm not in the military, so I don't actually answer to this General of yours," she said.

"Is that right," Alexander smirked and popped his helmet seal, and the armored brain bucket retracted and stowed away over his right shoulder. "Come here, you."

As carefully as he could, Alexander wrapped his armored arms around his armored wife and cautiously and a bit awkwardly leaned in and kissed her lips as passionately as the situation would allow. While the motion was cumbersome and clumsy, the sentiment wasn't. It was easier for the two of them to touch foreheads, and so they held that way for a long moment without saying a word. It was a long moment of just being with each other that both of them needed and had yet to have since Dee had been shot down. It was a long moment that allowed them to feed on each other's strength—a strength that had taken them through some very trying events. They would come through this together.

"She'll be okay when we get there," Alexander whispered.

"Of course she will," his wife whispered in return. "It is the only way I can see it and still function."

"Me too, baby."

Uh, sir, I hate to interrupt, but DeathRay is requesting an audience with you, Abigail said in his mind.

Tell him to come to my quarters, Alexander thought.

Uh, sir, he is outside your door now.

Oh, I see. Alexander opened his eyes and raised his forehead and looked at his wife's face, taking in every single freckle on her pale skin, her deep brown eyes, the corners of her eyelids that were only beginning to wrinkle as it had been ten or more years since her last rejuv, and the few dark hairs that had become unkempt and hung loosely from her forehead. He took in all of the detail and reminded himself of just how beautiful she looked at that moment and how exactly like that she had looked a century ago as she rescued him from the torture camps on Mars. She'd been through that with him and she had to go through this with him. Alexander sighed.

"What is it?" she asked.

"Boland is at my door. No doubt wanting to discuss the flight surgeon having grounded him for thirty-six hours," Alexander replied. "Got to get back to work."

"I should get back as well. We are moving the triage to the forward hangars and I should get back and help." Sehera reached up and retightened the ponytail of her long, jet-black Martian hair, and then tucked it back in as she deployed her helmet. "I love you, Alexander."

"I love you, Sehera. Stay out of trouble, please." He turned toward his chamber door and watched as his wife clanked through it.

"Jack." Sehera nodded to the pilot as she walked by him on her way out.

"Ma'am." Boland stepped aside and nodded to her as if tipping his helmet.

"Come in, Jack," Alexander said. "What can I do for you?"

"Sir," Jack saluted him. Alexander returned the salute and relaxed his posture a bit.

"At ease, Jack. It's just us in here. Say whatever it is and let's get on with it." Alexander wasn't in the mood for formality. He was in the mood to get this crazy-assed mission on with and to get his people, his daughter, to safety, and while he'd like to just go home whether they found some secret superweapon or tactic or jack shit, he knew he couldn't do that without making a statement to the enemy. They had spent too much time getting their asses handed to them and he was getting tired of that. The Chiata had to think of them as pushovers. Well that time had come and gone. It was time to show the Chiata what they were up against.

"Well, sir, as you probably know, because I managed to let myself get shot up, the surgeon has grounded me," Jack stated. "I truly apologize for that, sir."

"Let me stop you right there." Alexander held up a hand. "While I may disagree with the regs, the doctor, or even if I don't care, Jack, I'm not going to adversely impact our morale at this point by overriding, or attempting to override, a flight surgeon's decision."

"Uh, no, sir, I wouldn't think of it." Jack frowned, but with one corner of his mouth upturned into half a smile with a raised eyebrow. "Sir, as far as I can tell, there's not much flying to do on this mission anyway. Not without risk of putting more pilots stranded in this godforsaken star system, there isn't."

"Then what can I do for you, Jack?" Alexander sized the CAG up and could tell he was up to something.

"Well, sir, the flight surgeon's orders are very specific,

sir." Jack hemmed and hawed to the point that Alexander was almost getting impatient, but he had nearly two hours of just waiting to do anyway. "And I quote, sir, 'Due to the extensive injuries sustained by U.S. Navy Aviator Captain Jack "DeathRay" Boland,' that's me, sir, 'he is currently suspended from all flight duties for thirty-six hours mandatory for medical recovery. Upon which time he will be subject to a flight physical, whereas he may be, at the attending flight surgeon's discretion, returned to flight status.' Unquote, sir. That is what it says in the log, sir."

"Jack, again, what would you have me do?" Alexander could tell that Boland had an angle but he wasn't exactly sure how acute it was. "Spit it out, Jack."

"Well, sir, my records say nothing about ground duty." Jack looked Alexander in the eye with his deadly serious let's-go-kill-those-motherfuckers look and Alexander knew exactly where he was going with it.

Abby? Double check. Is he right?

Yes, sir, whether the surgeon missed it or not, there are no stipulations on ground service for Captain Jack Boland.

He's a clever sonofabitch, ain't he?

Yes, sir.

"I see, Jack. The records certainly do not say anything about ground duty." Alexander paused.

"Yes, sir." Jack stood at attention. "Captain Jack Boland volunteering to lead a team to find the Chiata megaship's bridge and take it, General."

"Jack, before I send you off on such a mission, volunteer or not, I need to know two things," Alexander said. He squared his shoulders to the man and looked him in the eye. "Number one, are you one hundred and fifty percent certain you are fit enough to take on combat duty right now?"

"Sir, you know as well as I do that the injuries are completely healed physically. Just ask your wife, sir. She's the one that fixed me up. The mandatory leave is for emotional and psychological stuff. I'm fine, sir. Yes, sir," Jack replied, thumping his right gauntleted hand against his armored chest.

"And number two, Jack, I don't want you doing this in any way feeling like you are repaying some sort of guilt or debt for Dee. I'm the CO. I ordered the combat operation. I am solely responsible for the results of the mission. End of story." Alexander judged Jack's facial expression as best he could, but Jack was as good a poker player as he was. "I mean this, Jack. Dee's predicament is what it is and is a consequence of combat. If you are going to do this, it needs to be for the right intentions and in the right mindset."

"Sir, I, uh, no, sir. That is not the reason. While I am Dee's squadron leader, her wingman, her friend, and dammit sir, almost a brother to her, I don't want to do this out of guilt. I want to do this because I'm the right man for this job and because I can improve the odds that we come out on the up side of this thing and we do get our people back home safely as one of the outcomes." Jack took a deep breath and looked back at Alexander. He was as sincere and hardcore as Alexander had ever seen the man.

He'd have made a good marine, Alexander thought.

Yes, sir. Abigail replied. *If you say so, sir. When you*

get a moment, the CHENG wants to go over something with you.

In a moment. Alexander looked at DeathRay, who clearly had more to say.

"Anything else, Jack?"

"Well, sir, I just wanted to say that we have lost too many people today, sir. And it's about fucking time for us to just go in there in kill every last one of those alien motherfuckers!"

"Assemble your team, Captain." Alexander nodded. "You have less than two hours."

"Yes, sir!"

Chapter 28

February 19, 2407 AD
Northern Region
Alien Planet, Target Star System
700 Light-years from the Sol System
Tuesday, 12:03 A.M. Ship Standard Time

It wasn't so much the pain any longer, because the pain had mostly subsided to a level that Dee could manage, but what troubled her most was that she'd been lying in the same spot for almost three hours bouncing in and out of consciousness, sleep, dreams, and thoughts and still wasn't sure she would be able to do anything more to help herself. She still couldn't move her legs no matter how much she focused her mind on the task. They just wouldn't move. The organogel and immunoboost had stabilized her vital signs, healed most of the critical wounds, and were now moving forward with fixing even the superficial ones, but her legs still were nonfunctional.

That was most likely due to the piece of alien body armor lodged in her spine just above the L4 lumbar vertebra. Dee looked through the mindview three-dimensional diagnostic of her body and suit and could see the material fragment that was the culprit. It was an alien metal that was tougher than the suit systems had dealt with in the past. The immunoboost was having a hard time dissolving the alien metal and therefore her spinal cord was cut off from her lower extremities.

Deanna Moore looked up past her mindview of her body at the stars as she fluttered into a more awakened state. The running clock in her mindview troubled her in that it likely wouldn't be more than a half hour or so before she'd be dealing with company again. She had to get up and start to figure out her situation. Perhaps the Chiata weren't coming for her again. Just maybe they wouldn't send another search party after her. She didn't really believe that.

Besides, curiosity was getting to her about the inside of the alien ruin and those damned beetles. Dee knew that this was as important for humanity as anything. She just knew it. Don't ask her how or why she knew it, but somehow, deep down she knew that she needed to figure out what the ruins were all about and she was probably closer to doing that than any other members of the Expeditionary Fleet. So, the job was hers.

"Shit. I've got to get up, Bree," she said faintly with a slight grunt. "My legs are still gone."

I can function the legs in the suit following your motion actions and your brainwave patterns. The damage to your body is done and isn't going to get worse or better until that alien metal is removed, her AIC told her in her mind. *Just intend to walk normally and I will keep you upright. If there is more pain, tell me and I will add more pain meds.*

I really don't want any more meds. The stims have my head pounding like I have a helluva hangover. There's a damned mecha convoy traversing from one ear to the other and around the front on a continuous loop. Anything we can do for that? Dee thought.

Drink more water, Bree told her. *I'll administer more fluids and electrolytes into your system. I would have thought the pain meds would help with that, but there is a saturation point.*

"Saturation point, my ass. Unnhh, damn, here goes nothing." Dee pulled her armored hands from the Chiata rifle that rested across her chest and pushed her elbows underneath herself. She grunted as she pushed upright. She looked about and then down at herself and realized the headless Chiata body was still draped across her legs. Instinctively, she kicked her feet and jerked her knees upwards to make the alien body roll off, but nothing happened. Her legs just simply didn't respond. The headless and mangled alien body still lay draped across her.

She leaned forward and felt a tightness in her lower back, but not pain, and grabbed the armor around the alien's torso and used the strength of the suit to roll the carcass off her. She looked to her left and then right and saw the M-blaster in the burned vines only a couple steps away. She had been so close to it all along. With hindsight, she actually preferred the alien's rifle. It packed a bigger punch than her blaster or HVAR.

"I'm standing up, Bree," she said. An outside observer looking at Dee would not have been able to tell that she wasn't getting up on her own accord, but Dee knew. She felt awkward and off balance the entire time and felt as if she would fall over.

Don't worry, Dee, Bree assured her in her mindvoice. *I've got you. I will not let you fall.*

Is there a way I can reach that shrapnel myself? Dee reached behind her back but could only feel a hardened lump of suit seal scabbed over there. *I'll cut it out myself if it will help.*

I'm afraid not, Dee. It is deep in and lodged into the bone. You need a surgeon to remove it since the nanomachines cannot seem to dissolve it.

I was afraid of that, Dee thought. *Better hope I don't have to do any real fighting again.*

I agree.

"Shit. We've got to get off this fucking planet."

Deanna attached the alien firearm across her chest. The weight of it was different than the standard issue hypervelocity automatic rifle that Marines were issued. The weight was even stranger considering the fact that she had to keep the severed alien hand wrapped around the trigger mechanism in order for her to fire the weapon. It was fairly gruesome, and Dee actually hoped the sight of it might give the alien bastards a bit of pause before they fucked with her again. She doubted it though.

"Alright, what first, then?" She looked down at the dead alien at her feet and then over at her blaster. She decided to pick up the blaster as a test of Bree's walking and motion control support. Bree anticipated her movements well, Dee thought. The two of them had been together since she had been a teen so they knew each other very intimately. They had been there for each other over the years as best internal friends. AIC-to-human relationships became close because the two shared thoughts that nobody else in the universe would ever hear. So, it didn't seem like a big stretch that Bree could anticipate and help make Dee's walking movements. Even so, the walking still felt awkward to Dee because she was along for the ride and not piloting, but the motion itself was fluid and seamless.

Dee leaned over and picked up the blaster with her right hand. The suit bent perfectly at the knees to allow her to squat and then it managed to raise her back upright. Dee twirled the blaster with her right hand and then slapped it into place on her thigh. She didn't feel the click of the holster extending, the click of the blaster into place, or the snap of the holster closing. She heard it all and could see it, but there was no tactile response from her body. It felt weird and isolated.

"Not bad," she said. "Not great either."

She hit the water tube in her helmet for a short burst to quench some of her thirst. The pounding in her head was still there, but it was getting better. She turned back toward the headless alien body and grabbed it by the foot with her left hand. She dragged the body across the charred black vines, occasionally stirring up red and orange embers, and small flames would spring to life, but the vines were for the most part burned away. She continued to drag the body, and the alien armor screeched, metal against stone, on the roadway underneath. The eerie screeching noise caused the local wildlife to hold deathly quiet and still. Dee pulled the body across the road to the nearest of the beetle mounds and then deployed her knife blade from the left gauntlet forearm slot. The blade shot out and locked in place with a zinging sound, and Dee quickly sliced through the alien's leg at what she assumed was the knee. There was little blood left in the creature's mangled corpse, but Dee hoped there'd be enough.

"Well, here goes nothing." She tossed the leg over on top of the beetle mound and waited. But she didn't have to wait very long.

Hundreds of the beetles poured over the edge of the mound and onto the Chiata's body part, devouring it almost instantly. Quickly, Dee knelt down and grabbed at one of the beetles about the back. She missed it. The damned things were very fast. She grabbed at one and had it between her thumb and forefinger, but as soon as she grabbed it, the bug turned itself around within its own skeleton and stuck a five-centimeter proboscis through the armor in her glove and into her hand.

"Ouch! What the fuck!" Dee stood up and flung herself backwards awkwardly, shaking her hand trying to free the beetle from it. The beetle wouldn't let go and it pulled itself closer to her hand with its legs and mandibles. "Bree!?"

Calm yourself, Dee, Bree told her. *I'm analyzing it now.*

Do I yank it free or what? Dee did her best to stay calm. Just what she needed was to be paralyzed even further by some alien toxin.

Dee, you are not being injected with venom of any sort. Relax. I think it is taking blood samples from you, Bree told her. Then the proboscis retracted and the bug sat still on her hand.

Dee stood motionless for a long pause and took in a deep breath. Then, cautiously, she looked at the alien beetle that sat motionlessly in the palm of her right hand. She zoomed in on it with the visor instruments, and at max zoom she wasn't so sure that the creature was actually biological, or at least not completely.

This thing might be a bot, she thought.

That would make sense, Bree agreed. *Now what is our play? The clock is ticking, Dee.*

Right. Let's go. Dee turned toward the ruin entranceway with her new friend resting comfortably in the palm of her gauntlet.

As she pressed into the ruin the awkwardness of walking was becoming less and less a problem. Dee was getting more of the hang of letting the suit walk for her, but she still felt really strange with each step. There was no feedback from her feet and legs to tell her she'd made the steps and motions she was making, and it was actually overwhelming to her mind. Even when walking mecha in bot mode, the mind received sensor information that was passed through the body's nerve endings and sensory points. Walking with no feedback just felt odd.

Odd or not, she was making it work. Finally, she made it back into the large cavernous room with all of the dead Chiata stuck to the force field and the wall covered with the alien glyphs. The floodlights from her suit illuminated the large room with bright white light, causing long shadows to move about with each of her movements. The rapidly moving shadows kept her on edge, not sure if one of the Chiata was going to spring to life and jump out at her from the shadows. Dee just kept telling herself to stay frosty.

She centered herself in front of the wall with the largest set of ellipses and curves and the one marked as what Dee interpreted to be representative of the ruin she was standing in. At least she hoped she was reading it right. The picture of the star system and planets matched and the continents on the planet matched. As far as she could tell, the wall was pointing out the ruin she was standing in. It looked like the Chiata had figured the same thing out as well, but they had taken that information to their grave.

"Here goes nothing," she said, and carefully picked up the beetle with her left hand and placed it against the divot in the stone wall that looked like it had been carved out just for the alien bug-bot.

Dee held it in place and pressed it against the wall. Nothing happened. She pressed it harder against the wall and still nothing happened.

"Damnit! I thought that was going to work." She wasn't sure what to do next.

I thought it might as well, Bree agreed. *Don't give up. We will figure this out.*

Right. We WILL.

Dee started to retract her hand from the wall, but the beetle didn't move from its place, and then she realized that she couldn't remove her hand from around the bug. She was stuck in place, and the horrific looks on the decaying Chiatas' faces stood out in her mind. Had she been trapped only to die in place, never to be let go?

Bree! I can't remove my hand! she thought in a panic, and with each pull of her hand she seemed to be stuck even tighter to the wall. *I'm stuck!*

Calm down, Marine. Calm down!

Then a ripple of blue and white started to form around the periphery of the bug and Dee's hand. The wall rippled like she had dropped a stone in a puddle. The waves splashed outward across the wall and built up in width and depth. A cone of white light sprayed outward around Dee's hand and filled the room, blinding her momentarily and saturating the suit's sensors.

There was a frying bacon sound, and more dancing whites and blues and arcs of light and ripples of quantum foam churning about her. And then it was dark. It was completely dark, wherever she was.

What happened to the floods, Bree?

The suit diagnostics say that they are still operating within normal parameters. They're on, Dee.

Bullshit. It's dark in here. And I still can't move anything.

Chapter 29

February 19, 2407 AD
U.S.S. Sienna Madira
Target Star System
700 Light-years from the Sol System
Tuesday, 12:47 A.M. Ship Standard Time

Sir, I'm not receiving Dee's blue force tracker ping at all, Abigail said in Alexander's mind.

Keep looking.

Yes, sir, but it is like she isn't even on the planet.

Keep fucking looking.

Yes, sir.

"Fullback, keep those bastards off our nose and lay down cover until you can't lay it down any longer!" Alexander ordered over the Fleet-wide open tac-net. His four ships were in tight formation, cruising like Orcas looking for the right seal to pounce on, all the while Admiral Walker led the remaining eighteen supercarriers out a few tens of thousands of kilometers ahead, creating a perimeter in front of them and using their hyperspace jaunts effectively to disrupt the Chiata formations. "As soon as we pick our prey, you start jaunting all ships at a once to a chosen singular target. Just like we planned."

"Roger that, General! Good hunting!" Walker replied and cut from the net. Alexander looked at the mission clock in his mindview and noted that they'd been in system less than two minutes and the Chiata were already responding with heavy resistance.

"Alright, let's find our target!" Moore pulled up the DTM battlescape of the system and started looking for the right response tactic. There were over twenty Chiata megaship porcusnails already responding to their attack, and he expected more would show up soon enough. In fact, he was counting on it. Alexander twisted the ball around in his mind until he found the enemy ship he wanted to go for. "That one right there!"

Abby, transfer those coordinates to the Fleet.

Done, sir.

"Why that one, General?" the XO asked. From the contorted look on her face, she was clearly studying over the DTM battlescape in her mind, trying to understand the logic from the General's decision.

"Because it is dead center of the ball right now. If this shit works out, that is right where we want to be." Alexander explained and then he toggled the channel on the net to ship internal. "All hands, all hands, this is General Moore. Prepare for a short jaunt and then an impact on the aft section of ship. We are on the attack! Moore out."

"Sir, all ships in Alpha wave are ready for jaunt." The Nav said.

"Well, don't waste time telling me about it, Nav! Go!" Alexander watched as the vortex spun up in front of them, and then as soon as they were in hyperspace they were out and only a few tens of kilometers from one of the porcusnails.

"Blue beams, General!" the STO shouted. Alexander held tightly to his chair and waited but the beams didn't hit the *Madira*. Instead, several of the Admiral Walker's Beta wave popped into reality space at just the right moment to draw the enemy fire. "Yeah! The *Thatcher* is drawing their fire, sir!"

"Damn good, Fullback!" Alexander smiled. The plan was working so far. "Nav, you know what to do! Let's ass-end the bastards!"

"Aye, sir!"

"Gunnery Officer Banks."

"Sir?"

"Target that shield generator with everything we've got and soften it up," Alexander ordered. "I want that spot soft when we ass-end it."

"Aye, sir."

"General!" the Air Boss looked up from his station. "The search and rescue teams have been dropped, sir. Full stealth and decoys. So far, all resistance is staying on the main attack waves."

"Good. Keep me posted." Alexander turned back to his mindview, but the Air Boss wasn't finished.

"Uh, sir," the Air Boss continued. "We have no location ping on Major Moore. I'm not sure where to send the SARs team for her extraction."

Abby?

No, sir, still no ping. She simply is not there, or is being cloaked or has her transmitters turned off. None of those solutions seem to make sense.

Alexander wasn't sure what to do. While he wanted to give Dee every opportunity to escape, he also couldn't just send a team to a random location on the planet's surface and hope that they guessed right. He couldn't send them in if he didn't know where to send them. He had to wait and hope that whatever was happening, Dee would find her way on top of it in the end.

"Have them support the first team then. We'll deal with Major Moore once we find her," he said reluctantly.

"Yes, sir." Alexander could tell the Air Boss didn't really like the order either.

"Impact on enemy shield generators in fifteen seconds, sir!" the Nav shouted excitedly.

"All DEG batteries direct hits on target, sir!"

Alexander watched out the viewport, on multiple screens and in his mindview of the battlescape as the *Madira* accelerated the last few kilometers toward the alien megaship. Smaller spires were firing plasma weapons from the surface of the ship, which were redirected by the Buckley-Freeman barrier shields. They were too close for the megaship to use the blue beams of death from Hell on them, but twice the large tuning fork belched forth lightning blasts of the blue beams into Admiral Walker's formation of supercarriers. Several of the other alien ships were firing their beams as well. Alexander could see in his mindview that Walker's formation formed a phalanx and drove at a single Chiata megaship. All of the weapons of the supercarriers in the formation focused on the one alien porcusnail and before the ship could generate a targeting solution, it burst at the middle, exploded into a large orange and white plasma ball, and ripped from bow to stern in a fiery death.

"Yes!" Alexander cheered under his breath. "Go Fullback!"

As instantly as the alien ship exploded, the entire Beta attack wave vanished into hyperspace and reappeared seconds later on the opposite side of the ball. Alexander nodded in approval of the execution of the plan.

He quickly zoomed in on his target and noted that the *Hillenkoetter* had already rammed the ship on the opposite side. The two clone ships hitting the megaship on the aft section generators were within seconds to impact. As far as Alexander could tell, the *Hillenkoetter's* shields and hull plating had held up during impact. Mr. Buckley's calculations had been spot-on and the supercarriers could not only take a beating but could dish one out.

"Ten seconds to impact!" the Nav announced. "Nine, eight, seven,"

"Brace!" Firestorm shouted.

"Six, five, four . . ."

Alexander clenched his teeth against his mouthpiece and clutched his gauntlets around the chair arms. He wasn't sure but he thought he felt the metal give way under his grip because he was holding on so tightly.

"Three, two, one, impact!"

The shields of the supercarrier generated a quantum uncertainty field that caused energy and matter to be redirected randomly at the potential barrier location. As the alien ship's shield system, which appeared to function in a very similar manner, made contact with the Buckley-Freeman shield, each of the fields did their best to redirect the energy vector of the other into random directions. It became a fight of uncertainties as to which shield would hold. In the end, it was the barrier shield that was able to generate the thickest potential barrier that won out, and that meant the one with the most energy density in the area of impact.

Alexander watched the numbers and graphs and diagnostics in his mindview. He and the CHENG had gone over the simulation many times and he hoped that real life would work as well. The plan was to put all the energy from the hyperspace projector into the shields at the instant of impact and hope they could overpower the alien's shields, especially after having weakened them with the DEGs on the attack run. Just like in the simulation, the shields of the *Madira* held and the generator on the alien ship buckled and exploded as the barrier came into contact with the structure. The barrier shield tore against the super-hard alien alloys and dispersed them in spacetime, with an ionizing ball of plasma forming in its wake. The entirety of the rear section of the supercarrier pushed into the alien ship dragging hull plating, conduits, and a sundry of other alien technology down as it did. Metal against metal vibrated and resonated throughout both ships and fires began to break out along the aft sections of the *Madira*.

But the shields held.

"CHENG to CO!"

"Go, Joe." Alexander kept his grip tight on the chair arms but eased up on his gritted teeth.

"The shields are holding, General! I'm ready to release the bots on your command." Buckley said excitedly over the net. Alexander thought his excitement was well warranted.

"Nav! Are we full stop?" Alexander asked.

"Aye, sir! All progress full stop!"

"XO, let's give the Chiata bastards a present."

"Yes, sir!"

Firestorm turned to his console, and both he and the Ground Boss began giving orders over the net for the shipboard teams to deploy into the alien ship and start bringing hell. Alexander watched the battlescape as the aft hangar doors opened and the shields were dropped. The first line of attack were hovertanks in tank mode and they instantly started blasting away at the interior of the alien ship. Alongside the tanks a river of buzz-saw bots flowed into the ship, programmed to seek out any Chiata and fight them to the last rivet. Behind the battle bots were two teams of armored soldiers. The first team was back up to the bots and numbered at almost one thousand. Alexander had taken ground troops from the clone ships to support the numbers needed for the ship-to-ship assault. The second team had twenty-five soldiers in it being led by DeathRay. Moore followed the action in the battlescape and noted how Jack was biding his time, and waiting for the tanks and bots to create openings in the Chiata defense before he pressed inward. But all things considered, the plan seemed to have caught the Chiata with their pants down and it was working.

"Alright, Mr. Buckley, it is time to release the bots."

Chapter 30

February 19, 2407 AD
U.S.S. Roscoe Hillenkoetter
Target Star System
700 Light-years from the Sol System
Tuesday, 12:51 A.M. Ship Standard Time

"Push the tanks forward and keep on them for cover!" Commander Davy Rackman shouted over the net at the Franklin clone leading the tank squadron and the Malcolm clone leading the armored environment-suit marines. Davy ducked just in time as a blue plasma ball separated a buzz-saw bot from its blade. The blade flew between him and the clone, only missing them by centimeters. "Holy shit! Move!"

The Franklin clone dropped back down into the tank and closed the hatch and Rackman spread himself out flat in prone position just to the right of the big gun, bringing his HVAR up and blasting on full auto as his targeting Xs turned red in his visor. A red and green blur roared up the middle of the corridor, slinging the bots off of it in every direction in sparks and pieces. The Chiata trooper was formidable and laid waste to several of the bots. But the bots were too numerous for the single Chiata, and it started to stagger. The armor on the alien started to flicker, suggesting that its shield generators were being pushed to the limits. Rackman put a red X right dead center of the creature's head and released several rounds. The hypervelocity rounds *spittap*ped out of the weapon and ionized the air in their path all the way up to and through the alien's head. The blur stopped dead in its tracks. Green viscous fluid was sprayed across the sea of killer battlebots as it fell. The bots simply moved on to the next target once they realized that their current one was dead.

"Franklin, we need to keep moving on this route. The CHENG's map cuts right and down in about fifty meters." Rackman highlighted the map in the clone tank-driver's head. "And we need to be laying down better suppressive fire. I'm tired of these damned bots getting blown up all around us."

"Roger that, Commander Rackman," the clone replied. "If we get stuck, just say the word and I'll blast us a new doorway."

"Right," Davy said and then nodded at the AEM clone nearest him. "Keep that flank clear. I don't want one of those fucking blurs to come zipping through a hatch or dropping down on top of us. Eyeballs peeled!"

He looked to his right and over his shoulder and could see tanks two and three behind them, making a Vformation. Several other tanks were further back protecting their rear and the builder bots as they started in on their important tasks.

Where the *Hillenkoetter* had rammed into the alien ship had created an impact zone the width of the supercarrier and several false bulkheads deep. Where the aft end of the ship had finally come to a stop was a large cavernous hangar-sized room that looked like a hurricane had hit it during an atomic bomb test. Bulkheads were collapsed and crushed and bent metal dangled about from every structure. Sparks and fires flashed at every corner of the area and there were multiple conduits that appeared to have ruptured and were venting plasma jets. What once was likely a pristine area of the alien ship became a disaster area after the supercarrier rammed it. Davy looked behind him and could see the extreme aft end of the *Hillenkoetter* jutting out into the room, and tanks, bots, and AEMs deployed almost continuously into the Chiata megaship.

They were on the port side just forward of the giant blue-beam tuning forks. There was a cavernous room that led to multiple corridors heading off in multiple directions. Davy led them along the corridor that had the least amount of distance between the power source and the impact zone. The STO and the CHENG were using instruments aboard the *Hillenkoetter* and in conjunction with Commander Buckley on the *Madira* to guide the team to the target power source. He could only assume that the clones in the ships that attacked the aft sections were doing the same. He didn't have time to play armchair quarterback in his mindview.

Rackman pressed forward, down, and deeper into the alien ship. The corridor they had taken was just large enough that the three tanks could fit with a little room to spare on either side. There were clone AEMs on the tanks behind him and on foot, bouncing about, firing their rifles at targets of opportunity. Davy had expected heavier resistance, but so far they had only seen a few handfuls of Chiata ground troops. With the buzz-saw bots and tanks, the numbers had been on their side.

"Commander Rackman, my red force tracker cannot get a solid read on enemy numbers in here," the tank commander told him. "We could be leading ourselves into an ambush and not know it."

"Yeah, I don't like that either, Franklin, but what can we do about it? Just keep pressing forward. If we get caught up in an ambush, we'll deal with it then. That's why we brought tanks." Just as Davy made the statement, they turned the corner into a barricade covered with red and green blurs firing blue energy bolts at them, filling the void between them with bright flashes of ionization trails and molten materials as the bolts hit. A bolt caught the AEM Malcolm clone on the right of Davy square in the face. The clone never knew what had hit him. His shields held on the first shot, but the second one vaporized the clone's body from mid-torso up.

One of the red and green blurs rushed toward the center tank, firing a continuous barrage of blue plasma bolts. Rackman returned fire and tracked the blur as best he could, but it was just too fast for him to track. His hypervelocity rounds splattered behind the alien every step of the way. Then the alien dove forward firing, and one of the bolts hit the tank just beneath where Rackman was laying prone. The plasma burst against the forward shields of the tank and burned through to metal. The forward bulkhead of the tank glowed red hot but was undamaged otherwise. Davy, on the other hand had taken a faceful of the molten metal spray, and his helmet was peppered with pockmarks. His suit diagnostics and alerts started going off in his mindview.

"Screw this!" He ducked his head and popped a grenade from the shoulder launcher. The grenade *thawoomp*ed out of the tube and exploded at the feet of the Chiata attacker tossing it off balance but not killing it. Several battlebots jumped at the alien but it dodged, rolled, and at once stood up, grabbing one of the metal killer bots in its hands, and two tendrils of amorphous armor shot out from within the alien's torso and harpooned through the bot, destroying it.

"Shoot those bastards!" Rackman ordered as he rolled backwards off the tank and to his feet. Just as he came to rest on one knee, with his rifle firing full auto into the multiple advancing blurs, the big gun of the lead tank fired twice. The hundred millimeter rounds exploded against the barricade, throwing shrapnel, plasma, and alien body parts in every direction. Davy continued to fire as buzz saw bots poured in around them and crossed the barricade. Tanks two and three fired a round each into the alien barricade. The fighting didn't dwindle at that point. Instead, Chiata screamed as they fought to their last breath and more and more of them seemed to just crawl out from anywhere. Rackman kept pressing and pressing until their line finally broke.

✧ ✧ ✧

"Commander Rackman," Nancy monitored the team's progress in her DTM view while at the same time doing what she could to fight off the Chiata in the ball around them. "We need to be making faster progress."

"Yes, ma'am!" Rackman replied over the net. "We ran into a couple of snags along the way and the bastards are holed up and putting up some serious resistance. We've started taking on casualties, ma'am, and I'm afraid we're at a slow grind down here until we come up with a better plan or bigger guns. I've sent in the buzz-saw bots, wave after wave, but I think the Chiata have figured out how to neutralize them."

"Quit sending robots to do a SEAL's job, Commander," Nancy ordered him.

"Understood, ma'am. I'll keep you posted."

"We have to take this objective, Commander! Do you understand?"

"Yes, ma'am."

"Gunner, keep targeting and firing. I don't want you to stop until the DEGs overheat and melt, do you understand?"

"Yes, Captain." The Malcolm clone gunner continued operating his console emotionlessly and efficiently. Nancy counted up the ships that were still functional. In less than five minutes they had already lost two of the Beta group and several were approaching the questionable mark. The four that had rammed the megaship had done their jobs and were now fighting towards the interior of the alien ship with hopes of exploiting the latest Buckley maneuver. The builder bots were working feverishly right behind the buzz-saw bots and ground troops, pushing ever closer, centimeter by centimeter, toward the alien power sources.

"Captain, the Admiral just lost another ship." The Air Boss and acting XO announced. Nancy saw the ship in her mindview vanish from space through a hyperspace tube. It was damaged beyond fighting and all it could do was escape. They'd hopefully catch up with it at the rendezvous point after the battle.

At least they got away, Nancy thought to her AIC.

The Beta attack wave is taking a very severe beating, Allison told her. *According to my simulations, if they continue with the same attrition rate, they will not be able to hold off the Chiata for the full duration of time we will need in order to connect the shield generators to the megaship's power source.*

We need to tell that to the General, Nancy thought. *Perhaps we need a new tactic.*

I have already transferred this information to Abigail. She assures me the General has a plan.

Any idea what that plan is?

Yes, I do.

Well, don't leave me hanging. What is it?

DeathRay.

I see. Nancy both smiled and frowned inwardly at the same time.

Chapter 31

February 19, 2407 AD
U.S.S. Sienna Madira
Target Star System
700 Light-years from the Sol System
Tuesday, 12:55 A.M. Ship Standard Time

While the General had agreed to let DeathRay lead the ground teams into the alien ship with the goal of seeking out, capturing, and holding the bridge, he'd probably assumed that Jack was going to attack wearing just an armored suit. But Jack had decided to game the orders, perhaps, just a step farther than was actually within the spirit of them. While he had no intentions of doing any "flying" whatsoever inside an alien megaship, Jack had figured that he was safest and, more to the point, most lethal in his own mecha rather than in just a suit.

Once the first attack wave of tankheads, ground-pounders, and battlebots tore through the Chiata ship from the *Madira's* aft hangar, DeathRay led the second team right in behind them. But where the first team turned downward and aftward to find the power sources Jack's team turned up and aftward, headed for the little bump that stuck up between the blue-beam spires that was suspected of being the bridge.

DeathRay pounded forward in bot mode in his Ares-T fighter mecha, clanking hard against the alien deck plates and blasting holes through bulkheads rather than looking for alternative pathways to the objective. Jack had decided that the shortest distance between the two points, A, where he was, and, B, where he needed to be, was a straight line filled with explosives. Several of the Archangels followed behind him, pounding down the alien corridors and firing from the hip the large sixty millimeter plasma cannons at any of the Chiata that dared to blur in their general direction.

"Fish, you keep our six clear and blast the shit out of anything that doesn't ping blue force," DeathRay said to his second in command and former wingman. "We need to push through these bulkheads and up five floors at least."

"Roger that, DeathRay." Fish replied. Jack could see in his battlescape view that the bot-mode mecha of his squadron were moving swiftly in a diamond formation with Jack at the point and Fish at the rear in an Ares-T. The two side points of the diamond were filled with USMC Lieutenant Wiley "Bridge" Cruise and USMC Second Lieutenant Dimitri "Backup" Romanov, both piloting FM-12s. Several other mechas filled in the gaps of the formation. The mecha pilots burst through the alien corridors like bulls in a china shop, tearing away at everything they passed.

"Hold up!" Jack held up his giant bot hand as he came to a crossing in the corridor. He hugged the mecha back against the wall, bringing the barrel of his cannon up. "I've got nothing on active sensors, but that might just mean we're getting cloaked."

"I say we go full floods and hope we flash blind some of the bastards," Bridge suggested. "At the least, we might make them shit their armor."

"I'm good with that," Jack thought. "Floods on then. Hell, I'm going full on everything. They know we're here, might as well see if radar and QMs can get anywhere."

"Understood." Fish replied. "We're all going full sensor suite on."

"Okay, on three," Jack said and then counted to three, leaping out into the corridor with his cannon at the ready. Immediately, targeting Xs appeared in his mind and flashed from yellow to red.

Several blurs screeched down the corridor and slammed into him, causing his shields to flicker blue and white flashes of light. Jack turned his mecha sideways and grabbed at the shoulder of one of his attackers, but it moved out of the way. While the aliens in their body armor were a good three meters tall, that was still like a lapdog barking at the heels to a full-up bot-mode mecha. So, the alien ground troops were like angry insects swarming up on them. That made Jack recall how it felt fighting the smaller bots over the past few years before they had found the Chiata. He needed to use those types of fighting moves against the multiple smaller foe.

Jack stomped the floor with his mechanized boot as hard as he could, shaking deck plates loose from their moorings. The impact took the Chiata ground trooper nearest him off balance and Jack swatted it like a fly with the back of his mechanized hand and then swiped the one to its left with the barrel of his cannon. The first alien's shields flickered out, and the impact of its body against the bulkhead likely broke its neck. The second one jumped up, but not in time to keep Jack from stomping it into the deck plating with his giant bot-mode foot.

"Go to auto DEG targeting for the ground troops!" he ordered.

Candis, take them out.

I've got them, Jack, but I'll have to target optically because they are jamming the radar and the QMs still don't work.

Understood. Just do it, he thought.

Roger that.

Directed energy beams fired from the shoulder mounts on all the mecha bots, targeting the red and green ground troop blurs. The Chiata moved so fast that they were barely visible to the human eye, but to the high-speed optical cameras on the mecha they might as well have been sitting still. The AIC supercomputers quickly developed a tracking algorithm from the optical sensor data, and the squadron of mecha using their directed energy beams cut them down as quickly as they attacked.

Jack left the beams on full auto at his AIC's discretion and bounded through the line that the Chiata megaship crew was forming. He fired his cannon several times, scattering molten debris and aliens in all directions. It looked to Jack like the Chiata ship's crew had used anything they could get their tendrils on to create a makeshift barrier a few tens of meters across the corridor leading into a larger high bay area that had a stairwell and a ramp leading upward. Jack wasn't sure if the aliens knew he was headed for the bridge or if they were just the aliens that got in his way, but it did appear to him that the closer he pushed his team inward and upward, the heavier the resistance got.

"Listen up. That ramp ahead on the other side of the barrier is our target. I think that will take us up and closer to the bridge," Jack told his squadron. "We need to push through there and then up a few decks."

While the resistance got heavier, it was mainly in numbers of ground troops. It seemed to Jack that the Chiata must have been arrogant to the point that they didn't believe anyone would ever board them. Either that or they were really slow at responding within their own ship. But he thought about that and wondered how quickly a response would be mustered if the *Madira* had been boarded.

As soon as Jack had that thought, a deafening boom resounded in the corridor and a very large fireball pounded into the mecha to his left, knocking Bridge off his feet and making his shields flicker.

"Holy shit!" Fish shouted. "AA fire!"

"They've got an anti-tank gun!" Fish exclaimed. "Bridge, get your ass up and take cover!"

"Fuck that," DeathRay added. "Fox!"

He fired a missile down the hallway into the bulkhead and out the other side, waiting to detonate it until it had passed the barricade and penetrated all the way through bulkhead behind the ramp. As the missile exploded the bulkhead, it bulged and vaporized into a fireball that slammed against the Chiata troops and their barricade structure. Shrapnel rained against his mecha, making it ring like a bell, and the blast wave nearly knocked him off balance.

Shit, that was too close for missiles, he thought.

I would agree, Jack. Candis replied. *I don't recommend that again.*

Right.

"Warning! Enemy targeting radar lock! Warning! Enemy targeting radar lock!" his Bitchin' Betty chimed.

"Shit! Move!" DeathRay ordered. "They've got guided weapons on us! I'm locked up!"

"Guns, guns, guns!" Fish shouted, and DeathRay could see the fireballs splattering against the bulkhead with thunderous booms and flashes of plasma. "Guided weapons, hell! Check your tracker! There's mecha in here!"

Fish was right. As soon as she'd said it, Jack's red force tracker lit up like a Christmas tree with bogies. There were at least five porcupine mecha craft bouncing about across the corridor and behind that barricade. One of the porcupines bounced up and over and came down on top of DeathRay. He had just enough time to fall back and roll over in a backwards judo roll to avoid getting stomped on.

"Guns, guns, guns!" DeathRay grunted as his mecha

sprang upward to its feet. The targeting X flashed red and Jack held down on the trigger. But the mecha was faster than Jack's response. "Shit."

It slipped past him into the middle of the squadron's formation and grabbed Backup around the shoulders, slamming him against the wall with a thunderous screech of metal on metal, and then a tendril shot out from the porcupine's torso and pressed clean through the mecha's shield generators. Fish was quick to respond and grabbed the alien mecha about the head, yanking it over her shoulder and throwing it across the room. As the alien was flung over, a second tendril wrapped itself around Fish like a boa constrictor.

Bridge dropped to a knee, firing his cannon into the torso of the alien mecha, cutting free the tendrils that had constricted Fish and Backup. All of this happened so fast that DeathRay barely had time to think, but what he did think was, "Fox three!"

The missile cut out across the room and exploded almost as soon as he fired it. The alien's shields failed, and secondary concussion waves from the blast knocked all of them backwards. Jack kept his balance and bit down on his bite block, making himself be patient for just a fraction of a second longer. Then the targeting X turned red.

Again, too close for missiles, Candis scolded him.

No shit?

"Guns, guns, guns!" He said. The cannon rounds ripped through the alien porcupine mecha, shredding it to pieces and throwing sparks, debris, plasma, and red and green viscous fluids about.

"I've got several more coming in!" Bridge said.

"I've got 'em, Bridge! Stay on my wing!" Backup acknowledged him.

DeathRay took a quick glance at the mindview battlescape image with the hope that he'd see an obvious weakness to exploit in some sort of a plan. But it was pretty straightforward. The aliens were on one side of the room guarding an up ramp, and the Archangels were on the other side of said room wanting to go up said up ramp. It was going to be straight out head-to-head, force-on-force combat. There was nothing left to do but to go in there and kill those motherfuckers.

"Attack, Archangels! Attack!" Jack ordered.

Chapter 32

February 19, 2407 AD
U.S.S. Sienna Madira
Target Star System
700 Light-years from the Sol System
Tuesday, 1:02 A.M. Ship Standard Time

"Thank you, Captain! Keep me posted," Alexander said
to the Teena clone who was captain of the ship taking the
port-aft shield generator of the alien megaship. The clone-
driven supercarrier was efficiently taking on its mission
and had already completed the initial connections
between the supercarrier's shield generators and the
power source. Alexander wondered if it was because that
section of the megaship was where they had encountered
the least amount of resistance, but he couldn't be certain.
That Teena clone might have just had one hell of a crew
and been one hell of a captain.

"Sir, the Beta wave just lost another ship!" Firestorm

told him. "They're down to a baker's dozen. Casualties are stacking up, sir."

Sir, I have gone through the simulations that Allison has completed and she is quite right, Abigail alerted him. *We are going to fall short by almost three minutes. DeathRay has less than five minutes to make it to the bridge of the alien ship if his team is going to be of any assistance here.*

DeathRay will make it. Alexander knew he could count on Jack. But he wasn't sure about the builder bots. *But if Jack has to buy us more time than his op will afford, then we're in trouble.*

Yes, sir. I agree. Somehow we need to speed up the builder lines.

Right. Only way to do that is to stop the Chiata in those sections of the ship. Alexander thought about how to do that and he didn't have any good ideas. They already had all hands fighting or building. *Our troops are doing the best they can.*

Yes, sir, but we are moving way too slowly.

"We are going to have to move faster than this," Alexander muttered to himself as he thought about his plan briefly. The XO looked over at him as if she were going to add something, but he could tell she must have thought better of it and just kept her mouth shut. He was beyond beginning to worry that they had bitten off more than they could chew in such a short period of time and with so few ships. Something else was going to have to happen. "CHENG, this is the CO!"

"Yes, General?"

"How long, Joe?" Alexander asked. "How long until we can fire the weapon?"

"Sir, the aft section is all but connected. But the forward port side is still several minutes out. The resistance is so heavy there that as soon as the bots build a conduit, the Chiata take it out. If I can ever establish the connection it will be difficult for them to turn it off."

"Understood, Joe. Are there any partial options?"

"Not really, sir, no. We might could engage partial shields or something if they start attacking their own ship, but I'm not sure what good that would do."

"Alright then. Just, well, get this thing working as soon as possible!" Alexander felt as though he were sitting idle with his thumbs stuck up his posterior. There was nothing he could do but sit and watch his fleet get picked apart and wait for a bunch of robots to build a weapon system while under fire. They were all in on this. He had committed four ships to their doom if this didn't work out. Alexander knew deep down, though, that if things didn't work out here today, then humanity was likely done for as well. Oh, certainly, humanity would survive for a few years as the Chiata approached Sol, and they might even have enough escape out the back door to survive in colonies. But, if they didn't win here, today, it was very likely that humanity as they knew it was over. In essence, this was his all-out Hail Mary play.

And at the same time he had no idea where his little girl was and how to get her home safely. While the reports showed that the SARs teams had made it to ground safely, they were overwhelmed almost immediately before they could fly out. They ended up being stranded with the rest of the ground teams in the canyon basin. Alexander had to do something to turn the tide. And, he had to do it quickly.

He brought the force tracker view up in his DTM. The teams from the *Madira* and the *Hillenkoetter* had faced the most resistance within the alien megaship. The *Hillenkoetter* even more so. He mapped out the pathways the ground teams and bots had taken, and they were directly juxtaposed to each other on either side of the alien ship. The ground team from the *Madira* was only a few hundred meters from the ground team from the *Hillenkoetter*. Both teams were stalled and ground down in close-quarters combat. They needed something to give them a shot in the arm. Alexander sat in his chair and considered their predicament for a second longer. Admiral Walker had control of the Beta Fleet and was doing all she could to keep the Chiata busy and from turning on them. While she was overwhelmed by the numbers game, she had it under control as good as or better than anyone could under the circumstances. There was little naval-style fighting he could do while stuck to the larger enemy ship. There was literally nothing to do but sit and wait. Alexander hated waiting. Alexander hated sitting.

I'm tired of sitting in this chair, he thought. *I think I need to get involved a little more directly.*

Ooh-fuckin'-rah, General! Abigail replied in his mind. *Is it that time, sir?*

Yeah, it's that time, Abby, he thought. *Ooh-fuckin'-rah.*

About fuckin' time if you don't mind my saying so, sir.

Alexander stood up and clenched his fists briefly. He flexed his chest and shoulders in the suit and rolled his neck left then right. Finally, he took in a long deep breath and then relaxed his body with a long exhale. He looked about the bridge and decided that they were a good crew even if they were brand new. They could do the job. He looked over at Firestorm and knew she could handle whatever came her way with few to no problems. They didn't need him sitting in that chair. They did need him out there being a Marine.

"Firestorm, you have the bridge," Alexander said.

"Sir?" Sally looked at him and Alexander could tell by the look on her face that she knew exactly what he was about to do.

"General Rheims, I'm going for a stroll. You are in command," he said.

"Excuse me, General," CMC Sowles interjected. "If you don't mind sir, I'd like to tag along."

"That isn't necessary, COB," Alexander replied, not sure if his Chief of the Boat was going to try to stop him or join him.

"I know it ain't necessary, General. But, all things considered, I sure would like to join you."

"Suit yourself, COB."

Alexander didn't waste any time getting to the elevator, and the COB clanked along right behind him without saying a word. The mission clock in Alexander's head continued to click precious seconds away, and he thought that with each second, there was another blue beam blasting away at the Beta Fleet. The elevator doors opened and the two men stepped in almost in unison.

Override the controls and take us on the fastest path to the engagement zone, Abby, he ordered his AIC. *Have somebody at staff armaments waiting on me when I get there.*

Yes, sir. That will be down the control spire to the bottom deck and then all the way aft. Abigail paused momentarily. *That will take about forty seconds, sir. The Sergeant at Arms in the aft hangar bar is ready and waiting. There are weapons and ammunition stations already in place for the insertion teams, sir. You can choose from those when we arrive.*

I waited too long. That's forty seconds we don't have. Alexander sighed inwardly. *Forty seconds Dee doesn't have. Where are you, girl?*

Alexander didn't say a word or think in his mindvoice to his AIC for the rest of the trip down the command tower and back to the aft of the ship in the elevator tube. His mind was singularly focused on one thing, and that was bringing Hell to the Chiata between him and the power source the bots needed to get to. They had to succeed.

The elevator door opened at the back of the hangar bay. Alexander bounced as soon as the door opened with his jumpboots full throttle. There were several muster stations set up and triage units evacuating wounded out and up through the various elevators and ladderwells. Alexander bounced right on by them, stopping twice at the armament bins to grab extra ammo belts, grenades, and two rifles. The sergeant at arms watched as the general and the COB grabbed at the weapons and ammo.

Alexander didn't hesitate. Time was critical and his feet were never still for longer than a second at each of the tables and bins, and then he was bouncing past the mechas and AEMs standing guard at the hangar entrance and into the alien megaship. At that point the general was out of the ship and in enemy alien territory. The chief of the boat was hot on his jumpboots.

Alexander has left the building, he thought. *Alright, Abby, lay out the path for me. Get me to the forward AEMs.*

The actual front line is presently being held by Lieutenant Colonel Jessica894120 with thirty-three remaining clone AEMs and a considerable contingent of battlebots, sir, Abigail explained and highlighted a path in his mind. He could see the blue dots of his teams and the red dots of the Chiata bouncing about.

The repair bots were working like maniacal worker ants and bees, running and buzzing about cutting, welding, printing, melding, and all other sorts of construction imaginable. Alexander marveled at the conduits and cables that were already physically connecting the alien ship and the supercarrier, and the connections stretched for hundreds of meters into the belly of the alien beast.

A few tens of seconds more and the sounds of construction changed to the sounds of destruction. The familiar *spittap*ping of HVARs, the *zing*s of M-blasters, and the *thwoomp*s of grenade launchers rang and boomed. The sounds of thousands and thousands of buzz saws spinning against metal, screeching so shrilly that it made Alexander's skin crawl, resonated through the alien metal hallways. Alexander also heard blasts that he hadn't before, and he assumed he was hearing Chiata weapons fire for the first time. They turned one last corner and there was the front line in all its blood and glory.

Almost as instantly as they had turned the corner several red and green blurs danced about to take up aim point advantage on them, but it was neither of the men's first rodeo. The two scattered in opposite directions and dove for cover. The COB landed behind a pile of twisted-up metal tubes that looked like exploded power conduits and Alexander bounced in behind a blown-out hovertank, landing right beside the clone commander an AEM lieutenant colonel.

"Sir. I was not sure if I should have believed my blue force tracker when I saw your icon bouncing in here. You shouldn't be here, sir," Lieutenant Colonel Jessica894120 said.

"Everyone has to be somewhere, Lieutenant Colonel." Alexander bounced up to the top of the tank, looking for targeting Xs to turn red, and when they didn't, he fired his rifle at yellow ones. At full sprint he dove off the tank into a forward flip, releasing two grenades from his shoulder launcher as he did so into a mix of blurs that had flanked the clone AEMs.

The highlighted path in his mind showed him what he hoped was a downladder just on the other side of the bulkhead. He needed to drop down beneath the line if he was going to change the stalemate. The grenades burst into the bulkhead, throwing red-hot shards of metal and orange plasma onto the deck plates. Alexander rolled to a stop on the deck, firing his rifle through the hole in the wall he'd just made. Hundreds of battlebots rushed into the opening after the blurs on the other side. The Chiata troops fired their blue plasma bolts and fought hand-to-hand with the bots. Alexander fired several rounds from his rifle as he stood and rushed head first through the hole to the downladder. Almost out of nowhere, the COB bounced to the other side of the opening, laying down cover fire for the general as if it had been their plan all along. The two of them burst through the opening and down the ladder, dropping like a ton of metal to the deck below, both of them with their rifles firing at anything moving and blurry.

"When you go for a stroll, sir, you go for a fucking stroll!" Chuck Sowles shouted over the sound of *spittap*ping automatic hypervelocity gunfire and the occasional grenade *thwoomp*ing out of a tube. Alexander didn't have time to keep an eye on his COB, and at the same time, he didn't need to. The navy warrant officer was exceedingly efficient at killing shit, and Alexander highly approved. At present, there was plenty of shit that needed killing.

"Chuck, we need to press forward though the left flank on this wall." Alexander paused to highlight a path in their DTM view. "Blow through that passageway and into the next ante-chamber. I think if we drop down underneath the bastards there we could bring the floor out from underneath where they have the bots stalled."

"Hell of a plan, General! Hell of a plan!" Sowles growled over the net. Alexander turned just in time to see the man spinning like a whirling dervish wrapped up in the tendrils of one of the Chiata troopers, but the COB wasn't trapped at all. He used his wild spin to generate angular momentum that sent the alien off its feet from the centrifugal force. Chuck popped out his blade and sliced the alien free with his left hand while firing through its chest with the rifle in his right. Alexander held his rifle in his right hand and set his targeting X on one of the two alien creatures attempting to get the drop on the COB during his mad spin and took the alien out without Chuck ever being the wiser. He pulled his blaster up with his left and fired at the other, forcing it to take a cover position.

Abigail, keep that path lit up and don't let me make a wrong turn.

Understood, General.

Chapter 33

February 19, 2407 AD
U.S.S. Sienna Madira
Target Star System
700 Light-years from the Sol System
Tuesday, 1:05 A.M. Ship Standard Time

"DeathRay! I've got your six, just go, dammit!" Fish shouted over the tac-net at her former wingman. Jack didn't hesitate, if Fish said go then she needed him to go. He kicked the thrusters of the mecha's boots and burst headfirst through the doors of what Jack had decided were mecha elevator platforms. The metal was weaker than he'd expected, and he almost lost his balance as he tumbled the rest of the way into the large elevator. The doors behind him were bent inward and mangled from the slides to the point that they wouldn't close again.

Three Chiata porcupines stood facing him as he entered. It looks as if they were being readied for takeoff as the platform lifted to the upper hull. The alien mecha in the middle raised up on amorphously shaped legs and rippled with lightning as blue bolts of energy shot from the spires on its back at Jack. But Jack was expecting company and he didn't have time to play around with these bastards anymore.

"Guns, guns, guns," he shouted while falling forward and rolling so that he landed on his back. He kicked his boot boosters in, skittering him across the deck of the platform, throwing sparks as well as cannon fire. The thrust from his boot boosters pushed him right up underneath the middle porcupine, and DeathRay raised his cannon and fired it full auto at point-blank range on the alien mecha.

The rounds burst through the shields and into the armor plating as DeathRay continued to fire into its empennage. The mecha ruptured and exploded out the topside and then split in two. Jack pushed his mecha upward through the exploding alien mecha, tearing it out of his way. He jumped upwards and fired again at the alien ship on his left, then crashed down on top of it with both metal boots of the bot-mode mecha. Jack could see the alien creature inside the cockpit looking up at him as he depressed the firing controls. The shields gave way and the cockpit exploded. This time the blast was a little stronger than Jack had expected, and he was thrown backwards and off balance. Almost instantly, the third of the porcupines was on top of him, wrapping him up and firing plasma rounds at him, but DeathRay managed to squirm about and stay mostly unharmed.

Then an amorphous alien tendril shot through his

shield generator and wrapped around his right arm near the shoulder brackets. Metal and machine squealed against the stress from the alien constricting tentacle as DeathRay fought against it. Jack grabbed at it with his left hand but couldn't quite reach it. The Chiata porcupine transfigured to some other odd amorphous shape and slammed DeathRay against the deck plating so hard that Jack saw stars. He bit at the bite block to release some stims and air, and then kicked his back thrusters on full, forcing the two of them upwards in the platform shaft all the way to the top. Jack threw wild mechanized punches, knees, elbows, and headbutts along the way, all the while dodging and grappling with alien tendrils spearing at him and constricting him.

"Fox Three!" Jack shouted as a missile zipped out in front of them blasting a hole in the top of the shaft. DeathRay could see stars on the other side as the two of them burst through the fireball into open space on the hull of the megaship. "Oh, shit!"

Jack grunted against the acceleration as he turned his boot thrusters on full throttle. Grabbing the HOTAS and yanking it to the left while stomping on the left lower pedals he toggled the bot over into fighter mode. The Ares-T transfigured under the strain of the alien's constricting tendril, but the transfiguration mechanisms were strong enough to snap him free. The porcupine fell backwards from him almost a meter or two before it reached out with new tendrils to grab him. But the mecha in fighter mode was too fast for it, and he pulled away.

DeathRay watched in his DTM until he knew he was out of reach of the tendrils, and then he toggled the fighter back to bot, falling head over heels into a Fokker's feint and drawing his cannon from the hip, dumping over a hundred rounds into the alien fighter in an instant. The porcupine exploded as Jack landed on the outer hull of the alien ship with a thud.

"Shit, I hope that don't count as flying or I'm gonna get busted back down to ensign." Jack pursed his lips and made a motorboat sound to relax and focus his mind. Then he hit the stims as he toggled his mindview. "Well, one thing about it, I got where I needed to be."

Jack dropped back into the elevator shaft he'd just blown out and hovered at the top-floor doorway. Reaching up with his two giant bot hands, he jammed them into the opening slit and forced the doors apart. The secondary doors wouldn't budge. They were made from some stronger material.

"Fish. Where the hell are y'all? Get up here," he said over the net.

"On our way, DeathRay. You gave us the slip," Fish said. "Thought you weren't supposed to be flying."

What do you think, Candis? He smirked. *Too close for missiles?*

Don't, Jack. Jack!

"Fish, y'all better take cover for about five seconds." Jack kicked back to the opposite side of the large elevator shaft and gritted his teeth against the mouthpiece.

Jack!

"Fox Three!" he said, and fired a missile into the wall. At the same time he cut his propellantless drive and fell downward toward the rest of the Archangels. The elevator shaft once again filled with molten metal and plasma, but since it was now evacuated to space the fireball didn't last near as long. Jack fell to his feet with a thud against the rising platform.

"Going up?" Fish, Bridge, and Backup clanked beside him and Jack could just imagine the smug look on Karen's face while she spoke. "Penthouse. Lingerie, alcohol, and alien megaship bridges."

"Where's the rest of the team?" He checked his DTM, and they were underneath the platform, covering their exit if they needed one. "Oh, I see. Alright, this is it, stay frosty."

Four porcupines dropped through the blown-open elevator shaft opening from outside the ship. Fish didn't hesitate and neither did Bridge. The two of them kicked their thrusters, and were in death grappling matches with Chiata almost instantly. Backup stood his ground beside DeathRay and both of them raised their weapons, firing at the other two.

"Fox Three!" Jack shouted.

"Goddammit, Jack! Would you quit firing missiles in such tight quarters?" Fish said all the while grunting as she fought the Chiata mecha on her back.

"Oh, fuck it! I'm gonna get court martialed anyway." Jack mumbled to himself, kicked the bot over into fighter mode, and screamed back up the shaft, bursting through into a rolling and yawing mad spin with targeting Xs filling his mindview. "Guns, guns, guns."

Backup was right behind him and going to guns as well. The four of them tied up with the aliens for precious seconds, and Jack finally realized that he was wasting far too much time. He rolled over with his cockpit facing the megaship and took a deep breath and a hit of stims.

Start pukin,' Candis! Now!

Deathblossom in three, two, one.

There were only four alien fighters on top of them and there were a handful more inbound, but none of them were expecting what Jack was doing. The Ares-T spun up, firing DEGs and cannons and targeting all of the alien fighters within seconds. Jack barely had time to place himself in his "zone" before the targets were neutralized and the Deathblossom spun down. Jack clenched his jaws on the bite block and breathed through his nose doing his best to keep from regurgitating. Somehow he managed to choke back the bile.

"We've got to move it!" Jack gasped as he opened his mouth and swallowed. He dropped back through the elevator shaft hole and then through the top-floor opening his missile had made. He bounced in and looked around. The concussion from his missile had taken out all six of the ground troops, or more likely command team, or bridge crew of the ship, and there were mutilated and mashed-up alien bodies and amorphous armor stuck to the bulkheads like someone had thrown a plate of red and green spaghetti in a blender with the top off. The shit was everywhere.

"I guess they weren't expecting us," DeathRay said. "Fish, get in here and keep my exits covered!"

"Roger that, DeathRay!"

What now, Candis?

I was expecting you would ask that, his AIC said. *I'm in direct contact with Allison. First things first, get out and look around.*

Right.

Jack popped the hatch and dropped to the floor. His

jumpboots hit the deck plating solidly with a bit of a crunching sound and he noticed that there was frozen alien goo all over the floor. He looked up and for the first time had a second to notice the Beta Fleet engaged with over two dozen Chiata megaships in the ball around him. The porcusnails were zipping those fucking blue beams of death from Hell across the sky, and one of the Fleet ships burst at the seams.

"Shit, they're getting hammered," he thought as he checked the battlescape. The Beta wave was down to seven ships. He crunched across more of the alien body parts and goop.

"This place is gonna need a shitload of floor cleaner." He walked to what he thought was the captain's chair, if you could call it a chair. The Chiata were odd beasts with legs, yes, but they were amorphous blobs that changed on a whim. Jack wasn't even sure that sitting meant anything to them. But it was a station, whether it was a chair or not. "Alright, Candis, I'm looking at what I think is the Captain's station. Can you handshake with it?"

Allison and I are on it. It would appear as if propulsion is locked out and the shield generators are offline.

No shit, Jack thought. *What else?*

It looks like that there is the weapons station, Jack. Candis lit up a panel in his mindview. Jack turned to it and pushed the dead Chiata torso off the panel.

Okay, so it does. Yeah, this looks like a targeting link here and there are the fire controls. Is it locked out?

I'm not certain, his AIC replied.

Well, it is certainly not in any language I've ever seen. Jack stood in front of the console pretending he was the alien gunner for a second. He looked out the transparent bubble in front of him and could see the giant spires of the tuning fork reaching out above the ship. In the distance he saw one of the alien megaships taking up position on a Fleet ship's six o'clock. Jack laid his hand against the alien handprint on the table and flexed his trigger finger. Nothing happened.

Did you think it would be that easy? Candis asked.

You never know. What now?

"Jack this is Nancy, copy?" His wife's voice cut into his speakers on a private channel.

"Copy, hot stuff." Jack said. "What can I do for you?"

"Allison says you have to find some sort of transmitter or implant from one of the alien bodies. They must use some sort of wireless interface that is encrypted at the user. She is having no luck cracking it from the outside," Nancy told him. "The consoles are likely biometrically locked out."

"Okay, hold on. You seeing this?" He asked.

"Yes, I've got you in my mindview. Keep looking."

Jack foraged about the bridge and the mangled and frozen bodies until he found an alien's head. There was an implant on the left side of the earhole that looked as if it went all the way into the thing's brain.

"That's it, Jack!" Nancy stopped him. "Pull that out."

"How did I get the gross job?" He carefully pulled at the implant until he felt bone snap and then it pulled out of the alien head with green brain matter still connected to it. "Ooh, shit, that's nasty. Now what?"

"Open up your universal data port to your suit and snap that thing onto it," Nancy told him.

The alien implant didn't have any sort of connection that would fit into his suit, but the UDP was basically a wideband full-spectrum antenna. Any connections were wireless. Jack waited for a second longer.

"How is this going to help? If you couldn't get in wirelessly already, what difference will this make?" Jack asked his wife.

"The ship's system was locked out. But Allison believes she can hack in through this creature's wireless interface and get us in. Maybe the creature wasn't locked out before the system was shut down." At that, the bridge lit up and the panels came to life.

"Son of a bitch," Jack stammered.

"What I used to do for a living, remember." Nancy sounded pleased. "Now just use your battlescape mindview to highlight a target and Allison will relay that to the targeting computer and fire the system."

"Okay, that one." Jack pointed out one of the alien megaships. Nothing happened.

"Allison says that should have worked," Nancy said. "We're missing something."

Jack looked around the panel and at the dead body on the floor next to it. He looked at the panel again and looked closer at the hand print indention. Then he looked back at the alien body.

"How about this?" Jack pulled the dead alien's hand up and placed it on the handprint on the tabletop control panel. Then he looked in his mindview and focused on one of the Chiata megaships. As soon as he did, the panel jumped to life with lights and the tuning fork began flashing lightning like a thunderstorm. The hair on the back of Jack's neck stood on end as a blue beam of death from Hell burst forth from the top of the porcusnail's antennae and zigged out before them and then zagged twice, hitting home dead center of the alien megaship.

"Hot damn! Hit it again, Jack!" Nancy exclaimed. Jack did.

Chapter 34

February 19, 2407 AD
Northern Region
Alien Planet, Target Star System
700 Light-years from the Sol System
Tuesday, 1:06 A.M. Ship Standard Time

Deanna Moore stood motionless in what at first was a sea of blackness, and then there was something that was lit up in the distance. Maybe it was a wall. Dee wasn't sure. But it was a light. A light aqua color with rippling white flashes dancing across it. The wall was perfectly square and it appeared to be approaching her; therefore, the scale of the wall grew while the aspect ratio remained the same.

What the hell is that, Bree? she thought. *It looks a lot like a QMT gate.*

I'd have to agree with you, but every one we have seen before is round and not square.

So? Deanna wasn't an engineer or a STO, but she figured the shape of the gate was in the engineering of it and not the physics. *So what?*

I have no response to that other than there are no readings on any instruments.

Keep looking.

The square continued to approach her until it was within a meter from her, and the quantum foam rippling effect before her stretched in all directions as far as she could crane her neck to look. The center of the square right in front of her formed a circular wavefront that propagated outward along the surface of the quantum foam and then a figure stepped through it.

At first Dee thought it was another human, but once the lighting from the gate, or whatever it was, illuminated the being's face, it was clear to her that it wasn't human. Humanoid, yes. Human, no.

"Hello?" Dee asked timidly. "Who, who are you?"

The creature stepped very close to Dee, almost to within millimeters, and appeared to be sniffing her suit. Then it reached up an extremely long set of fingers, six on each hand, and poked at her visor. The alien made some sort of facial expression that Dee didn't understand and then it pointed a device in her general direction. When it did that, the beetle that was stuck between Dee's hand and the wall back in the ruins on the planet in the target star system crawled up her arm and jumped into the alien's outreached hand.

For the first time Dee realized she was no longer standing in the alien ruins, or if she, was she had somehow moved further into them. She wasn't really sure just where in the universe she was and she wasn't sure what was going on at the moment.

Dee, we are being scanned and I'm being sent connectivity handshaking protocols. They don't seem malicious yet, Bree thought to her.

Talk to it, Bree. This is why we're here.

The creature stood silent for a moment and Bree didn't respond any further to Dee's thoughts. At first Dee was getting concerned that the alien was taking over the AI and longtime friend in her head. But then an expression that looked like relaxation washed over the alien's face.

Dee? You hear me?

I'm here. What happened to you?

I think this creature just downloaded everything I know. It was so overwhelming I could do nothing but let it happen.

Are you okay?

Uh, yes, thank you. I'm fine.

"Human? Interesting." The creature said in perfect English. "United States Marine Major Deanna 'Apple1' Moore. Why are you here?"

"Uh, I was looking for you." Deanna wasn't sure how to respond, but she knew she needed to be diplomatic and not blow whatever chance this might be. She thought briefly to herself about what her father would do.

"Looking, for me?" The creature started to do something that resembled laughter. "No, I highly doubt you were looking for me."

"Well, I was looking for someone? Or something that could help."

"Of course you were! Ha, ha. Well then, you have found me. Help you how? What do you want?"

"Uh, wait, you know who I am, so why don't you tell me who you are?" Dee was doing her best to think her words through before she spoke. She had no idea if this alien was finicky or easily insulted. She didn't want to create some intergalactic incident with a first contact by saying the wrong things.

"Very well. Mru." It said.

"Mru? Is that your name or what you are?" Deanna asked maybe a little too abruptly.

"Aha, yes, my name is Mru as yours is Deanna. I am Thgreeth as you are human."

"I see. Where am I, Mru?"

"You are here," it said with a pause. At first Dee thought the thing was being funny, but it was merely pausing to find the right words. "Here is a pathway between places. Give me a moment as I'm still assimilating your speech."

"This place is a teleportation facility? That's what all the star maps and trajectories on the ruins mean, right?"

"Yes. As the scourge covered the galaxy from the outer rings inward, my people moved ahead of them and placed these safe havens and escape passages through space. Our hopes were to enable multiple attack fronts unavailable to the enemy in the oncoming war. You have found how to access one of them. This is important in that no other species as of yet has been judged by the automated guardians as trustworthy enough to allow through. Perhaps they allowed it or perhaps you manipulated it. Either way, you are here now."

"Automated guardians, you mean the beetle bugs? That thing didn't like the way I tasted," she said.

"Yes, I see this. That is exciting and intriguing for me. In seventy thousand years, no other species has triggered the tunnel system. But through testing your blood and reading the history stored in your artificial counterpart, we could see that we should at least have a conversation with you," Mru explained. "That does not mean you are trustworthy."

"Great. We are having a conversation. What now?"

"You still haven't answered my question. Why would you put yourself through so much pain to come here? Tell me, Deanna Moore of Earth, why are you here?"

"My race is about to be invaded by this scourge you speak of. They are moving rapidly through the galaxy like locusts and within two more years they will devour my homeworld. We came here hoping to find answers and perhaps a way to fight the Chiata horde. We are looking for something, well, something that will give us hope. Any kind of hope is more than what we have now," Dee said.

"Oh, no, you are mistaken. The Chiata are not the scourge I spoke of." Mru hesitated as if searching for words again. "The Chiata are only doing what is within their nature the same way a swarm of insects would. They devour what is within their path. True, they are destructive, but that is simply what they do. Doing what is natural isn't evil, it simply is."

"The Chiata were not the scourge? Seems like it to me." Deanna was confused. "Scourge or not, they are about to wipe my people out. We have to stop them."

"Do not doubt that the Chiata must be dealt with. This

is why we left the guardians behind on all of the planets we have traveled to. But there is a much more malignant species bent on being overlords of all that is not them within this galaxy. They are amorphous parasites. When we first encountered them they had enslaved a race of large sentient mammals and used them as parasitically controlled slaves. They attempted to enslave us and that is why we disrupted their technologies nearest our outposts. To the Thgreeth, living in freedom is the most precious and sacred concept. We could not coexist with this evil. We will not be enslaved."

"Wait, you mean you were not fighting the Chiata?" Dee realized that the Chiata didn't have quantum membrane teleportation technologies, so, clearly the dampening fields that rendered the QMTs useless were not meant for them. She also knew who had the QMT technologies and how humanity had come by them. Knowing that gave her pause and frightened her even more than the Chiata. "Someone worse than the Chiata?"

"We were winning the war and seeding the galaxy with bases that would enable a clean sweep of the parasites, but that is when the Chiata came. Their numbers were so great that we did not desire the loss of life required to stay. This was the last planet we had made it to and we were not finished here when the Chiata arrived here. So, we left the inner galaxy and relocated our civilization to what you know as the Monoceros Ring around this galaxy. We have remained and will remain there until such time as we can retake the galaxy in peace or leave it altogether." Mru paused and studied Deanna closer. It looked at the instrument in its hand and then back at her. "You are very strong, Deanna Moore of Earth. Yet you are still very damaged. I see that you must depend on this mechanical suit for support because of injuries you have sustained."

"Yeah, well, I'll live," she said. "What I need to know though, is can you help me stop the Chiata from destroying my homeworld?"

"Oh, I cannot help you, not really, as you see, I really am not here. This is a real-time projection of me. I am tens of thousands of light years away from here. But that isn't to say that you are not able to help yourself." Dee was tired of the riddles the alien spoke in. She wanted it just to come out and explain itself.

"Help myself? How?" She asked.

"You now know how to use the tunnels. The map is complete on the walls of the evacuation centers. Use them to your advantage as you see fit. The walls are interactive once you figure them out. They will help you plan your attacks or escapes as needs be. We used them to evacuate entire worlds before the Chiata devoured them," Mru told her, but Dee wasn't buying it.

"Without our QMT engines we can't move to those tunnels fast enough. Being limited by just our hyperspace travel puts us at a much lower advantage than the Chiata. These tunnels would be useless to us." She wanted some sort of super Chiata killer, but Mru was being too cryptic to give away something of the sort. Or maybe it was like her grandmother had told her, Mru was just too alien for her to completely fathom.

"Yes, I see that," Mru noted. "Very well. As long as your people remain trustworthy allies, you will be able to use your teleportation technologies within range of the evacuation centers and forward operating bases. But do not expect them to bring you all the way to us. We will not allow that. I am uploading the key sequence to your counterpart who can then disseminate it to your people. But be aware, as soon as a non-trustworthy entity attempts to use it, the key will be changed."

"That's it? Nothing else? No super weapons that eat Chiata?" Dee was disappointed.

"Perhaps something, more than nothing." Mru held up his hand and the beetle jumped from the alien's hand to Dee's shoulder and perched there briefly. "This key is yours. Learn from it. Perhaps it is what you are looking for. You should have your bigger minds study it, but note that it is yours, Major Deanna Apple1 Moore. It is yours to command and control. It will only answer to you. Your people have returned and I think it is time you do as well."

"You mean the Fleet has come back?"

"Yes. But before you go I will do this one more thing for you."

"What?" Dee was puzzled at first, but then the beetle scurried over her shoulder and buried its nose into the armor in her mid-back. The mandibles moved as fast as the buzz saw on the killer bots her grandmother had invented.

The beetle clawed through the armor and bit a long gash across Deanna's side and lower back large enough for it to crawl through before the armor sealed itself. Dee could feel the bug crawl underneath her skin and dig into the muscle tissue all the way to her spine. It hurt. Bad. Very. Bad.

"Oh, Jesus!" she screamed in pain and the feeling of

the ping-pong-ball-sized beetle digging into her back near her spine where there was already a piece of alien metal lodged was enough to make her faint. But the beetle kept on digging. Dee came to with a jolt from the stims being administered to her by the suit and could feel the metal in her spine being moved against the bone. The pain was worse than any pain she'd ever felt in her life. It was so overwhelmingly painful that even the medication administered to her via the suit couldn't numb it. She felt a tug and then felt the metal pull free from the bone. Dee passed out.

Deanna! Can you hear me? Deana Moore?! her AIC shouted into her mind.

Chapter 35

Lieutenant Colonel Jessica894120 and the rest of her clone AEM squad were completely pinned down. There were still twenty-seven of the AEMs fighting alongside the battlebots, but Chiata reinforcements had strengthened the line and stopped the progression of the power conduit construction butt-cold. Alexander knew that once lines got settled in a conflict it was difficult to breach them and even harder to move them. He couldn't let the Chiata make their foothold stick.

"Chuck, if my AIC's calculations are right, and they usually are, we should be right under the Chiata barricades by two floors," he told his COB. The Chief of the Boat had fought alongside him all the way across the line and down through heavy Chiata ground troop resistance like a sailor possessed. The COB wasn't bad for a Navy squid.

"Aye, sir! What are your plans?" Sowles asked.

"Well, you see that power conduit right there that is running across the ceiling and through that bulkhead?" Alexander pointed it out with the laser sight from his rifle.

"Yes, sir, I do." Chuck smiled, and the grenade tube extended from his right shoulder armor.

"My sentiments exactly, COB." Alexander extended his launcher as well. "Listen, Chuck, as soon as that bulkhead goes, the Chiata are likely to fall right in our laps. It's probably going to get shit thick in here very quickly."

"Wouldn't have it any other way, Captain," Chuck replied as the targeting system blinked. Alexander could see the Xs forming through the man's visor. He turned and switched his system back up as well and targeted the conduit.

"Alright, Chuck, let'em have it!" Alexander ordered.

"Aye, Captain!"

Thwoomp! Thwoomp! Thwoomp!

The grenade tubes fired, releasing balls of energy into the conduit. On impact they exploded with orange and white fireballs, and then the conduit breached and the explosion was about five times larger than Alexander had expected. The thunderous boom filled the corridors of the alien ship and shook metal bulkheads free from their moorings. The blast wave knocked both Alexander and the COB backwards against the hatch they'd just bounced through. The two men in the armored suits clanked against the wall and rolled to a stop, sounding like a hubcap banging around in a clothes dryer. Metal from the ceiling bulkhead creaked as a white-hot jet of plasma screamed from the busted conduit like gamma ray bursters from a black hole's accretion disk. The metal glowed red then white and then collapsed completely, dropping several tons of structure two full floors. The crash was so large that the falling material burst through the floor that Alexander and Chuck were on. The two of them barely had time to scramble into the hatchway of the ladderwell for cover.

Alexander could hear the COB laughing almost uncontrollably as the floor and ceiling of the alien vessel continued to collapse. Then two porcupines and several Chiata ground troops fell as well. They fell past them to the floor beneath.

"Now, COB!" Alexander jumped to the edge of the hatch and *thwoomp*ed two grenades into the hole with the aliens. The grenades exploded, scattering and confusing the alien mecha and knocking two of the troopers off their amorphous feet.

Alexander went to his standard two-gun mojo with his HVAR in his right hand and his M-blaster in his left, firing at any targeting X that dared to blink red. One of the mechas hovered upwards right in front of them and fired a tendril into the door. The amorphous glowing green snakelike appendage darted just between Alexander and the COB. The two of them would have been speared had they not reacted as quickly as they did. Alexander fell back to the left side and Chuck to the right. Immediately, both men extended their forearm blades and sliced at the tendril. The mecha appendages were stronger than the troop ones and the blades wouldn't cut through.

"Screw that!" Alexander turned and dove through the hatch onto the top of the porcupine. "Cover my ass, COB!"

"Damned right, sir!" Chuck shouted, all the while firing with both weapons at the mecha and the other troops that continued to rain downward through the hole the two men had created.

Alexander bounced onto the top of the porcupine and grabbed a handhold on one of the spiny protrusions with his left gauntlet. With his right he stuck the barrel of his rifle into an open vent, at least he thought it was a vent, and fired it at full auto. Several rounds *spittapp*ed into the alien mecha and flames began to shoot out of the vent like a kiln being hit with the bellows. Alexander ducked back just in time, because another amorphous snakelike appendage darted out from the mecha just beneath his jumpboot. The mecha jerked and rolled, throwing him onto his back, but Alexander managed to grab a handhold and was flung over face-first into the canopy of the porcupine.

Alexander held on and was staring face to face with the Chiata pilot. He pulled up his rifle and fired nonstop into the canopy until the integrity field gave and the transparent material started to crack. The alien inside worked controls with amorphous tendrils feverishly, shaking the mecha wildly, trying to shake him free. One of the movements slung Alexander outward away from the ship, but he held on and used the strength of the suit to pull his jumpboots down against the structure and then reverse his momentum by kicking the thrusters. He flipped back around and brought his boots crashing through the canopy and into the alien's torso. Alexander let go of his handhold and jammed his rifle barrel into the alien's face, pulling the trigger. Green and red viscous goo exploded against the interior of the cockpit as Alexander bounced himself outward. The mecha fell uncontrollably through the hole it had come up through.

"Hot damn, sir! We're all of a sudden blessed with plenty of targets!" Chuck told him as he bounced back to the cover of the hatchway. Alexander skittered backwards through the hatch and banged to a stop against the bulkhead underneath the ladderwell. "You all right, sir?"

"Fine, Chuck! Plenty of targets, huh? Blessed, are we?" Alexander collected himself and crawled to cover position at the edge of the hatch, firing his weapons.

"Yes, sir! Can't think of a better blessing than to have plenty of these alien bastards to shoot at! We won't have to fight over who gets to shoot at what. I'm just glad you left some for me to kill!" Chuck was almost laughing as he fired both weapons into the room at the blurs and the mechas as they poured through.

"Lieutenant Colonel Jessica894120, now is the time if there ever was one," he called over the tac-net to the clone AEM commander.

"Yes, General Moore!" the Jessica clone replied.

AEM clones and battlebots dropped in from all directions on top of the alien troops. The abrupt change in the battlescape confused the Chiata's defensive posture, and now the AEMs were on the attack. Alexander and the COB most certainly weren't going to let the AEMs have all the fun. The two men bounced into the fray from the side and mixed it up with the blurs. Then two hovertanks fell in from above as well. The bot-mode mechas banged through the remaining alien mechas like they weren't even there. The General's actions had been the snowflake needed to trigger an avalanche.

The line is crushed, sir! Abigail told him and illuminated the path to the power source in his mindview. *We can push through on this floor.*

Understood!

"Keep moving along the following path!" He sent the map to all the ground team. "We've shifted the momentum, so we cannot let up!"

"If I were a jarhead, sir, I'd yell ooh-fuckin'-rah or some such nonsense!" Sowles interjected between volleys from his grenade launcher.

"Nobody's perfect, COB. Were I a squidboy, I'd say it was a perfect Navy day!"

"Hooyah, Captain. Hooyah."

"General Moore! This is DeathRay, copy?"

"Copy, DeathRay, Moore here. Go." Alexander didn't pause to listen to Jack; instead, he pushed forward with the rest of the AEMs and battlebots and the COB. They were seconds from their objective and he wasn't going to let up. He could see the builder-bot icons in his mindview closing in on their position. He realized he needed to check on the *Hillenkoetter* insertion team's status.

"Sir, we have the bridge and are in control of the main gun. It works damned good, sir. But something just lit up all the lights up here, and we believe the alien chicken shits have triggered a countdown to self-destruct the ship. Check your red force tracker on full ship zoom, sir," Jack told him. Alexander did. He panned out and could see the red dots jumping ship as fast as they could reach the outer hull. They were so close, they couldn't lose this engagement to a damned self-destruct sequence.

"Shit! How much time, Jack?" Alexander asked, and then pinged his AIC.

Abby, get on this!

Yes, sir.

"If I am reading these damned alien clocks right sir, we've got seven minutes and forty-seven seconds left. My AIC is pinging clock to all the Fleet AICs," Jack said.

"Then you have seven minutes to stop that clock, Jack! Do not let those bastards destroy this ship!" Alexander ordered. They could not lose now, as far as they had come.

"Uh, yes, sir. We're working it."

"Keep me posted, but get it done, Jack."

"Yes, sir."

Sir! Deanna's blue force tracker just came online!

Where?!

Chapter 36

February 19, 2407 AD
Northern Region
Alien Planet, Target Star System
700 Light-years from the Sol System
Tuesday, 1:08 A.M. Ship Standard Time

Colonel Delilah "Jawbone" Strong was at a full sprint in her bot-mode mecha bouncing across the top of the canyon basin cliffs. The search and rescue teams had dropped down in three starlifters, enough to carry the tankheads and AEMs out with the Maniacs flying support, but as soon as the starlifters breached the bottom of the ball, the Chiata dropped porcupines on them and brought them crashing down into the forest several klicks from the canyon. Delilah wasn't about to just let the Chiata take the SARs down and then finish them off, and neither were the rest of the Maniacs, the Slayers, or the Juggernauts. She scrambled what was left of the Maniacs, and the seven FM-12s were fighting in the thickest upside-down bowl they'd ever been in with hopes of rescuing the would-be rescuers.

"Stick, you and PotRoast watch the southern flank! We don't want those bastards cutting us off from the canyon," Jawbone grunted over the tac-net. She bounced her mecha at full thrust upward through the tree canopy head first into an energy line with two porcupines firing blue beams at her as they approached on her three-nine line. She juked and jinked and dropped over into a feint, going to her guns. "Guns, guns, guns! Coffee! Where the fuck are you!?"

Orange tracers filled the sky upward through the tree canopy, burning holes in the atmosphere as they tracked into one of the porcupines. The shields flickered and the cannon rounds kept coming.

"Guns, guns, guns!" First Lieutenant Sara "Coffee" Ames, Jawbone's wingman, shouted in guttural grunts as her fighter-mode mecha ripped through the top of the trees, throwing a rooster tail of greenery behind her. "Fox Three!"

The mecha-to-mecha missile twisted and turned and slammed into the porcupine just as the guns finished off its shields. The missile exploded, separating the outer hull armor from the interior of the alien fighter in a fireball, and the amorphous creature inside ejected just as the fighter disintegrated. Coffee blasted through the fireball, yawing her fighter around, firing guns just across Delilah's nose.

"Great flying, Coffee!" Jawbone toggled her bot over to fighter, did a corkscrew spiraling roll across the other alien's energy line, and reversed her energy vector, putting her on its six o'clock and choking back bile from the extreme forces on her stomach. "Fox Three!"

Jawbone didn't take the time to watch the missile drive home. She cut her upward momentum into a free-falling stall and nosed over into a dive straight at the ground. She looked through her mindview at the battlescape and could see the red dots closing in on the downed starlifters. The tankheads were almost on top of them, but they were going to need some cover.

"Take it to the deck, Maniacs!" Jawbone ordered her squadron. The canopy of trees screamed past her in a wild flurry of greens, browns, and yellows. She flared her approach into a strafing run across the line of blurs, bouncing it at the SARs teams. There were several of them manning plasma cannons and HVARs, and they were holding their own for the time being.

Delilah weaved in and out of the trees and threw her mecha over, toggling back to bot, hitting the ground running and bouncing on her boot thrusters, firing from the hip at the blurs and porcupines, giving the downed crews a much needed break with the cover fire. The rest of the Maniacs followed suit, mixing it up on the ground and in the trees as the tankheads rolled in, firing their giant cannons and blasting holes through the forest.

"Colonel Slayer, we've got you clear up top. Push quickly and let's get the SARs over the cliff back to the ruins," Jawbone told the leader of the hovertank squadron.

"Roger that, Jaw! We see 'em. Damn blurry bastards got 'em pinned down!" Colonel Slayer replied. "Nothing a few tanks can't jar loose. But the numbers game is still against us. We need to move it to cover fast."

"Roger that!" Jawbone looked at her force tracker and watched as the AEMs moved in with the tanks in perfect cover formation. It didn't take them seconds to take up the flanks on the downed planes and then pull them out with them. The hovertanks weren't still for more than thirty seconds before the SARs and the AEMs loaded their wounded and they were on the bounce.

"Maniacs, keep them covered over the cliff wall. Drop to cover after the tanks go over." Jawbone watched in her force tracker as she bounced about the trees and then twisted over to fighter, pulling up above the canopy briefly, looking for targets of opportunity. There were too many and she was afraid if she engaged one she'd bring ten on her ass. "Coffee, stay below and low."

The mindview of the battlescape flashed and then a new blue dot dropped into the canyon basin. Jawbone zoomed in on it just to make sure she read it right.

"Well, I'll be damned," she said.

Deanna Moore, are you with me? Bree shouted in her mindvoice. *Major Deanna Moore!*

"I'm here, Bree," Dee whispered faintly. "Where is that damn bug?"

Dee breathed in deeply, and as her abdomen expanded with the breath, she felt pain against her sciatic nerve that shot all the way down her left leg to her toes. The pain was excruciating, but she could feel her toes. The diagnostic of her suit and body showed the gash at her back, and the beetle crawled out and up to her shoulder and over to her hand. She looked at it and then placed it in her chest ammo pocket.

The immunoboost is now responding to your back injury. You should regain use of your legs very soon, Bree told her. *I'm giving you pain meds in the meantime.*

Thanks. Now, where are we? She toggled over to her battlescape view. She was hundreds of kilometers from where she'd started and was much farther south. She was only a few kilometers from the rest of the ground teams according to her blue force tracker. Dee scanned her whereabouts and realized she was in a cavernous room not unlike the room in the ruins she had been in before. There were glyphs on the walls and she could see a river outside the opening of the structure. There were also several of the beetle mounds along the river banks.

"Major Moore, glad you could join us," a familiar voice sounded over her speakers. The blue force tracker icon for Colonel Delilah "Jawbone" Strong popped up.

"Yes, ma'am. I have useful intel and I am relaying to all of the blue force dots here a key code to trigger our QMTs!" Deanna replied.

"If you can do that, do it now! We need to evac to the *Madira* ASAP!" Jawbone ordered.

"Roger that, ma'am!"

You heard her, Bree. Do it.

Dee looked at her surroundings as they changed once again. There was a flash of light and the long-missing familiar sound of bacon frying. Then Dee was looking about the aft hangar QMT pad on the *U.S.S. Sienna Madira II*. There was a staging area with weapons tables set up, a triage filled with incoming wounded, and AEMs and tankheads standing guard at the open hangar doors. Engineering teams were running about like worker ants, and builder and repair bots scurried in all directions. Several other QMT flashes popped around her and AEMs, tanks, and FM-12s appeared on the pad.

"Bree, you should probably walk me to medical," she said audibly. "And transmit the key code to the Fleet."

Done, Bree replied. *The suit stood her up and started walking her toward the elevator. I'm checking you in with the medical teams.*

Where are Daddy, Davy, Jack, and Nancy? she asked, and then their blue dots appeared with labels in her mindview. Her mother's dot had already popped up in the med bay. The locations were so strange. She had obviously missed a lot. She zoomed out and looked at the battlescape and studied it as her suit walked her forward.

This is the craziest battle plan I've ever seen. Looks like four supercarriers rammed a megaship, Dee thought.

Yes, they did. I have downloaded the battle plan and will play it through for you, Bree explained. *Dee, did you note Commander Rackman's current predicament?*

He's a big boy. He'll fight his way out. And now he can flash out if he needs to.

Let us hope so.

Chapter 37

February 19, 2407 AD
Alien Megaship
Target Star System
700 Light-years from the Sol System
Tuesday, 1:10 A.M. Ship Standard Time

The combination of all the supercarriers and the alien megaship shook violently as secondary explosions rocked the forward section. The Chiata fleet had turned from the Beta Fleet of supercarriers and focused their attack on their own megaship. DeathRay did his best to fire the blue beams at the Chiata to keep them at bay, but the numbers game was getting the best of them. Admiral Walker's Beta Fleet were beat up, but they were still mixing it up, and with the QMTs back online they became much more effective at fighting.

There was still the problem of the megaship on a countdown to self-destruction, and the ground team from the *Hillenkoetter* had yet to push through to the power source for the builder bots. Several teams of Chiata troops and mechas had stayed behind to hold them at bay. Commander Rackman's team was stalled only two floors beneath the objective, but they were pinned down and the lines were being drawn. The ground team hadn't moved in over two minutes.

"Rackman, you have got to move forward or we are sunk, do you understand!" Nancy told him over the tac-net.

"Yes, ma'am! We are pushing as hard as we can with the troops we have! We need reinforcements!" Rackman replied. Nancy turned to her blue force tracker and noted that the Demon Dawgs and the Utopian Saviors mecha squadrons on the *Madira* were sitting in their mechas and waiting to be deployed. She had an idea.

"Hold on, Rackman, I'll see what we can do." Nancy turned to her mindview for a moment and tapped open a direct channel to the CO of the *Madira*. Firestorm answered the call.

"What can I do for you, Captain Penzington?"

"My ground teams are pinned down. Can we QMT one or both of your mecha squadrons into the AO? That would turn the tide I—" Nancy didn't finish the sentence before the ship shook so violently that it tossed her forward. She grasped for the chair arm so quickly that she couldn't control the strength in her gauntlet and she bent the metal almost into two pieces.

"Blue beam impact on forward generator section, ma'am," the clone Air Boss who was her acting XO told her. "Secondary explosions are ongoing and that section is venting to space."

Nancy brought up her battlescape virtual view of that area of the megaship and there were no blue dots or red dots in that section of the ship.

"No!" Nancy's hair stood on end and her stomach turned. She clutched the chair's arm and pulled herself back upright. "Get me eyes in there now!"

"Ma'am," the XO said calmly, "I'm sorry. There are none. The entire section has been destroyed for three decks vertical and several horizontal."

"Any signs of survivors that were blown into space?"

"Looking, ma'am, but none yet." Nancy's heart sunk. There were over thirty clone AEMs, a handful of tankheads, and Commander Rackman in that part of the megaship. They were all vaporized in an instant.

Davy, Dee, I am so sorry, she thought.

Do I tell Dee?

Alert her AIC.

Done.

"Send the repair bots in to reroute to the power source. There shouldn't be any resistance there anymore." Nancy squinted as blue beams burst out from the megaship at the ship that had fired on them. DeathRay was still giving them hell. The beams zigged and zagged and then ripped through the alien ship, sending it in thousands of directions at once in pieces and ionized plasma. Admiral Walker's Fleet QMTed in just behind the beam and went to full DEGs on the megaship's wingman, bursting it at the seams just underneath its tuning-fork antennae. Rackman's blue dot was still not showing up on the tracker.

"Captain, the repair bots are rerouting around the

damaged portion of the ship. They need approximately two minutes and fifty-three seconds to connect the system," the STO told her.

Too bad they didn't blow out the self-destruct system, Nancy thought.

Not a bad idea, Allison replied. *Hold that thought for moment.*

Allison? Don't leave me hanging here. What have you got?

We can take that system out. I just ran a multi-sensor cross-correlation on all the data we have on the alien ship from every bot, soldier, and mecha sensor. In order for that ship to self-destruct, they'd have to run a positive feedback loop on the hyperspace projector. We had that happen to us before, if you recall.

Okay, good. How do we stop it?

Simple. We take out the hyperspace projector.

"Penzington to General Moore!"

"Go, Nancy."

"The self-destruct is the hyperspace projector tube, sir. We need to destroy it!" Nancy told him.

"I've got my hands full here, Penzington. You'll have to get it done!" Moore said it as more of a fact rather than an order or a suggestion.

"Understood, sir. Consider it done." Nancy replied.

"XO. You have the bridge. Be ready to throw that shield system on as soon as Commander Buckley gives the order." Nancy didn't wait for a response. She tapped the controls on her wristband and there was a flash of light and then the sound of bacon frying. She materialized in the hangar bay of the *Hillenkoetter* just long enough to grab as many grenades as she could stuff in her suit, and then she grabbed a blaster and a rifle. She flashed out just as fast as she had flashed in.

The frying bacon sound subsided as she materialized in reality space deep inside the alien ship. The coordinates Allison had calculated for the alien hyperspace jaunt projection system turned out to be a very large room with massive conduits running from back to front, bottom to top, and left to right. The conduits were at least ten meters in diameter and the room had to be over a hundred meters across in any direction.

Where is my target, Allison? she asked her AIC.

The infrared systems and the QMs both show huge energy readings building up in the centralmost conduit overhead running stern to bow. Allison lit the particular conduit up in her visor.

Roger that. Nancy sized it up and realized that she didn't bring enough grenades. *I don't think twenty grenades would make a dent in this thing. I need to rethink this.*

I think you are right.

Nancy tapped her wristband and snapped back to the hangar bay of the *Hillenkoetter*. She looked around at the parking deck and picked out an FM-12 that was on the flight line and ready to go. It just needed a pilot. Quickly, she bounced to it and had Allison start handshaking with the mecha's flight computers. Nancy bounced into the pilot's couch and cycled her QMT system before the cockpit had completely sealed. The mecha started springing to life as it rematerialized in the belly of the alien megaship. Nancy could feel the ship lurch forward again as if they'd been hit by another blue beam. She didn't have time to worry about that at the moment.

"Targeting systems, on." She toggled the fighter over to bot mode and the mecha flipped over and stood upright. The targeting Xs in her mind lit up and she placed one on the central conduit. "Fox Three!"

The missile twisted out from the back launcher deck of the bot-mode mecha, and just before it impacted the conduit, a porcupine blurred in between it and the missile, taking the hit and protecting the self-destruct system. Red targeting Xs lit up in her mindview and Nancy counted four other targets in the room with her.

"Warning! Enemy targeting lock! Warning! Enemy targeting lock!"

"Shit!" Nancy hit the boot thrusters and rocketed upward as she stomped the left lower pedal and slammed the HOTAS full back and to the right. The bot-mode mecha pirouetted like a figure skater as blue beams from the porcupines filled the empty spaces all around it. "Guns, guns, guns!"

Nancy fired her guns at the nearest porcupine, hitting it dead to rights before it had time to move out of the way. The alien mecha's shields flickered and went out just as she landed shoulders first into it. She drew her cannon upwards, shoved it through the armored torso, and fired again. "Guns, guns, guns!"

The mecha exploded all around her as she pressed through where it had been. She rolled over backwards, hit her down thrusters, and threw the HOTAS forward full throttle. The targeting X for the conduit stayed locked on so she gave it another shot. "Fox Three!"

Just as the missile jumped from the launcher tube on her back, a glowing green tendril wrapped around it. The porcupine it was attached to slung the missile around, using its propulsion to spin them up like a merry-go-round. The alien used the centrifugal force of the missile to redirect it back at Nancy and then it let it go. Nancy barely had time to react. Barely.

With both feet stomping hard against the top pedals, the mecha hovered upright and Nancy turned her body away from the missile. As the missile swung past, she reached out with her mechanized hand and grabbed the tendil holding the missile. She yanked it until it snapped, letting the missile fly free into the bulkhead on the far side of the room, exploding against a non-important target. She held on to the tendril and yanked the alien mecha toward her as she fell over sideways, stomping her mechanized boot through the backside of the porcupine. The shields flickered and several of the spines on the craft were crushed, but the ship managed to squirm free of her grasp.

That didn't matter. Nancy feinted over just as she'd seen DeathRay and Dee do a million times. As as the mecha toppled over playing dead, she fired again. "Guns, guns, guns! Fox Three!"

The guns took out the alien, creating a thunderous echoing boom in the cavernous engineering room. Orange and green plasma fire lit the room. The missile twisted around the fireball and upwards into the conduit, crashing against it just as Nancy felt something puncture her chest and could see metal twisted out of the way on her dashboard. The conduit exploded throwing purple and white-hot plasma swirling in every direction, and like a chain reaction the other conduits traversing the room ruptured at the seams and gave way. Nancy felt as though something were ripping her body apart. She looked down and saw two alien green glowing tendrils protruding from her suit at the abdomen and chest.

There was no blood. The suit had sealed off around them. Then a third tendril pushed upward through her right thigh. Nancy was too shocked to scream. She reached for her wristband but a fourth tendril wrapped around her hand and tore it cleanly from her arm.

Nancy screamed in pain but did her best to focus her mind on turning the mecha over into fighter mode. As she did so the last of the conduit explosions threw her wildly across the room against the bulkhead, knocking her free of the Chiata porcupine that had grabbed her. The tendrils quickly retracted from her body, but not before a blue beam cut the right wing free and clear from the fighter.

The mecha skittered into a flat spin across the deck of the exploding room, and then the propellantless drive went critical.

Eject, Nancy! Eject!

Nancy cycled the ejection seat and was tossed free as the mecha exploded around her. The ejection seat tossed her upward into the larger fireballs that were consuming the engineering room, on a direct trajectory through one of the white-hot plasma jets spraying from the vortex projector tube.

Oh, God, Allison. I think this is it. Did we at least stop the destruct sequence?

I'm pretty sure we did. It's been a great ride, Nancy.
Yes, it has. Please upload the file for my family.
Already done . . .

Chapter 38

February 19, 2407 AD
U.S.S. Sienna Madira II
Target Star System
700 Light-years from the Sol System
Tuesday, 1:10 A.M. Ship Standard Time

Alexander flashed into the bridge alongside the COB. The two of them were covered in green and red glowing goo. As the frying bacon sound settled and he got his bearings, he could see the damage reports and casualty lists rolling by in his mind. The attack had gone too long and there was little left of the Beta Fleet. Another solid hit to the megaship, and it would be gone as well.

"CHENG! It's now or fucking never!" Alexander shouted over the net.

"Twenty seconds, sir!" Buckley responded.

"CO! CDC!"

"I see them, CDC!" Moore responded before they

could warn him about the thirty-eight megaships that had just joined them out of hyperspace.

"Buckley!"

"Okay, sir! Now!"

"Engage the weapon!"

There was little to notice at first, but then a flickering blue and white field protruded outwardly from the shield generator at the nose of the *Madira*. Alexander could see it spreading out before them, and several blue beams bounced off the barrier as it grew.

"STO, project a full megaship view in here for all of us," Moore ordered.

"Aye, sir."

A holo projection of the megaship filled the room over their heads. The alien porcusnail looked like a strange alligator with the four supercarriers jutting out as legs. From the nose of each of the supercarriers projected the blue and white flickering energy barrier. As the shields drew power from within the alien starship, they spread and grew, and the barrier thickened and darkened. It continued to spread, and the multitude of blue beams that zigged and zagged into it had little if no effect.

"Alert the Beta Fleet to QMT the hell out of here ASAP, XO!"

"Already done, sir! The Beta Fleet are free and clear!"

"Good. Now let's hope Commander Buckley ain't as crazy as we all think he is." Alexander smirked.

"Honestly, sir, I hope he's a helluva lot worse!" Firestorm added.

The field reached an energy level at which the four projected barriers bounced into each other and melded into one giant spheroid. The shield continued to grow until it became a perfect blue and white shimmering sphere around the megaship and the four supercarriers. The Chiata fleet continued to attack and pour blue beams of death from Hell into the barrier to no avail. And then the beam flickered and shimmered and pulsed like a gluonium bomb explosion and a supernova all at the same time. The blast wave left the spherical surface at near the speed of light, washing through the Chiata fleet and vaporizing the megaships on impact. The Chiata had no clue what had happened to them; they had just been killed.

"Hot damn, Buckley!" Alexander shouted. "XO, STO, CDC, I want full reports on any Chiata ships left in this system. Full-up sensors sweeps now. Now that we have QMs back, we ought to be able to find the rest of them if they are hiding out."

"Yes, sir!"

Sir, you need to check the casualty lists. Both Commander Davy Rackman and Captain Nancy Penzington are listed as KIA, sir.

Hell. Alexander collapsed into his seat with the wind knocked out of him. *Nancy, no.*

Yes, sir.

Do Dee and DeathRay know?

Yes, sir.

Oh, hell, I'm so sorry. I didn't mean for Penzington to . . .

Yes, sir.

Epilogue

February 28, 2407 AD
Arlington Cemetery
Arlington, Virginia
Earth, the Sol System
Wednesday, 9:30 A.M. Eastern Time

Dee held her jaw clenched as tight as she could; otherwise, her mouth would start quivering and she'd start to cry. She bit the inside of her bottom lip and squeezed her mother's hand tightly for comfort. There was little comfort to be had for her. Even leaning her head against her father's wide shoulder, shoulders that had borne the weight of the world, didn't help. Dee continued to cry.

Jack Boland sat beside Alexander, and a couple that turned out to be Nancy's real parents sat to his right. Dee could see the tears forming in the corners of Jack's eyes, and his cheeks were wet where they had been flowing already. The sight of him, her larger-than-life pseudo-big brother, of DeathRay, Captain Jack Boland with tears in his eyes was all it took to push her even farther over the edge.

As the President finished speaking, she turned and faced the seven Marines to their left. The soldiers then raised their guns and fired. They fired again, causing Dee to jump. They fired a third time and the twenty-one guns saluting the ten soldiers being honored there that day rang out across the hillside by Robert E. Lee's mansion. It had taken Alexander pulling some strings to have burials at Arlington, as it had been closed for almost a century to new funeral locations. But Dee wanted this for Nancy and for Rackman, and for the other members of the *Madira*, their family, that gave their lives for the greater good and the survival of humanity, and she convinced her father to pull those strings—however many it took. Her father had been happy to oblige his little girl.

The ceremony finished as the flags were folded and given to the next of kin of the ten soldiers. DeathRay accepted the flag, but then handed it to Nancy's parents with a nod. Dee watched as Rackman's father accepted the flag, and she broke down into sobs the likes of which she hadn't known since she'd been a little girl. It was uncontrollable and it hurt and Dee just couldn't stop the ache in her chest.

"I didn't get to see him again, Daddy," Dee whispered through her sobs.

"I know, princess. I know." Dee held onto her father's arm and buried her face in his shoulder. Her mother leaned to her and patted her on the leg as she hugged her.

Dee watched the others being given flags. She knew

them all by name but didn't really *know* them. The only other casualty she knew was the CHENG's second. Commander Buckley and Gunny Howser sat together behind Commander Benjamin's family. Dee could see Rondi's hand turning red from Joe's grip on it. She wanted to hold Davy's hand like that.

As the funeral service ended, the President had long since been scurried away by the Secret Service, and the large Clydesdale horses had been led away. Only a few family members and friends remained. Dee watched Jack as he knelt over Nancy's gravesite with a single rose in his hands. He was muttering something to his lost wife as he carefully placed the flower by her headstone.

Dee looked down at Davy's resting place and continued to cry. All that time on the alien planet she thought it would have been her who died. She thought it would've been her who would be taken from Davy, and she never even knew for sure that he loved her as much as she loved him. Dee fell to her knees with her hands on her face, and she felt a hand on her shoulder. At first she thought it was her father, but she could see him farther away in her peripheral vision consoling some of the other families.

"He spoke so highly of you, Ms. Moore," a man's voice said from behind her. "He told us so much about you that, I'm sorry, I feel as though I know you already. I mean, other than you being the daughter of a famous president and all."

"I'm sorry, I—" Dee turned and could see it was Rackman's father. He held the flag in one hand, and his other was on her shoulder.

"No no, don't be sorry," Mr. Rackman told her solemnly. "Davy was doing what he loved and he was with the people, or person, he loved the most. He wouldn't have had it any other way. It's just a shame that you young people didn't have more time for each other."

"I loved him," Dee said to Mr. Rackman between sobs. "Did you hear that, Davy? I'm not too chicken shit to say it now. I love you."

"Sweetheart, he knew that. And he loved you with all his heart." Mr. Rackman knelt beside her. "Remember him and you can love him forever. But do us all a favor and don't let it keep you from living and loving again."

Dee didn't know what to say to that. She looked at Davy's father and could see her SEAL's eyes looking back at her. It broke her heart even more.

"Thank you, Mr. Rackman."

"Anytime. And you can call or visit anytime you'd like." He told her.

"Thank you. I'd like that." She nodded and turned back to the grave and wiped the tears from her cheeks.

"I think that Davy would too," he said. She could feel Mr. Rackman's hand retract and heard him shuffle away behind her.

Dee stood after a long moment and forced herself to move forward. Rondi Howser and Buckley approached her and gave her a hug. Dee reciprocated, but she was numb and sort of just going through the motions. She had no idea what to say to her friends at the moment, because all she could think about was how bad she wanted to see Rackman alive and well again. And her mind raced with how much she wanted to talk to Nancy Penzington again.

The grief was overwhelming. She somehow managed to make her way to DeathRay who was still kneeling over Nancy's grave.

"I loved her like a sister, Jack," she told him. Jack looked up at her and then stood and hugged her to him.

"She loved you like a sister too, Dee," Jack said through sobs. "So do I."

"We lost her, and Davy, and . . . what do we do now?" Dee asked. "I'm not sure if I have the stomach for it any longer."

"The Chiata are still coming, Dee. This is just a small taste of what is to come." Jack took in a long breath and then turned and nodded to Rackman's grave. "He deserves better than to have those fucking aliens desecrate his final resting place. I know she does! If we lose Earth, they get this place and who knows what the alien bastards would do with it." He nodded at Nancy's grave.

"No, he doesn't deserve that. And I guess humanity doesn't deserve it either. I, uh, I just don't know. I feel gut-punched." Dee hesitated. She wasn't sure what she felt. She just knew she was tired and so very sad. She felt like she couldn't go on any further, but she knew that somehow she had to. "I guess somebody has to stop them, even if it means dying in the process."

"Oh, make no mistake, Dee. We're not gonna be doing any dying anytime soon. You understand me. We WILL not be dying anytime soon," DeathRay told his wingman loudly and with anger, and it was enough that several heads turned and looked their way. "You don't have to worry about that. Do you understand me?"

"How do you know that, Jack?" Dee could see Jack's jaw tighten and the fire in his eyes. He was angry. He was turning his grief into something else and he expected her to do the same. She could see the familiar look just before they would go on an attack. DeathRay was pissed. The aliens had killed his wife. It was time for Dee to learn from her big brother and roll the grief into a fire inside her that would burn so bright that she became unstoppable, like DeathRay.

"How do I know we're not going to be dying anytime soon, Dee? Because, Dee, you and I, well, for them," Jack pointed at the graves and took in a snarling, deep breath. "Well, we've got way too many of those green alien motherfuckers to kill before dying."